Monsieur

Monsieur

Emma Becker

Translation by Maxim Jakubowski

Constable • London

Constable & Robinson Ltd
55–56 Russell Square
London WC1B 4HP
www.constablerobinson.com

First published in the UK by Constable,
an imprint of Constable & Robinson Ltd, 2012

A copy of the British Library Cataloguing in
Publication data is available from the British Library

ISBN: 978-1-78033-476-9 (hardback)
ISBN: 978-1-78033-521-6

Printed and bound in the UK

1 3 5 7 9 10 8 6 4 2

'The worst tyrants are those who succeed in getting themselves loved.'

Spinoza

Monsieur

I bumped into Monsieur's first-born on Line One, at Charles-de-Gaulle-Étoile. Classes had ended and hordes of noisy schoolkids were laying siege to the trains. I had to get up from my seat to allow a new batch to fit into my already full carriage and it was only when I felt a sharp elbow dig into my back that I looked up from my book for the customary exchange of indifferent apologies, neither of us bothering to disconnect from our iPods. As ever, I was only half convinced of the need to apologize. Why should I? Because I just happened to be there? Because I was in the way?

I can't pretend that his voice, which I could barely hear, triggered it. For some reason, I looked up at him, and knew instantly, without any shadow of doubt, that it was his son. There was no magic involved, but the likeness between them struck me with all the power of a spell. With immense effort, I dropped my eyes from his. They were wide, heavy-lidded, weighed down by the sensuality he had inherited from Monsieur and of which he was no doubt unaware. *It's him it's him it's him it's him it's him*. I realized I was staring at him and pretended to return to André Breton – I couldn't think of anything else to do.

I had never thought it would be so painful to be close to him. I didn't even notice the train reaching my station – I could have followed him anywhere.

Charles. The eldest. That morning, in the blue room of a hotel in the fifteenth *arrondissement*, I had surprised Monsieur by listing his boys: Charles, Samuel, Adam, Louis and Sacha, the spawn of a life I could barely imagine. I knew things about the eldest that even he

1

might no longer remember: the heated argument over dinner about some historical battle during which Charles, in a fit of rage, had slammed his fist on the table, almost earning himself a paternal slap; the afternoon when he had come in from school totally high, his thick black hair still smelling of grass. Monsieur loved him with a passion – beside which the tenderness he had once shown me was a drop in the ocean.

The train lurched and, again, Charles bumped against me. 'Sorry,' he said, with a pinched smile.

I recognized his father's dimples, the same white teeth. It was as if Monsieur was gazing at me, for the first time in six months, in a way that explained everything: his children, his wife, everything he had built his life on. I could have been kind, I could have been compassionate, but Charles was somehow unable to move away from me, offering a series of apologetic smiles (each evoking an image of Monsieur after our lovemaking). I wanted to scream, *Stop!* I don't want to look into those grey eyes, which don't belong to you. None of your features truly belongs to you – not even the long nose your mother gave you. I was biting the inside of my cheeks, pressing my lips together tightly, avoiding the unformed questions in his eyes.

Who am I? My name is Ellie (which means nothing to you but, God knows, there was a time when it meant everything to *him*, more than drink, food, sleep and everything in between). I'm about your age, a couple of years older – I haven't changed much since the days when I was carrying my maths books around in a moth-eaten old rucksack, and I'm looking at you like this because you remind me so much of your father. In your dark eyes I recognize the same unconscious languor that once frightened me, the hunger for women that attracted me. Right now, I'm reminded of those eyes peering over his mask when I watched him operate at the clinic. Of course, Charles, I know it shouldn't affect me in this way: I'm almost forgetting you're just a rough sketch of him, but thirty years younger.

I was once his mistress and I loved your father with an all-consuming fire. I can imagine one random evening coming across you at a party, sharing a joint with you and watching your eyes cloud over, as his did, learning what makes you laugh and contemplating your so familiar lips. It would be so easy, so natural, to become your girlfriend and meet up with you every evening outside the lycée. I'm not too old for you, just old enough to help you discover the realities of life, but I feel twenty years older. I heard so much about you from your father that in my eyes you're almost a child, asexual. If I were now to kiss you, as I desperately want to, it would be with despair, because you are the son of the man I cannot forget, and your kisses would have the same effect on me as the methadone prescribed for a recovering heroin addict. I've encountered so many Almosts and Not Quite Rights since he and I parted . . .

Hi, Charles, I'm Ellie. You've never spoken to me and you'll probably never see me again, but I know the name of every member of your family because I have held your father, of whom you happen to be a disturbing copy, in my arms. So, although I don't really know you, I truly

3

know you . . . It's like a Truffaut movie: a strange woman among thousands walks into the same Métro carriage as her lover's son. She recognizes him; his features are familiar from all the photographs she has seen of him, of his family. With your father, it could have been anyone, but it just happened to be me. It was me he would meet up with on Tuesday mornings when you'd all left for school; it was me he was already thinking of when he kissed the top of your heads. Me, with my Bensimon jeans and my ponytail. This face. These hands sweating over a paperback in the stifling atmosphere of the Paris Underground but which, *barely six months ago*, Charles, were digging their nails into another pair of hands, the hands you felt on your back when you were learning to ride your first bicycle in the Luxembourg Gardens. You know none of this, and you're peering at me in the way you probably do at all girls – but I should be the person you despise most in the world because all I want is to hide in your pocket and spend the evening next to him at your dinner table. Just to see him. To witness some of the moments you barely notice, like your conversations, his kiss before you go to bed, the first words he says when he crosses the threshold every evening. Just five minutes at a table with all of you. Five minutes of your comfortable life, you arguing with your father, who is so annoyed that he has stopped eating, your pretty mother sighing at this male aggression, your four younger brothers fearful of taking sides, and me, stuffing myself with images to conjure up when I'm alone.

At Châtelet, Charles shot me a final glance from beneath his long black eyelashes, then disembarked amid the flow of passengers. I watched his silhouette until he had disappeared among a hundred anonymous heads, walking, I knew, towards Line Four and, later, emerging onto the Île Saint-Louis. A door, a number, a key granting access to the large family apartment where his mother was listening to his brother Adam telling her all about his day in first year. Monsieur would get home at around nine, after the children had had their dinner. But they would cross his path in a thousand ways, brushing against him as they cleaned their teeth in the bathroom before the goodnight kiss. And Charles would fall asleep with no memory of me. The Métro carriage felt so empty now that he was gone.

Cry. Scream. Burst out laughing. Whistle. Get back to your book.

My chin quivered like that of a little girl whose hand had been smacked. I pulled my collar up, and all the way to Nation, serenaded by Offenbach's *'Belle Nuit'*, I sobbed my heart out. It seemed the only thing to do.

Book I

'Dear me, how beautiful you were on the phone tonight!'

Sacha Guitry, Les Femmes et toi

Lolita, by Nabokov. A book that led me on the path to damnation. I don't think you could find a more guilty title in my library. I had journeyed through de Sade, Serpieri and Manara, Mandiargues, Pauline Réage, but none had produced the itch that literally threw me into Monsieur's arms. I see it clearly now. I should have been kept well apart from the yellowing old copy that stood innocently on the shelf. It was there I learned all there is to know about a particular type of man, worldly but weary, whose gaze is invariably drawn to young girls, and how those men focus on bodies that are no longer children's but not quite women's. It's the book in which I learned about the inner voice that draws them to nymphets. I learned how to decipher the vice beneath their respectable appearance, their adoration of the tousled goddesses they name Lolita.

Lolita. Demanding beyond reason, possessive and jealous, drawn into an endless war (which she has already won) against all other females, looking down on them despite her diminutive stature, her slender limbs and her age: she is fifteen years old, the age at which Nabokov killed her. The men we are talking about, in their serious suits and oxford brogues, kneel at the altar of these little darlings, for reasons that are wrong, and sordid to many: their innocence and the softness of their skin; their arses and breasts, which defy Newton's laws of gravity; their fingers, which lack shame, their small hands manipulating in childlike fashion – hands that have probably held nothing larger than a Magnum ice-cream (isn't there playful appetite in the way they hold this new delicacy?); their eyes, which are like harpoons because invariably, with men, they hold their gaze, in the street, despite the presence of parents, because they have no sense of shame. I now know all there is to know of men's attraction to them, but does anyone know what the nymphet is looking for? What draws her away from long-haired boys towards men as old as her father? Nabokov never let us into what Lolita was thinking when she sat on Humbert Humbert's lap on that pale summer morning. Or why, a few pages earlier, she was jumping across his knees, deliberately mistreating him, knickers flashing, twittering while her worshipper attempted to stem an almost adolescent effusion. It's this parallel reading of the book that I missed, the impossibility of discovering how the story would have unfolded had Lolita been allowed to speak. It was with this in mind that in the previous October I had climbed into the bed of a forty-year-old man. I shall ignore the almost accidental frolic I had when I was fifteen with a young company executive: there are men, and then there are men in their forties. Should you consider the distinction insignificant, I can assure you that not a single member of my tribe has ever confused the two. Nymphets and forty-year-old men attract each other.

That man – what was his name? – hadn't left me exhausted with delight in the morning but neither had he killed my attraction to his sort. I will go further: it was his abysmal lack of *savoir faire* and sensuality that propelled me on my quest. Maybe I was too demanding; maybe I was hoping too much to fulfil all the perfect scenarios I had imagined: myself, bent to the strength, will, hands and words of a professor, open to anything and prey to every manipulation my body would allow him. I had no wish to talk, and neither of us said a word until four o'clock when I got tired of having him inside me. It was a world away from the excesses that had previously crowded my mind. It was while I was jerking him off that I realized the list of those who could worship me as I wanted was endless. I smiled when he came, thinking of the men in my future.

The following day, scampering towards the Métro, still bone tired from lack of sleep, I realized I knew no more than I had the day before. That older men can sometimes find it difficult to get hard was no surprise. The experience had not been psychologically exciting as I had expected; he had said none of the words I had hoped for, and my body showed no evidence of added maturity, even though I was twenty. When the phone rang and his number lit up, I didn't answer and, after a few weeks' silence, I received this message: 'I'm tired of pursuing you, Ellie. Stop playing at being Lolita. You're too old for that sort of game, and I have no intention of becoming Humbert Humbert, even if I wanted to, which I don't.'

I didn't know Monsieur. I had heard his name a

thousand times over meals with my uncle Philippe – they were not only colleagues but close friends. For me, his name evoked the hospital. I didn't *know* Monsieur. If I'm honest, it's all my mother's fault. In February this year I was slouching up the stairs from my room in the basement, holding my Bible under my arms (*La Mécanique des femmes* by Louis Calaferte), wondering what to do with myself during the students' strike. It's impossible now to determine what Mum had in mind when she mentioned the surgeon's name. According to her, he was the only person apart from me who appeared to want such a filthy piece of literature – in fact, he was *obsessed* with it. At first, I couldn't have cared less: Philippe's work colleague belonged to another world, whether or not we were obsessed by the same book, and I couldn't see myself arriving at the clinic to discuss erotica with a man of forty-five.

Forty-five.

Forty-five.

An insidious form of boredom allowed the idea to take root in me that I should meet this man. I would repeat his name aloud, surprised that I found it increasingly attractive in a dangerous sort of way. I searched for it on Facebook and gazed at the only hit, trying half-heartedly to come up with a reason to make him a 'friend'. I had to enter his world like a spy, with literature, a charming Trojan horse, concealing my true purpose. The need to discover everything about him was like a mosquito bite I had to scratch. I had put two or three cunning questions to Philippe and learned that when I was still small I had passed the famous C.S. in the clinic's corridors when Philippe and he had been visiting patients. I plumbed the depths of my memory and recalled my uncle's birthday, two years ago: I had spent an entire evening among a crowd of elders without noticing the man who read the same books as I did, and just happened to have a twenty-five-year start on me. Twenty-five years: such an enormous gap. Twenty-five years spent caressing the bodies of women, subverting procreative sex, while I was still an innocent sucking milk from my mother's breasts. Must I also mention the strong ties connecting Monsieur and my family, thin but strong, like a nylon cord, with the same cutting edge? The heads of twenty-year-old girls are full of improbable romantic scripts: there's the one about the student and the surgeon, where she knows nothing and he knows everything and, standing between them, the dear old uncle, unaware of the drama unfolding around him. (Were he to find out, the erotic tale would swiftly turn into a drama by Racine!)

In March, I moved closer. I no longer needed a face for Monsieur. That he was a surgeon, that he harboured the same tastes as I did, that he was married and had a family made him stand out from the crowd easily enough; those attributes confirmed him as an inhabitant of an almost parallel world, that of Adults (it would be an aberration to define people of my age as such). I didn't need to find him physically attractive (just as long as he wasn't disgusting . . .). As I write, I can hear his theatrical indignation: 'So you would have been content with any old fat guy!' To which I can only answer, yes, probably.

But let me reassure him: as the story unfolds, we will see that his trap was perfect.

One day I became tired of circling him without his being aware of it. It was April. The shimmering month of April. Pollen was floating down from the chestnut trees and I was bored. The strike struggled on, I wasn't seeing anyone and, as spring came around, I spent my days sprawled on the terrace, sunbathing. I was desperate to meet up with people, men, and experience fever, ecstasy, passion, anything but this deadly lethargy. I had gone over and over the situation in my head and lay in wait, crouched in the shadows, for the moment to reveal myself to Monsieur.

Good evening.

You probably don't know who I am, even if you have kindly added me to your Friends list, so let me tell you: I am the niece of Philippe Cantrel who worked at the clinic until recently. It was through him that I learned you are a reader of Bataille and Calaferte, and I am curious about men who have read and appreciated *La Mécanique des femmes*. It makes me feel less alone . . . !

My name is Ellie, I'm twenty, studying literature, and I've published articles in an erotic magazine. You'd know this already from my Facebook profile, but I thought it would be sensible to introduce myself.

I have no doubt you're a very busy man, but I would be grateful if you could find the time to explain, in just a few lines, what pleases you in Calaferte. I am currently attempting to write 'Mécanique des hommes' so everything is grist to the mill.

Have a lovely evening.

Ellie

At the time I was selfishly fearful because I had no idea how Monsieur might react: I imagined Philippe learning from his shaken colleague about my cunning manoeuvre and screaming at me, 'What's wrong with you, trying to chase a guy of his age? Just wait until I tell your mother! See how clever she thinks you are!'

And me, red in the face, sweating like a pig as the rope tightens around my neck: 'What do you mean, *chase*? I only wanted to talk about erotic literature!'

Explain yourself, Ellie. Try to explain to the man who changed your nappies and gave your first boyfriends dirty looks the subtle difference between discussing *Story of O* and shameless flirting. Philippe would see beyond the words. In the dry tone that always gave me the willies he would say, 'Do you think I'm a complete fool? Do you think a *guy* knows the difference between talking about erotic literature and the chance to have it off?'

Maybe the subtle difference is that there is no difference: I was never stupid enough to believe that an appreciation for writing alone would provoke Monsieur into a response. I just wanted to see how he'd react. Compare my scruples with his. Assess the power of my youth, determine how much weight it held against a marriage and children. Already, in my absence of principles, I was toying with a seductive postscript, providing him with the assurance of my total discretion as long as he would show me what a man was like, a real man, a man who could fill my body *and* my mind.

MONSIEUR

Ellie,

I am moved to discover that a twenty-year-old is interested in such writers. Actually, I don't remember mentioning this particular cultural interest to Philippe. I have an enormous interest in erotic literature, and own a significant collection centred around Andre Pieyre de Mandiargues. Apart from my work, it's the true passion in my life.

We can meet up and chat whenever you wish.

What magazine have you written in?

(And, by the way, there is no need to be formal with me.)

See you soon.

At first I didn't mention my secret to anyone. It was like keeping a surprise in my pocket, or stifling a scream. On the evening that Monsieur answered me, Babette came to mine for a sleepover. She knitted her eyebrows, concentrating, as she read the first two messages, carefully weighing up every word, while I stood behind her and spilled out my fears.

'No, really, Babette. *Really*. Do you think that's what he has in mind?'

'I do.'

I was far from reassured by that. 'I just suggested we chat by Internet. He's the one suggesting we meet.'

'He's "*moved*",' Babette added, like an amateur detective.

'It's not uncommon to be *moved*. If all he wanted to do was talk, he could have written, "I'm surprised" or "It's unusual to come across people who read Mandiargues."'

'I reckon he's thinking about it.'

'What should I do?'

'I don't know. What do you want to do?'

We were in my room in Nogent. I lit a fag. 'Generally speaking? I'd like to meet him, talk to him.'

Babette stood up and raised her eyebrows. She was dubious. 'Even though I know how you feel about erotic literature, it'll be difficult to have some sort of innocuous relationship with him, if that's what you mean.'

'You asked me what I wanted to do, *generally speaking*.'

'Basically, you want to find out what he's all about.'

'He's married, he has five kids, he's forty-six and used to work with my uncle. Should the situation ever become ambiguous, it would only mean the guy has balls.'

'Or that he's a pervert.' She had picked up one of my old copies of Bataille and was leafing through it.

I sat down at my desk and stared at my computer keyboard. 'So what is perversion at the end of the day? For me, it's just the opportunity to track pleasure down wherever it's hiding out. I don't know of any men who search for it in books. Especially this kind of book. Maybe it's worth taking a few risks. Well, I think so at least.'

ELLIE

Good evening,

I recently wrote for a literary erotic magazine called *Stupre* that a friend of mine had set up and which has so far published three issues. Its distribution is fairly limited so it's unlikely you've come across it.

I would be delighted to meet up with you this week, if your work schedule allows; as far as I'm concerned, I have all the time in the world, as my university faculty has been on strike for an eternity and is likely to remain so for some time to come.

I assume you're not on Facebook that often so let me give you my phone number. It'll be easier to communicate that way: 06 68 . . .

I hope we'll see each other very soon,
Ellie
(I will try not to be too formal in our dialogue)

(but then again . . .)

MONSIEUR

There is nothing wrong with being formal, although it makes some forms of dialogue somewhat awkward, which, however, I appreciate. Informality is a reflex, while formality is a choice.

I shall attempt to get hold of *Stupre* and read you before we meet so I'll have some idea of the way you . . . think.

My own number is 06 34 . . . and my email address is ******

I'll call you soon.

Until then.

'Surely, you're not going to fall into bed with this guy!'

Having read the mails, Alice was rolling her eyes. I hadn't expected that. Or maybe I had, just a little. Once upon a time I might have reacted similarly, although I haven't a clue when.

'Come on!' I said, looking her straight in the eye, with an assurance I knew I couldn't sustain.

'Well, that's the way it looks.'

'But he's thinking about it, no?'

Maybe Alice could see hope in my evasive gaze. She let out a deep sigh. 'It's *you* who's thinking about it.'

'But he is too! And I'm not going to sleep with him just because he feels like it.'

'So if you have no intention of doing so, why are you furnishing him with such heavy hints?'

'I'm not providing him with any hints whatsoever. All I'm doing is talking about erotic literature, which I agree is a bit much, but this guy reads the same books as I do. To discuss our taste in reading is not an invitation to fuck.'

'Why couldn't you have simpler tastes, like sport or animals?'

For a moment, sitting cross-legged on my bed, we fell silent. That's how our conversations go when I shock my sister. We were watching our feet, fags in hand, music in the background connecting us. I'm never worried about losing Alice: she's as corruptible as I am and has the same sense of humour, and I knew that if I could find something funny in this story about the surgeon, she'd soon jump aboard. The only problem was that I couldn't see any humour in the situation, not yet at any rate. That it would be easy to corrupt the man amused me, but perhaps I would be the only one to laugh.

'Anyway,' she went on, 'I can feel it in my bones you're going to do it. No point in trying to deny it.'

'So don't ask the question.'

New awkward silence. Alice probably hated me then, and was clinging to every scrap of sisterly love to defend my course of action. As for me, a perfect egotist, all I needed to find was the perfect lie, or the perfect excuse. I could have sworn to her that I wouldn't touch the man, but the story was already taking shape, whether I wanted it to or not, and I knew I could never keep from her a single detail. My next words rushed out of me: 'He interests me. OK? It's bad, it's immoral, nobody must know, but he interests me. I don't know if I'll sleep with him, but I probably will if I get the opportunity. So, come on, have a go at me.'

Alice, wearing her I'm-beginning-to-give-in-but-that-doesn't-mean-I-like-it face, mumbled: 'If Philippe knew . . .'

'I don't see why he should. And at this stage the guy's suggesting we meet, not me. He's taken the first step.'

ELLIE

Good evening,

Herewith my masterpiece. You won't have to search for a copy of *Stupre*. My story's in the first issue, which has possibly now become a collector's item, although I will bring it along if you wish. It's my first time in print so you might find it a bit ingenuous, but I'll say no more, except that I won't forget how I felt when I first held the magazine in my hand. Bloody proud. My family pretended they'd never heard of *Stupre*, although I noticed that the magazine moved from room to room, almost as if by magic. My uncle didn't realize the narrator was a man, and I had a hard job convincing him I wasn't a lesbian . . .

As far as formality in our dialogue is concerned, I had no intention of making you feel awkward. Do as you wish. Feel free to switch to informality along the way. I've actually devised a theory about the erotic nature of speech, which, no doubt, only makes sense to me, and I'd love to explain it to you whenever you're willing to listen.

I remain at your total disposal . . .

MONSIEUR

Thank you for letting me see the story – although I will still want to acquire a copy . . . and get it signed . . .

You're only twenty? What have you read? How have you lived? I'd love to know how all this made its way into your mind. It's not that ingenuous – not always at any rate, with the way you move so effortlessly from 'pussy' to 'cunt' . . .

You intrigue me. And your uncle failed to understand you were Lucie? . . . Maybe that's a good thing . . .

Do tell me your theories on the erotic nature of speech. George Steiner, in a recent piece of writing titled, I think, *My Unwritten Books*, devotes a whole chapter to the subject, although it's more about the way the colour of eroticism varies according to the language it's written in.

'Total disposal' covers a lot of ground, but I like it. And 'along the way'.

See you soon.

PS I can't resist sending you this poem by Baudelaire, '*The Jewels*'.

The lovely one was naked and, knowing well my prayer,
She wore her loud bright armoury of jewels.
They evoked in her the savage and victorious air
Of Moorish concubines upon a holiday.

When it gives forth, being shaken, its gay mocking noise,
This world of metal and of stone, aflare in the night,
Excites me monstrously, for chiefest of my joys
Is the luxurious commingling of sound and light.

Relaxed among the pillows, she looked down at me
And let herself be gazed upon at leisure – as if
Lulled by my wordless adoration, like the sea
Washing perpetually about the foot of a cliff.

Slowly, regarding me like a trained leopardess,
She slouched into successive poses. A certain ease,
A certain candour coupled with lasciviousness,
Lent a new charm to the old metamorphoses.

The whole lithe harmony of loins, hips, buttocks, thighs,
Tawny and sleek, and undulant as the neck of a swan,
Began to move hypnotically before my eyes:
And her large breasts, those fruits I have grown lean upon,

I saw float towards me, tempting as the angels of hell,
To win my soul in thraldom to their dark caprice
Once more, and lure it down from the high citadel
Where, calm and solitary, it thought to have found peace.

MONSIEUR

She stretched and reared, and made herself all belly. In
    truth,
It was as if some playful artist had joined the stout
Hips of Antiope to the torso of a youth! . . .
The room grew dark, the lamp having flickered and gone
    out,

And now the whispering fire that had begun to die,
Falling in lucent embers, was all the light therein –
And when it heaved at moments a flamboyant sigh
It inundated as with blood her amber skin.

ELLIE

Les Fleurs du mal, Monsieur! Your aim is true! This is why I read: for such epiphanies.

My theory of formality: well, the word 'theory' is possibly a bit far-fetched. Rather some sort of aesthetic of formality that I've fine-tuned as I've grown up. At the age when I began to take an interest in men I noted there was a somewhat heady charm in formal speech, a tension that had, as you pointed out, an ambiguous effect on the relationships. If you stick for some time to that unnecessary formality there's a remarkable change in the atmosphere when you switch to informality. And doesn't it make for an ironic paradox? To be formal in a certain context can almost become a form of indecency. I hope I'm making myself clear, I'm quite tired this evening . . .

The questions you raise are thorny. What I have seen, what I have known . . . both a lot and not much. Enough, I believe, to have written what you have read, not enough to be willing to use 'cunt' from the very beginning of the story. I am now twenty, not eighteen, as I was when that story was published, and I think I'm more articulate now. I hope so. It would be a pain to harbour such love for words and not be able to use them properly . . .

What I have known: I don't believe it's necessary to have known many men to be able to write about them. Calaferte was almost sixty when he wrote *La Mécanique des femmes*, and even though I guess he must have spent many hours in his own bed, I detected several awkward mistakes in his descriptions, which betrayed a still imperfect knowledge of women. For instance, there is a line where he has a woman saying something like 'Anyway, if you hadn't come round, I would have grabbed the first man I saw. Just a cock.' At my age, and with the experience I have (for what it's worth), I am sure that a woman cannot crave only a cock and nothing else. I believe that female desire, however complex and fleeting it might be, has some sort of life instinct that draws us towards tenderness with men, even though at the same time we are motivated by an animal need to be filled. I'm trying to say that I've never desired just a piece of a man's body. And many women I know cannot conceive of a cock with no torso, back, hands, smell and breath, and the words of the man that go with them.

So, writing about men when I'm only twenty . . . There are likely to be mistakes in what I write, but I don't believe that knowledge is the foundation stone of the whole malarkey. It's not only about the desire to know men – a task that will never be completed anyway – it's the intention that counts: the willingness to dive head first into their world of large hands and dark voices in an attempt to understand them. For now, it seems to me to be a beautiful vocation.

What have I read? A lot. The story you've seen was, I

think, fairly influenced by Calaferte, who was something of a revelation to me. I'd found his book a few months earlier in our cellar, and liked the way he described male flesh. At the time, you see, I was with a boy, had been for a year, and wanted to write all sorts of things for him, but he was incapable of writing a single line in response. So when *Stupre* suggested publishing me, I took great pleasure in reversing the roles . . . As you correctly guessed, there is something of Lucie in me, and that scene actually took place. I must say I'm curious to learn how you came to that conclusion.

I've also read two or three titles by de Sade, but I'm no great fan, and I feel I know all there is to know about him having just read *Philosophy In the Bedroom* and *120 Days*. Which a friend of mine, who is heavily into de Sade, finds particularly annoying . . . But, then, this is a guy who hates Queen and the Beatles.

Bataille, of course. I loved *The Dead Man*, although the Régine Deforges adaptation was stupendously poor. *My Mother* affected me a lot, but I'm still not totally into it: Bataille's literary style is awkward.

On the other hand, it bugs me that I'm telling you a lot and still feel I have so much more to say. But I know so little about you. What a pity. Worth a coffee? Or a glass of wine? I have so many questions for you. I have an indecent fascination with men who read. Particularly these books. An interest in erotica is very telling. But let's have this conversation another time – what if you had nothing to say? Am I boring you?

As I mentioned, I remain at your disposal whenever you'd like.

You have my number.

Ellie

(I don't think I'm boring. I can even be very funny, given the chance. I hope.)

I have to admit I was waiting for your mail with a guilty sort of impatience.

I firmly believe that, in spite of your delicious, impressive and precocious sensibility, time and experience do allow us to expand our erotic universe. I discovered the erotic in literature when I was ten and came across Pierre Louys. At the time, he seemed to me to be the *nec plus ultra* of subversion. I then began reading a lot and some of my reading revealed sensations, excitement, emotions I couldn't understand and would only come to understand much later. I do believe, in fact I know, that a woman under the right circumstances, when things are intense enough, can desire any old cock . . . I've witnessed it, lived through it, have been told so, even if, as you correctly point out, she is also thinking of a back, a smell and all those things you write so well about. But there is a moment when everything teeters, and in a flash the object of desire can, in a marvellous way, swing in another direction, change: anyone, any cock, and that's what Calaferte is writing about.

De Sade established the early principles others built upon and his writing is not very sensual, which is a bit shocking for us today. But what he writes about is fundamental. It's about the disconnect that eroticism generates, the proximity of violence.

And then there is Bataille, whom you are aware of. To understand the theory better you must read *Eroticism*. And *Story of the Eye* is sublime, *Madame Edwarda* too . . .

I knew you were Lucie after I spent time looking at your photos on Facebook with awe – your smile, your eyes, your skin.

Write to me soon.

PS Don't show my mails to your uncle . . .

My shaft against your cheek
Helmet grazing your ear
Slowly lick my scrotum
    Your tongue soft as water
Your tongue raw like a butcher-woman
Red like meat
Tip like a smiling bird,
My shaft leaking spittle
Your rear is my goddess
Opening like your mouth
    I adore it like the sky
I worship it like fire
I drink inside your tear

EMMA BECKER

I spread out your naked legs
I open them like a book
Where I can read my death

Babette had just rolled herself a cigarette and begun smoking it, when I yelped.

'What? What?' she cried out, springing to my side.

'I've just received a disgusting poem,' I squeaked, half smiling, reading the first lines, amusement mixed with loathing. 'A poem about cock slapping.'

I answered him hurriedly, Babette endlessly repeating 'shaft' and 'scrotum' behind me. Then she said: 'Don't you see? That man is already in your bed. Worse, he's thoroughly enjoying himself there.'

ELLIE

My dear, of course no one is aware of anything, and least of all my angelic uncle . . .

The final verses are rather pretty . . . When can I see you?

MONSIEUR

I'm certainly keen to see you but shouldn't we
wait a little longer?

ELLIE

Wait? Why should we? Do you want some more
poems?

> There is something magical in discussing crude
> things without knowing each other . . . but I know
> I won't be able to resist much longer . . .

'I like your first name. Ellie. Ellie. Ellie. Ellie.'

'A pleasant mantra. But it doesn't surprise me – I've always known I had a bedroom name.'

'Strange how different you sound from your texts.'

'Different? Would you like me to be wittier?'

'Witty? How funny . . . No, I like you as you are.'

'But still, you haven't asked to meet me.'

'It's all I dream about . . . but I'm enjoying our conversations . . .'

'This . . . literary tension is quite nice. Keeps the tummy warm.'

'Exactly. Delicious . . . Tuesday morning?'

'What a good idea!'

'Where could we meet?'

(Maybe Monsieur is wrong to provide me with so much rope. Maybe Babette was wrong to leave so early. Once I'm alone, I promptly abandon all my principles.)

'I do have an idea, but you might find it indecent.'

'Nothing is indecent – and, anyway, I like indecency. Where?'

'I often work in hotel rooms. It's too noisy at home. So really I'm just inviting you to meet me at my office. I'm often in the fifteenth, rue des Volontaires.'

'Fine with me . . . How intriguing. Rue des Volontaires, then. I have to go. Write to me again.'

'I will.'

'Sometimes in my dreams . . .'

'Report everything to the doctor tomorrow.'

ELLIE

My dear,

A late response to a point in your letter that was bothering me.

You wish to thwart my youthful assumptions with your manly experience. Fine. So, a woman can crave a cock. I shall eagerly await the moment when this comes true, although I just can't see myself ever saying, 'Anyone, any cock.'

Or maybe it's already happened to me. Although to reach such a state of mind and body, I must have been travelling through Ohio or somewhere close.

Damn it, what about the poetry of it? It pains me to believe that a woman can turn into such an animal that all she can conceive of is that part, however fundamental, of a man.

Although I'd have to forget all those nights I've spent tossing and turning in my bed, in torment, nailed to my sheets in a crucified pattern of passion, forever hungry. But maybe you're right. Maybe that's all I was seeking . . . insofar as I spent the evening with a girlfriend who had once experienced the very same thing. All very Peter Pan-like in the telling, but I'm sure you'll appreciate it. It takes place at night, then. Not just a single night, as there are many of them. A dark night, late, and the Young One on the first floor, confined to her blue childhood room, is twisting and turning between her damp sheets, unable to find peace, literally crucified by the imperative need to be filled, the craving that happens to be the only phenomenon capable of turning a young girl into a woman. Aware that any attempt at self-satisfaction is useless, as any climax thus achieved is just another hollow stimulation; as soon as the orgasm fades, all those thoughts would just come charging back. And, on so many occasions, I just lay there spread out in my bed for someone to open the door, anyone, and take me. Anyone, the son of the neighbour who seems to spend his life spying on me, the guy who comes to repair the boiler, a burglar even. The body of a man; no more, no less. The body of a man, the hands of a man and the demands of a man and the undescribable, delicious and profoundly shocking smell of man. That's what I was waiting for, when I was smaller, for Peter Pan to come to me. It's quite funny this Peter Pan story. Not long ago, I was writing to a boy, 'Did you know that God invented nighties so that girls can wear them without knickers? I think that's why Peter Pan came to visit Wendy. The little slut must have been sleeping with her legs open.'

Have you read the actual J. M. Barrie novel? I believe it's both the most beautiful and saddest story about the death of children and their early erotic awakening. In fact, I'm quite certain she wore nothing under her nightie . . . and what about the pesky Captain Hook?

All this to explain how affecting the cravings of young girls are, despite the insomnia they generate, how despairing and full of paradoxes. I know so few girls of my age who have experienced a true orgasm in the arms of a man, 'true orgasm' meaning one initiated simply by penetration.

I don't know the reasons. That at twenty our bodies are still unexplored continents? That boys of our own age don't properly understand us?

At any rate, the only pleasure available to us is of our own making. And when we experience that almost hysterical craving for sex, it's a total waste of time to try to reach it alone. The specific part of our body isn't screaming. It's a desire that takes root in the deepest part of the gut and demands, animal and instinctive, a man's gut to rush against, because that's the way things are. It's a physiological fact that we are made to be filled by a man. Whether we come or not is beside the point. So, in a way, you may be right. 'Just a cock.'

It ain't easy – it's even humiliating – to be belittled thus. Reduced to crawling, begging.

Changing the subject, I just remembered you basically telling me you had no memory of discussing your taste for Mandiargues and

Calaferte with my uncle. You did actually talk about it, one weekend in Jersey or thereabouts, with my mother. The facts, just the facts: six months ago, my mother caught me yet again with the Calaferte volume in my hands and said, 'I don't understand how you can read that book over and over again!' To which I responded that it was possibly one of the most beautiful books ever written. And I think she answered, 'How funny. You'd get on well with one of Philippe's colleagues.'

Me : '?'

Mum: 'One of the surgeons who works at the clinic. He's heavily into erotic literature.'

There you are. That's why we've been writing all these mails over the past days. Of course no one else needs to know. But you are as conscious of that as I am.

3.30 a.m.

Once again, do forgive me for the clumsy style and any spelling mistakes. It's that time of night when I'm no longer quite in control of myself . . .

Ellie

MONSIEUR

I'm often startled when I read your mails . . . as if you were a wonderful creation conjured up by my subconscious and my memory. *Peter Pan* . . . my very first unforgettable conscious erotic memory . . .

Yesterday I read every line of your blog while watching the photos on your Facebook profile. It was later reflected in my dreams. I'm eager for you to wake up properly . . . not that I have any objection to imagining you sleeping, alone and lasciviously clad in some unknown garb, the thought of which gives me shameful and delicious ideas . . .

I'm slowly waking up . . . My room is all red. Lascivious . . . I like your choice of words, Monsieur. I am lascivious and barely awake, waiting for the boiler repairman to arrive.

This is where I regret spending fourteen years studying surgery while a boiler repairman's certificate would have sufficed today . . .

You have no sense of poetry! There is nothing more beautiful than your job. Anyway, maybe I need medical attention. You see, I've just twisted my wrist. I need you to call on me. To look after it, of course.

Of course . . . to look after you . . . but are you alone?

My father is working in his study. Why? Did you want to come round?

How could I resist? My mind's all scrambled . . . Tuesday seems so far away still . . .

Doesn't patience feel like a row of teeth biting into your stomach?

Beautiful . . . Toothmarks exploring your flesh . . . your skin shimmering with impatience . . . and me behind my desk sitting awkwardly in an attempt to conceal the incongruous rise beneath my trousers from the gaze of all eyes in the waiting room.

Enough! You almost make me want to break my wrist!

Can't have your wrist out of action. You wouldn't be able to free the stranglehold of my belt . . . your light-coloured eyes wantonly seeking mine.

My dear, I'm in a meeting with some journalist friends. You'll make my cheeks go all red.

(The truth: I'm burrowed inside my bed like a helpless cock-teaser running out of ideas, unable to come up with the right response to his provocation, even incapable of imagining myself looking into his eyes while I open the flies of his suit trousers.)

I like making your cheeks go red . . . You have also . . . affected me . . . a lot. Is it a bad thing? Is all this wrong? And if so, would it change anything? Can I call you?

This man, on the other side of Paris, at the other end of the line, light years away from me, showed such old-fashioned delicacy as soon as he guessed I was taken aback by his masculine banter. Now that I've revealed myself to him in words that vibrate from his mobile, he wants to hear my voice. And I'm absolutely terrified to listen to compliments about my body or my mouth – which he has never even seen. I can't imagine his voice; can't imagine the way he might chuckle at my possible wit or because he knows I'm going red in the face. But I'm sure his voice will be the voice of the devil, whether it's deep and dark or clear and precise. And because I can't confront the devil with any form of assurance, I can only contemplate this call with the guilt of a kid who fucks guys around in Internet chatrooms.

Later that afternoon, as I had little else to do, I went to avenue Daumesnil to get waxed in a salon more used to older women. At least, that was what I assumed when I asked for a full Brazilian and the beautician gave me a puzzled look. In my handbag, my mobile was buzzing. Unknown caller. Unknown caller. Unknown caller.

Once I was hairless, I found the nerve to answer.

'Ellie?'

I knew it was him. It could have been anyone, but the voice had had a first name. Standing alone in a puddle of sunshine, my Wayfarers perched on my nose, I answered: '*Bonjour, Monsieur.*'

Did I mention how nice the city smelled that day? A lingering sun turning all the buildings slightly orange. Standing motionless in the middle of rue Dugommier, I bit my fingers while I weighed up the sound of his voice, the depth of his laughter. All around me, people moved in the slow motion that only belongs to summer, unaware of the story that was about to begin right there under their gaze. In spite of the muted heat of the waxing, a strange buzz was spreading under my skirt and, fearful that Monsieur might notice – God knew how – I moved the conversation into inconsequential areas. He answered, slowly, politely, complacently even, but somehow it was better than talking about sex. This man knew. This man had read my words. Maybe he was being gallant, pretending to believe my innocent-student spiel. Was that the impression I was giving? Was it really me?

And then, out of the blue, anything but spontaneous, I had to say something else: 'Your voice sounds so young!'

He burst out laughing, and I did too. Then, embarrassed by my gaucheness, I floundered in a sea of clumsy explanations.

'Not that you're old! It's just that your voice sounds young in comparison to . . . I mean, I was expecting . . . '

'An old geezer!' Monsieur was still laughing.

'No, just a *deeper* voice!'

Under my silk blouse, my back was wet with sweat.

I miss your voice already . . .

When I said you had a young voice, it was meant as a compliment. You have a lovely voice, clear and serious. Young, which you also happen to be. Well, not as young as me, I'm just a baby, even more so after what the beautician just did to me.

Hmm. I love it . . . My lips are already quivering at the thought of assaulting you there . . .

Stop saying things like that! You almost made me swallow my cigarette!

Things like what?

When you referred to my depilation.

I can't stop imagining the likely crimson hue of your mound following the recent treatment.

You're the devil incarnate. I just confessed I was now smooth and vulnerable, and you're already taking advantage of it by text. I just hope that in the flesh you'd do the same.

I will . . . totally . . . You'll find out how much by feeling how hard I would be against you . . . rock hard . . . against your smooth baby skin . . .

What shocking sort of perfume might you wear?

Habit Rouge by Guerlain. My sort of smell.

Do you talk? I mean, during.

I speak, I listen.

Cool.

(When you are five years old, the advent-calendar chocolate is the equivalent of a morning erection, peacefully waiting to be unsealed. Fifteen years later, Monsieur's mails are like the onset of a heart-attack.)

I've just arrived in Holland . . . My thoughts are full of your wisps of blonde hair, your cheeky smiles and adolescent sex . . . I am obsessed with you, Mademoiselle . . . I'm counting the hours . . . I'll be silent . . . I'll undress . . . and my tongue will move towards you and lick your drowsy stomach . . . My inquisitive hands will invade you . . . My sex will feverishly seek you out . . . You will pretend you're asleep . . . but once my tongue has begun exploring you and I've tasted the dew dripping between your thighs . . . felt your breath rise in your chest . . . your hands grip the sheets . . . I will bite your neck and almost trigger a scream that will linger in your throat until the moment my hard cock dives deep into your little pussy . . . while my fingers delve into your shuddering little arsehole . . . my cock plunging even deeper . . . making you beg ever more indecently for things I cannot write down here but which I promise to do to you . . . You try and hold back the pleasure and it's oh so terribly painful . . . but the expectation of an even more intense explosion helps you hold on longer . . . You shamelessly growl . . . impaled . . . restless . . . sweating profusely . . . eyes wild . . . the tip of your little pink tongue emerging between your half-open lips . . .

Did you get the text messages I sent last night? Was I too crude?

No . . . not at all. Crude, most definitely, but enjoyable. I'm working, can't answer you right now. Can you wait a bit longer?

It's not easy to wait, Mademoiselle. I'm under your spell. May I call you?

I'm in my father's car. You mustn't make me blush!

I feel it's my duty to make you blush.

Tell me how you will be on Tuesday when I enter

the room – and tell me about your breasts . . . I've just had a walk in the cold outside so my jeans won't betray me.

I have small breasts. Round. My nipples get hard terribly fast. Because they're small, men tend to neglect them, and small breasts are more sensitive.

I promise I will not neglect your breasts. I will worship them, kiss them, caress them, crush them, lick them . . . and maybe you'll help me come between them.

Between my breasts. Not just over my face.

A bite of sandwich has just gone down the wrong way.

See what happens when you become too perverse! Although I should take full responsibility for that.

Tell me about your arse.

My back arches a lot so my bum looks big, but it's my favourite bit of me. Big maybe, but hard and round.

I'd like to spread your arse cheeks open . . . while you're on all fours and watch my tongue slowly insinuate itself inside your small door . . . opening

for me like a shimmering flower, sucking me in
like a divine leech . . .

'How do you reply to a message like that?'

I handed my mobile to Alice, who was smoking by the
bathroom window.

'He's so FILTHY!' she cried, almost throwing the
phone into the washbasin.

'What should I do? How should I answer?' I asked, as
I spread the soap across my skin.

'Maybe you should just wash your divine leech. Make
sure it's clean.'

Let me call you.

I'm in my bath.

I'd love to be there, pushing your stomach against
the bathroom's cold floor, your face squashed
against the tiles, entering you . . .

Now you've made me truly wet. I'm quite curious
about what we might get up to. Loads of possibilities. Unless you die first, choking.

Not a chance. My whole body is drawn to you, as
is my soul . . .

ELLIE

As I said, but I'll say it again: an endless day. From eight in the morning to eight at night (twelve hours later) I've been wrapping pots of lily-of-the-valley and almost cut myself every time a new text arrived. 1 May's balance-sheet: my legs are painful and right now, slipping into my pyjamas (my girlfriends are deep in conversation in the next room), I can't even look at myself in the mirror. I don't know how you've achieved it but you seem to have taken possession of my eyes – every time I peer down at my body I burn up inside. Give me back to myself.

I'm so totally amazed by the fact that we did once come across each other before. I just keep on thinking about it. It means that a year or so ago while you were operating on some wide-open stomach I was watching you, and you could feel my eyes on you, but neither of us knew anything about it at the time. No doubt you already had the same eyes, the same mouth, the same hands, the same body, the same voice, and there I was so close to you, hidden under a uniform that probably suited me no better than crotchless pants would Golda Meir . . . We still didn't exist for each other, I was only the vaguely inconsequential niece of Dr Cantrel and I made no impression on you whatsoever . . . no more than a baby.

Prediction: in approximately two days you will be deeply embedded inside me.

Notions of good and evil: what we are doing is indeed evil. I don't think anyone could truly justify our course of action. Even worse to think that it's so exciting because it's evil. (At any rate, and I'm firmly closing the book on him here, by de Sade's standards we're still choristers clutching our crucifixes.)

It irritates me to remember that my ex-boyfriend thought me wanton. Maybe it was a joke. But I don't think so. I'm sure he believed I was something of a whore. And he was far from wrong. I freeze when I think of everything I got up to with him. I provoked him into saying awful things and, in the throes of lust, I surprised myself by coming out with words I couldn't record here.

So, I have been filthy and depraved and still, now, manage to be shocked when I read your texts.

You're invading my territory.

Usually I'm the one who takes innocent words and plays around with them to come up with . . . I don't know . . . 'Send me any message you wish, promise me everything, and Tuesday I will hold you so tight and captive within me, I will be warm and incandescent and melting around you, my little-girl hands so tight around your cock that you'll find it tough to hold on even a couple of minutes more.'

Or 'I might sound naïve on the phone, but I know that in the flesh I'll hold on to you with total abandon.' Not so explicit.

Or I could be quite vile. Example: 'Were it not utterly wicked, I would tell you I'd like to crawl under the table

55

where you're sitting and suck you off without letting you come in my mouth.'

Why not quote Calaferte? 'Thinking of it. Nothing else. Strongly. My cunt and your cock.'

I want to be both a whore and a little girl and I will be what you want me to be.

Tuesday is at the same time too near and too far. And I'm already in such a state on D-Day-minus-two that I can't even bear to think of how I'll survive Monday night. I don't want to touch myself anywhere. I cherish the sensation that I've been on fire for a thousand years.

Listen to Velvet Underground. It'll be a delight for me to explain why I find their music extraordinary. Though I doubt you're aware of it. There's one song in particular, '*Heroin*', so full of sexual electricity. My favourite, by far. And then there's '*Venus In Furs*' (whose sounds make love inside my ears every time I listen to it on my iPod), '*I'm Waiting For The Man*' and '*After Hours*'.

I've only had a single glass to drink so far and I'm not doing too badly, am I? Anyway I'm off to meet up with the girls. They're probably wondering who I'm talking to.

Fortunately God created mobile phones. I'd go mad without mine, and without those texts of yours that keep my heart fluttering wildly.

The heart of a

not a   slut
a truelittle   hypocrite

(connect the right answers. Level-four difficulty exercise.)

56

The hours are going to seem even longer. I wake up with my mind so full of images of you . . . a landscape of photos of you stolen from your Facebook page and the texts you've sent me . . . as if the motionless person in the photographs began moving, smiling, slowly undressing . . . My cock is so hard this morning . . . Having licked the palm of my hand and made it wet, I almost negligently caress myself . . . imagining your eyes watching me, conjuring the smell of your cunt on my tongue . . . Imagining your arse triggers convulsions in my wrist and I know that pleasure is advancing . . . but I hold back. On Tuesday I intend to burst within you, flooding your dark, moist, secret, forbidden place . . .

The room I enticed Monsieur to on that first morning in early May was – and still is, I guess – in the fifteenth *arrondissement*, an area I had seldom set foot in, and never have since. The window looked out on the rue des Volontaires, some decaying buildings and a miniature hospital surrounded by an incongruous cocoon of greenery.

'Well planned. There's even a clinic over the road should I faint in your arms!' I wrote to Monsieur.

It was Monday night and I was quivering like a dead leaf, smoking fag after fag on the balcony. Behind me, the room was a pitiful mess – scattered clothing, the sheets stained with the juice of fresh blackberries and overripe mangoes. Six thirty p.m. Babette was spending the evening with Simon, Ines was in Deauville, Juliette and Mathilde had gone to the movies. I was on my own and likely to be until ten the following morning. Not a friendly soul to hold my hand throughout this endless and heartbreaking period of expectancy. From time to time, Monsieur would parsimoniously send me one of those riveting yet revolting messages that helped both shorten and lengthen the flow of time; that was my only contact with the rest of the world. Every time my mobile vibrated I was close to jumping out of the window. And as soon as I had read the message, there was a second or two while I wondered whether I should gather up all my stuff and leave like a thief, without warning Monsieur that in the morning he would find the scene of the crime empty. So many things encouraged me to do just that: the thought of my uncle, of my sister, who had seen me leave the house carrying all those nibbles, but most of all the immense fear of facing the man who, for the past five days, had thought of me as the most emancipated of all the girls he had held in his arms. In reality, alone in my vast cast-iron bed, I was rehearsing a multitude of positions that might hide from him the dubious extent of my depilation and the dimple on the left side of my bum, a blemish from puppy-fat days. I was consumed with fear. As two whole seconds slowly ticked by, a small squeaky voice in my head asked, *And what will the skin of such an older guy feel like? Will it be supple and firm or soft and wrinkled? And what happens if he doesn't even like me? If he's ancient and balding and his stomach sticks out? If he sweats like a pig? If he's toothless? What will I do if it turns out – and it could easily happen – that he's totally repulsive? And what about his cock? How do they get hard when they're so old? How hard can they get?*

Incoming message during the course of my inner monologue: 'I'm dying inside at the thought of being with you.'

As if it had been a waking dream, I retain few memories of the evening I spent with my friends from *Stupre*. There's the leather notepad in which Benjamin sketched my face in the style of Francis Bacon, drops of strawberry juice spread across it like dried blood. There's the photograph Kenza took while I was leaning against the bed post staring into nowhere, a cigarette in my hand. It's the only image in existence of me with my head so full of him. Two months later, I think my face has changed so much already. Maybe not its shape – although I did lose weight – but my eyes, a look in them that I've never seen since. I miss it terribly.

Later, already deep into the night, I washed my hair for hours, or at least it felt like it, even if I only spent fifteen minutes at it, lost in an alcoholic coma and senseless dreams. The room's mirrors were set up so that my naked figure in the shower spread right across the room – the optical illusion that we had found fascinating from a photographic point of view now felt disturbing, as if the room already knew everything of the future. From every angle, the small ill-proportioned room with its heavy curtains and dark wallpaper was already vibrating with the sheer essence of Monsieur. The mirrors I travelled between were searching for his unknown silhouette. And the immaculately made bed throbbed with anticipation. The sparse furniture was probably wondering what role it might play when he finally arrived.

Wearing a towel that was much too short, I leaned against the window and smoked yet another cigarette. Neither Paris nor the fifteenth *arrondissement* felt normal: there was a tremulous tension in the air, as if I were expecting the devil or the Messiah. Or the end of the world.

My mobile vibrated: a final message from Monsieur as if my nervousness reached him: 'I'm about to go to bed. My next words will be for your ears only.'

The dreadful finality of that text assailed me and I flung away the cigarette. It landed on the roof of a car parked in the street. I felt on edge. I had given Monsieur the number of the room, the floor; he could appear at any moment, and there I was with my hair dripping, my face caked with streaming makeup, my legs still unshaven. And that was far from all of it: I was convulsed with so much more than the fear that I might not please him. The memory I had of him was terrifying: I could vaguely invoke his face, the shape of his mouth (why his mouth?). I drew back from completing the ghostly identikit portrait in my mind, even though it had been lingering there for days. The spectre haunting me was surrounded by a fuzzy mist, no nose, no eyes, no distinctive features, just that mouth. THAT mouth.

How good it feels to remember that evening now, some months later. Half-drunk in the Métro, I write it down lovingly with pencil on paper. I remember every single gesture. I could make a movie of that night without missing out a single detail. How I went to bed watching a report on the Arte network about young Belarussian rock 'n' rollers, transfixed by my appalling lack of interest in those people and their plight. How I set my alarm for six in the morning before switching off the lamp and the telly, left alone in the blue light of the empty streets. The anonymous smell of hotel sheets, always a bit too rough and not warm enough, but just then the level of discomfort I needed. I had no intention of spending a comfortable night.

When I started awake, the room was red. A beautiful, barely luminous shade of red.

It was a radiant beginning to the week. The uncertain light of a beautiful day threaded through the curtains. The sky was uniformly blue. I lay there waiting, apprehensive, like before an exam, my stomach in knots. The tenuous arpeggio of desire quivered deep inside me: I recognized its insistent vibrato drowning below the din of white noise. In a foetal position beneath the enormous white duvet, I watched the hours go by and the sun climb in the sky, torn by lack of sleep and seized by a sickly form of lethargy interspersed with dreams that were evocative of fever, as if I had fallen ill. I was acutely aware of every sound on the stairs outside, confined as I was to that small room with its blue walls. There was only one thing I could do while I lay there: count the number of flowers in the pattern of the wallpaper, catalogue them, analyse the blooms. Wide-open pink tulips, three-headed buttercups in a flurry of petals. A lily, leaves unfurling, was carved into the dark wood of the chest near the window.

The possibility that Monsieur might not prove attractive had occurred to me but I hadn't worried about it. There was something else, though: the certainty he and I shared, even if it was only over the phone, that we were reaching for something infinitely more important than a mere Tuesday morning in a Paris hotel room, something more subtle than the physical. It was not love, but the attraction we shared to a relationship that would be intellectual and immoral. I still had enough time to flee and stop thinking of how exciting sleeping with Monsieur would be: I was in love with the idea of being twenty and waiting naked, but for a pair of hold-up stockings, for a former colleague of my uncle aged forty-six and married with five children. A man who was slightly older than my father. But the absence of morality in this liaison held me there as if it were a ball and chain. I had never experienced such excitement, a curious blend of hunger, fear and finely chiselled expectation. Beneath the reassuring darkness of the duvet, I felt my heartbeat under the tight skin of my chest. The hours passed. I was waiting for Monsieur to free me, allow me to breathe again without pain.

I was pretending to be asleep, experimenting with my breathing, when Monsieur pushed open the creaking door I had left ajar. A man's slow steps, muffled by the carpet. My heart stopped. Until now it had only paused each time I'd heard a step on the landing, only to resume its monotonous beat, in unison with the silence. I could feel the new presence in the room, the intrusion, the movement in the air, thick and sweet like candyfloss, hear the door handle being turned (no one else is expected; what is to happen is just seconds away), the whisper of a coat being draped across a chair, but mainly the softness of his approach, almost imperceptible. In fact, with my eyes half open beneath my fringe, I found it difficult to focus on where Monsieur was standing. He could have been everywhere and anywhere, and my only clue was a purple shadow moving across the blue walls.

I was still seeking him out when my doubts disappeared: the mattress, to my right, sagged under his weight. The heaviness of him.

Strange how, sometimes, you can surmise with a degree of precision a man's state of mind by the way he sits beside you on the bed. Some are like tree trunks, paralysed by their desire. Others, impatient like children, move swiftly to caresses. But with Monsieur, there were a few brazen moments when I felt his gaze move across my naked back and shoulders, then the slow rise of a hand through the air and its slow landing on my neck, fluid and determined. I could hear his breath, intuit his calm. He was in perfect control. The way the fabric of his jacket brushed my skin, the click-click of the watch on his wrist, a tapestry of perceptions that betrayed civility: no doubt he had nodded politely at the receptionist two floors below as he walked across the hotel foyer. Even the fingers lingering on the back of my neck felt elegant and relaxed. For a few minutes they fluttered down my spine, reaching disturbingly for the depths of my soul.

Paris held its breath.

The infinitesimal portion of my brain not engrossed by the journey of his long, thin fingers along my shoulder blades was moving rapidly through the gears: I was grasping for a detail that might crystallize in one thought where those fingers had originated and what memories they held. I had to establish that those hands were his and not a stranger's. Why those caresses were anything but anonymous.

When his hand took hold of my arse, I stretched out like a cat, in perfect imitation of the sudden awakening of a child from heavy sleep. This was when Monsieur understood that I was aware of his presence. He whispered something I couldn't understand, muted as it was by the rustle of the sheets, but I recognized his voice, deep and grainy.

A distant church bell rang at ten o'clock as Monsieur, pressed into the curve of my back, ran his fingers over my body. On my shoulder the softness of a freshly shaved cheek, the silent epiphany of a kiss. Monsieur said nothing. His regular sighs contrasted with my gasps – he seemed unaware of the torture his belt buckle was inflicting on me. I was terrified of turning over and seeing him, afraid to disturb the hitherto cerebral desire I felt for him, a blend of attraction and repulsion I couldn't explain. His patience was wearing me out – that he couldn't see my face clearly didn't bother him. Like me, he was happy to tease out beauty and wantonness wherever it might exist, even if he was missing the whole picture. All I knew was that his hands were soft and his skin smelled good. Which told me that the entirety of Monsieur would not disappoint me.

Initially I thought I could play with him, as I had done with most of my thirty-year-old-lovers, holding the reins and controlling him by rubbing my arse against the hardness of his cock. But he stared at me with a perfect combination of naked desire and adult tenderness, which disarmed me. I realized there and then that Monsieur might well pretend he was yielding control to me, but that this was an illusion: even silent, facing my back, his eyes could tie me in knots.

His fingers sprang into action, seeking my folds, my openings, wandering wherever my impatience had left me vulnerable. I watched myself struggle against him, but Monsieur took control and, in an instant, my legs were wide open, my arse cheeks spread, and my attempts to free myself were those of an animal caught in a trap. The light of day, even muted by the curtains, meant I no longer had any intimate secrets from him. He knew how wet I was.

(The room smelled of old waxed wood and dust. It was the familiar odour of a bourgeois house, saturated with furniture polish, that I could smell as Monsieur held his hand to my mouth and I gasped for air, stuttering, 'No, no,' into the sleeve of his jacket.)

My cheeks heated as I became aware that Monsieur was looking between my legs, with the elusive expression men reserve for gazing at that part of a woman's body. In that moment the connection between his eyes and his fingers felt eternal. I suppose it was a look of love, which I would continue to witness on every Tuesday morning that he parted my thighs. A form of love I had yet to tame, new to me and intimidating, scorching and rough, which I had come across only in the verses of Apollinaire or the colours of Courbet. It was then, I think, that I knew Monsieur would please me, beyond any physical consideration, with a love so fiery. I'd thought it didn't exist, but it does.

Finally he touched me. And I *knew* at once, from the depths of my confusion, that I liked him. And I was glad that he knew I was willingly cushioned against his thumb, hard under his forefinger, swollen against the palm of his hand, touched with awe and precision, like a painting or a precious doll. The quiet strength of his hand in my hair and across my skin.

In one single bound Monsieur was naked, and I'm shivering as I write, remembering his heat against mine, his cock against my arse. I still don't know how he managed to undress so fast, so silently. It took him seconds – I barely had time to wonder whether I should be flattered or offended: I had grown up with men whose idea of seduction focused on the slow shedding of our clothing. I had little time to dwell on it: Monsieur's immense shadow loomed over me. I felt the tremor of his breath, and then the room melted around us. At the moment he took me, I opened my eyes and saw his hands on my hips, thin, long hands, the sharp reflection of his wedding ring.

If there is one single thing – among a hundred others – that I have never forgiven Monsieur for, it's to have mounted me without protection that first morning, so fast I was unable to stop him. (I didn't worry about it for long.) It elicited in me a misunderstanding that was later to destroy me: that I was the only one with whom he had taken such a risk (which extended to his wife – she would have been far from amused to learn that I had passed on to her an STD). Monsieur penetrated me inch by inch until he reached my depths with a wet slurp that shattered my soul – it was like some obscene sound effect in a porno movie. I prayed he hadn't heard it, but the silence was such that it couldn't have escaped his attention – along with anything else that related to my arse or the burning intersection where his body and mine were now joined.

Two months later, the heat is oppressive and I am sitting at my desk, wearing the nightie I had with me that Tuesday. Writing is a slow chore and it's silly that the moment of penetration is all I remember with absolute clarity. I have forgotten everything about our first embrace, apart from its beginning and end, overtaken as I was by wonderment at being filled by that man, filled by the hardness of his cock, hard for me. I was too busy surrendering myself to the moment and have no memory of pleasure or pain, only that, gasping wildly against him, I knew I wanted to see him again, and again, and again. There was a fire burning inside Monsieur, offering me glimpses of worlds unknown through half-open distant doors. Flash memories: me, sitting in his lap, panicked at the thought I had exhausted him. Me, crawling over his stomach, sniffing him; his flat stomach, the firm, soft skin of a thin man that the passing years had barely altered, just blemishes here and there that only I could feel against my cheeks, beneath my fingers.

I know I gazed at Monsieur before I took him in my mouth; I stared at his body, fascinated as always by the shamelessness of a man's erection, the pride he displays in his spectacular nakedness. Monsieur's legs were wide enough apart for me to find refuge between them, and through the curtain of my eyelashes I could see the brown silk blanket through which his cock surged. His taste blended with mine. This was mostly new territory for me. As much as I would have liked to impress him with my appreciation and knowledge of a man's body, I didn't want him to think that, at only twenty, I was as wanton as he.

Another flash memory, so crude: after just a few seconds, he pulled out of my mouth and turned me onto my stomach, so fast I almost bit him, as the stream of cum he had been unable to hold back flew down my throat. I heard him speak, but I could barely understand a word he was saying, moaning as I was, lying in the gutter of my mind with the filth of his voice, that still ownerless voice for I hadn't yet looked at his face . . . I was mortified to realize that Monsieur was silent, watching me calmly, listening to the broken rhythms of my breathing. What I had taken as an insult was the sound of his cock sliding rapidly in and out of me, his belly thumping against my arse. I had to strain my neck to see the evidence for myself: my arse quivering like jelly with every thrust while Monsieur held me pinned down, his hands outstretched, his nails digging deep into my flesh. Even from that awkward angle, I could see his cock sliding inside me, and the sound it made as it slammed against the back wall of my cunt was loud enough to take physical form and colour. I was embarrassed but crazily excited, and I began to moan louder, if only to drown those sounds. But what came from my throat was more like an echo of Monsieur's movements inside me, mimicking their strength and depth, their powerful vibration. The sounds of a bitch in heat.

Monsieur pulled away from me, and I was left gaping, pink and vanquished, my body still shaking convulsively, flat on my stomach. Before I closed my eyes, I glanced for the first time at his face as he held his cock and leered at my body.

I had known the taste of his cum before I had seen him properly. Now I opened an eye and he was there. His large grey eyes were full of the sensuality he shared with his eldest son (I had come across a photograph of Charles a few days earlier) and the soft curves of his mouth betrayed his enjoyment of love. His nose was perfectly positioned between eyes and mouth, a nose made to ferret between my thighs and tango across my neck. All of Monsieur invited me to purr like a cat in his presence.

Or maybe I was already triumphantly corrupted by the submission that ran from my cheeks to the aqueduct of my mouth.

Who were you, Monsieur? Who were you *really*? What did you conceal in yourself to make that ordinary Tuesday morning what it became inside my head? Had I been in your shoes, I'm almost certain I would not have pushed open the door to that room, or at any rate not with your poise, as if you felt you already owned me. You looked at me as if you'd hungered for me all of your life. I saw how you moved around the bed, how you took control of me. I allowed myself no protest: that room would always be ours.

Do you remember the twenty minutes after we had made love? I was stuck against you, your torso weighing down on me as I wiped the cum on to the sheets. Thinking I was trying to move away, you tightened your grip on me: 'Stop fidgeting!'

Further captive caresses. I only truly got used to them much later, after the time for tenderness had passed. How sad.

For a long time we didn't talk. I was scared of looking into your eyes. I was studying the structure of our silence. I was the first to speak.

'So, you came.'

It was all I could think to say. I was still surprised, shocked that you'd had the guts to leave your flat and journey through the streets separating the Latin Quarter and Convention to climb the twisting stairs of the tiny hotel to our room after four days of holding your hard cock in your hand and reading our texts.

I can't summon the subtlety of the dialogue we exchanged, and it's a pity: I'd give anything to be able to screen in my mind the film of my first morning in your arms! I listened to the tone of your voice, echoing like music. The perfect voice of the hundred faceless lovers who had hitherto kneaded my body for ten minutes before I fell asleep each night. Until you held me down for the first time.

'You didn't imagine it would happen as it did?'

'How?'

'That I'd be like that. Did you think it would be so gentle?'

(So gentle, Monsieur. How true.)

'That I would enter the room silently, that I would caress you and wait for you to wake? I could have rushed in, jumped on you and raped you. Torn your stockings apart and sodomized you.'

Sodomized me? Monsieur! How crude! I have only a faint memory of the moment, but I think my ears shrivelled to hear that. I felt a brief spasm of disgust, thinking that 'arse-fucked' would have sounded so much better from your lips (as we soon discovered when you whispered the dreaded word into my ear on another Tuesday morning). Anything but 'sodomized'. One day, Monsieur, I will be accepted into the Académie Française and I will expunge that word from the dictionary, if it's the last thing I do.

Do you remember, later that morning, you released me reluctantly and I put on a Liberty slip rolled down to the waist? I lit a cigarette, leaned back against the cast-iron bed posts and displayed myself, like a tramp, as you watched, constantly caressing the tips of my breasts. I could see myself reflected in the large mirror facing the bed and, fag hanging from my lips, I postured, talking about books, university, the friends I'd been with the previous evening. A veritable ballet of open thighs, studied lazy stretches all the way down to my toes, contortions against the bed posts, then bending over in a pretence of picking up my hair slides so I could show off my bum. Your smile was both sexual and paternal, just right for the situation, blessing the spectacle of my youth and your maturity with perfect insolence: Monsieur sprawled in a hotel bed with his naked, post-adolescent Lolita still gaping from his ministrations.

It was one of those mornings you only get in May. The sun rising slowly while time stands still, immutable.

From time to time, you would interrupt to say: 'You're so beautiful!'

And I felt like a star among stars. (Much later you would ask yourself how I could have surrendered myself so completely and develop such a passion for you. The spiky adoration I had for you surprised you: you were unable to determine at which stage our traditional roles had switched. I don't know. But I'm sure that the compliments and love in your seductive eyes had a lot to do with it.)

I lay down against you, between your arms and knees, and you cupped your hand around my right breast.

'This little tit is going to be lonely when I leave,' you predicted.

The truth is, it took me a week to miss the caresses and the rest. Remember: attraction, repulsion. You fascinated me. There was something highly toxic about my unholy attraction to vice. As my hands neared your hips without touching them, I was almost fearful of looking you in the eye. You held me tightly against you, stroking my hair, quietly calming me. As if there was nothing wrong with you freely coming over my face, then being playfully tender with me. Lying motionless by your side for a few minutes, I felt as if my whole body was burning from the inside. You didn't understand: my frequent little treks from bed to window annoyed you as time ticked on and you were growing hard again.

You must have known how much in awe of you I was. The day before, I had sent you a truthful text message: 'It's all a bit scary.'

You had answered: 'Don't be scared, I'm the gentlest of them all.'

But, Monsieur, you knew that was wrong. You knew all too well that your softness and tenderness were unconnected with your illusory gentleness. You were just readying yourself to jump. I could see it in your eyes as we talked, as we began some sort of competition to see who would lower their gaze first. A competition I lost.

You allowed me to escape, with a grin of amusement. While you still can, your eyebrows seemed to say. Faced with silence, you took an old edition of Mandiargues from your medical bag. It was encased in a dainty ultramarine cardboard box. Oh, Monsieur, the way you made me feel just then! As if all my Christmases had come at once. OK, so I had reached out to you for your love of erotic literature, but for this to be confirmed with such elegance . . . Father Christmas had turned up in the middle of May. I hardly dared turn the yellowing pages, shrieking like a kid at a Disney movie, eyes wide. Then I handed it back to you, almost sad at having had the privilege to glimpse your world of rare books and limited editions. I worked in a flower shop for four hundred euros a month and slept surrounded by paperbacks, which was all a student could afford. And you said to me: 'No. Keep it. It's for you, a gift.'

I protested, squeaking like a piglet, as I handed it back to you, but you pushed it towards my chest with a smile, and I was forced to accept it. Later I would slip it into my overnight bag between my laptop and sponge-bag. It would share the space with a tube of toothpaste.

(Do you know what I did as soon I got home, far from parents in my pink basement room? I tore off a piece of paper and, between the divine pages of Mandiargues, I slipped a note I had scribbled with a ballpoint pen: 'Given by C.S., on 5/5/09'. Just like a junior courtesan.)

For a brief moment, I might have felt like a whore. But then I changed my mind: even Zola had never imagined a whore being paid for her services with rare books.

And then you mounted me again, doggy-style, and all I could smell was the overripe mango I had brought with me, its fragrance gliding over my skin like oil, its heady odour of turpentine and alcohol blending with the Guerlain on your fingers (the persistent sweet fragrance of men who love women). I barely dared open my eyes: to see would have detracted from the magic conjured by the sensation of fullness. I felt like sobbing every time you withdrew from me. How could you know our two bodies would fit so well together? Before I knew you, the possibility of such osmosis was just a pleasing idea. It wasn't lust that was blinding me, but the fluid way we fucked, the communion of movements orchestrated with a hypnotic sensuality, the perfect conjunction of your breath and mine. Me, Ellie, twenty, a tiny plump body still trying to get rid of its baby fat, and you, Monsieur, with so many years of caresses, together in a clandestine bed, at the time of day when all the people we knew were leaving for work. You came inside me with a final gasp, while I held you tight as a nutcracker, every muscle in my body straining.

'Good thing I have a coil,' I said later, with a smile, as I sat in your lap. 'A good thing I take precautions. You didn't even ask if it was safe to come inside me.'

'I was confident you were careful,' you replied, pinching my nipples.

'You can't be sure I'm clean. Maybe I sleep with all and sundry without using condoms.'

'But you don't,' you concluded.

I was flabbergasted by your adolescent carelessness. I decided to be like you: forget about Andrea, the risks, your wife. I would have to trust to the fact that you were married and that, in theory, you couldn't allow yourself to catch an STD. My mistake.

'You should come and watch me perform an operation,' you suggested, a few minutes later, nibbling my neck.

It would be so risky to join you at my uncle's old clinic in that pretty part of the Marais, where hordes of nurses might recognize me as the little girl with flat shiny shoes running up and down the corridors when nice Dr Cantrel visited. I would have to invent university coursework to justify my presence and lie to at least twenty people to drag the sexual tension and sheer wrongness of our affair into the aseptic operating block.

'That would be so cool!' I answered.

And then you left, in the middle of a fascinating conversation rudely interrupted by your damn phone. I jumped from the bed, scattering cushions and pillows, shrieking wildly, 'No! Stay a little longer!' In truth, I was strangely anxious to be alone so that I could examine my memories with forensic attention. There was little I could do while still in your presence: I could store away precise images of you, fragments of conversations and the sound of your velvet voice. Maybe I already knew how much I would miss the aura that surrounded you.

'I can't, sweetheart. I have to go to work. But believe me . . .'

Another meaningful gaze.

'. . . it's the last thing I wish to do.'

I would hear many similar excuses, punctuating the course of our narrative. Weren't we characters in a script? Remember how you took flight, that final, pensive look in your eyes as you reached halfway down the stairs, me standing with naked breasts on the landing, framed by the door, still steaming with lust. As if you were exiting stage left. Once I returned to the room, traumatized by your departure, I went through the motions of an actress after a show, packing up my makeup, folding my clothes, bone tired but happy. I smoked, sitting on the bed, facing the open window, absolutely starving. Physically, it felt much like the first time, the same recognizable lassitude; a deep craving to fill myself with pasta, chips, peanuts, shandy, to feel complete again.

But when I got home, having hurled my bags onto the bed, I couldn't even summon the strength to walk up to the kitchen. Spread out beneath my bed cover, I closed my eyes, trying to muster the energy to heat a saucepan of something, and woke at five o'clock, refreshed. My sister watched me drown a whole packet of *biscottes* in cold milk and frowned. Perhaps she'd noticed the purple rings of makeup and fatigue around my eyes.

'What's up?' I queried, somewhat aggressively.

She was sitting next to me at the table. I could hear the distinctive murmur of her breathing.

'Nothing,' she answered, without looking at me, and I knew that she knew.

Something had betrayed me.

ELLIE

I'm writing to you from the large, cold bed in my small room, at my parents' flat (such a pity you can't come here, much too dangerous – I have an immense mirror on the wall facing my bed, and the images we could reflect in it would be so amazing).

I was going to proceed with a full debrief of this morning's events, but whatever I come up with will lessen what I treasure in my mind. I have no intention of cheapening the sensations with a series of superlatives and stupid adjectives. It was all superlative, anyway.

I'm filled with diabolical ideas. Especially since I read *Irene's Cunt*. I have a limitless admiration for men who truly appreciate cunt, having listened to so much crap from men of my own generation (or even older ones, in truth). I would not have tolerated a single negative comment about my own, but I know from having discussed the subject with many twenty- and twenty-five-year-old men that they find it ugly. So, maybe I'm being subjective, having lived for twenty years with one between my legs (and having no intention of changing, as its uses can be so delicious), but I've decided I'll never go to bed again with men who are incapable of tenderness for that part of the female body. If *I* am to spend the rest of my life literally worshipping men's bodies, I expect the same in return. Further, if I were a man, before I fucked any girl I would spend at least five minutes just gazing at her from top to toe. I mean *truly* looking at her. If only for safety reasons. It astounds me that so many of them are willing to stick their cock in without any idea of what might be lurking inside. Like sharp teeth. Not only is it rude, it's also annoying.

If I tell you I'm distracted now, it's because a previous lover of mine was attempting to chat about sex on Facebook a moment ago. I disconnected for fear of what I might say. Today I have no intention of pleasing him.

I've been thinking, it's best I don't tell my uncle if I come to the clinic on Wednesday. He's in England at the moment and can't be contacted anyway, but he'd probably say I can't watch an operation because he no longer works there. And it would be awkward to persist – 'But surely if you asked your friend they'd let me in . . .' Tell me what you think. I doubt that any of the anesthetists or nurses will phone him to let him know I was at the clinic. Anyway, I'll do what you want me to do. As far as Uncle Philippe is concerned, I'm still four years old with a strawberry lollipop in my mouth and spend my days frolicking in the Luxembourg Gardens with a helium balloon. He has no idea.

At any rate, tell me what you think. You might have a different perspective on it.

I lied. I slept badly last night, constantly waking up and checking the time. At six, I finally got up, had a shower and fell asleep again at nine thirty. Every time I closed my eyes, I had spasms in the small of my back from all the anxiety. I dreamed of you. I even thought it was real, that you were lying in the bed next to me and I could feel your thigh between my legs, and got all aroused. When I opened my eyes, I saw I was alone and the sun had barely risen. My heart was beating wildly when I was waiting for you to arrive. Mind you, it behaved in a similar way later. But it made me feel better. I was back where I'd wanted to be for the past five days.

I'm now going to have a lie-down before I cook myself something for supper (a prospect as entertaining as having toothpicks inserted under my nails). I will write to you again at greater length afterwards . . .

Ellie

PS I've just had my bath and I found one of your hairs. Guess where. Easy, eh?

A good thing my mother is still asleep. I would have found it pretty awkward to explain why I had dressed like this on a Wednesday morning during the student strikes. At eight o'clock. Without even being conscious of it, I'd done myself up like the perfect tart. The world surrounding me may be unaware of it, but I'm not. It's the way my legs hurt from wearing these heels, and my skirt's designed to be pulled off in one movement.

I stop a taxi, the posh way to reach the opulent Marais district. I'm already late anyway. By at least twenty minutes. All the way to the Gare de Lyon, I alternately watched the cab's ticking meter and my watch. My mobile phone didn't ring. Afraid. I can't even be a proper mistress. I'm twenty, I'm jobless, I spend my life sleeping: I should always be on time for Monsieur.

And then, I don't know how, everything changes. I see the Saint-Paul church, its slate roof bathing in the warm early-morning sun, all the fools in their two-piece suits strolling like robots to their tiny offices, while I'm sitting here, oblivious, in my skirt and high heels, travelling to the man who had me years ago (or was it just two days ago?), to watch him perform in his surgical scrubs, laughing in the face of danger personified by the doctors and nurses who dined at my uncle's when I was only five, my head in the clouds. I must talk to someone. I must call someone or I'll start to scream: it's happiness, stage fright. If not I'll explode into a million pieces. I must call Babette. It's ten to nine and she'll kill me, but no matter.

Babette must have gone to bed late and smoked a lot with

her boyfriend. Her voice has the charm of a betting-shop manageress's.

'Is it important? If not, I'm falling asleep while you're talking.'

'Don't go back to sleep. I must share this amazing moment with you!' I'm like a cat on hot bricks, watching the rue de Rivoli speed by outside the cab window.

At the other end of the line, Babette is shaking herself awake. Knowing her, she's already sitting cross-legged and lighting a Lucky Strike. I like Babette. Ines would have hung up on me without a second thought.

'Guess where I am?'

'I haven't a clue. Somewhere that makes you happy.'

'I'm in a taxi, near Saint-Paul. I'm about to watch Monsieur at the clinic, operating.'

Seconds pass, and Babette is totally silent. I'm dismayed.

'And . . . I don't know . . . I just had to tell someone . . . explain how madly happy I feel. Not that it seems to have had any effect on you.'

'May I point out to you again that I've just woken up? So, you're going to see Monsieur, then?'

'Absolutely.'

'But you saw him yesterday!' she shrieks, as if it were now her turn to be agitated. 'Are you mad?'

'I promised him I'd go to the clinic and watch him operate.'

'And you're trying to justify the fact that you give in to his every whim.'

'Maybe . . .' I admit, red-faced but proud to have become his whim.

Whims are so underrated: the way they consume you from the inside, evidence of immaturity; it's easy to forget how vital they can be, the craving they represent for beauty or more. After all, I'm only twenty. What more could you expect of me? I don't care that I have to rise at seven thirty in the morning on a strike day to fit into Monsieur's timetable, so that he can see admiration as well as desire in my eyes. But Babette doesn't share my view. 'You'll kill me,' I tell her. 'There I was, flying through the cloudless sky like a seagull, and you're taking aim at me all the way.'

'Not at all. Anyway, you know that you and him, it can't go anywhere. Might as well enjoy it while it lasts.'

'Did you have to say that?'

The driver manoeuvres the taxi into the rue du Roi-de-Sicile (we're getting so close and my whole body is on edge), and Babette bursts out laughing. Then she says, 'I just don't want to have to pick up the pieces. Anyway, go ahead and let Monsieur pinch your tits under those awful blue pyjamas.'

'So I have your blessing? *On the right, here, please.*'

'Sure. Although I know I'll regret that when you come to me with tears in your eyes, but we're all fallible. We can't predict the future, can we? Who cares? Two seconds of pleasure versus two weeks of pain? Just go for it.'

'OK, I have to hang up. We're almost at the clinic and you're giving me the creeps.'

'Go and get drunk with happiness.'

I can't help laughing, but I sense that Babette's last words will come back to haunt me. I get out of the taxi, almost stumble, and there I am, at the clinic. Remember,

Ellie, when you were only ten you hated to be brought here, and now a few years later you've actually spent thirty euros to get to the place faster.

Those were the days, when I tried to hide around the corners in corridors to escape the visits: twenty minutes of being stroked by patients who gushed at the sight of the cluster of little blonde girls hanging on to Dr Cantrel's coat, in rooms stinking of ether and pain, and as a bonus, the occasional sight of enormous, bleeding lines of stitches across the knees of sobbing old women. I can remember how my sister Louise was unable to eat the piece of chocolate she had been offered by the nurses, arguing it must taste like the scabs she had seen on the shin of an Algerian workman. We spent hours – or so it felt to us – in the waiting room, Alice hiding from the doctors behind Philippe's legs. Disgusted as I was by the spectacle of wounds and the heavy smell of medicine, I was endlessly fascinated by the way others looked up at him with respect and gratitude. You could be a famous surgeon and still run around the Luxembourg Gardens with a swarm of brats in your wake, or take hold of our small hands, sticky with popcorn, to guide us across the rue de Rennes. It was only, many years later, when I visited the clinic that I *realized* we had a doctor in the family. That was also the first time I came across Monsieur, or at any rate the anonymous pair of grey eyes he then was.

Another real-life-encounter memory. It's all coming back to me, like a dream, or maybe even a sequence from a good erotic movie. An evening party on the occasion of

85

my uncle's birthday: I was barely eighteen, and we must have ignored each other.

(How curious it is that the men we love already exist in their own right before our perception changes them and they enter the familiarity of our world.)

How nice it would have been if he had already known then that the plump, blonde schoolgirl sitting at the table across from him would one day encircle his body with her legs. I can almost feel the tension in the air: halfway through a formal conversation I could have whispered in his ear, 'I will become your mistress,' then moved away from the table, still wearing my school uniform, leaving him to guess at the shape of my breasts under the T-shirt, and what the whole body he would caress two years later actually looked like. Sliding like a snake between tables and chairs, spreading my smell across him, like a spell, as my hands waved in the air. It would have been nice to be able to watch him silently, and then, under the cover of innocence, speak to him, make him laugh, imagine myself naked against him. I can picture an evening spent moving together from room to room, not daring to do anything. Then, in a neglected corner of the house, Monsieur and I would begin to debate literature, he sitting in a deep armchair, me cross-legged on the bed at the other end of the room. The door wide open, he would not have tolerated any suggestion of impropriety, even though those few stolen minutes away from the other guests would have been full of unspoken cravings deep inside our guts. Monsieur understands perfectly what lies behind a young girl's eyes, when she is at an age that makes men reluctant to respond to her smiles. He is one of those men who recognize the way blushes spread across cheeks, the initial listlessness clouding the eyes, and responds accordingly, already so cleverly aware of what lies in wait beneath the mask.

Go and tell your uncle that that's why you're standing in front of the clinic today.

I call Monsieur. I can hear his smile when he says, 'I'm on my way, darling.'

A blonde secretary stares at me, as if she has overheard our conversation. I have absolutely no intention of justifying my presence to her. I turn to the window and gulp the last drops of my coffee, suddenly filled with the anguish of Tuesday morning. The silence in the small blue room is so oppressive that I start humming as I read the hygiene warnings Blu-tacked to the wall. Someone is walking about behind the door on the left, which leads to the operating theatre. A few steps away from me, the secretary is restless, shuffling her paperwork. I wish my whole face could be pixellated, fearing she might recognize me as Dr Cantrel's niece and want to chat. Fortunately, just as she is about to open her mouth, the mysterious door half opens and Monsieur emerges, regal in surgical scrubs, his hair beneath a blue skullcap. I feel him draw back from taking me in his arms, even though I rush towards him, my cheeks on fire and my eyes shining, as if my lights have been switched on. Monsieur's smile is like a caress, even though his hands remain in his pockets.

The clinic's geography is such that we are invisible to others as we walk a few metres down a twisted corridor. In a flash Monsieur is all over me, his mouth assaulting mine, his tongue working with such speed and determination I almost faint, and lose all sense of place and time. I submit to the urgency of the kiss. It speaks to me, says, 'I can't resist.' I understand where the subtle mix of repulsion and magnetic attraction comes from: while I'm fascinated by the fact I'm having an affair with such a brilliant and sensual man, I can also see how pathetic it is for him to sleep with such a young girl behind the backs of his wife and kids. Maybe I made it too easy for him or Monsieur isn't much of a seducer. Maybe he tries not to resemble those old guys hanging around the school gates whose hearts are broken by a nymphet. There are times when I see so much pain in his desire that I'm unsure whether I should be flattered or take pity on him. I feel a form of power surge through me, which overwhelms me. Should I use it?

In the changing room Monsieur hands me a pair of pyjamas and watches me with close attention. While I attempt to find some privacy behind the wobbly shelves, he seizes my handbag. 'I'll put it in the locker, darling. Just keep your mobile.'

For an instant, my heart stops. Hidden by the locker door, I mumble: 'What did you call me?'

'I call everyone "darling",' Monsieur explains, and I feel like slapping his face.

A nurse helps me stuff my ponytail inside the white skullcap. I now look like an egg. Facing a large mirror I try to improve my appearance while keeping an eye on Monsieur. Even though I am trying to be discreet, I'm sure the short brunette standing next to me notices my efforts to look a bit sexier before Monsieur turns to me again. She doesn't seem concerned about it, which suggests to me that I'm not the first young girl to pass through this changing room on the arm of Monsieur. He's unlikely to compromise himself with the young women in blue coats, but no doubt they whisper about his activities behind his back. Monsieur is not the type to be bothered or embarrassed, or to look away when he sees someone he lusts after. He has no fear; this is his kingdom. Women can chatter away to their hearts' content, but for now he's dragging me towards the cavernous lift carrying the operating staff to the theatre. Surely they know this is a moment of truth. And, of course, as soon as the doors close Monsieur, so immense next to me in the restricted space, pins me back with a kiss that tastes of so many forbidden things, but that's nothing in comparison with the long fingers slithering beneath my pyjama jacket, the feeling I have of slowly collapsing into a hot bath and my muscles turning to jelly. This man is like a symphony of inquisitive fingers spreading across my breasts and inside my trousers. I put up a token struggle, my face flattened against the side of the lift, Monsieur's growing erection grazing the small of my back. The problem is that desire is rising fast inside me, triggered by his feverish groping. As the lift doors open, I'm panting hard. Any observer would have concluded in a flash that I was getting wetter by the minute at the mere thought of that eternal cliché: a masked anonymous medic seeking to enslave me by trying to grip my wrists behind my back. Not a single word passes between us, the quiet broken only by our uniforms rustling, a silent dialogue.

'Do calm down, Monsieur! Not here, not in the lift, not in the clinic!'

'I'll do whatever I want with you, right here and now, whether you like it or not.'

'Please, I beg you, stop!'

'Quiet, learn to give yourself! At least a little!'

The whole scene lasts about six seconds, but I'm praying no one will notice that the eminent surgeon has a pronounced hard-on, and the small masked blonde girl at his side is evidently responsible for it.

As soon as the doors open, I recognize some of the orderlies and anesthetists. It's extraordinary how elegant and noble Monsieur looks, cruising down the corridors of the surgical block; he's lost the superior air he usually wears, as if he owns the place. Just the way he moves, spreading his particular scent that even the ether can't obscure. There is something magical about Monsieur's movements as he strolls from room to room, leaving his mark.

I find a corner where I am out of the way while he introduces me as a literature student here to research a paper on the body (I can imagine the obligatory face-to-face discussion with Monsieur behind the locked doors of his study). It's crazy, all these women here at his beck and call, instinctively adjusting his scrubs, preparing his instruments, voicing his name as they soothe the nerves of the first patient. All the kindness, the lack of condescension Monsieur displays in the presence of the person now lying on the operating table is unlike his usual rather cynical attitude. How can he move so quickly from arrogance to this? He's now bending over the table, whispering instructions into his microphone, such a benevolent picture of kindness I'd be willing to have my nose shattered into a thousand pieces if only to be smiled at like that.

'Can we go ahead, Doctor?' a nurse asks, opening a pack of sutures.

And the ballet begins. Beneath his surgical mask, teasing me, Monsieur reminds me: 'If you begin to feel faint, you can always walk out and sit in the corridor.'

'Don't worry,' I answer, with a dire attempt to emulate his honeyed smile. 'I don't faint easily.'

His gaze is insistent, so, in a tiny voice, I add: 'Some years ago, not that long, I wanted to become a pathologist.'

'A pathologist?'

His eyes are like fingers touching my skin under the surgical blouse, almost laughing because this tiny blonde girl with her pink bum and careless words had considered spending her life in the realm of dead, silent flesh.

'How amusing,' Monsieur says, with irony, while my cheeks grow redder by the second. Then, holding his scalpel, he leans over the man sleeping below him, as if suddenly aware that his tone almost betrayed us. The fear and awe inside my chest are coming to the boil at the elaborate precision of his movements. Amazing. Now that I am aware of this, I will be able to concentrate better on the ways in which he manipulates me, assess whether his surgical skill can be detected among the folds of our sheets.

'If you happen to faint,' Monsieur continues, without glancing at me, 'we have everything here to bring you back to life.'

'Blood won't make me faint.'

'Oh, there are many reasons for fainting – pain, hunger . . .'

Still not looking at me, his large hands dancing above the operating table, hesitating briefly between instruments, he continues his inventory, but I already know where it's leading.

'. . . fear . . .'

I lower my eyes, red under the surgical mask. Would he dare?

'. . . pleasure . . .'

I bite the inside of my cheeks and blood floods my mouth.

'. . . and oppression.'

His large grey eyes fly across me, watching me attentively, defying me.

'Although, technically, there is little difference between fainting and a swoon.'

I try to pull myself away from this invisible battle of wills, oddly fascinated by how Monsieur is playing with me, echoing every perverse word I have used in my text messages to him. I suspect he is grinning under his mask, as he returns to his work, and my heart pounds. God knows how many times this morning he's almost given me a heart-attack.

He doesn't allow the nurses to put in the sutures, stitching the wound himself with fierce, gentle determination.

'Just imagine how important the nose is. The way it punctuates a face. The size and beauty of the scar are of paramount importance.'

Monsieur says 'beauty' where others would have used

'appearance': a subtle nuance that transports me back to a moment in the small blue room. He was caressing my hips, and I noticed that my naked skin was caught in the unforgiving glare of a band of sunlight. But I couldn't have cared less. I smiled. 'Are you looking at my stretch marks?'

And Monsieur, ever serious, whispered into my neck: 'They're pretty, you're striped. Like a little tiger.'

As soon as he puts down his instruments, a nurse reminds him of the visits to be made on the lower floor. Back to the lift, and its intolerable pressure. Before he's even touched me, I feel his hardness against me, a hardness that will only increase when, a few hours later, I send him a text full of my usual filth. I savour the intoxicating aroma of coffee on his breath. On the ground floor, I'm shaking with need next to him. 'But what the fuck am I going to do? Tell me.'

A rhetorical question to which he responds with a deep sigh, his eyes caressing me.

I'm sitting in the waiting room, waiting for him, staring into space, when my mobile buzzes. Monsieur, telling me: 'I really like you!'

(Even though these pyjamas don't suit me, I'm as naked as the day I was born beneath them. When he noticed this, Monsieur nearly went mad.)

Encouraged by the knowledge that I'm unlikely to be violated inside the clinic, I send him an obscene answer, and quickly regret it. He reappears, his face unreadable, just like a doctor after his rounds. But I know he's on fire inside: I know this man is capable of performing operations or anything requiring the utmost concentration while still allowing other things to fester in his mind. (Dear God, I am no doubt closely involved in them. I shudder to imagine what would happen to me right now if everyone in the clinic were suddenly to disappear.)

By text, I had said he was a dirty old perv. In the lift, Monsieur pretends he's angry, as if he can't perceive the affection beneath the teasing insults.

'This is all going to end badly,' he growls, pinching my nipples under the jacket. 'Next time you're available to me, there'll be major spanking.'

Being spanked by Monsieur would likely entail black and blue fingermarks across my arse for at least a fortnight. I'll have to come up with some lie for my dear but naïve Andrea (maybe a fall down the stairs?). But now getting myself unscathed to the end of this corridor looks like a perilous undertaking. I'm already giggling, knowing my nipples are so hard they're visible through the material of the jacket. I just don't know how Monsieur can persuade people to ignore his spectacular erection. And here he is again, the mighty professor gliding into another ward, to examine someone's stomach. I bombard him with, I hope, relevant questions. Amazingly, while he never ceases to open, spread, cut or cauterize, he answers me politely. Not a trace of the condescension I've noticed in surgeons much younger than him, always talking down to me and seldom explaining anything, as if to emphasize the gulf between their world and mine. On Tuesday morning, he showed me how breast implants were inserted, cupping my breast in his hand. I felt like a mannequin of flesh being spread open in an amphitheatre full of medical students. I swooned.

In the main operating theatre, Monsieur's next patient, a woman, is being given her anesthetic.

'Come and have a look. It's really interesting,' he says, sensing that I'm flagging.

I make myself as small as possible, standing in a corner, while the young woman sobs. The anesthetist, whom I'm sure I know, sticks the needle into the white hollow of her arm, causing her to shriek. No doubt the anesthetist has to go through this procedure at least five times a day, but she looks sincere as she sympathizes with the patient.

'Is the anesthetic painful?' I ask her, while the orderlies wheel the bed towards the ward, where Monsieur is joking with another patient.

'It is for her,' answers Dr Simon. (That's it. I remember now that I held on to her legs when I was younger and watched Philippe do liposuction on some enormous woman! God!)

And while she diplomatically explains to me that this patient is something of a drama queen, I hesitate to look her in the eyes from beneath my mask, as any normal person would. Since I arrived here earlier, I have come to understand how much your eyes can betray you when the rest of your face is blank. There are wrinkles at the sides of her eyes when she smiles. If her memory is as good as mine, I'm done for. There's a good chance she's dined at our house: my uncle is always inviting colleagues to his Sunday lunches. I can't tell if she has unmasked me or not, as she attentively watches all the others come and go, chattering. But every time our eyes accidentally connect, doubt assails me: there is a moment when it looks as if she is about to ask me to remind her of my name (and who I am and why I am here, all questions to which I would have no answer). Then I hear Monsieur ask where the hell I am, like an angry father who's misplaced his brat in some supermarket. Hearing 'Ellie' called, Isabelle Simon's eyes pierce me like knives. I'm truly fucked. She's put two and two together: it's the young Cantrel girl, and what on earth is she doing here chaperoned by the sprightly Dr S? Knowing the man, it's certainly not out of the kindness of his heart. Evidently, the situation is simple and despicable: the young girl and the family man are having an affair. Who cares how it might have begun and what it might mean to them? All that matters is that they're impudently advertising it here of all places.

'It's not what you think,' my eyes say to her beneath the surgical mask. 'Well, maybe a little . . .' my reddening cheeks confirm.

Tough luck. As soon as I slip away the telephone in the corridor rings loudly.

'Doctor, it's your wife!' a nurse shrieks, making her way through the small crowd surrounding the sobbing female patient.

The shadow that looms above us. Isabelle Simon gives me one final lengthy stare and turns on her heels. I make myself small again, in a corner of the room, stuck between two women for whom I represent, from different perspectives, an intrusion. He exchanges some rapid banalities, without any note of tenderness in his voice, which serves only to emphasize the strength of their bond, the untold complicity that has little use for the words other lovers rely on. Monsieur's wife: evidently a Dark Continent as immense as the couple it represents. Look at the man, whose beautiful Oriental eyes are drawn to every specimen of the female species, and remember that his voice, his fingers grasping the phone that connects him to his family, will never change. He might travel to the four corners of the planet with twenty different girls, each one even younger, as tempting as the uncut pages of a book, but he always returns to Her. Maybe a divorce would cost him too much, but that's not the point. Monsieur is not the sort of person who leaves a marriage on the spur of the moment for another woman. And he's not the sort of guy who's likely to fall in love with the girls he fucks in secret, not even me, though I happen to be his current obsession. He can smother me with sweet nothings, but it's all too clear he needs his roots, the immovable foundation stones, to enjoy his freedom to roam. Monsieur loves his wife, and has done so for such a long time that he is no longer even aware of it; it's the way people his age love. She's under his skin, a part of him.

Monsieur hangs up and, without looking at me, standing pressed against a partition wall, leans across his patient as she clears her throat, muttering to him. In Italian. He begins to speak to her in the same language, soothing her calmly but firmly. In quiet control of the surgical landscape they inhabit, he may be annoyed by her theatrical shrieks, but he doesn't complain. He doesn't even try to silence her. Such compassion; I didn't think he was capable of it. A nurse strokes away a few strands of the woman's dark hair as it spills from her skullcap, informing her that her new teeth are beautiful.

'Show them to the doctor so he can see how pretty you are!'

The young Italian woman, between sobs, attempts to smile. It's an old technique to make her forget she is in pain, but it appears to be working. Monsieur obligingly joins in and in a simulacrum of seduction ups the odds. 'See? She really is beautiful. And soon her cute little nose will be too.'

Now the young woman can't help smiling. I yearn to catch Monsieur's eye; I want to know that, even though I am shapeless beneath my pyjamas, so near but so far from him, he is still aware of my presence.

'And haven't you noticed, Doctor, how much weight she has lost?' the nurse continues, hoping he'll take the hint as their patient is wailing again.

'Indeed,' he says, 'but you should still lose some more, you know, all these days of being inactive and lots of French food . . .'

The young woman chuckles. I'm ashamed of how vulgar she sounds. I gaze at her, daggers in my eyes. And still Monsieur is flirting outrageously with her, jokingly listing the culinary delights responsible for the size of her thighs.

'How could you say such things to her?' I ask him later, as he removes his scrubs and his surgical mask.

'When she arrived at the clinic, she was truly enormous. Now, she's just fat. Still much work to do. That's all,' he answers, washing his hands.

(I love the way the foam spreads through the soft hairs of his lower arm. So virile.)

'I'd hate to hear you talk about me like that,' I say, after a few seconds' reflection.

'That will never happen.' Monsieur smiles at me as he calls the lift. 'You have an adorable little body.'

An orderly passing us prevents Monsieur moving closer to me. But, as if all the inanimate objects assembled in this clinic are at his beck and call, the creaky lift appears and, once again, a catastrophe is miraculously averted.

We rush in, my mind clouded with apocalyptic thoughts. Just as, out of sheer relief, I release a sigh, I am assaulted by my own breath and its lingering smell of stale coffee and empty stomach. That's why coffee drinkers always carry chewing gum. All of a sudden, I no longer care about Isabelle Simon, the fat patient or the orderly: the whole world revolves around my putrid breath and how to prevent Monsieur smelling it. Here he is, drawing me towards him, his soft hand grazing my neck, pecking at my nose with his lips. His fingertips toy with the elastic of my surgical mask.

'Stop!' I'm squirming like an eel in his arms, but Monsieur has other ideas. He can't understand why my mouth is so close to his but remains unavailable. I despairingly attempt to justify myself: 'All I've had this morning is a coffee. My breath stinks!'

'I don't care,' Monsieur blurts, as the lift doors open

and we reach the changing room. 'I'm a doctor. I know every smell there is to know in the human body.'

For what it's worth, some nurses are looking at us.

'That's not the point,' I answer, pulling away my mask, feeling almost as if I'm unveiling my cunt to him (knowing Monsieur and his love of symbolism, it's probably all the same in his mind). I have heard him fall back on his profession a thousand times when we argue about my possible unavailability and I come up with random pretexts to avoid him. It's irrelevant to me. I've never thought of Monsieur in that way: he's always a man before he's a medic, affected by the same stimulations as all of his sex, whether he's aware of it or not. He unknowingly confirms this when I ask him to pass me my handbag from the locker and he takes advantage of the situation, allowing his extended arm to slide over my arse. With a knowing wink, he takes the clitoris-pink sheets of paper on which I've scribbled a series of Byzantine words for him.

'For me?' he whispers, and stuffs them into the pocket of his jacket.

I nod, for the record.

In a corner of the changing room, while I am slipping my skirt on, Monsieur undresses. He is soon in deep conversation with another doctor, who's just walked in. They're talking about a colleague, François Katz; I clearly recall being held on the man's lap some ten years ago.

'Ah, that rascal Katz has calmed down a little,' Monsieur remarks, chuckling softly, as he stretches out topless.

I love the colour of his nipples, the quiet strength and

inner fragility his body conveys, whether he knows it or not. The smoothness of the skin, as soft as a woman's, makes him look younger than he is, while the fire still burns inside. The fire always burns.

'Remember the row he caused when they changed the operating theatre's schedule!' the other surgeon continues, and Monsieur laughs while untying his skullcap.

His hair, salt and pepper, falls to his neck and, with a swift movement of his hand, he smooths it down. I'm standing there, my breasts almost on display, but I'm oblivious of the fact, hypnotized by the sophisticated architecture of his arms. His long, powerful animal muscles are evidence that he belongs to a world he has never needed to tame. Below his navel the road to Damnation stretches, cleverly drawing my gaze, capturing my imagination in a thousand wicked ways. How can I watch the path disappear inside the waistband of his blue trousers without simmering? Framed by his narrow hips, it's like a postscript indicating that the chaste hairs of his belly will blend into a fiery burning bush.

I'm falling headlong into a daydream filled by the landscape of Monsieur's cock, when my mobile brings me back to my senses. It begins to vibrate: my mother. Wanting to know where I am, what I'm doing, with whom. When I'm coming home. The first excuse I can think of isn't necessarily the best: I'm playing poker at Timothée's. Yes, at eleven thirty on a Wednesday morning. My mother pretends to believe me, although I know she's far from convinced. I can't allow her the slightest clue that Ellie is at a clinic, so my speech is succinct, monosyllabic.

'Well, if that's what you want to do,' she concludes, in the high and mighty tone I hate.

'Mum, where would you like me to be?'

In just a few seconds, she's put me on the defensive. As I raise my voice, Monsieur throws me a querying glance.

'I don't know, Ellie. Anyway, what does it matter?'

(Oh, the endless sigh that says, 'My daughter is a total social failure'! Sometimes I could kill her. With my bare hands.)

'I hope you have your keys, because I'm not at home.'

'You don't believe me, do you?'

'Do what you want to do,' my mother says. 'Have fun.'

That's just what she would say at the end of a conversation to put further pressure on me and prevent me having fun, like a cartoon cloud that pours litres of cold water over me as I walk along.

'What's happening?' Monsieur asks, buttoning his shirt, next to me.

'Nothing. My mother just wanted to know where I am.'

'What did you tell her?'

It's clear that he's worried. You bastard, is my only thought. My mother's short call reminds me that all our recent arguments have been caused by my spending so much time with Monsieur, in real time and on the phone. On Saturday night, although I hadn't met him then, he'd pushed me into a corner. I'd just got back from work and the phone had rung as I was hanging up my coat. With no word of explanation, I'd walked out again with him filling my ears, tempting me. For a quarter of an hour, we had chatted about lingerie and vaginal orgasms while my dog was left sobbing behind the door, begging to join me, and my mother repeatedly called me to the table, as she moved about the house. Once I was back inside, she made it her business to find out who I'd been talking to. It was clear that she'd overheard some of our conversation so I called her bluff.

'Just a friend.'

A friend? I'd been speaking to him or her so formally!

'Yes, Timothée. We're very formal.'

Why was I talking about sex with him?

'You've got a nerve, listening in to my conversation!' My mother had overheard me brazenly discussing the advantages of open-crotch panties.

'You were talking very loudly.'

'If you'd stayed in the kitchen, you wouldn't have had to hear me,' I pointed out.

She didn't say any more, but I could see she was aware that we were entering a tangled skein that had little to do with Timothée.

So, any moment now, I'm about to initiate chaos within my family because of him. All Monsieur seems concerned about is whether I'm involving him in my downfall.

'I told her I was at a girlfriend's.'

His eyes won't let go of me. He's far from reassured or willing to believe that I'm capable of misleading my parents, so I mockingly come up with the necessary cliché: 'Don't worry.'

He doesn't hear the irony in my tone, and continues:

'Still, be careful.'

I've always been aware that, at heart, Monsieur is a terrible egotist: you have to be to react with such alacrity to the advances of a young girl when you're married with children. You have to be to risk bringing a young woman whose family you know to your place of work so that you can witness the admiration in her eyes. Only an egotist would bet on the odds of a whole life against a few hours' pleasure. Monsieur is motivated sometimes by irresponsible childlike desires, although at others he's in complete control, in the way he caresses and kisses me, even determining the alias I give him in my phone. But on every single occasion he is the one who endangers us, and he's convinced that the outcome will be decided by my carelessness. I already have enough on my plate in taking care of myself, and now I have to deal with a forty-six-year-old baby, who likes to play at scaring himself and terrifying me. However, however . . . every time I gaze into those eyes, so different from mine, I understand how similar Monsieur and I are. Deep in his eyes, there is no mask and I recognize the artfulness and egocentricity we share, even if we labour in different ways to achieve our desires. If I rush straight into the trap Monsieur is setting for me, it's because I identify with the childlike immorality, the polymorphous perversion, or at least that I know he resembles me enough to intrigue and please, in ways I can't yet understand.

'Can I drop you off somewhere?' Monsieur asks me, outside the clinic.

'I'll be OK,' I say.

'So, you're really going to take a taxi?' he asks, with a

smile that hurts me.

It's as if he's conversing with the perfect courtesan, who came here by cab and is about to depart likewise, living in his own financial world. I am still at the age where every five euros count; where my pragmatic student soul is ever at odds with the laziness of a penniless tart who wouldn't think twice about taking a taxi, but it's not simply a question of cost.

'I'm off to see a girlfriend, just a few Métro stops away. Don't worry, I'll be OK.'

Monsieur doesn't understand. He's enjoyed driving and speed for too long to understand that, after such a morning, the only thing I'm looking forward to is spending an hour on a train with my iPod, replaying every scene, analysing it, and brooding over my craving to see and possess him, without the handicap of thirty people surrounding us. Monsieur isn't aware that I seek solitude.

Unsteady on my legs, my eyes heavy, I have the slow demeanour of a woman who's just got out of bed. I feel as if I've made love to him all the time we've been together in the clinic.

'Kiss me one last time,' Monsieur whispers, his hands in his pockets, just like the student he must have been twenty years earlier, rakishly relaxed.

And there, within the neutral angle of that small sun-splashed street, where no onlooker can see us, I raise myself up, eyes closed, and Monsieur takes my face between his beautiful lover's hands. The seconds tick by as if our rapture shields us from the rest of the world. His scent eclipses that of the flowering chestnut trees, his thumbs on my cheeks protect me from the cold breeze. Then he recalls that we are not quite as isolated as we were within our Tuesday-morning cocoon. The atmosphere changes: a sense of urgency returns, and Monsieur kisses me, or am I kissing him? At any rate, we're kissing. For an instant our faces merge below the Paris windows.

'It's awful,' I stammer, my lips puffy.

'What is?' Monsieur asks.

My smile is sad. 'You know all too well what's awful about this.'

His silent answer, his eyebrows conveying some mysterious empathy, an unreadable map of responses I am unable to decipher. *You are you and I am me. We live undeniably incompatible lives, your wife, your children, my parents, Andrea. It's awful that I can no longer think about them. Look at me. My boyfriend left for Brazil a week ago, and before I met you, all I did was pine for him. Now I dread the day he comes back because I don't know how to negotiate that relationship alongside ours. I don't know how I can juggle two men in my brain – right now you're occupying all the available space in it – and I don't want to. I can't. That's what's so awful.*

'I'll see how we can get organized for next Tuesday,' I say, taking a few steps backwards.

'You don't know how much I'm looking forward to it,' Monsieur answers, grazing my skin one last time with his fingers.

It's the same for me. Lust cannot be tamed. Jogging towards the rue de Rivoli, all I can think of is the way my arse sways when I run. I don't have to check, but I know that Monsieur will be watching me until I'm round the first corner.

'You're beautiful,' he texts me, two minutes later.

MONSIEUR

Your letter . . . like a hand grenade with the pin
pulled out.

ELLIE

I think you don't fully understand the problem I have with the nerve in my leg. Let me explain it again, because I think it might be serious and you might have to operate on me. These are the symptoms: the moment you start speaking to me, my right leg goes limp and heavy, as if I was turning into a slug. The same thing happens every time I think of you, wherever I might be. At some critical stage, the numbness rises from my thigh to my arse and I lose all sense of decency. Every movement I make arouses me even more. Even walking becomes a form of foreplay. I'm not really that bothered, but if I'm not alone, it's embarrassing. Almost as if I had an orgasm every time I yawned, a bit indecent.

I don't know the name of this particular nerve, but I think you should shed some light on my problem. I have no wish to become a female oyster: they spend their days gobbling the sperm of male oysters as it floats in the sea. Filthy whores each and every one of them . . .

Still, let's not worry too much about this as I've

discovered there's a seminar on Tuesday morning to discuss the nerves in my thigh. A rather short but useful seminar. I have no objection to being experimented on, as long as the right treatment is found and I'm provided with some relief. As I write, I've become almost incapable of moving my leg.

Also, as you don't appear to have received my message about what I did between the sixteenth and seventeenth hour of yesterday, I must insist on the Titanic aspects of my evening orgasm. I'm lucky I've never been caught doing it by my parents, but it would have been humiliating had they rushed into my room that evening on some flimsy pretext. As it is, even with a normal, mediocre orgasm it's difficult enough to keep a straight face and a clear conscience and tell Mum, 'Noooooo, I don't know where your Hermès wrap is. Just leave me alone!' Anyway, I think I usually manage to look almost decent – my eyes don't go white or my ears crimson. However, on this occasion, I almost swooned.

And there you go, talking about swoons at the clinic. I sure was red in the face after that.

I still haven't solved the case of the strange scratch marks that appear on my back every time I see you. I was thinking about guilty stigmatas, but that's not possible as I have no sense of guilt. I feel as if I'm untouchable. For the last two days I've been on fire.

All of this to say it's imperative I see you on

Tuesday. And when we speak on the phone, I have no wish to hear the word 'maybe' again.

So, I'm off to bed.

So, I'm going to touch myself.

So, I will think of you.

So, I hope I didn't bother you this morning.

And that there was no camera in the lift.

And tell them they need an even more decrepit lift, so it takes even longer to climb through the floors.

See you tomorrow.

Ellie

MONSIEUR

I miss you.

Sweet nothings exchanged with Monsieur on the phone at eight in the morning while I'm still buried beneath my duvet.

'Did you write a bit yesterday?'

'Not really. Just thoughtless scribbling,' I confessed, annoyed and ashamed.

'You *must* write!' Monsieur stormed.

'I know, I know . . .'

'Seriously, Ellie. You know what you should write about?'

'No.'

'Write about us. Our story.'

'Eh? What could I write about us?'

'I don't know! You're the writer! When I read all your old mails, it's like reading a novel. Write a novel about us!'

I touch myself lazily as we speak, spurred on by the frustration of hearing his beautiful voice, his hard-on voice, singing songs of desire. Oh, the writing, the writing . . . These days, Monsieur is insistent that I should be writing. Come to think of it, it's all a bit of a cliché, a story about a married man with the niece of a colleague. But I shouldn't offend his literary pride.

'Why not?' I know all too well that yet another strike day will just see me faffing around.

'Give it a try, at least,' he answers. 'I'll call you tonight, or at some point during the day if I can manage it. OK, my love?'

'OK.'

'Where are you now?'

The conversation is changing direction.

'In bed. I've just woken up.'

'Completely naked?'

'I'm *always* naked. Like the day I was born.'

Between clenched teeth, Monsieur releases a painful sigh. 'You make me hard!'

I chuckle contentedly, stifle a protest. 'But I said *nothing* to provoke it!'

'You said enough. My imagination does the rest. How's it going to look if I get to the clinic with an erection straining at my trousers?'

'It'll fade,' I predict, stretching, even though I know that, given the chance, I'll make sure it doesn't. A fact Monsieur is quite aware of.

'It'll fade, and you'll send me obscene text messages and I'll get hard again. Do you think it feels comfortable when I'm operating?'

'If you'd rather I didn't . . .' I smile.

'Are you crazy? Send me photos of your arse. I'll look at them between appointments.'

'And then you'll sport a mighty erection in the presence of your lady patients. Not very professional.'

'To hell with them. It'll relax me getting hard for you. You'll send me pics?'

I rephrase a small anodyne promise, a witticism, the foundation stone of most of our telephone conversations. What makes me wet, my version of hard, is knowing it's so easy to excite Monsieur. To think of him in his expensive suit, or his surgical scrubs, clearly erect, concealing his embarrassment beneath his mask, and all because of me. My fat arse stirring up such feelings inside him.

'We'll speak tonight, darling,' I warble, still stretching.

'Your voice arouses me,' he says, then brusquely 'Till tonight.'

After an hour on Facebook, I summon the energy to open a new text folder, and stare at its emptiness like a chicken confronted with a knife. The problem of the white page is how full of emptiness and expectation it is. If you jot down a few words, the white void seems to shout, 'Feed me!' How can I plumb its depths? I, who, for the last year, have been sleeping on the laurels of my one and only publication. For more than six months I've felt like a dried-up well from which only drops of muddy water have been painfully drawn. So, yes, I write. In notebooks I lose after a few days, across the virgin pages of my diary. Stupid thoughts. All the nothings that are part of my comfortable student life. Am I capable of more today?

I think of Monsieur's voice on the telephone as he expressed amazement that I knew so much about his private life over recent years, neglecting to mention that my mother had told me about that weekend in New Jersey long before we first met. So, with no thought of success, I improvise a few lines, like a compliant courtesan, to oblige him. I write:

> He always seemed amazed that he had long been a part of my life, although before our first conversations he had been something of an abstraction. I was building a whole world with the facts I could glean, or plunder, about him. Monsieur enjoyed erotic literature; this was the

detail that set me on my quest. For a long time, I had been alone in my appreciation of Calaferte, André Pieyre de Mandiargues and so many others that I had even come to think of myself as the sole reader of their masterpieces. To learn that a man who had a similar burning passion was so close to me seemed a miracle.

Men who read. There is a whole universe that revolves around men who read, who dive in and out and drown in this ever so feminine reverie, and, God, it makes them charming. The dazzling charm of their fingers turning pages, turning down the corner of a page, their eyes absorbing each letter, line, word. The abyss I can only dream of behind the wrinkled brows contemplating yellowing pages.

Knowing this, I reread Calaferte's book and found it tasted different. For hours on end, I would lock myself in my room, rediscovering with delicious discomfort the crudest paragraphs, aroused by the thought that his grey eyes had also read them, providing a new freshness to the passages I knew by heart. How did he contemplate all these words – cunt, arse, cock, moistness, cum, buggery? What sort of impact could such words have on a forty-six-year-old man, who had lived enough to distinguish between the vocabulary and the reality? What does the word 'cunt' evoke for him? Whose cunt does he think of as his eyes glide across the four dark letters of the word? Which woman has corrupted his memory with her scent, her presence, scattered across every page of erotic writing?

Through all my readings, I was picturing him, considering the mystery of older men and the promises they make to us without even opening their mouths.

I sent Monsieur a copy of my musings.

'It's great. Go on with it!' was his response.

The following day, for the first time in weeks, I got up early and rushed out to buy a notebook.

'How did you spend your day, dearest?'

'This afternoon I sunbathed on the deck-chair in the garden, with my legs wide open. I think the family next door now have an intimate acquaintance with my knickers.'

'What sort of knickers were you wearing?'

'Actually, I wasn't wearing any. But I thought it would be in bad taste to let you know that from the off.'

'You do make me laugh!'

'Is it possible to make you laugh and give you a hard-on at the same time?'

'It's essential.'

'I'm a knickerless clown.'

'And most appetizing at that.'

'That's the nicest compliment.'

There are moments in the story I love recalling. Images that come to mind and make me smile, whatever the time of day, whatever my mood. The morning we spent in our small hotel on place de Clichy is in this exquisite garden of memories, every flower as precious as the next. Time can't change them.

I was sleeping heavily – but restless because of the vodka Babette and I had consumed the previous evening. A room decked out in red, with a stucco fountain in one corner, and there I was, snoring like a drunkard wearing only my Agent Provocateur pants. You can just imagine what a vision of bad taste I was when my mobile woke me up on the stroke of ten.

'Another ten minutes and I'll be holding you against me,' Monsieur said.

I jumped out of bed as if I was on springs. I had ten minutes to rediscover my young-girl freshness and jettison my bad breath. There was not even enough time to experience the pangs of waiting, the tightness in the pit of my stomach. I threw myself under the shower, toothbrush in my mouth, eyes distorted with panic. I kicked the empty bottle under the bed. I was a mess, my hair all over the place, my eyelids puffy, but I knew that after just a few words Monsieur would see none of this. He would see all of me.

I crept out onto the landing, wearing only knickers, half a joint in hand. Sat down, legs through the banister, swinging in the void, watching the ground floor. The vertigo I felt had nothing to do with the height. Next to me, my telephone vibrated with languid insistence.

'Hello?'

'What are you up to, sweetheart?' Monsieur was smiling at the other end of the line, and I was about to coo when I realized I could hear his voice twice: in my ear and on the ground floor.

'Not much.'

Quivering, I stood up, without losing sight of the stairs unfolding beneath me. I tiptoed back along the corridor to my room.

'I'm in bed. You?'

'Very close, darling. See you soon.'

Monsieur was testing the temperature. I buried myself inside the sheets, a flash of arousal coursing through me, almost as if I was playing hide and seek.

Have I ever told you about the sound of his steps on the stairs? Or, rather, as I think about it, an absence of sound, the magical way he moved from ground floor to second without making the slightest noise. Only a well-trained ear would have detected the subtle creak of a floorboard or the squeak of the carpet beneath his shoes. The ambient air changed texture, smell, density: a wave of goose pimples covered me from head to toe, while beneath my small breasts, my heart beat fast, its echo racing to my ears, eclipsing all other sound. With a whisper, the door handle swung from left to right. The ray of light now bathing the floor seemed to flow from Monsieur. As I was still in the embrace of the sheets and the curtains were drawn, he was making me a gift of the new day and doing his utmost to see it began well. After all, wasn't he the master of everything he surveyed?

For a moment he was just a motionless shadow on the

sunlit threshold. Lasciviousness, as I came to know it that morning, had black and golden hair. He was smiling, a childlike glee in his eyes, and staring at me, as if I added a touch of freshness to the room, the best possible accessory for the bed. He rushed to me, barely allowing me time to set my joint in the ashtray. I squeezed him between my legs with all the strength I could summon and Monsieur murmured into my ear, 'A whole week without you!' In his frantic kisses I recognized the power I held over him, and how weak he was becoming. I hadn't known it, but I'd been yearning for him to say something like that to me. It was like a lullaby and, dear God, it shouldn't have been. Monsieur's big nose met mine, as he whispered, 'You're such a beautiful little whore . . .' He frowned. 'What do you smell of?'

I laughed, high on joy and smoke. 'Grass?'

Monsieur grinned. 'You've been smoking?'

There was half a joint in the ashtray.

'I love that smell,' he whispered, kissing me. 'Such a pity I can't smoke today. I have an operation lined up. One day, though, we'll share a joint.'

'You smoke too?'

'Whenever I can.' He rose, his back to me. 'How the hell did I manage not to tear all your clothes off on Wednesday at the clinic?'

'You almost did in the lift.'

'You liked it,' Monsieur stated.

I let out a strangled sound, confirming my guilt.

'What an arse,' he said then, his fingers kneading me carefully.

So, this was to be a morning when my arse would

be the focus. My cunt was already complaining that it wasn't to be the centre of attention. Monsieur delicately pulled my knickers down. This man ran a series of operating theatres, with crowds of uniformed women at his beck and call, but this morning his powerful fingers were caressing a young student in perfect health, all for the sake of beauty – or was it?

A crude detail: Monsieur's thumbs wandered to the heart-shaped hollow separating my thighs, mapping my jewel case. I heard myself gurgle with wetness, a noise that could only have originated inside my thighs. But my idea of modesty was already twisted, and my only reaction was to place myself on all fours and arch my arse further towards him. I somehow expected him to remark on the innate vulgarity of my arousal. Not at all. Monsieur stood up and, in a flash, I remembered his text messages and realized what was about to happen. He moved into position and I was unable to escape his grip. I thrashed like an animal caught in quicksand, protesting wildly, but Monsieur ordered me to keep still. Instinctively, I curled up.

Not that, I silently implored, as if he might change his mind and proceed to make love to me politely.

In those circumstances, the grass no longer had any effect. I regained lucidity when Monsieur's mouth came down on me, his hands firmly holding my arse cheeks open. This was followed by his tongue and I screamed with sheer embarrassment, praying he would stop – *how could anyone want to do that? How could anyone like it?*

(Later, when I described the whole humiliating episode to Babette, she cleverly remarked: 'In that position there is just no way you can ever forget he's licking your arsehole. That's the point of it.')

It was a sensation I didn't want to find pleasurable, and Monsieur understood that, not even objecting to my body's rigidity. Whenever I tried to move, he pressed my face into the mattress. As a last resort, I tried another ploy. Squirming, I rubbed my cheek against his cock, although it was still beneath his grey-flannel trousers. As he watched, I undid the few buttons separating me from his penis, and took him into my mouth. Monsieur remained motionless, his hands in my hair, pulling it. Eventually he threw me back with a regal gesture, signifying that I had no choice in what would happen.

Monsieur was still fully clothed, his cock still wet with my saliva. He whispered: 'No, I want to see your cunt first.'

I shuddered and wriggled, vainly attempting to close my legs. Out of the question: his predatory hands held me open and, for an endless few minutes, he leafed through me as if I were pages in a rare edition of the Bible, all of his fingers journeying inside me with infinite care. Whimpering in shame, I raised my eyes and saw, with a shock, that the man who loved the same books as I did was gazing at my cunt with the same reverence he would read a rare Bataille vellum edition, with words like 'labia', 'cunt', 'slit', 'clit'. *Oh, Ellie, look at the delicate firmness of his hands, the precision of his fingers, the flame deep in his eyes. This is a man who appreciates cunt. This man must dream of a world where he floats in a sea of cunts of all races, all shapes and configurations, all day, all the time.* Although instinct told me to protect myself against his curiosity, I didn't feel as if Monsieur was judging me negatively. When I was younger, I had always been afraid that one day a man might find my cunt did not fit with my puppy fat; I worried about the dichotomy between my body and my face. But he seemed to approve, evidently understanding that my cunt was the perfect spokeswoman for the whore he knew I harboured deep within. Monsieur was all appreciation. In fact, just a little later, his voice cut across the churchly silence: 'I really like your cunt, you know.'

Right there and then, I would have liked to be a boy, so that I could make a girl get hard as he had just done. No one could have felt better than I did, facing Monsieur naked, wide open, wet, dribbling, numb and craving to be fucked. And how could it be possible to feel any better when the sharpness of freshly shaved bristle and thick lips touched me in a place I couldn't quite locate but was so full of nerve endings that a 220-volt electrical discharge raced along my spine. I think I jumped, and his smile was that of Satan, telling me: 'You know you love it. You're depraved, and depraved women enjoy melting inside the mouths of men.'

I am lost, I thought, and there was nothing scary about it.

'And I very much enjoy the taste of your cunt,' Monsieur added, his lips shining.

He licked with the attentive precision of a man expert in caresses, like a pianist of genius, who allows himself artistic, unstructured improvisations while never quite losing the thread of the melody. I could feel myself getting hard, harder and wetter, like a river, all slack against his face. I was captivated: this kiss was the most venomous in the world. Because it was definitely a kiss. Monsieur certainly knew what he was doing.

He rose above the bed, still pretty hard, and as he pulled my thighs apart, he licked his lips. 'I don't know where to fuck you first,' he said, glancing from my cunt to my arsehole. Then, looking me in the face again: 'Which would you prefer, darling?'

God alone knows why I answered, 'Behind.'

Monsieur possibly misunderstood, accustomed as he was to using the word 'sodomy'. He indicated that I should turn round.

'Not like that, not on all fours.'

Which was when I realized that the grass was affecting my speech. Undoing his buttons, I tried to explain to Monsieur: 'I want you to . . .'

'You want me to what?'

'I want you to fuck me in the arse. But on my back,' I added, as if I wanted him to ignore the initial clumsiness of my request.

I don't know if he grasped what a huge leap forward I had just made. I threw myself back and he moved towards me to fold my legs into position, and I knew he had been aware all along of what I had in mind, words had been unnecessary, and he fully approved. He understood that I enjoyed this position because he could see all of me, and he liked my willingness to reveal myself in such a crude way. He penetrated me very slowly, attentive to every sound he drew from me, firmly, never retreating from any territory once he had invaded it. Monsieur could feel from the way I was tightening around him when the pain was overtaken by pleasure.

I sighed, and Monsieur plunged deeper inside me, his voice interrupting the sharp buzzing in my ears: 'You love it, don't you, darling?'

Monsieur was fucking me in the arse. Incredible how noble it was when he was involved. The supreme way in which he respected me. Ironic in the circumstances: he knew that taking me in this way illustrated my submission to him. And he was entirely aware of my desire to submit. But there was something magical, too, in the way Monsieur behaved, something I had never come across with anyone else: somehow he could convince me that what he was doing and the crude words he spoke were for my own good. And every time he called me a tramp, a whore or mentioned my cunt, all I could hear were sweet endearments that broke down my defences. But I was incapable of speech. Monsieur cooed: 'Tell me you love it, darling. Talk to me. Tell me you like it when I fuck you in the arse.'

I shrivelled, my shoulders drawn in, red-faced, while Monsieur moved inside me with elastic ease and whispered: 'Look at me.' With one hand he gripped my chin. 'Look at me.' He spoke sternly. I couldn't respond. When he continued, he was all sweetness: 'Look at me, darling. Look at me.'

Still overtaken by shame, I opened my eyes. 'I can't.'

'Don't you know you must always look straight into the eyes of a man who has his cock dug deep in your arse?' Monsieur said. I was listening to him as if he were reading *Lolita* to me, with the same awe. 'You have power over me. Even if I happen to be the one buggering you.' *I bit my lip until it began to bleed.* 'I am a prisoner of your arse, and you're driving me crazy.'

He pulled my thighs up slightly, to make the missionary position obscene. Then, in the same breath: 'Don't you feel like a real filthy tramp the way you are now? With my cock inside your arse? Tell me how you feel.'

I half opened my eyes and saw my cunt raw and wide open and, below it, his cock slowly coming in and out of my arsehole: Monsieur was enjoying the same panorama. I shivered with delight. 'I feel like a tramp.'

Monsieur, that infamous corruptor, took advantage of the situation, grazing my ear lobes with his lips, inhaling the true scent of me. 'Show me how you caress yourself.'

I froze, reluctant to expose something so intimate to him. The prospect of making myself come in front of Monsieur, with his cock digging deep into me, was petrifying.

'Do it, darling. Show me how you do it. I know you must be oh-so-beautiful when you touch yourself.'

With the pretence of a courtesan, I took flight: 'But I've *never* done that!'

'Do it, my love. Caress your little cunt. You can feel how wet it is.'

'No . . .' I groaned, in an effort to move my fingers.

Finally, I allowed my hand to approach my lower belly. It came to a halt. I cried out with frustration, like a small dog pulling on the end of a leash. But Monsieur was in no mood to take pity on me.

'Wank. Do it, or I'll stop fucking you.'

If only he'd known how much I wanted to obey, how desperate I was to do it and please him. That I felt as much a victim of my unexpected wave of shame as he was.

That word, however arousing it was coming from his mouth, had shocked me. I wasn't sure I truly wanted to *wank* in Monsieur's presence. If only I could make him understand. Then maybe he wouldn't have to resort to blackmail. Monsieur ceased all movement. I threw myself back towards him, but with both his hands on my belly, he stopped me.

'I swear I'll stop fucking you. Wank for me. Didn't you know you'll have the strongest possible orgasm when you touch yourself while being buggered?'

('Buggered'. He pronounced it with the nobility of the most beautiful pages in the world of erotica. It was no longer the insulting word that my girlfriends sometimes mutter. When he said it, I could almost feel the awe in which I held it when I first came across it in a libertine novel from the seventeenth century. Ah, the treasures of language.)

Annoyed by his intransigence, I gave him a dark look. Which he ignored. Then, I yowled: 'No, fuck me!'

But Monsieur was cleverer than I. 'Wank.'

And, from his tone, I understood that he had meant what he'd said, that he was capable of retreating to the edge of the bed and masturbating in front of me, until sheer frustration obliged me to do likewise. I moved my fingers towards the stickiness of my yawning slit. It was awful: my whole body was on fire and I found it hard to sketch even a simulacrum of caress. When I was in motion, though, Monsieur's gaze froze me and I shrank in shame between the damp sheets. But he began to move inside me again, taking me anew, sliding inside, whispering, *Ellie Ellie Ellie oh Ellie, caress yourself, do it as if I wasn't here and you were on your own*, as if I could ever forget his presence. I was transported: his need to take sex to the ultimate shores of intimacy, this was a world to which I had never before been granted access. With Alexandre I had believed I had reached a new level of perversion, but now . . . There was undoubtedly a perverse beauty in what he was attempting to draw out of me.

Tears overcame me, my hand still reluctant to perform the ballet I knew by heart. Every time I stopped, Monsieur would hold it in position. I no longer knew who I should hate more, him or myself. My eyes pleaded, and I think he realized from the way I kept wrinkling my brow that we were heading nowhere fast. He gave me a look that told me I was a bad pupil that morning, but also that he was willing to accept that I had reached my limit. With his two thumbs, he eloquently took over my travails, and I asked myself how much of a genius this man was to have sensed from my fingers' movements the perfect way to drive me crazy. I was just seconds away from erupting, but I wanted to see Monsieur come before I did. So, with my cunt hoovering up his fingers, I squeezed his cock hard between my sphincter muscles and, my nails digging into his arse, I forced him to fuck me faster. So he could concentrate, he stopped talking, and his eyes closed. All of a sudden, he was no longer Monsieur, and it was no longer that particular room. It was more than an older guy mounting a slut of a girl who could have been his daughter in a rundown hotel in a rundown area of Paris, the two of them wallowing in filth. I wasn't sure

I liked it without him gazing at me: when he looked at me, I could almost forget that our affair was worse than immoral. His eyes gazing deep into mine reminded me that we were not only sleeping together but talking, from time to time, on the telephone or in writing, which felt good. It would have been a shame to waste it. For five minutes or so, making love with him seemed boring.

Please, God, don't let this go on for hours, I thought. (A stupid request: I would regret it a few weeks later when I was alone, with no news of the elusive Monsieur.)

All of a sudden, the face above mine came back to life and Monsieur said: 'I'm going to come inside your arse.'

Breathless, I became attentive to the exquisite rise of pleasure as it coursed through his long, thin body, the final quivering in and out motions and then the ultimate thrust, hurling him deep inside me. He cried out, a single note, rough, raw, which affected me so strongly I almost came in unison. I fell into a deep concentration, trying to focus on his spurts, but all I could feel were the frantic spasms of his cock, then Monsieur modulating his breath as he buried his mouth in my neck, still hard inside me.

'I'd been missing your arse,' he said, withdrawing from me, and I was overcome by a sensation of physical loneliness. Even after I had come, I wanted more and more of him.

Afterwards Monsieur was seized by frantic tenderness, pulling me across him, pleading and emotional. 'Kiss me! Look at me! Don't you want me to cuddle you?'

'Of course I do,' I protested, twisting in his arms, like a rattlesnake. 'I'm looking at you all the time!'

'You know very well that's not true. You never let me

cuddle you. You squirm away from me. I can fuck you in the arse but you won't let me cuddle you.'

'Of course you can,' I answered, barely concealing my impatience.

As I sighed, betraying my unwillingness, I allowed Monsieur to turn my chin towards him. Then I drew away from him. 'I was smoking earlier. I don't want to face you.'

I stood up with as much grace as I could summon and picked up my laptop. As the screen lit up, Monsieur noticed the photo of Andrea. 'Who is he?'

'My boyfriend,' I answered, reviving the half-joint in the ashtray.

'Great.' Monsieur leaned back against the bolster.

'Must I apologize for having a life?' I said, regretting the indifference of my tone.

I put a Turtles album on and took a puff, then sat across Monsieur, legs wide open, providing him with a spectacle that no longer concerned me. For a moment, he stared at me, his fingers on my knees. Then he smiled. 'I have something for you.'

I jumped up and down on him, my eyelashes fluttering like a geisha's. 'What is it?'

'You told me you hadn't read Aragon's *Irene's Cunt*, didn't you?'

Another puff on the joint. A broad smile crossed my face. 'You told me about it on the phone.'

Monsieur held out a hand for his briefcase. He'd told me about it the night before while I was smoking a cigarette stark naked in the kitchen, shamelessly parading in front of the large window. Later I'd received some lines from the book in my in-box. They hadn't inspired me. But when he set the book down beside me, with its gaudy mass-market cover and ridiculous author pseudonym (Albert de Routisie), my innate hunger resurfaced. How wonderful that Monsieur had bought me a paperback, perfect for the poverty-stricken student.

'Oh, thanks!' I cried, with too much spontaneity, and Monsieur smiled, visibly touched.

I was about to nuzzle up to him, but Monsieur brusquely seized the book and opened it. 'Read the first two pages.'

If only I could explain the way I felt right then, sitting naked and cross-legged across the carpet of his body hair, in the warm darkness of that room. Never had I felt so high: I'd reached some stratospheric level where everything felt right. Just as I looked down at Aragon's opening lines, the chorus of '*Elenore*' burst into the moist silence like a whirlpool of love. At the same time, the opening lines spoke to me of sleep and pain, the voluptuousness of the black night. Transported, I threw myself back, smiling. 'These lines, this music . . . It's just amazing.'

I think he understood. I began reading voraciously, every sigh escaping my lungs like a heavenly form of punctuation. How can I even describe such a moment of profound loneliness and total bliss? I felt as if I'd seen, touched, the Messiah, and I knew that Monsieur, in his sobriety, would never understand how close we were to the divine. Sure, the joint had helped lower my defences and allowed me to absorb the magic. But I wanted to explain it to him. He had to understand how that particular moment had come to crystallize everything we had been reaching for. For the first time, I think, I spoke his first name. Then came the post-joint babble: 'How can one possibly write so beautifully? It's not only a case of writing well, it goes miles beyond. I've never read anything as beautiful and truthful. In these pages, Aragon makes me think of Mozart. If you took just a single word away, moved a comma, it would collapse. Perfection.'

And Monsieur didn't understand. As a would-be writer, I was torn between awe and jealousy, or perhaps it was dismay. Just as I had when I first read *Lolita* (oh, Nabokov), I saw that every sentence, miraculously fine-tuned with the care of a goldsmith, had little to do with work or application. It was a thing of genius. To carve such a beautiful stream of words would have taken me hours, locked inside an empty room. And I knew I hadn't the talent to join the ranks of such writers. I was serene in the knowledge, as you are when you accept the realities of life. But it hurt.

'It is beautiful, isn't it?' Monsieur said.

Right then, even if he was incapable of understanding my frustration, I found him truly exquisite and intoxicating. I loved sharing my appreciation for words and the flesh with him, that I could see in his maleness a woman's inclination to hours of reading, living half of her life by proxy. And especially that he could watch me talking about Aragon while his eyes coveted me alongside the renewal of desire.

Monsieur took the book back and opened it some pages further on. While I changed the music, he began to read a passage that was to transform my admiration for Aragon into worship: his description of Irene's cunt. Every time I heard the words 'cunt' or 'vulva' (Aragon, from my own feminine perspective, is the only person who can write about a vulva without provoking waves of disgust in me), they had me squirming with pleasure and embarrassment, despite my veneer of worldliness. From the glint in Monsieur's eyes, his delight in our situation, I could see that it still excited him to talk dirty to a young girl. During the conversation that followed, he told me about all the rare editions he owned. I adored Monsieur for his private library and imagined myself spending two nights and days there, collapsed in a large leather armchair, a cup of coffee in one hand, naked beneath one of Monsieur's shirts, which, on the stroke of every passing hour, he would pull away from my skin.

For a brief instant, I buried my nose in his hair and rubbed myself against him. I was passionately obsessed with him, but clumsy in expressing my love and desire. I found it so difficult to caress his chest or kiss him. My face in his armpit, I watched him. An invisible observer would never have guessed he'd just fucked me in the arse. Now Monsieur was all softness, like the pages of the book he was holding. Soft, soft.

First lovers' tiff between Monsieur and me. Out of the blue, he asked me: 'Did you fuck this week?'

'What sort of question is that?' I moved a little away from him while I tried to work out the right thing to say.

'It's nothing. I just wanted to know.' He appeared quite calm.

Shrugging, I said: 'Yes.'

Then I asked him the same thing. Monsieur laconically confirmed that he had.

Oh, tell me more!

'How many times?'

'Twice.' He was not offended by my intrusion into his sex life.

'With your wife?'

'Yes. And you?'

'With my boyfriend.'

The facts were the facts.

Maybe it was then that I first became aware of the trap into which I would soon fall. I was dying to know how she and he made love, after twenty years of marriage, the automatic movements of his hands across her body. But the thought released in me a jealous streak I hadn't known I had. Like a moth drawn to the brightness of a lamp, I asked: 'How is it with your wife? After all, it's such a long time you've been sleeping together.'

'It depends,' Monsieur said, in a strange tone to his voice. 'But overall it's fine. After all these years, it's still good.'

'You must know each other very well?'

'Of course,' Monsieur replied, without further revelation.

I was consumed with the need to know everything, every single detail. How Monsieur fucked the woman who knew all his perversions. What was her body like? What did her face look like when she came? When did they do it? Did they have favourite positions, preferred techniques? Habits? Were there things they had never done? She was Monsieur's wife, and her shadow oppressed me.

'And you?' he continued. 'I'm sure it was pretty awful.'

'Why should it have been?' I was offended.

'Because boys of your age know nothing about women.'

'He's thirty.'

'Thirty?' Monsieur cried, eyes popping out of his head.

Was he joking? For a couple of seconds I stared at him, trying to assess whether his surprise was genuine.

'Another older guy!' he said, the beginning of a smile on his lips.

'So now you're jealous!' I smiled back. 'You're shocked because I happen to have a boyfriend.'

'I'm not jealous. I was just wondering why you always seem to go for older guys.'

He moved an inch or so forward across the bed, watching me intently. Then, he changed his mind: 'Maybe I am jealous. Not a good idea, eh?'

'No doubt about that,' I answered, surprised that I could make a man jealous, more so *this* man.

'So, what do we do about it?' he asked.

'What do you mean?'

'We can go on as we are, can't we?'

And, in truth, I couldn't envisage pretending he didn't exist. The idea of living so close to him, knowing he was just a few kilometres away *but being unable to reach him* took my breath away. I strove to understand him. To unravel his mystery. And I wanted so much more. But all I could say was,'Yeah, why not? We go on.'

We go on, even if I already know where it's leading. To disaster. I can feel in my bones that the coming summer without him, and that's just the beginning, will be unbearable. And I have no wish to be like the other fools who fall in love with married men.

One of the things I always admired in Monsieur was the way he became erect. So easily, so fast. He could talk to me for hours, casually playing with my nipples and earlobes, a rich intellectual discourse with his courtesan, discussing André Breton as freely as sex, making an inventory of authors still unknown to me. His breath on my neck spoke words of love interrupted by literary wit, then kisses and gentle bites. Halfway through one of my answers – I was about to contradict something he'd said – Monsieur mounted me in one swift movement. His first thrusts overwhelmed me, leaving me unable to breathe or speak, not that he needed any sign of my submission.

'You like it in your little pussy, too, don't you?'

'Have you slept with anyone else since we've been together?'

'No. Why?'

'Oh, nothing,' I lied.

It upsets me enough to imagine you making love with your wife but the idea of another woman underneath you hurts deep in my soul.

Monsieur raised himself beside me. 'Are you jealous?'

There was a touch of jubilation in his voice, which irritated me. 'Absolutely not!'

'You're jealous as hell!' Monsieur insisted, feasting on the idea.

'*Absolutely not*. I just wanted to know, that's all.'

'Yes, you are. You want to know if I'm sleeping with other girls to establish that you're the only one. So, darling, you are most assuredly jealous.'

My lips barely parted as he kissed me.

Slipping his trousers on (oh, the curve of his back): 'Of late, I haven't wanted to touch anyone but my wife and you. I'm always thinking of you.'

His gaze burned my back.

'I think of your arse all the time. When I'm operating, your arse is all I can see. You, in that position.'

I was on the bed, contorted, with my bum in the air, my face under my hair, watching him dress. I loved how the light danced around him. I found him beautiful. He put on his pristine white shirt, which clung to the contours of his body. Do men ever consider the chasm between their nudity and the moment they unthinkingly rebutton their shirt? The way their fingers slowly manoeuvre upwards, all the way to the collar, sealing themselves away when, just a few minutes ago, they were on full display. Some, like Monsieur, however elegantly they may dress, still have an aura of nakedness. The suit jacket they add to the ensemble makes no difference: it's so easy to pull off again. Now, watching Monsieur's thighs inside his expensive grey trousers, I could already trace the contours of his next erection.

The handcuffs.

'And I think of your body all the bloody time, not always in terms of making love with you. Just to feel close to you. I'm not aware of the age difference when I talk to you and listen to you.'

I smiled. Then I asked: 'Are other girls of my age different?'

'Yes. They're much more passive. They take, never give much back.'

'I wasn't very obedient this morning,' I said, half hoping this would prompt Monsieur to propose a date for our next meeting.

'It's not a question of obedience. I enjoy the random things that rush through your brain.'

'Anyway,' I said, 'you'd be a total bastard if you were sleeping with your wife, me *and* other girls of my age.'

'You only say that because you're jealous.'

'Once again, I'm not. It's just . . . you know . . . the situation . . .'

'Jealous, darling.'

'*No.* All I'm saying is you'd be a real bastard. Mind you, what with what we're up to, we're in no position to judge!'

Monsieur's mood darkened. He fell silent as he adjusted his shirt collar and came to sit beside me on the bed. 'I don't like it when you call me a bastard.'

'From me, it can be an endearment.'

Which was true, but his eyes were so dark that I thought for a moment he was about to hit me, or that I had hurt him. 'Don't look at me like that,' I whispered, wrapping myself against the cold material of his suit. 'When my girlfriends and I talk about bastards, it's in a nice way. Affectionate.'

Monsieur appeared unconvinced, but he kissed me at length.

I added: 'Anyway, I'm as much of a bastard as you.

What with my uncle, all my family in fact, I have so many reasons not to be sleeping with you.'

'There's nothing wrong about what we're doing. Other than that I'm married.'

'Can't you see? We're immoral. You used to work with my uncle. You spent three days at a seminar in Jersey with him and my mother. All my family knows you. And I happen to be the young niece and daughter.'

'It's not as if I were sleeping with his wife.'

'It's almost worse. My uncle adores his nieces. He doesn't want to know that other men touch them, particularly men he knows. Especially if those men are married and have children. Have you any idea of the unholy mess there would be if anybody found out what's going on?' The tone of my voice no doubt betrayed how much the wrongness of the situation excited me.

'So, the only problem is that I'm married, no? If I happened to be your uncle, I'd rather like to know you were with a man of my age, someone with experience, rather than with a young fool who'd treat you badly.'

'Come on!' I was exasperated. 'Don't you realize that if Philippe sees you with me, he won't give a damn about experience or status? Even if he were to ignore the fact you have a wife and children – and I'd find that difficult to believe – the situation remains the same: you're his age, you worked together and he likes you, which would certainly make you one hell of a bastard in his eyes. No way you could ever hope he might forgive you. He'd also despise me, but because he's my uncle he would always love me too – somehow. If he ever found out about you and me, *which will not happen*, all he would see is one thing: that you're fucking his niece.'

Monsieur sat next to me, his hands on my hips.

'But should anyone find out about us, all I'd have to do is open my in-box and they'd know you came looking for it.'

I looked into his smiling eyes and saw the hint of a threat. Or was it? Perhaps it was the expression of a thug telling a newly arrived shopkeeper: 'We're going to play a little game which will be to both our advantage. As long as you play fair, so shall I. If you ever betray me or put me in an uncomfortable position, I can blackmail or hurt you and wouldn't hesitate to do so.'

I remember thinking, Fucking bastard, as I watched Monsieur without blinking, trying to see if he was serious. If he was capable of defending himself by throwing me to the wolves. From the determination I saw in the depths of his eyes, I knew he was. Indeed. Monsieur was that type of man.

Wordless, smiling back at him, I lay down against his legs, coiled like a cat. I was being held hostage, and Monsieur was now as much an adversary as a lover. He controlled me in vile ways, but the more I thought about it, the more it aroused me.

Monsieur. Monsieur and his lips.

As he began to fade away, already mentally on the way back to his medical and conjugal life, I became his slave. I was lying flat on my stomach and observing every movement he made. He settled back on the bed, taking my hands in his. As if he were about to kiss my neck. Which would have been enough for me.

'Talk to me of love before I leave.'

My eyes widened with amazement and incredulity.

'How could I not be a little in love with you when you feel the same way towards me?'

I understood he wouldn't leave unless I said something, and I was dying to know where all this was leading. Maybe I did love him, in the contemptible way cheap tarts do, or was I just attracted by the idea of love? Who knows? 'I am a little in love with you,' I admitted.

Monsieur's smile was silent, and I felt like slapping my face.

There was nothing cataclysmic about my defeat at his hands. I can see that now. Defeat is just an accumulation of minor acts of surrender. One. And then another. Until the noose around my neck choked me.

ELLIE

I've said it already in an SMS, but I have to write it down now. Ten words on a mobile phone mean nothing.

I was thinking of you, your body, your voice, your smell. I was thinking of that morning when I was ashamed of what I was doing. I was thinking of all the things you said to me (words cutting through me to my nerve endings) and I realized I was going to find it really hard to hold out until next Tuesday. You can't imagine the state I'm in. Every time I think of that morning, my stomach twists, goose pimples spread up my arms, my right leg is paralysed, and I can feel my cunt flickering open and closed, like my eyes do when I am tired.

Can I tell you a secret? Why I'm reluctant to touch myself in your presence? It's shame, I think. The thought that if I did that, I'd immediately become an object of contempt. Which is paradoxical insofar as it doesn't bother me in the slightest to be fucked in the most disgusting ways possible, or be called abject names.

Never take pity on me. If I don't obey you, I'll be going nowhere. I'll likely reach the ripe old age of sixty without an orgasm. Use me, manipulate me, turn me into your ideal mistress. Free me. I know you can do it. I've never come across anyone more capable of doing it than you. I know that if I don't manage to come for you, it's just because of the stupid conditioning I've imposed on myself. Listen, when you were taking me from behind this morning, I was overcome by pain, or discomfort, whatever, for five or six minutes. On the other hand I was terribly wet. See the way I am? My body displays a life of its own. It ignores all the obstacles I place in its way and devours every caress you bestow on it. You must help me or I'll never become one of the women they write about in the books, Irene (I've just finished it by the way) or any of the others. Those women whose only ambition is to come, with no concern about being pretty or dignified. You can't be dignified when you're being fucked. It doesn't work.

I so want to talk to you right now, but I'll hold on until tomorrow.

Earlier, I was reading *Irene's Cunt*, and I could smell you all over the pages. A little.

I love the word 'cunt'. And the fact other people dislike it so intensely fills me with joy. Cunt. Cunt. The only female counterpart to cock. When you think about it, cunt is so apposite. So easy to say. Cunt, all so literary and unsettling, full of a charm most people can't process. You have to be a keen reader to fully appreciate the sharp sound of the word 'cunt', read, fucked, licked, all woman. Or to be a woman and listen to the word whispered in her ears by a man like you.

So, I had my shower when I got home and – how can I make this sound part of the story? – when I washed myself, the soap stung me. I was still quite open, as if you had just withdrawn from me. Is the devil in the detail?

I have to stop now. Monday night. Sleep with me. Or come at night, go home to sleep and return the following day. But I want you as soon as possible.

TUESDAY, 11 MAY 2009, 04.25

I don't know where the surrounding décor I invent when I'm playing with myself comes from. When I think of Monsieur, the mystery deepens; around us, blue swirling drapery, with a life of its own, full of haphazard breathing and sighs. The walls and the whole world gasp and vibrate to an obscene rhythm. Here and there, a window, the edge of the bed, the smell of a room; a random pot-pourri of all the places where Monsieur has followed me, trapped me, cornered me.

I'm at the hotel in the ninth *arrondissement* but I'm also everywhere and nowhere. Do take note of the fact that it's half past four in the morning and I still can't sleep. And I have no sleeping pills or grass and only my two fingers guide me towards sleep and liberation.

So, I'm lying here, sprawled out. Naked. The mirrors in the ceiling capture an image with all the purity of a painting, my body at the heart of crimson sheets, a bad-taste odalisque, as kitsch as this 'Chinese' room.

It's weird, this adversarial relationship I have with my pussy, and how it never presents Monsieur with a problem. Why are all men so irresistibly attracted to *it*? What do they see? What is so fascinating about what I have between my legs? Two lobes of flesh and a thin carpet of fur, shining like a seal's skin, disfigured by a deep gash. All these '*gracious undulations, the lacework of love*', as Aragon puts it, how is it possible for Monsieur to find poetry there? How can I not see beyond the superfluous folds of my flesh? Wouldn't it be nice if I had one of those exquisite sealed pussies in the shape of a shy mouth, slit barely opening when touched, widened by fingers. A sea shell carved from almond paste, harbouring minuscule nacreous lips, the tiny muzzle of the clitoris, a miniature rampart in need of courting before it consents to display itself. But I inherited this loud, lippy, porno-movie pussy, ever gaping, open like an obscene smile even when lovemaking is the last thing on my mind. Open-legged in front of Monsieur, I feel as if I'm displaying so much more than my sex. And it's never enough for him. In such close proximity to my pussy, he wants to watch it come alive, squirm beneath my fingers as it does when I am alone. How can I tell him, face to face, that I'd like to hear him say I'm as beautiful there as I am elsewhere? Monsieur wants to watch, spend hours studying me there, dissecting me until I become catatonic with discomfort. In his ideal world, Monsieur wishes to pin me down like a butterfly with wings extended, pulling and pinching to his heart's content, but all those assaults on my modesty would exasperate me and render me sopping wet. God only knows how much worse it all is when I'm wet. I become bloated and expand, unable to conceal the fact that mine is no virginal cunt shedding just a few parsimonious drops of inner dew. Doesn't Monsieur know this already? It's like a waterfall. A flow of gummy lava streaming down to my arse crack;

evidently, even if I look the picture of innocence, the dark folds of my pants betray the mark of the devil. There is no way I can even open my thighs without making untold promises of shameful sex. Maybe that's what makes his cock grow so hard.

Maybe, maybe. The mirror above the bed has its undeniable charms. The finger I slowly slip inside disappears within the slimy moistness, and the stale odour of the sheets is overcome by my sickly fragrance. A smell that undeniably operates as a spell on all men, strong enough to turn them into murderers. It's a bit like walking into a cider-house, where the perfume of the apples becomes too much. Maybe it's this very smell that turns men topsy-turvy so that they find everything beautiful and right about the bodies of women. And now I know this, it's impossible, IMPOSSIBLE, to proceed with any semblance of normality. Lust makes my slit open and close like a real mouth, and all these silent utterances make me blush. I am annoyed by the nuances of this language I fail to fully understand, and hate the fact that I don't like watching myself do what excites me when other girls do it.

I'm like an amateur movie. I can't watch; I'm still blushing. I can't look at my own face without wincing. Have I ever known what I look like when I come? How do those delicate contractions in the pit of my stomach reflect in an onlooker's eyes? I'm sure I pleasure myself as much as anyone else, if not more, in every imaginable or possible position, standing, sitting, lying down, with my hands, my thighs, the showerhead, all the ordinary objects of everyday life my unquenchable vice summons up for assistance. But never in front of any of the thousand mirrors spread across my house. And now that I have met the man, whenever I touch myself I feel as if I'm being watched. Just three days ago I surprised myself by checking my own room (within the walls of the family home) for hidden cameras. And tonight the red reflections of the super-cheap galaxy painted across the ceiling in this room are like a gang of informers reporting my activities back to the Île Saint-Louis castle, more precisely, the mythological study where he hides my accumulating letters, between volumes by Mandiargues and Baudelaire. Improbable, I know. But I'm on my guard.

It would be so much better if Monsieur were actually here. At least I'd know why I was shivering. There would be something tangible to fear or lust for, no longer these twisted fantasies that I wouldn't reveal to him even under torture.

Can you hear me? With your animal intuition, can you feel that somewhere in Paris, as you fall asleep against your wife, I'm spreading my thighs all the way open until it's painful and I'm thinking of you, standing by the door there gazing at me? And because I'm a paradox, closing my eyes to my reflection in the mirror doesn't stop me imagining you ordering me to spread my legs wide, still wider, *even more*. A touch red-faced, I improvise a scenario in the style of the Marquis de Sade, a tale full of orders and insults, and – would I ever have the courage to tell you in real life or confess its details to my girlfriends? – the moment that captivates me most, binding all the other scenes together, is the one where I hear you say, your voice calm but peremptory, unwilling to accept any refusal: 'I can see your pussy, Ellie, but I can't see your arse. Pull your legs up.'

And I watch myself in the mirror following orders. (Imagining you imagining all this, troubled by it as you read a book, numbs my fingers and I find it difficult to write.)

As if your almost invisible presence wasn't enough, you appear out of nowhere and come to me, kneeling by my head, your nails digging into my calves preventing any further movement. Bewildered, I watch as my stomach divides, just a few centimetres away from my nose, and above it how my cunt and arse cheeks painfully conjugate with the spreading of my thighs.

'Look,' you order me.

In the mirror, all my holes are quivering; the stray hairs surrounding them appear to be drenched with sweat. But the worst thing is the way your eyes follow mine across the surface of the mirror, how your gaze travels over my hips, my breasts squashed against my knees, and focuses on the geometric centre of my shimmering, unveiled machinery now purring like a well-oiled engine. The violence of your will and the smells surrounding me suffocate me. You take a firm hold of my hand, set it against my clit, like my piano professor crushing my fingers beneath his to force me to learn difficult scales. There you are, holding me captive like a puppet, with all my wires tangled, leaning towards me. I hear the sound of your zip moving downwards, like the sharp echo of a circuit-breaker or a guillotine blade racing towards its target.

'Touch yourself. You're open. You can see every damn thing. I want to see you wank.'

I barely have time to open my mouth in protest when you brusquely interrupt me: 'No, Ellie, no. No bargaining. I don't even want to hear you breathe. Touch yourself, you fucking bitch.'

I have no sense of ridicule when I'm in the throes of lust. Right now, whatever I do next, I'll look like a whore. Eyes closed, my lips sliding along the material of your trousers, I rub myself gently.

(Presently, if there is any rightful order in the world, your intuition should be waking you: I bite the flesh of my thighs as I slip my fingers inside.)

You stroke my hair. *Very good, darling. Make yourself come.* On another planet, such curt orders would feel like a slap, leaving me breathless and – oh, dear God, maybe I'd enjoy being slapped. Maybe in this parallel world, where I can say or do anything and still emerge fresh as a flower, I'd want you to spit on me, inside my mouth, yes, after licking my lips, then slapping my cheeks. Because it would feel good. For no particular reason. Just to take me to the edge of a nervous breakdown. Am I some sort of monster? Would it be so awful and decadent to ask you for yet more?

'Put your fingers up your arse.'

The filthier your sentences are, the more I squirm within your grasp. I reach the point where I no longer need your commands to explode: to hear you mention fingers up my arse brings me to the brink, all those mysterious compartments in the pit of my stomach contracting suddenly. One of your hands briefly abandons my thigh and rises all the way up to my cheek, pinching it hard between your forefinger and thumb.

'What is it you really want, Ellie Becker? You want me to hurt you? Do as I say. Put your fingers up your arse.'

(I obey, still licking the blue scars left by my teeth across my thighs.)

'One more.'

'I can't!'

'Of course you can. You have no idea how much you can take. One more.'

You give a single glance at the mirror that is impassively reflecting the whole dreadful scene, your words so full of menace. My arsehole spasmodically squeezes my fingers and the flesh inside me shudders, gripping me with the energy of despair.

'One more.'

I half open my bitch-in-heat eyes, look through my parted knees. I no longer have three but four fingers inside, your hand painfully crushing my clit, and I'm dying for more.

'Open yourself wide. I want to be able to glide all the way to the depths of your arse, like sliding through butter. I will not tolerate the slightest sound of protest when I bugger you. Further, Ellie.'

All I can now hear are the gurgling, suffocating sounds struggling in the back of my throat, muted squeaks. If I close my eyes, I find myself back again in a world so like ours, a hail of smacks landing on my arse cheeks and your saliva forcing its way down my throat.

'Show me, now.'

You pull on my shoulder, emphasizing your last

word, and however much I bite my lips and try to look sorry for myself or hide behind my fringe, any outside observer, unaware of how the whole scene began, would come to the conclusion that I'm just a whore. And my parents. Jesus Christ, my poor father. How will I ever be able to look him in the face again, explain I was forced to do it, that their daughter is more than just this filthy bitch split all the way up to her belly button, rubbing her cheek against the cock of a family friend, her cunt dripping like a river, her thighs all red, shamelessly begging for it?

'But it's what you wanted, Ellie,' you whisper (because, naturally, in this particular world our brains communicate instantly). 'That's why it all began.

'From the very first text message you sent me while touching your clit in your little-girl room, I knew you yearned for this, to be bent over, my nose digging deep inside your bitch cunt, watching it melt like butter in the sun. Your messages betrayed the fact that you're a cheap whore, whose only need is to be shown the sheer infamy of her holes. And the more I hurt you, stretch your limits, the more you'll beg me to continue. There is no longer any need for you to say anything. I watch your holes open and close like the gills of a fish out of water. You need it. You crave it. I must say, come to think of it, wouldn't it be an atrocious sort of spectacle for your parents to witness, or are you actually thinking of that too?'

'Why should I ever think of such a thing?'

'I could pinch your nipples and make you come right now, just as you are, on all fours like a dog, or maybe I could bugger you, get you screaming, eh? I can already hear the sounds, the dry slap of my stomach against your arse cheeks, one thrust followed by another, all the way in, deep . . .'

The voice I am imagining is a deep bass, slow and deliberate, its tone a blend of desire and determination. My mouth remains wide open and silent.

You continue: 'You could be open wider, but I want to fuck your arse the way it is now. Feel myself plunge deep inside your stomach.'

There is no transition in my mind between the words emerging from your mouth and the moment you breach my arse. Maybe you'd asked me to spread the spit you'd dribbled over my open arse with my fingers.

A second later, you're deep inside me and the only thing I can see, even though my eyes are closed, is your cock violently thrusting deep into me, then withdrawing slowly, pale with slime, a lazy but steady rhythm. Any movement I make brings me closer to an orgasm.

'Look at yourself. I want you to recall every single image tonight, back in your own bed. As soon as you close your eyes.'

'Aah, you're about to make me come . . .'

Well, that's what I was planning to say, but your fingers are inside my mouth and the bass note of your voice glides across me: 'Shut up. I don't want to hear a sound, understood?'

I keep on looking at you despairingly, greedily chewing anything you place between my lips and your orders change: 'Come.'

If only you could imagine the shrill impact of such a simple word in the depths of my twisted brain. I think of it so much I forget everything else.

'I said, come now.'

'But . . .'

'Shut up. Touch yourself. Like that. Faster.'

Your fingers bruising my lips in a semblance of anger.

'Faster. I'm allowing you a further ten seconds to come, OK? After that, I'll cease fucking you and I'll get very angry. Nine . . .'

I'm wanking as fast as I can, my hand and wrist cramping. A strangely pleasurable sensation. Like the odd spasms I used to have at school when a teacher would announce the end of a test. All the desks surrounding me emptying, the barrage of whispers fading, the schoolmaster gathering the papers, and I'm still busy with mine, a few words away from the ending, and I would feel my fingers going numb with an unwelcome but rapturous feeling coursing through me, preventing me from writing anything legible. Tracing the final letters, I would be forced to bite my lips to restrain the tears. My back wet with sweat. The same sort of twisted feeling I used to experience when I was only five months old and tightened my buttocks when swimming; I could have allowed myself to sink to the bottom of the pool to fully enjoy the tingling, but kept thrashing around like a frog, overcome with pleasure. In both instances, I wasn't touching myself, didn't know how to then, but now that I was twenty and, dear God, the effect of these deep-seated contractions as I'm ordered to do so. *Just imagine if at five years old in Sainte-Maxime you had known how to rub that small nub of flesh between your legs. It would have been miraculous. Just imagine the uproar, a hand buried beneath the desk in class B36.*

I feel sorry you're a man and unable to experience such an exquisite feeling that it makes you want to scratch, bite, suck until the blood flows.

'Eight . . . Do I have to describe how you look, with your arse in the air and your gaping cunt? Do you want me to tell you what I see so that you can imagine it too, Ellie? Maybe you want me to fuck you harder.'

The more I think of it, the more the cramp spreads, intensifies, blood rushes to my face. I keep repeating the seductive accompaniment of your countdown ('Seven . . . six . . . five . . .'), I must come, fuck, I MUST come, bloody hell, menaced, under orders, threatened with danger or acute pain; only you know what sort of terrible things you might conjure to punish me further. The new obscenities you could throw in my direction. A torrent of words, filthy bitch whore tramp, can't you feel me tearing up your pussy can't you see watch watch watch? The moment is approaching, I end up folded back on myself like a religious icon, consumed by shame, streaked with spit, and an endless stream of your cum criss-crosses my face from mouth to forehead, dripping all the way down to my tits (and if it covered the whole of my body, it would be absolutely perfect).

'Two . . .'

'Almost, almost!'

Yes, it's rising inside me, nerves twisting around each other, releasing their invisible but devastating conflagration around the mast of your cock inside my arsehole. I'm just centimetres away. (Is it really a question of centimetres? Shouldn't it be another, much more complicated, form of measurement, a bar, an ampere, or some obscure scale in the quantum vocabulary? How do you calculate the strength of an implosion?). I'm just a hair's breadth away from the finish line and still you keep on muttering at me: 'One . . . Come, you stupid little bitch, come now . . .'

I bite my shoulder and it always hurts when I sleep on my side.

The following day, Monsieur pushed the small door open. In the darkness his eyes miraculously created light as he took in every detail of the room, a smile spreading across his lips. I was waiting for him, crouched open-legged on the bed, drinking in the joy of his reaction. Then, familiar gestures: Monsieur taking his coat off, placing it on a chair, followed by a few seconds of unbearable tension, sensing how every muscle in his body hardened as he readied himself to throw himself against me, over me, into me. My favourite moment: when Monsieur was no longer a man but a hurricane through which I could just about recognize arms, legs, the perfect hardness of a cock, the sly fragrance of masculinity, lips full of expectation, his silver-grey hair.

A quarter of an hour or three centuries later, his voice whispering: 'Touch yourself.'

Me, ever obtuse: 'Aah . . . stop looking at me.'

Once I had begun this indefinable and unreal relationship with Monsieur, meals with my uncle Philippe became fascinating and full of fear. I recall a particular evening when they came to dinner, on some anniversary: Monsieur occupied all my attention. Under the table in the salon I was answering his texts, trying to conceal the lubricity of my smile. Only Alice, facing me across the table, knew who was causing my BlackBerry to vibrate, and was throwing me dirty looks I preferred to ignore. It was one of those informal meals where the conversations merged into an indistinct hubbub, and I was half involved, answering questions politely, the sort of meaningless chat my family had engaged in since time immemorial. What about university? When would the strike end? How were the mocks being assessed? And how is your boyfriend getting on? Occasionally, it was the turn of my two sisters to face the random interrogation, Alice confirming for the nth time where her new art school was located and how she was revising for her baccalaureate exam, and our eyes would meet across the table and I would recognize in hers the impatience I was experiencing to leave the table and go to my room to smoke a joint or two. She appeared to be even more bored than I was – she didn't have a lover who had spent fifteen years working alongside our uncle. How could I ever describe to her the delight I was experiencing that no one at the table knew of the words Monsieur had whispered in my ear or the way his hard cock had lodged deep inside my stomach. What a whore I had become, how much I enjoyed it.

'By the way, weren't you planning to show me your fat?' Philippe's memory always came to life at the most inopportune moments. 'I think a bit of suction around the thighs would do the trick.'

I stood up, still unsteady from my glass of red wine. 'I've lost eight kilos, but it just won't go away.'

'No, not worth operating on,' he answered. 'I, for one, wouldn't risk it. It would be criminal.'

'But it's a bloody cushion! Wouldn't Dr S operate on me?'

Alice knew I was buzzing inside and glanced at me fiercely.

'None of my colleagues would ever agree to do it. Tell me, Ellie, why don't you take up jogging instead?'

'You surgeons are a hopeless bunch. Why should I run when you've got all these new techniques available to you? Or starve myself?'

Philippe burst out laughing, as if he knew I was kidding. I pretended to change the subject. My sister wasn't fooled when I jokingly said: 'Did you know I have S on Facebook?'

'Really? What does he have to say?'

'Not much. I basically added him because Mum told me he was fond of Calaferte.'

He frowned. 'Who's Calaferte?'

'A writer,' I responded.

Like many family members, my uncle kept as far as possible from my interest in erotic literature. My mother, sighing, added: 'He writes about sex, of course.'

'You say that because you've never actually read *La Mécanique des femmes*,' I pointed out, annoyed.

My mother's disparagement of Calaferte had thrown me into the arms of Monsieur. She had never opened any of his books, but she knew they were erotic and felt, foolishly, that she could express an opinion about him. She raised her eyes upwards.

'What do you mean? I'm the one who bought the book!' She turned to her brother. 'It's the one where he describes a woman peeing over the pages.'

Inevitably most of the people around the table were laughing nervously, displaying their stupidity. This was one of the things I had not dared express to Monsieur, for fear he would guess from my tone how I sometimes found my family contemptible. There were moments when I truly hated them, wondering why we were so different when it came to certain subjects. Irritation rising, I almost shouted: 'That's enough, Mum! You might have bought the book, but you evidently haven't read it. At no stage does Calaferte describe a woman peeing. I know because I've read it at least ten times. And even if he had done, it's possible to write well of such things.'

'You're quite right,' my aunt said, patting my arm. In an attempt to defuse the situation, she changed the subject. 'Philippe, what was his name again, the photographer who liked to take pics of young girls weeing in fields? We saw his exhibition.'

'Anyway,' my mother continued, 'I'm not surprised S likes Calaferte. He's a sex maniac.'

'I don't see the connection,' I retorted. 'As it happens, sex maniacs don't read Calaferte.'

'Philippe, do tell her what a sex maniac S is! When we were in Jersey, it was all he could talk about.'

'All men are sex maniacs,' my uncle said philo-sophically. 'It's just that some conceal it better than others.'

'Maybe,' I said, clumsily sitting down again. 'But in the meantime he's the only person with whom I can discuss the books I like.'

'No wonder, if you raise the subject of sex with him . . .' My mother sighed, clearly hoping the conversation had come to its natural end.

'How can you not understand that discussing literature is not automatically a matter of talking about sex? Do you really think I'm some sort of tramp?'

'Ellie, I was joking!' she said.

And everyone was laughing. At me. I was ready to defend those books with tooth and claw, but for them it was just a pretext to talk about his love of sex. When he had offered me *Irene's Cunt*, I had spent the whole evening behind the locked door of my room, sprawling across my couch, smoking cigarette after cigarette, breathless. Beyond the literary beauty, I was thinking of Monsieur. If he'd made me receptive enough to read the text, it was because he approved of Aragon. That was the night when I had elevated Monsieur to a pedestal and had come to understand that he was the only soul who could keep me company on my path through erotic literature. It bound us together.

I had crawled to the kitchen where my mother was cooking dinner. I wasn't expecting a miracle, but I had to attempt to explain the divine nature of the work I had emerged from. The mere thought that I would ever be capable of expressing myself in the same way consumed me. I sat on a stool, and began reading aloud, daunted by Aragon as much as my audience. I hadn't been angry with my sisters for laughing when I'd used the word 'slit', but I had never hated and despised my mother more than when she had burst out laughing as I read: *'"... the moist folds of her outer lips yawned ..."'*

'It's disgusting!' she cried.

I kept my lips sealed in a rictus of scorn.

It was far from easy to begin reading again, starting where I had been so rudely interrupted, conscious that she was now already concentrating on the next pretext to belittle Aragon's sublime verbal violence, and I stopped reading two lines further on. I felt foolish.

'Why did you stop?' My mother was surprised.

'You're not making the slightest effort to understand the beauty of the text!' I was indignant.

'Come on, Ellie, we're just having a laugh!' she said. Then, serious: 'Do you really like this sort of stuff?'

'Yes. *I like this sort of stuff.*' I repeated her words, backing away with all the dignity I could muster, *Irene's Cunt* held against my chest, rejected.

I had been offended enough that evening when Philippe said: 'I didn't know he was on Facebook.'

'Why should it surprise you?' my mother interjected. 'Typical of his sort!'

'Why hasn't he friended me?'

'Probably because you didn't ask him to,' I answered. with pained indifference. 'People don't automatically become your friends. Anyway, you don't know how to use Facebook.'

'You're right,' he confirmed. 'But if I asked him to become my friend, he would, wouldn't he?'

'How would I know? It's up to him to decide. There's no reason for him to turn you down, is there?' (Apart from the fact that he's fucking your oldest niece, I didn't say.)

'Did I tell you I saw photos of his children?' my mother broke in. 'They look so much like him. They're darlings. And his wife isn't bad, either.'

'I've met her a few times. She's good fun.'

'I've always wondered how she can live with a guy like him. Such a skirt-chaser.'

'She's probably up to the same tricks,' my stepfather said, and everyone around the table pretended to be shocked, as if it would have been something out of the ordinary, the secret arrangement of a couple.

'I couldn't live like that,' my mother added. 'I'm just not selfish enough.' For the first time that evening, I was in total agreement with her.

'A lot of married people do,' my aunt observed. 'It doesn't prevent them living together in harmony. Either they know and tolerate it, or they keep it a secret.'

'After twenty years of marriage, I don't see how you could avoid knowing about it,' my mother objected. 'She's like an ostrich, with her head buried in the ground. As for him, he probably doesn't know his wife's cheating on him and thinks she hasn't a clue about him. Men think women are stupid.'

Once we'd disposed of a birthday cake, much too rich to follow a veal casserole, I rushed back to my room. With a quick trawl through Facebook, I found a stack of photos of her. In most of them, she was lost among a crowd of unknown faces, but I always knew which one she was. She stood out from the others as if I was shining a light on her.

'Who is it?' my sister asked, as I was zooming in on her features.

'His wife.'

'So now you're spying on his wife. Oh dear . . .'

'I'm not spying on her. I'm intrigued, that's all.'

'This will all end badly,' Alice predicted.

I kept the page open for the hour Alice and I were surfing, watching silly clips from the eighties. From time to time, I'd close a window by mistake and her face would reappear, large black eyes circled with dark makeup, pretty white teeth, a smile like a question mark making a rendezvous with me for later when I would be alone.

Estelle. A name I seldom hear that will for ever be attached to this woman, his wife. When I pronounce its dull, old-fashioned syllables, it sounds like a refugee from a bad Mills & Boon novel, but from Monsieur's lips it would sound like a caress. I don't know. I'm terrified of hearing him say 'Estelle'. The gulf that separates her from me would be evident in the way he pronounces our names.

Monsieur has no idea how much respect I demonstrate in the way I say 'your wife'. Deep in his grey eyes, I search for her, for a footprint of the love and how different it might be from the tenderness he extends to me. When Valentine or Babette pity her for the metaphorical horns on her head and use the odious 'cuckold' word, I explain to them how she differs from the provincial trophy wives who avert their eyes from their husbands' peccadilloes and suffer in silence. I am intimately persuaded that life at his side has taught her what sort of man shares her bed and brings up their children. I've looked at photos of her for hours, and she has a fierce intelligence: she shines with the awareness that she will never change Monsieur. Has she ever tried? It's just the way he is: fascinated by women, but in love with just one. I've never been tempted to think I could rival her. All I am is a parenthesis in his life, a parenthesis among others already forgotten, while Estelle remains, year after year, sitting on the same pedestal, and that is no metaphor: there is a photograph, taken on their third son's birthday, in which she is floating around on a chair held high by a dozen friends. And there is Monsieur, too, about to burst into youthful laughter, gazing at her with eyes full of love and admiration. Dazzled, I remained still for several minutes observing them, my heart bleeding.

In all the photos of them together, mostly taken without them being aware of it, if they are not in each other's arms, they are never far apart, their shoulders, arms, cheeks or eyes magically converging in the same direction, their bodies merging. It's evident this woman has managed to tame Monsieur and his impulses. I could never attempt it. Domination is a strong aspect of his character, manifesting itself in the beds we share. He cannot accept any kiss he hasn't planned; whenever he's taken by surprise, he says, 'I am the one who's kissing you,' and then his lips devour mine. That's the way we always communicate, verbally and physically. I'd thought he could never bend to anyone's authority until I came across another wonderful photograph, also taken on Louis's birthday. The shot is focused on a single image: the two faces seemingly welded together, as if capturing the precise moment of a spontaneous kiss, Estelle's pretty hands unfolding like a fan, stroking and holding Monsieur's freshly shaven cheeks. Their eyes are closed; at the corners of Estelle's the trace of a small wrinkle betrays that the embrace has caught her in the midst of laughter. Monsieur is partly obscured by his wife's long fingers, but across the upper part of his face, there is no evidence of resistance. At first glance, there is nothing special about this photo. But it showed me where my power over Monsieur ended, and Estelle's began. That she had tamed Monsieur for the duration of a photographic flash was beside the point. What mattered was deciphering the good fortune that emanated from the image: a woman happy because her child was growing up, all her friends had joined her for the occasion, and kissing that child's father was the best way to express her joy. The woman in the photo is profoundly in love with her husband.

Monsieur has never made me shine in the same way. Monsieur has never been present to smother my joy with his lips. Monsieur has never granted me entry to the kingdom he has built with Estelle. And while I feverishly hold on to the power he almost accidentally afforded me, and shudder at the thought of the other, unknown, women, Estelle reigns supreme, so untouchable that she allows Monsieur to roam free: he will always return. Over twenty years the seductions have multiplied and he has always come back to Estelle, his harbour. So many other men among his acquaintances have become soft and harmless, like fat, neutered cats, exercising their blunt wiles on unworthy prey, but Monsieur continues to fine-tune his art.

Maybe she *is* up to the same thing. Monsieur and she are not even friends on Facebook.

What led Estelle to cut Monsieur so much slack? How did she come to understand that none of his mistresses mattered? They must have clashed over it. You don't become an expert in deceit without getting caught out once or twice. That's how you learn the business.

I have a very cinematographic vision of the whole improbable scene. Nine o'clock in the evening, Monsieur in the lift waiting to reach his floor, while a short distance away his young wife, who's just finished feeding the baby, is watching the TV news, her mind switched off. Agitated, she is thinking of the phone call that tore her day apart: around two in the afternoon, a woman had asked to speak to Dr S. Estelle, her heartbeat resonating in her ears, had tried to recognize her mother-in-law or a secretary, two women who would normally have no reason to call him at home at this time of day.

'He's not home yet,' she'd said. 'Who's that? Maybe I can pass on a message. I'm his wife.'

The unknown woman had immediately hung up, leaving Estelle holding the receiver, assailed by the thought that it could only have been one of *them*: she had never been stupid enough to believe that Monsieur would restrict himself to a *single* mistress.

Estelle had spent the rest of the day with her hands shaking, unable to think beyond what had just happened. She was mad with anger and pain. Humiliated. When the baby was having his afternoon nap, she had stood for a few minutes in front of the open wardrobe of Monsieur's clothes. She had instinctively slipped a hand inside the pocket of a jacket, hating herself for acting like a typical betrayed wife but hating him more for having placed her in this situation. Just a petrol receipt and a few ten-franc coins. Fifteen other suits beckoned her, now that she had begun searching for evidence, had actually become that sort of woman. In one, there must be some tangible proof, something to provide her with more pain. Come on, Estelle, turn all of this upside-down, open every drawer, unfold every pair of trousers. Here they must be, all the bitches he fucks between consultations, during his nights on call, all those girls who know his body as well as you do. If one of them has his home phone number, there must be something to betray him in this wardrobe, don't you think? While the baby sleeps, and can't see how ugly an hysterical mother looks, investigate. When he returns this evening and you mention the phone call, he's bound to have an excuse. He'll say you're crazy and, anyway, you haven't an ounce of proof.

Avenge yourself: among the thousands of scraps of paper folded at the bottom of sundry pockets, how many do you think will provide you with clear evidence? And we're not even talking about all the blonde, brown, red hairs, all the white stains on his shirts and trouser legs. If we could talk to each other, I could tell you how they climb on to his knees, naked under their dresses, when his office is locked. Which dry cleaner's he goes to so you won't come across the lipstick of all those whores, most of whom haven't half of your class or beauty, but have him running around in circles because they smell so strongly of no-strings sex. Search, Estelle. Do it for me. If he was you, he'd have turned the apartment inside out, not that he would find anything: women are much too cunning. But men are stupid: there's always something they've forgotten to hide. Don't let him turn you into of one those shrews everyone takes pity on. Defend yourself, while you're still young and pretty. Change him. Cut him off at the knees. We women can do that, no?

Eyes closed, Estelle had moved away from the cupboard, jaw clenched, stomach tight. All afternoon on the couch, she could feel the pernicious call of temptation vibrating inside her, beckoning her. She'd thrown herself recklessly into games with little Charles. At eight o'clock, he'd begun to cry and, for half an hour, Estelle held him to her breasts, full of milk, without taking her eyes off him, smiling mechanically. Once he was sated, the baby had let go of her nipple and she had held him tight against her chest.

Charles burped quietly, and Estelle wiped his lips with her sleeve. It was almost nine and she still hadn't dressed or combed her hair. Her makeup kit had been lying on the kitchen table since the telephone call. She should have prepared dinner, but the idea of setting a saucepan full of water to boil on the stove was too tiring.

Monsieur's keys turn in the lock. Estelle's heart is beating wildly. Charles's eyes are round and questioning as he sits on her knees.

'Here's your daddy,' she says to him, and the baby appears to understand her.

The door opens and this man she finds so beautiful appears, dressed in his grey suit, holding his briefcase, the weariness of a long day's work drawn across his smiling face. The thought of another woman hanging on to the scented flesh of his neck appals her. She composes her features into a semblance of neutrality as Monsieur takes Charles, who has instantly recognized him. However tired he is, he has always enough strength to hold his baby. And Estelle realizes that, watching the two similar faces smile at each other, her husband's lips kissing the child's tiny nose, she is incapable of not loving Monsieur. There is no way she can ever love her son without worshipping the man he takes after. Monsieur never complains when he has to get up in the middle of the night when Charles has colic. Monsieur never hesitates when the child wishes to be held in the air like an aeroplane, even if it ends up with Charles giggling until he's sick over Monsieur's suit. Such a beautiful spectacle, it always breaks Estelle's heart.

'How are you, darling?' he asks, before tenderly kissing her.

He holds the baby against himself with his large masculine hands, in love with the trio they form. But Estelle can't find the energy to lie. 'Not good.'

'What's the matter?' Monsieur asks.

She'd thought it would take her hours to find the right words, but it all comes out quickly. 'You have a mistress.'

Monsieur opens his eyes wide, as if rehearsing some theatrical monologue, but Estelle sharply interrupts him: 'Please, don't say anything. Don't start lying.'

She feels like screaming. Her throat tightens and she brings her hands to her mouth, closing her eyes, the lashes already full of tears. She loves Monsieur so much. So much.

'Don't start lying to me because I know you lie so well that I'll want to believe you.'

Monsieur takes the baby to his play-pen, by the entrance to their room. When he returns, he seems sad, his tall silhouette bending under the weight of what Estelle assumes is guilt or remorse.

'Darling . . .' he begins.

'I had a phone call today. A woman who wanted to speak to Dr S.'

'Many of my patients have this number,' Monsieur explains. 'If it's urgent, they can reach me at home. You know that.'

'When I said I was your wife, she hung up immediately,' Estelle continues, burning with shame. 'No real patient would do that. Anyway, no patient has ever called you here. So, please, *please*, don't lie to me. Not to me. I'm not one of those girls. I am your wife.'

'Listen, darling, I don't understand,' Monsieur says, shaking his head, looking so confused she can feel herself weaken.

Part of her, so much of her, wants to accept any excuses he might come up with so they can go on as usual. Estelle recognizes the innate talent her mother always had for closing her eyes to any problem likely to disrupt the peace of the family life. But out of pride she can't agree to be blind and cowardly.

Like a machine, Monsieur keeps on talking: 'I don't understand.'

'Well, you're the only one,' Estelle answers, louder than she wants to. 'Stop lying to me.'

'She didn't give her name?'

'If she had, I wouldn't be so upset.'

'What did she sound like?'

Her nerves on edge, Estelle bursts into tears. 'If you're cheating on me, fine, as long as you don't rub my nose in it! But it hurts when you lie to me.'

In the play-pen the baby is shrieking.

'Please, don't cry. You're frightening Charles.'

'That's what all this is about. The baby and me. I'm only asking for one thing. Don't make me ashamed to be your wife.'

Monsieur is reduced to silence, his eyes darting around the room.

'I don't want to blush with embarrassment when I tell people I'm Madame S, and I don't want Charles asking me one day who all these women are when he answers the phone. And when you lie to me and an unknown woman hangs up on me when she learns you're married, I'm ashamed of you and of myself. I'm ashamed of you and it hurts because I love you. So don't do this to me. If you love me, if you have ever loved me, tell me the truth. Tell me you're fucking another girl and she's the one who called you. Or I'll go mad.'

Monsieur's grey eyes stare back at her. He is horribly aware of the sheer chaos a few wrong words would trigger. The pain he would inflict on Estelle, whom he loves so much. Without looking away from her, he says: 'There's this girl, at the hospital, a patient, who came to see me back in March with a bad deviation of her septum. I had to operate and she came back on several occasions for check-ups. Most of the time I looked after her. We got on fine and I gave her our home number in case of unexpected pain. She fell in love with me, or so she told me the last time she visited me. I immediately took her off my list of patients and referred her to someone else.'

Estelle listens to her husband; she will never know if his story is true or a fabrication. The tears on her face dry, turning her cheeks into a mask. Charles stops crying and the random sounds from his play-pen soften.

'I hadn't told you about it because it wasn't worth it. She's obsessed. Now she has our phone number, there's not much I can do, apart from change it. I'll call her tomorrow, get rid of her. Darling . . .'

He touches her cheek. As if stung by a wasp, Estelle jumps back.

'Did you fuck her?'

'No,' Monsieur answers, not batting an eyelid.

She feels almost ashamed as the weight lifts from her chest. 'Why should I believe you?' she asks.

'You *must* believe me. I have no proof, but you must believe me. Good God, the woman's over fifty!'

And Estelle vaguely remembers the grainy, frayed voice, a smoker's or an older woman's. But how can she untangle the false from the true? How can she know he hadn't planned it, an experienced womanizer, familiar with amorous intrigue? Monsieur loves women. And, for a man like him, wouldn't a fifty-year-old prove a delicious trophy? As he leans towards her to take her in his arms, Estelle leaps up.

'Leave me alone. If you touch me now, I think I'll scream.'

'Believe me, please,' he says, his hands seeking her.

'Leave me alone!'

173

'I can't allow that woman to harm us. I'll get the cops on to her!' Monsieur shouts, with an impulsiveness she has seldom seen in him.

'Why? It's *your* fault. *You* gave her our phone number. No judge, no cop can do anything about it,' Estelle says calmly.

She goes to fetch Charles, holds him tight, heavy with love as she smells her husband's scent on the small downy head.

'I'm going to put him to bed,' she says, her voice white and cold. 'If you're hungry, there's some of yesterday's pasta in the fridge. You can warm it up.'

And, baby in her arms, she turns round, no longer stuck to the same spot, cooing into the tiny uncomprehending ears, trying not to hear Monsieur calling Estelle Estelle Estelle brokenly. She walks into their bedroom as if facing the gallows.

A few hours later, in the dark, Monsieur finds her lying on the still made-up bed, her eyes dry and closed. In his cot, their child breathes softly, like a satisfied little bear. Before she can say or do anything, his long body spoons against hers, overlaps, holds her tight, taking away any thought of resistance. She is overwhelmed by unexpected tenderness, and tears spring to her eyes.

'I love you so much,' Monsieur sobs, into the hollow of her neck. 'Believe me, darling, I love you so much. I could never hurt you.'

His words hurt Estelle so much more than the image of him thrusting between the legs of another woman. She is aware that he has unknowingly confessed everything, and she turns towards him (*dear God, this is what pain is about*) and holds him tight against her. 'Don't give our number to patients again. I thought I was going mad.'

'I swear I won't,' he answers.

The ghost of the other woman floats across their bedroom, and Monsieur whispers: 'Tell me how I can make you happy. I don't want to see you sad because of me.'

She closes her eyes tight, wraps her hard thighs around his back as he moves above her, dries her eyelashes against the soft material of his suit through which his scent lingers. 'I want to make love.'

It's the only solution the instinct for survival dares suggest, that she should open herself to this man, own him, body and soul. And Monsieur, who is quite incapable of watching or touching his young wife without wanting her badly, gets rock hard in her embrace. Maybe he wasn't yet the relentless explorer I know him to be, always inventing new perversions, reaching for more extreme limits; tonight, at any rate, all he wants is to give her pleasure. Between his fingers he feels the hard nipples, and reckons they're the only part of Estelle's body to retain some hint of anger. The rest of her is compliant, willing. The extra curves gained during her pregnancy are still beautifully present. Estelle is on offer, has lowered all her defences. He's never looked at her as a mother: for him she will always be the young girl who awoke his desire in the South of France. He still gets as hard for her as he did on their first nights together. Sometimes all it takes is for her to move slightly in her sleep and he wants her with a vengeance. This woman is magical. This love is magical.

'You're so beautiful,' he says to her, inhaling her smell. And Estelle groans, 'I want you inside me, darling.'

Monsieur is so hard he fears he might hurt her. He penetrates her slowly, amazed as ever at how tight she always feels. With other women, frantic arousal results in a form of passive openness, while Estelle contracts and convulses repeatedly. Monsieur takes comfort in their togetherness against all the odds. She bites his arm to stop herself howling and waking the baby, and her cunt sucks his cock like a leech. Estelle kicks beneath him. She whimpers, 'Fuck me,' and he has to hold her still with his hand firmly against her chest, touched to tears by his deep need of her, but he is already facing the abyss and Estelle is impaling herself on his cock, fucking herself, drawing his thrusts towards the cushioned pit of her stomach. As she does so, she shamelessly touches her clit, her fingers racing against the hard nub, making Monsieur feel even crazier (she is the one who taught him how women caress themselves and initiated his fascination with it; she never asked for his approval, just did it of her own accord). What man would be able to hold back more than a few seconds, trapped within her small warm box, the only landscape in his sights the hypnotic panorama of a woman's fingers teasing a tiny pink excrescence of flesh? Of course, he's studied anatomy and knows all the technical words for this area of the body, but as a man he remains fascinated by the clitoris. Estelle, on the other hand, is just wanking, a word few medical tomes list.

'Let me fuck you,' Monsieur then says, launching himself towards her depths, holding her thighs apart like the pages of an art book.

While Charles is lost in infant dreams, Estelle and Monsieur almost come at the same time, the surgeon's large, clever hands lost in his wife's mane, just their clenched toes emerging from the cocoon of the bed. Monsieur's powerful body is heavy on hers. As long as Estelle's nails are digging into his arse, he will not retreat from her. He will never retreat even though he has already filled her to the brim, even though her cries are muted now, dying on the waves of satisfaction.

'I love you,' Monsieur says.

'I love you,' she answers.

As Estelle slips into sleep, she once again remembers the love and fear she had witnessed earlier in her husband's eyes. These are things only she can trigger.

It's all so pathetic and beautiful, a scene involving Estelle and Monsieur.

Book II

'He took Marie by the hand and they danced an obscene java. Marie gave herself to the dance with all her soul, nauseated, head held back.'

Georges Bataille, The Dead Man

BOOK II

Today I have no idea where Monsieur is. It's three months since I've had any news from him, a few weeks since I ceased the drip-drip of our communications. Where are you? Sitting at the wheel of a car, leaning over that thick folder titled with a word that belongs to all men but only means you? Locked inside your office in an attempt to escape the unceasing stream of patients, leafing through the pages of our story? Do you hide in the toilets, late at night, away from Estelle and the children, as soon as their backs are turned? Or are you holding *Monsieur* casually, your fingers dripping with sun cream? Are my corners already turned down, pages covered with the sand your kids have thrown as they played with their beach ball? Have I somehow managed to infiltrate your family holiday?

Are you afraid? How much hate is there among all the possibly contradictory emotions I evoke (posthumously?) inside you?

Do you remember everything?

Even that particular day?

It was the first morning in June when the heat made itself felt. I was almost naked when I opened the front door of our house in Nogent to you and you fumbled with me, no preliminaries, on the kitchen table, among the sprinkling of breadcrumbs from breakfast. I had to beg you to come to my room in the basement. I ran down the stairs, as your hands searched for me.

'Switch the light on,' you commanded, noticing the skirts I had hung in front of the window in lieu of curtains. 'I want to see all of you.'

We undressed in silence, at each end of the bed,

panting loudly. I pretended I hadn't understood and, naked, jumped onto the bed. Hesitation in your eyes: you were torn between wanting to punish my insolence and the attraction of my arse. Then, in one bound, you took me in your arms, wrapping yourself around me. My face was in your neck and I could smell the musky sweat rising from the palms of your hands as they raced across my back. You pushed me down on my stomach, your hand hard against the back of my neck. I was still damp from the shower but even so I was uneasy with your perverse insistence on licking my arsehole before you moved on to my pussy. *What pleasure did it give you?*

Sensing my unease, or wanting to make it worse, you brusquely turned me over, your face approaching my gaping thighs, your hot breath already so much more powerful than a caress, and whispered: 'What is it you want, my love? Do you want me to eat your pussy or should I fuck you straight away?'

I cried: 'Take me!'

And you methodically penetrated me, behind, even though I was laid out on my back, your eyes fixed on my cunt, which gaped slightly with every thrust. I was moaning, swinging between pleasure and pain. I couldn't rid myself of a certain embarrassment, even as you loomed above me and filled my ears with a stream of seductive filth. I'm about to write it all down, but my ears still go red at the thought.

'Darling, you should always look into the eyes of men who are fucking you in the arse. Look at me now.'

I raised my eyes but I couldn't keep them on you: raw lust was written on your face. Then came the monologue.

I shudder with wetness every time I think of it. You tightened your grip on my wrists and whispered: 'Touch yourself. You have the right to do so. I understand, you know. With my cock deep inside your arse, it's quite normal you should want to wank.'

Truly, you were so convincing and my heavy hand sketched a caress, banishing my shame, as I wallowed in the obscenity of your words. Surprised by my boldness, I somehow managed to slip my fingers inside and felt the hardness of your cock sheathed inside my arse. A popular clip on YouPorn.com. We moved on quickly to a higher level.

It occurred to you to turn me around and position me on all fours, which is when I had a bad feeling: something was wrong. This wasn't the way I wanted things to be going. How could I explain it to you? (Just the thought of your smile somewhere in France sets my teeth on edge with feelings of shame and arousal.) It was like a smell. Maybe not a real smell. Maybe the seeds of doubt.

I was realizing that nothing good could come of our coupling, however long it lasted. I could already imagine the mortification, the scene endlessly repeating in my head months later, and the sight of you, unable to look at me as you did before. I wanted to get you out of there and, in some way, keep you in total ignorance of a possible diplomatic incident. Suck you, maybe. Anything to avoid you seeing me doing it.

Fortunately, it didn't come to that. Unaware of the drama hatching with every passing second, you came somewhat quickly, warning me with that dark voice of yours that I was about to be 'filled to the brim with cum'.

An assortment of witty responses came to my mind, but I kept praying silently.

It was after that that the doubt solidified. You rapidly withdrew from me, leaving me gaping, a vision I'd rather you hadn't seen. I spent almost fifteen minutes just staring at your cock, while you held me against you, knowing it was often the best position to get me to whisper to you the endearments I normally reserved for Andrea. But time, our time together, faded away and you had to have your shower.

'Why?' I asked, a touch hastily.

It was thirty-five degrees outside, and well over a hundred inside my arse. We were dripping with sweat and I had worn Shalimar, in a covert attempt to help your wife catch you out. But I needed you to say it. You smiled. 'I'm going to be at the clinic all day, as if you didn't know.'

So I followed you to the bathroom and sat on the edge of the tub, trying to dazzle you with my wit. Below my fringe, the machinery of surveillance and analysis women use on awkward occasions moved into a higher gear. It was just a total misunderstanding.

Back in the room, where our clothes were scattered across the floor, you gave me a lengthy look, smiling. 'I like you so much . . .'

And my anguish ended. If you liked me so much, you didn't know that I'd tried to fuck you up.

You kissed me one last time on the threshold. I watched you walk away and blow me a kiss as you sat behind the steering-wheel of your black car, the smile of a satisfied woman spreading across my lips. The scar of your nails dissected the skin of my thighs. I felt good. I ran for a pee, a cigarette hanging from my lips. And though I know you have read all of de Sade, the despicable scenes from Apollinaire's *Eleven Thousand Rods* and Mandiargues until you've memorized them by heart, and I am only twenty years old, I must warn you now: this is where the story becomes excruciating.

I was about to wipe myself clean when I realized I'd been right to worry. My head began to spin. I threw my fag into the toilet, ran with my knickers around my ankles to my room, already well aware, like in a horror movie, of what was waiting for me in the still warm bed.

'Two huge smears of shit,' I whispered to Babette over the phone, shuddering on the brink of manic (solitary) laughter.

Two huge smears of shit, which, as she noted an hour later, were the precise shape of fingers wiped across the sheet.

'I've come to the almost suicidal conclusion he must have touched his cock by mistake, seeing I must have covered it with . . .'

'Not at all!' Babette intervened, gazing at it. 'When he had you on all fours, he must have pulled out and held it in his hand before he entered you again. He needed to support himself against something for a second and wiped his fingers on the sheet. Mind you, he could have stuck his hand on your bum cheeks. It could have been so much worse.'

'Which might mean he didn't realize it was all over his

cock, and then his hand. I would have noticed if I'd been him. Definitely. Look at it. Those smears tell the whole story. He must have noticed.'

'Why don't you ask him?'

'I called him just before you arrived. Answer machine. Anyway, I'm not sure how I could raise the subject.'

'Just ask him if anything unusual happened this morning. He'll understand.'

'Of course he will. And he'll just say "*Yes, there was lots of shit.*"'

'At least you'll know.'

'But what do I say after that? What do we talk about?'

'He'll find something.'

'Sure he will. With his usual laughter, cunningly asking me *why I'm so embarrassed, these things happen when sluts get themselves fucked in the arse, eh, Ellie? Anyway, I enjoyed it, didn't I?* And he'll probably say it was all the more exciting.'

'No one could be that filthy.'

'The way that guy thinks, it was no accident. There's no place for accidents in Monsieur's sexual universe. Everything that happens is meant to happen because it's natural. I expect he believes I allowed myself to be fucked up the arse in full knowledge of the consequences, that it doesn't bother me. That I wanted it so bad I didn't pull back. But I'm telling you, Babette, there's no reason this should have happened to me.'

I couldn't bring myself to pull the cover over the sheet, unable to abandon the spectacle, even though the horror was fading. Babette sat on the bed, leaning over the smears to examine them forensically, looking for fingerprints or whatever. I slid down to the floor, my back against the wall.

'*Why* did this have to happen to me today and with that particular guy? I'd spent hours in the bathroom stuffing myself with litres of water – I should have been as clean as a newly minted coin. That slut Ines lets them all fuck her arse when she's bloated and nothing ever happens to her.'

'I know, but if Monsieur, from the depths of his dark soul, wasn't a bit drawn to shit, he wouldn't take the risk, would he? He wouldn't fuck your arse.'

'I don't think there's a connection. Of course guys know women have to shit, but they surely don't want it confirmed so obviously.'

'He's not your average man, Ellie.'

'I know.' I sighed.

I wasn't reassured.

It was still too early for me to begin to understand how you thought of women, how you love them. Your relentless hunger was not assuaged when sheer filth mysteriously encountered the sublime at some crossroads. Or when sodomy was the only way to unveil the link between a woman's purity and her carnal instinct. The point at which a woman's sanctity becomes twisted and corrupt, transforming her into the holy slut who invariably gives them a hard-on. Months later, I sometimes think of the two smears of shit that might have ended our story. If they caused you to stop calling me and sending me the intoxicating messages that set our days on fire. How could I know? You disappeared from the surface of the earth. And I was caught between two monstrous explosions: your unexplained absence and the incident that might have caused it. They must be connected. The thought of changing the sheets was grotesque, like getting rid of the evidence, and I slept in Alice's bed, my mind churning with unanswerable questions. The ridiculous idea that I disgusted you now was eating me alive. Everything I knew of men, everything I had ever read, all my recently constructed theories resisted this insidious thought, because, let's be clear about this, there was no reason for you to leave. Just the day before we'd been communicating like two lovers the whole world could not have pulled apart – or, at least, not so abruptly.

And somehow, all this time later, now that I have become an ex-mistress who is only required on rare occasions, after I've taken my revenge on your defection, I still blame myself a bit.

One thing stopped me rushing to the clinic with my frantic air of abandonment: the evening when Édouard, who had learned of my recent trauma, had fucked me, slowly, tenderly, exploring my arsehole, first with his fingers, then with his pulsing cock, screaming, *Oh fuck Ellie, oh Ellie oh your arse.* I came with a vengeance, leaking slime across the cream-coloured sheets, as his darling hands convulsively kneaded my tits.

'There's something so special about your arsehole, which other girls just don't have,' he whispered, as he fell asleep, having ejaculated over my tummy.

Before letting go of me, he always performed the same ritual: he twisted my hair around his forefinger, tickling my scalp and making me coo. But that night his right hand was nestling between my arse cheeks, unwilling to move away. When I woke up at five o'clock, his five fingers were deployed like a star across my pussy and my arse. I shook myself gently and Édouard laid a hand on my cheek, whispering, 'Stay like this.' It was the first time in ages that a man with whom I'd spent a whole night had insisted on being close to me for a full ten hours.

He was teaching the following day at nine in the morning.

'Just close the door when you leave,' he said, as he finished dressing.

I was lying across the still warm bed, fighting the impulse to sleep, resisting the idea of going home, leaving. I was about to get up when Édouard, dressed in brown, knelt at my feet and kissed my tummy. I stretched and turned over. And he, who had been so kind, suddenly spread my arse cheeks apart. I was too slack to react.

'Stop,' I mumbled. 'It's dirty.'

'What's dirty?' Édouard asked.

That was the first time I made love with a man's tongue.

JUNE

Dearest,

There's no way you'll make me believe that all's well with the world right now. I might not know much about men and life in general, but there's more than a hint of a problem.

If you think I'm totally naïve, you're wrong. It's now been two days since I've had any spontaneous message from you and I'm smelling a rat. So the mystery is what happened between you and me for you to be like this.

Don't tell me you're busy. You've always been busy and managed to find time to speak to me.

Tell me what it is or I won't be coming today.

I realize our relationship is far from normal. There's no need for one of us to be cowardly, as if we were an ordinary couple.

If you want to go ahead, let's do it.

If you don't want to, just let me know.

I did tell you I have no desire for pain, but now

it's beginning to affect me. And I don't like it at all.
Pain inside is so much worse than being spanked.
And that's as far as I'd ever go.
    Let me know.

There are so few things I could tell you about Monsieur.

I know he's forty-six, that his wife, a pretty blonde, is called Estelle. I don't remember his answer, but one day I did ask him how they had met. Some student party, I reckon, something banal and magical.

I know he has five sons: seventeen, fifteen, thirteen, ten and seven. Scandalous that they all look like him. They live in an apartment that I guess is rather plush in the centre of the Île Saint-Louis. An area I now visit sometimes; every step I take there is like an insight into the family life I know nothing about, drawing me inescapably towards it. Because I cannot ignore the fact that Monsieur is a father. Perhaps if he'd had a teenage daughter in the house, moping around in her underwear and smoking, he would have given more serious thought to the risk involved in touching up my bum.

Or maybe not.

I can discern no trace of morality in the vices he teaches me, although I know it's always in the background. The rooms we share on Tuesdays smell of tobacco, grass, cum, pussy and a total lack of guilt.

Monsieur wears Habit Rouge by Guerlain, but whenever he is naked, that is not his scent. His hands, for instance, have their own spicy fragrance. His neck is a blend of hair and the detergent Estelle uses to wash his shirts. And what about all the other smells I furtively learned about and never forgot?

Monsieur shaves daily, but I still find it hard to believe hair grows across his face, as his skin is so soft. In fact, that softness is often at the core of my repulsion: Monsieur's cheeks are as velvety as my father's.

Monsieur was a house surgeon and later a head of department at the Saint-Louis hospital when their wards had a somewhat poor reputation. No one knows what really happened, but I guess that's where he came to know the vast majority of his hundreds of women, unless he's boasting too much.

He stores every album by The Who on his iPod. One morning, as he was getting dressed, I heard him hum 'My Generation'. How to shed twenty years in a few seconds.

What sort of youth did he enjoy to have grey hair so early and acquire such an appetite for life? He seems to choose his age depending on what day it is, navigating between fifteen and thirty-two. Like a teenager, he is impetuous and easily bored, never in a rush to take important decisions. Even though he is married and the head of a family, even when he's in the clinic that's become his playground, Monsieur is like a cat on hot bricks, seething, all his soul seemingly screaming, *I want to live, LIVE*, and the pleasure he grants himself with me, the hours we steal from everyday life, make his eyes shine.

Monsieur has an eclectic taste in fashion. At the hotel and the clinic, I've only ever seen him wear a suit, determinedly elegant, devilishly seductive. But if I was with him for an evening, I'm sure I would discover another side to him: tight black jeans, crocodile-skin shoes, a matching belt and a leather jacket. When he described this outfit to me, I was nestling against him in a foetal position and bit my cheeks so I wouldn't offend him.

'No way can you fall in love with a guy who dresses like Johnny Hallyday!' Babette would later remark.

Monsieur often gets on my nerves: he's always so full of himself and the success he's made of his life. It doesn't anger me as much in him as it would in others, because there are so many things he can be proud of. I can forgive him for it, but other men's boasting just stupefies me. Every day, while I idle in bed or chat with my girlfriends, he's repairing noses, lips, malformations of which I had previously been ignorant. He's worked hard to sit at the high table of his profession. His status doesn't stem from mediocrity. But how can Monsieur, having been with me five times and mistakenly believing he knows all about me, think that cars, money and success matter to me? I prefer discretion.

Babette and Ines are much less tolerant than I am, lacking my patience, my intuition that Monsieur needs my approval. I've kept quiet a thousand times when I felt I should offer him my advice. I just raised my eyes with a half-smile, as he got things off his chest, seeing straight through him. On those occasions, I felt superior to him: this, I thought foolishly, was the ultimate barrier that would prevent me falling in love with him.

Only once did Monsieur make me laugh uncontrollably, but it cost me a lot.

One early morning, I was trapped beneath him when he decided on the spur of the moment to add a variation to our doggy-style posture. I could feel his heart beat against my skin as I held on to the bed posts, my face flat against the wall hangings. Monsieur gripped my hips, then my tits and, last, my hair, which he wrapped into a rough ponytail around his wrist. Then he slid his fingers into my mouth, stretching it wide. Like a horse's bridle. He'd acted so swiftly I had barely time to open my eyes before he was pulling me backwards. Somehow I left my body to observe the process. Dazed, I reckoned there was nothing wrong with being mounted like a horse; after all, I had allowed him to take me like a bitch. My mind rambled, my features disfigured by the jockey riding me, and the thought occurred to me that if the shady owners of the small fifteenth *arrondissement* hotel had installed a mirror on the wall facing me, Monsieur would have seen how crude the situation was: how would he feel fucking a girl whose face had turned into a Hallowe'en mask?

I wanted desperately to feel attractive and bit down hard on Monsieur's fingers, the clever fingers that had filled me with shame. It didn't make him angry, and later, or was it another day?, he repeated the scenario as he thrust slowly into me, every inch of his cock. Pinned down, like a butterfly, I was buzzing and struggling, my legs round his back. I couldn't escape. I fought tooth and nail, appalled by his lack of understanding, his desire to see me at my worst, but his hold on my neck tightened. My only way out was to bite his hand hard. For a few seconds, the mood in the room changed. Monsieur looked at his fingers, then at me, unsure what to do. I think it was the only time I witnessed a trace of hatred in him.

The following day, I rushed to Babette's, and I remember laughing as we cuddled up on the couch and I described what had happened to her in minute detail.

Monsieur had actually called me as Babette was giggling helplessly, and I had great difficulty in controlling myself. I had to bite my lip throughout the ten-minute conversation, feigning interest as he told me about his day. I relaxed only when he said something funny and I could laugh with him.

'When you grow tired of getting fucked badly by twenty-year-old idiots who can't distinguish between sex and penetration, you'll gravitate to men like Monsieur. They'll help you forget everything you know about sex and teach you all over again so that you'll never want to do anything else, every day of your life.'

That's me, talking to my girlfriends.

Because, I confess, sex in his arms is a playground in which nothing, absolutely nothing, is forbidden. I feel as if I'm tiptoeing naked through long grass beneath a perfect sky, and Monsieur is helping me reach new heights – like the girl on Fragonard's swing – it's like being drunk, the sense of release so deep that I can't find words to express it.

Sometimes when I opened the door to Monsieur I hardly had time to look at him before he had me in his arms, his hands disappearing under my dress. He is filled with passion for the crevice that lies below my belly . . .

Monsieur likes mangoes but has never shared one with me on our Tuesday mornings. He didn't want my orange juice either or my grass. In fact, I've never seen him eat or drink anything. I've watched him come, but never drink a glass of water (and I sucked his cock long before I had seen his face).

I don't even know Monsieur's handwriting. I'd like to be able to study it, even if only a note, like 'Approved', followed by his signature, which I guess is illegible, like all doctors' handwriting. But I'm sure something in it would tell me a little about him, something in the curvature of his letters.

Monsieur possibly made a pass at my mother, when they were all in Jersey. He talked about her, on that very first morning, as he caressed my breasts. 'I don't know how your mother is, these days, but when I first met her, she was a very beautiful woman. We talked a lot.'

('We talked a lot,' my mother told me, when I asked her as we drove. 'He was always asking me if I had read one erotic book or another. I was never interested, but he was OK. Always on about sex, but pleasant.')

'I could feel a current passing between us. We got on well. We laughed a lot.'

('He could be unbearable. Pretentious. We laughed a lot, but he wasn't really my type.')

'Your mother had just left your father, I think. She was a bit down. But a good-looking Israeli surgeon was staying at our hotel.'

('Yaacov!')

'Your mother liked him a lot. Made her feel better about herself.'

('He was so good-looking!' My mother was enraptured, full of memories. 'You can't imagine how beautiful he was.')

'You could ask her, but I think they really had a

connection. I don't know if anything happened between them, though.'

('Wouldn't you like to know, eh?' my mother said, sounding all mysterious, but her silence spoke for itself. Monsieur had told me of the tension between Yaacov and her. Just to muddy the waters, she continued: 'Oh, he was so sexy! We spent all our time together.')

'Your uncle, who's protective of his little sister, didn't notice a damn thing. We'd kid him that Yaacov had spent the night with some bird when we knew the last person he had been seen with the previous evening was your mother. It was hilarious.'

('Were you already divorced then?'

'No,' my mother replied. 'You were ten, and we divorced when you were twelve.')

Monsieur was turning my life into a game of Cluedo.

'I've never touched your mother,' he admitted, following a lengthy silence.

I wondered if that was true. At the time how could he have known he would one day sleep with the daughter?

'But she certainly was beautiful. I don't know why I held back.'

That's what we were all wondering.

'But you look a lot like her. Your smile. Except you're much prettier. You also take after your father, some features in your face I don't recognize.'

Monsieur has a best friend, a woman, and he told her about us long before he and I had met. She is suspicious of me, warning him to be particularly wary of a young girl who reads the same books as him and cunningly parrots their words, turning his madness into lust. Monsieur's friend is unaware of the reality of our relationship: when a man is forty-six, he finds it too easy to escape from furtive shadows such as mine.

Monsieur has a deep fear of dying, which makes him the most alive person I know. Again and again I hear the words he said on our first morning as he held me tightly against him. 'You know, there is a period of grace, between the ages of fifteen and thirty, when the whole world revolves around you. Everything men do is motivated by you. All they want is to please you and take advantage of the light you spread around you.'

'And then?'

'When you're forty, you see men gazing at schoolgirls as they walk past you.'

End of story.

Monsieur doesn't appear to understand the urgency that dictates my life. Although I'm less than half his age, I'm already condemned: I have a sell-by date. I've never worked out what made him say those things. I didn't want to think about it. I sighed. 'So, who'll want to fuck me when I'm forty?'

'I will,' he replied, kissing my shoulder. 'I'll always be here for you. You'll always be my little girl.'

There's something childish about Monsieur's *'always'*.

Monsieur is not over-fond of lesbians, unlike so many other men. They don't have cocks, he says. But I know that once, when I was waiting for him on a Sunday in our ninth *arrondissement* hotel, Babette had kept me company, spending the night with me, and he had wanted to find us tucked up together early in the morning.

Monsieur is an unyielding worshipper of girls' arses. I've always respected and been scared by this perverse form of love. With him, it's an obsession that acts as a counterpart to his passion for pussy. Monsieur can spend all day long visualizing my pussy, and often does, he says. His texts confirm it, in minute detail.

That's another of Monsieur's peculiarities: he loves to use my own weapons against me and to make me feel uncomfortable by using words I don't like. Monsieur knows I have to go to the Ladies when I'm at work to read his texts. Before we'd met, he would call me when I wasn't alone, forcing me to nod for minutes on end, a hostage to his words, unable to tell him this was not the right time without betraying myself.

'May I masturbate while I'm thinking of you?'

'If I said no, you'd go ahead anyway,' I said riskily, attempting to appear detached.

'True. And I have . . . I'd so much like to feel you against me and make love to you. For a long time. Lick you until you—'

'Could you call me back later?'

'Am I interrupting something?'

'Maybe.'

A cheeky laugh.

'I love the sound of your voice. The soft voice of an obedient little girl.'

'Really?'

'Why don't you call me as soon as you can? If I don't

answer, it'll just mean other people are around. I'll phone you back afterwards.'

'Fine. 'Bye.'

'Hold on, don't say anything. Just answer yes or no. Do you feel like making love with me right now?'

Usually, and as improbable as it might sound, it was at this point that the bus conductor, or whoever, would turn to me with understanding in his eyes. I cleared my throat.

'Yes, yes.'

Monsieur, as Ines puts it, loves to scare the shit out of shy virgin souls. Even when they aren't that virginal.

To say that Monsieur lacks any moral compass isn't quite right. His own sense of morality is mainly affected by pleasure. He is motivated by his inexhaustible libido, and his whole life is consumed by a socially perfect form of sexual energy, which turns everything into a feast of delight, passion, an intoxicating flight of fancy.

I reckon Monsieur is one of those rare people in whom each positive quality has a corresponding flaw, and vice versa. For instance, he is a great manipulator and is also brilliant. He twists me around his little finger, which irritates me but encourages me to to meditate and analyse. Monsieur is highly susceptible, but no other man I know displays such charisma. Granted, he is a bastard, but he's also a bottom-less pit of culture. Monsieur is pretentious, but passionate too. He is deeply sensitive, but keeps his feelings to himself. All you know of Monsieur is what he allows you to see.

* * *

Often I can't see anything beautiful or noble about Monsieur. Even his profession may be, for him, a means to an end – status. I basically hate him because of his arrogance and selfishness. I've even confessed to Babette a couple of times that I've never come across anyone as wicked as he is. In him, there is an undercurrent of sadism and the eighteenth-century libertine. Monsieur can be impatient, but never allows impulse to thwart his strategies. His artful trickery stems from his knowledge of women. When Monsieur acts unpredictably, it's just that he's decided to take a new path. His every silence is a killer: I'm always afraid he's been caught out by his wife or that he feels he's in danger. Now I know that if he doesn't answer me, it's just that he doesn't feel like doing so. That he's bored. He has no need to be polite because he doesn't owe a kid like me any explanation. Sometimes I come to the conclusion that Monsieur is evil at heart: he loves only himself and can feign some form of passion for others.

You learn about Monsieur in the way you assemble a giant jigsaw puzzle, meticulously putting it together a piece at a time. It's the only evidence I am left with, after I've spent weeks collecting all the facts I know about him. Whatever I have learned about him is intangible. All I know of Monsieur is a handful of words and smiles, absences and reappearances. Monsieur will not allow himself to be analysed, studied.

This is the man I am writing a book about.

* * *

Eight days since I've heard from him, and I am calling Monsieur at his clinic. I'm hopping up and down while the message at the other end of the line instructs me to dial one for the nurses, two for the nurses. There is no number for Monsieur.

The thought of having to confront the secretary is agonizing. I have no idea who I should pretend to be or how to ask for Dr S with the voice of a girl who's never held her whole body close to his. The need for some form of clumsy justification, to have to invent a set of X-rays I need to talk about, all the time knowing the worst I've ever suffered is a sprained ankle. I am a terrible actress.

'Who's calling?'

Miss Becker. It doesn't even sound like a real patient's name, more like the name a pretend patient would use when trying discreetly to get in touch with her surgeon lover. A name straight out of a *novel*, which is why I chose it. But right then I have no way of knowing how wrong it sounds, busy as I am with my tales of secretaries and X-rays.

'Please stay on the line,' she says, and I hear Monsieur's voice.

No way I can describe his 'hello', but that meaningless word journeys into my ears and through my body, awakening every hidden part of me with Pavlovian insistence.

'Monsieur S,' I mumble, instantly affected by the voice I know so well. 'It's Miss Becker.'

And then Monsieur, whom I hate and whose face I would slap wildly if he were with me, magically brings me to life, blowing on the ashes of my phoenix, his velvet tones, tender and amused, simply saying, 'Good morning, Miss Becker.'

Enchantment. Not that it helps me forget all the nights I was unable to sleep, the time I was on the verge of a nervous breakdown staring at my phone, but all the pain and anger fade away beneath a cloud blanket that mutes their strength. Because I can visualize him perfectly, sitting behind his desk at the clinic, one hand in his pocket and a wry smile on his lips. From the sound of his voice, I know he is not angry.

'Are you still alive?' I ask, clumsily attempting irony. The knowledge that he is somewhere in Paris is as euphoric as an injection of morphine straight into my vein.

'Absolutely,' he says pleasantly.

My words get tangled as I struggle for breath, but after a few seconds the line breaks up. I hold on to him as hard as I can, desperate at the thought of losing him so quickly, but it's all in vain. Monsieur, prompted by his fear of being compromised, has silently hung up.

'You're a fool, Ellie,' I whisper to myself in the mirror, staring at the unhealthy redness spreading across my cheeks.

This is what has become of me: I'm frustrated but transported by a brief moment of communication and the euphoria induced by hearing Monsieur's voice. How low have I fallen? If there was an expensive hotline on which I could listen to his voice again and again, I'd subscribe to it.

By the sink, my mobile vibrates, but I'm stunned by

the turn of events and knowing that Monsieur has sent me a text would be too much for me just now. However, the prospect of talking to him tonight is enough to curb the hysterical impulses he triggers inside me. I've been like this for ten days now, on tenterhooks every time Monsieur calls or texts. Not that anyone has noticed. Since I've known him, I'm only truly alive for two hours a week, and right now not even a second. I spend the rest of my hateful life watching my phone, collapsing into indifference when it rings and it's not him. I sleep. I try to think of other bodies, but there are none that interest me. I find this form of slavery intolerable. I can't remember what it was like not to know him, even though I'd spent twenty years oblivious of his existence.

A few minutes later, as I'm about to step into the bath, Andrea texts, asking me to come to his place in an hour. I remember the days when I'd jump for joy every time he called. Had I not been *in love* with this guy? And when did it fade away? Why don't I want to see him tonight?

Because Monsieur says he will call. I know what time he leaves work, and he'll ring when I'm at Andrea's. Maybe even as we're making love.

Wash hair, dig out a decent outfit. I can't be bothered with any of it if I'm seeing Andrea. I have the impression that going out or sleeping with me has become a polite routine for him. Later, I thought that if I were to caress myself in his bed, it would be when he was asleep. Andrea fucks rather well but, these days, he's too polite for me, just annoys me: it distracts me from my lethargy, but is too finicky to transport me to worlds of erotic amnesia. It's not powerful enough, at any rate, to overcome the looming shadow of my mobile phone on the bedside table. And, worse, Andrea suspects nothing. At no time over the past three weeks has he noticed my descent into lifelessness. On occasion, playing with him, I would mention Monsieur at the risk of betraying myself, and would have done so had Andrea been possessive. Out of the blue, I mentioned to him that a colleague of my uncle's had suggested taking me to Geneva for a seminar.

'So, are you going?' was all he asked.

'Of course not,' I answered, annoyed that I could be sitting naked on his knees and unable to generate any jealousy. 'You don't think he'd want to try it on, once we're in Switzerland?' I added.

'Of course he would,' he answered, and that was it.

Maybe, at the end of the day, Andrea doesn't want to know what's going on.

A radiant purple summer evening. I'm scampering down the corridors of the Métro, carrying my wantonness like a cross. Over the last two weeks, my seraglio has burgeoned and I stink of sex. Mentally, I'm miles away. I'm fucking frantically. Andrea, Zylberstein, Thomas Pariente and Landauer don't seem to have enough hands or cocks to appease me. It's Monsieur I'm deprived of. Everywhere I go I gorge myself with men, my eyes devouring them from beneath the curtain of my hair. The moment I find myself alone I miss men. I search everywhere for Monsieur and find him dispersed among my lovers, in Zylberstein's smart conversation and Thomas's eloquence, in Jerome Landauer's dark voice, in François's oval features. Facing every one of my 'friends', as he likes to call them, I have a good reason to give myself to them.

Except Édouard.

Édouard is thirty-six. My friend Mélie first told me about him when we were having a coffee on the terrace of a café near place de la Bastille. It was summer and the sun was making a welcome appearance, but Monsieur wasn't around. I was complaining about it. 'Now that I'm no longer seeing him,' I was more or less saying, 'I want a guy with the same curiosity and lack of inhibition but I can't find one.'

Mélie then told me about a university lecturer she'd slept with recently. One evening, as they were sipping glasses of wine on his couch, she had remembered she'd got her period, and decided that Édouard, like most men, would be turned off. She'd come clean.

'No problem,' he'd replied, with a smile.

'Really?'

'Is it a problem for you?'

'Not at all. Well, it's just that I feel a bit silly. I'm something of a poisoned chalice.'

'You must be joking!' Édouard had said, almost leaping out of his armchair. 'It's only blood. And it's the time of the month when girls are really hot.'

He'd drifted away to change the music on the hi-fi. When he came back to her, Mélie was still a bit shocked by what he'd said. They had kissed.

'But it was true – I did want it badly,' she told me.

In the middle of a passionate embrace, Mélie was down to her pants – her big old period pair – when she had sighed into Édouard's ear: 'I've got to go and take

EMMA BECKER

my tampon out.' She'd felt terribly self-conscious at the prospect of crawling to the bathroom, doing the deed and washing her hands, then having to apologize for sabotaging the evening. What a passion-killer.

But long-haired Édouard had whispered, 'Stay here,' and, without even interrupting their kissing, had pulled the tampon out and casually set it on an old copy of *Le Monde*.

'Are you kidding?' I said. I didn't believe her.

'I swear on whatever I hold dearest,' Mélie answered. 'I've been going out with the guy for five years, and I'm always the one who ends up red in the face. No way I could have invented it, Ellie.'

'I *must* meet him,' I said, slapping my hand onto the table.

It wasn't really a question of tampons. I was already dividing men into categories, from complete idiots upwards, and a whole universe of possibilities was opening ahead of me in which men could love women enough not to make them feel dirty.

A few hours later, I had a text from Édouard. Mélie had described me to him in such glowing terms that he was suggesting we meet up the following evening.

Stupidly, I had second thoughts: he wanted to see me for a glass of wine in place du Panthéon, but I was so tired I couldn't face small-talk, let alone sustain it. All I wanted was to fuck, endlessly. But you can't tell a total stranger you just want to go to his place. So I turned him down and didn't meet him until another mutual friend organized a dinner party. That was how we met. I never like to describe a man physically: it always sounds so banal. I could say he has brown hair, wide dark eyes, attractive white teeth and a body toned by all the tennis he plays, but that wouldn't tell you much. Édouard is good-looking. For an hour we discussed the art of the novel, which he felt was dying. I fought tooth and claw for Maupassant, and he countered me with Kundera. We ended up at his place four days later. Smiling wildly, I told him what had compelled me to meet him and he burst out laughing, which made me feel totally at ease in his Vincennes flat, with its phantom-like cat and empty wine bottles scattered around. Édouard is, I think, the first man, Andrea apart, in whose place I didn't mind spending the night: I didn't have to count the hours before I was free again. That night, I slept like a log, sated.

Édouard's in a category of his own, just like Monsieur or Andrea, even if he can't understand why.

'It's not really a category,' I was explaining to him one evening, after we'd smoked and drunk too much. 'I don't classify men like objects, or according to their function, perish the thought! It's like a network. On one side, there's Monsieur, OK? Then Andrea, who's my boyfriend. Then you have François and Timothée, who fit together. Then—'

'Wait.' He stopped me. 'I don't understand. Why do they fit together?'

'They're best friends. I met them at the same function – actually, the same evening I met Andrea. Then there's Thomas Pariente and Olivier Destelles – they fit together because they're filthy rich. And then there's Zylberstein, Jerome Landauer, Octave and Paul. They're all medics and friends.'

'So, how many doctors?'

'Five, if you include Monsieur. But it's not as if I *seek out* doctors. Once you get involved, it's a circle that keeps pulling you in.'

'And then?'

'There's you. I can't fit you into any specific category, although you're also part of a network, like Zylberstein. You're different.'

'Different *how*?'

I could have told him the truth: you're different because, for one reason or another, *you mean more to me than all the other guys. Is it because your attentions are so old-fashioned and you really seem interested in what I have to say?* But I was scared that if I told the truth I might appear clumsy and frighten him away.

'You're different because you're such a great fuck,' I said, with great difficulty.

Flattered, he laughed and, encouraged, I added: 'And it's also because I like you more than the others. You're nicer.'

Actually, Édouard is the best, on a variety of fronts. When I describe it like this, and my friends find out we see each other twice a week, someone invariably asks why we don't *go out* together. It's a question I always shrug off, as if the answer was self-evident, not that I know the answer. Because he's sixteen years older than I am. Because it would complicate the perfect relationship we already enjoy (why am I using such a fucking cliché?). Because he's not in love with me and I'm obsessed with and owned by Monsieur. In front of Andrea, I can pretend, construct all sorts of heartbreaking endearments, but

Édouard doesn't deserve to be on the receiving end of lies. He deserves the only thing I can freely give: simple but all-encompassing pleasure.

On rue Gracieuse, I walk along slowly, hoping Monsieur might have the grace to call me in the next couple of minutes. Even with my iPod plugged into my ears, it's all I can think about. I've been holding my mobile in my sweaty hand ever since I set out.

I swear silently in front of Andrea's building – Come on, you've got another thirty seconds . . . I'm already half an hour late, which would have made anyone else suspicious, but I know he won't have a clue, won't see anything beneath the mask I'm wearing. At moments like this I hate myself for not having the guts to leave him: he's not bothered about me, and I don't give a damn about him, but still we remain together. Maybe it's in the eye of the beholder: it's rather pleasing, isn't it, a cute young Ashkenazy Jew wearing glasses alongside a pink and blonde *shiksa*? All very *Portnoy's Complaint*. It's probably convenient, been that way for more than five months now, so why should I rock the boat? Andrea and I are running a lazy race: it's too tiring even to think of falling in love. Too easy, as far as I'm concerned. With Monsieur, it's all about pain, which makes the game all the more addictive. I can feel him infiltrate every pore of my skin as my body vainly tries to resist. I think I've always enjoyed pain, long before I came to love the men who inflicted it.

20.30
No one would believe me, but I hate to see Andrea like

this because of my lies. I'm no longer worried that I'm always play-acting. I'm accustomed to fucking a lot and with a whole gallery of men, and I don't mind admitting it. I've reached the depths of corruption, seeking in their arms sensations and intellectual stimulation that would once have disgusted me. But what I hate most is the ease with which I can lie. I lie all the time, about everything.

'You OK?' Andrea asks, opening the door to his small, well-lit apartment.

'I'm fine,' I answer, and my warm, cheeky smile is yet another lie.

I've become totally apathetic. Although it might seem that I'm keen to go to the restaurant, I'd be happier to stay here, sitting in an armchair, staring at my mobile. I flash Andrea to show him I'm not wearing pants and, well brought-up as he is, he pretends to be interested. The telephone rings just as he's pinching my bum. While he's on the line to a workmate, I look out of the window. His street is like a theatre set, a scene straight out of *commedia dell'arte*. Twitching, I watch the people on their way to meet friends for the evening. Everywhere there is laughter, the click-click of high heels on the uneven pavement, and I'd give so much to be elsewhere, far from this wide-open window. Fuck, I can't breathe. All I can hear of Andrea is his exuberant voice, and it's getting on my nerves. His laugh annoys me intensely. His once endearing habit of walking up and down the room and scratching his scalp while he talks on the phone is infuriating. I miss Monsieur physically. He's like a drug; from the moment he reappears in my life, however briefly, all my days in rehab are swept away and I'm quivering again. There are times when my heart is beating so fast that I feel almost faint, my head spinning and a voice inside it whispering, I need Monsieur. *I need him.*

'I'll only be a couple of minutes,' Andrea tells me quietly. 'Keep your coat on.'

Then I feel a dull vibration in my handbag – it sounds like the trumpets of Judgement Day. I freeze like a rabbit in headlights, seizing my mobile, noting the divine 'unknown caller' as it flashes on and off. Monsieur's sensuality forcefully invades the formal chill of modern technology. The words dance in front of my eyes, teasing me. *Pick up, Ellie. Take me. I know you're dying to find out who's calling you. Who usually calls you at a quarter to nine in the evening, if not the man who stops you sleeping at night simply because he happens to exist?*

I pick up. Damn everything else. At the other end of the line, that voice drills through me to my ovaries, tearing me apart. The impact is so powerful that my legs turn to jelly. 'There's hardly any signal. I'll have to go downstairs.'

'Wait for me outside,' he replies, readily accepting my lie. 'I'll finish my own call and be along soon.'

The mobile phone I'm holding is all that matters.

'Who were you talking to?' Monsieur asks.

'Andrea.'

'You're at his place?'

'I've gone outside for some privacy.' Which means I'm pacing up and down the street like a prostitute, wobbling on my uncomfortable heels, unaware of the pain they're causing. I feel nothing. I feel only Monsieur.

I must be strong. I should sound detached. He must

never learn how I've felt while he's been out of touch. I mustn't forget that the only reason he's speaking to me is because of my call to the clinic, which gave him the willies. It's a long time since I kept him waiting and, having called me four times without an answer, he had to send me texts, like a soft hand grazing my neck: 'Ellie . . .'

But that's no longer who I am. All that remains inside this small, carefully made-up and dressed body is consumed by the need to know why I appear to have done wrong, what I said or did to distance Monsieur from me and our anonymous hotel rooms.

'How are you?' he asks.

'Fine. You?'

'So-so. I'm depressed,' he says. The line is terrible, full of crackling. 'I'm feeling old.'

'Come on, you're not old!' I say, with surprising energy.

I know what he's planning to tell me. Just a week ago it was in one of his texts: 'Your twenty-year-old eyes and body are making me feel old.' That was when I understood how terrible the effects of youth can be, and the fact that there was so little I could do about it. How could I avoid childishly expressing my joy when Monsieur joined me on Tuesday mornings, even knowing that for him it was somehow a defect? I could have been slimmer, blonder, prettier, whatever, but I couldn't be older.

'You *must* believe me. You're not old.'

'Nothing I can do about it. You know how it is – I have days like this.'

'What about me in all of this? What happens to me?'

'I know, sweetie.'

'Sweetie': the word he used instead of 'darling' when he thought I was playing cute.

'I have no appetite for anything, right now.'

'Not even me?'

Monsieur deploys the indulgent smile I knew so well. 'The moment I see you, I feel like making love. And, by the way, those photos of your arse make me so horny.'

I smile. Like some cheap tart I'd tried to seize his attention with them. 'Do you want us to stop seeing each other?'

'I never said that.'

'So what do we do?'

'I don't know.'

'So what *do* you know?'

A couple walking by hand in hand glance at me, hearing me cry softly. I feel so alone in the world that I'm speaking too loudly, not noticing that, a few metres away, behind the corner of the building, Andrea is waiting by his car. He waves at me and his signal is like fingers circling my neck. For a moment, it's as if he's finally realized something is wrong, after missing a thousand clues.

'You're not the only one in this relationship. I exist too. If you don't wish to see me again, I'd rather know than live like a drug addict always hoping for her fix,' I say, lowering my voice.

I walk towards Andrea, unable to hang up. I'm so nervous I go on talking as I sit next to him in the confined space of the Fiat 500. All I hope is that he can't hear Monsieur's seductive voice as he defends himself:

'That's not a nice thing to say. Likening yourself to a drug addict.'

'Not nice for whom?'

'For me. My life isn't a bed of roses right now.'

(What about me? Do you think I'm enjoying this? Sitting like an oyster when you're not around, always wide open, awaiting your messages and calls, hoping to seize them from the air? Do you believe I enjoy having to force myself not to think of you for days on end, foolishly hoping that my silence will overcome yours? I'm drowning within your shadow: I Google you and learn things about you I already knew, then realize what a fool I am and, fuck, why am I doing this? Lately, apart from eating and sleeping, I've accomplished nothing I can be proud of, nothing that brings me closer to you, and, right now, my boyfriend is taking me out for the evening. I'd happily exchange that for five minutes with you. I'm twenty and I'm ready to devour the world, but I can't because you're eating me up inside. Who do you think is having a hard time? The wealthy and esteemed surgeon surrounded by his loving family and his admiring friends, or me? Who the fuck is suffering most?)

'It ain't easy for me either.'

'I know, sweetie. But why do you say you feel like a drug addict?'

'You know why. You just want me to say it.'

Andrea watches me calmly, waiting like a proper boyfriend for his girlfriend to end her call. The serenity in his pretty black-brown eyes hurts and annoys me.

'It's easy for you,' I say. 'You have the best of both worlds.'

'Not at all. You're the one for whom everything is

easy. Tell me, how many men would give everything they own to be in my place?'

'I don't give a toss about them.'

'You have no ties, you're free. I have to pretend nothing's going on.'

Monsieur has always underestimated the way young hearts can react.

'You're wrong. It's hard for me too. I go mad not knowing what's happening, whether I can help you.'

'You can't. It's just me. It'll pass.'

'So, you're not about to forget me?'

'I'll never forget you.'

'Swear.'

'How could I ever forget you?'

Ecstatic, I close my eyes. A few minutes later, this unhealthy joy will disgust me, bring me to the brink of tears, but for now it feels great.

'What do you want to eat?' Andrea whispers.

I break free of my opium dream and shrug. '*Whatever you want.*'

'Is the book making progress?' Monsieur asks, but now that Andrea is bothering me about the choice of restaurant, I can't talk to him any longer.

'It's complicated right now,' I say, fervently hoping he'll understand what I'm on about.

'You can't talk?'

'Not really, no.'

Monsieur has a strangulated laugh, reminding me of a rather indecent conversation we had, with my parents a short distance away. It seems the rules haven't changed.

'Shall I call you back tomorrow, when you're alone?'

'Yeah, that'd be good,' I lie, having resolved to leave Andrea's place, like a thief, in the middle of the night.

'Kisses,' he says, and it's over.

This car has never been so suffocating. I'm sweating like a pig under my trenchcoat. Behind the curtain of my fringe, I glance at Andrea, attentive to his expression. *So, what are we doing, darling?*

'Want to go Japanese?'

'Let's,' I say.

Then, as a strange silence settles over us, the sort of silence that usually triggers an argument, I fall headlong into yet another lie: 'I told you, didn't I, that we're having a party for my sister's birthday?'

'No.'

'We were thinking of hiring a free jazz band. I was speaking to a mate who thinks he knows a really good one. He's going to call me back.'

'Now? That's who you were talking to?'

'Yeah. I hope it works out.'

'It's a good idea, free jazz,' he remarks, parking the car on rue Monsieur-le-Prince.

'I love it,' I say, and hand in hand we walk into the narrow restaurant where, for the next couple of hours, thirty or so people will be able to watch me go through the motions of tenderness and lie through my teeth.

Thinking of Monsieur makes me witty and sparkling, and Andrea is a perfect audience, laughing at everything I say, stroking my knees under the table. I am the perfect criminal.

* * *

The following morning, on the stroke of eight, I open my eyes as Andrea is making love to me, gently and clumsily like a boy who has just woken up. His hands excite me. The way he caresses my breasts excites me.

'That's so nice.' I sigh. 'I just wish they were bigger.'

'They're perfect,' he whispers into my hair, his warm breath smelling of coffee and toast, as his fingers graze my nipples. 'They look erect,' he adds, and I start fucking him, my arse in frantic motion.

'You drive me wild,' I pant, sitting on him and caressing myself with my hands as I've never quite dared before.

Inside me, Andrea is hard and unyielding. In the pale early-morning light I watch, with fascination, his cock move in and out of my still sleepy cunt. Before I began going out with him, the mere thought of seeing him naked kept me awake. And after I did, all I could dream of was Andrea Levinger's cock. Now I am torn between the waves of pleasure and the shadow of my mobile phone sitting under my discarded pants on the floor.

Does Monsieur have any idea I'm being fucked right now? Does he have any idea how different I am, outside and in? He should be here so I could stare at him while I mechanically thrust myself against Andrea, my eyes dead as my body catches fire. I am a monstrous contradiction. No one could guess how much of my perverse sensuality is all pretence.

'Now?' Andrea sighs, as his taut back straightens like a buttress, his nails digging hard enough into my arse cheeks to make me scream, and I hate myself.

I hate myself because the only thing I can think of right

now, as his cum streams down my legs, is speaking to Monsieur.

'We'll call each other, OK?' I whisper into his neck.

'You're leaving now? So early?'

'I forgot my keys. I have to get home before my mother leaves for work.'

If Babette knew that, she'd call me a slut.

A few minutes later, I'm running down the Métro corridors, mobile in hand.

What's it like, Monsieur, to be a drug addict? It's just like it was that first Tuesday morning. Frantically waiting for you locked into that room with the shutters hermetically sealed until nine thirty. Falling apart as I realize you've forgotten me, despite yesterday's promises. Watching the day pass and shivering for an hour when I know you're on your way home. Yet again, like a bar of soap, you slipped through my fingers.

ELLIE

Darling,

I hope you're feeling better. That you've overcome the blues. My problem, right now, is that I feel like a downright beggar for wanting news of you, and it's something I can't bear. It's not a question of pride but I hate it when you see me like this. I know I'm better than that. And what I hate most is that our story (if you can call it that) is suddenly growing ugly, even if I was never sufficiently stupid enough to believe I was on the threshold of some mad romance. I know who we are, how we live.

Which is why I don't understand. It would be wrong for you to take pity on me; I'd rather you hated me. I'm just surprised by the lack of understanding I have of the current situation. I'd come to the conclusion that you were manifestly unwell, partly my fault, and there is little I can do about it. I reckon you don't need my assistance either; it would be somewhat presumptuous to think I could help. But I can't bear the thought you might forget me, and I have to know how you

221

are, because I have known you and, for me, that sort of detail is so important right now.

I've thought about it over and over, but you know I'm not too good at interpreting male hints, and can't decipher your 'depression'. It might feel clear cut to you, but put yourself in my shoes and try to spell things out. It would be so much easier and come as a huge relief.

I was under the impression that everything was going smoothly between the two of us. We talked so much and the suddenness of this break in communication is just killing me. I realize you're not always available, for a variety of reasons, but this is evidently different. You don't talk at all now. And I can't help thinking it's not my fault.

I'm a simple person, you know, in many ways. When I met you, I knew I shouldn't invest too much in the whole thing, that our contact would sometimes be minimal. I was never stupid enough to believe I could change things, and never wanted to. I entered into this relationship with the firm intention of being honest with you, and forbidding myself ever to get hurt by it. Which is why I believe it's only fair that you should keep me in the loop, in simple terms, letting me know how your feelings evolve as we go along.

I also told myself that my letters possibly made you think I was growing too attached to you. I'm fond of you, I confess, but it's the only way I can manage things, in the midst of this relationship.

Despite the violent strength of the passion that binds us, I need emotion too.

When I think back to where we began, I tend to say to myself: 'OK, something must have happened for him not to be in touch. He was fine when we last talked.' The only thing I did wrong was to ignore your cowardice. All men are cowards. As cowardly as women are complicated. At any rate, I can't believe you've been lying to me all along, playing a game just to get me into bed. It makes no sense because I was the one who came to you.

I've also come to the conclusion that, being married, you didn't want a normal sort of relationship, just the occasional encounter. If that's the case, I understand totally. I can understand everything, as long as it's made crystal clear to me.

I'm not asking for much. I'm not begging you to come back to me. All I'm asking for is an explanation. At most ten minutes of your time. I just want to understand, have things settled once and for all. And if you think I'm planning to hunt you down in a dizzy attempt to get you back, you're mistaken. I may have crawled all over the floor a fair few times for men, but not to that extent, and I'm not about to start now. What I'm proposing, and have been from the start, is childishly simple. I've never asked for commitment. Or love. Or anything that either of us might see as a chain. You're a fascinating person and I fancy you, and if you want me, I have so much more to show you, say and do to you. I have fun with you. It's that simple. If you don't want me any more, I won't stick around.

A few hours ago, I sent you a text asking for a clear answer. As you've not responded, I'm asking you, please, to give me a call when you can. If you don't want to do it for me, do it for yourself, and tell me to stop texting you. I can imagine how annoying you might find it.

Darling . . . I just cannot believe you didn't enjoy our Tuesday mornings. And everything we did. But I might be wrong, I often am. Make a small effort. Surely a man like you must know how irritating it can be to wait for others to show signs of life.

And it hurts to know you're sad. If I told you I understand how you feel about getting old, you wouldn't believe me, but I truly do. I believe it's even more tragic for a woman, to see her beauty fade. But you're still young, in the prime of your life – look, you have a twenty-year-old girl hanging on your every word. Surely that counts for something.

I'm touched by your sadness. That's why I was saying: 'Just use me.' I'm a sponge, and I absorb everything you teach me, do to me, say to me. There are a lot of things we haven't talked about, but I know how to listen. And if you don't particularly wish to be heard, I know other ways to help you forget everything. It might not sound much, but the power to make you forget is mighty. You can use me because I'm strong. I know I am. Sometimes I can feel myself bending in the wind, but I never break. And I can take over your grief, if only you'll talk to me.

I'll keep it simple. I can give you delicious early-in-the-week moments in small rooms, with my body at your disposal.

Ellie

(Oh, I know it's not the right moment, but if you've got the blues, maybe a photo of my arse might function like a really tiny fix of heroin. I quite like the idea of lurking inside a syringe . . .)

PS And the book is making good progress! But how in hell can I end it, if I don't know where to put the final full stop.

MONSIEUR

Please, please, don't stop writing *Monsieur*.

ELLIE

Damn it, really, what am I supposed to write? *Monsieur passed through my life like a flash of lightning and, if I'm to believe you, I had the same effect on you? Monsieur fucked me so well, made me realize how much more there was to sex, but only by a fraction, because at the end of the day he left me with the panache of a thirteen-year-old, just stopped communicating with me. Monsieur dropped me like a sack of potatoes, never had the courage to tell me why.* What sort of story can I concoct, with such a pitiful ending?

I'm angry. The last time you had me on the telephone, I gave you plenty of opportunity to say, 'It's over,' there and then. I was ready to accept it. I don't understand why you're behaving like this. I did everything I could to make you happy, never asked for anything in exchange. All I wanted was honesty. You couldn't even call me and talk about it. You've trodden on everything I gave you.

There are better ways of feeling young than acting like a spoiled teenager. I could have given you all of it, renewal, passion. No strings. God, I just can't pinpoint the precise moment I lost you.

I thought maybe I was too kind, but that's not it. I'll never blame myself for this, or for falling in love.

So, the only thing I'm asking of you today is to call me tomorrow. And let's sort it out. Because I have no wish to think you're an arsehole, as the Monsieur I once knew was anything but. Be that Monsieur again, charming, elegant, full of flattery, witty, but don't be a coward.

Do it for me. Leave me with the memory of a worthy man. It's the least you can do if you expect a book from me.

Somehow things are so much worse at the shop. It was hard enough anyway to summon the energy to get up at seven thirty on Saturday mornings, and now I was on the verge of tears at the thought of the long, long day behind the counter, when all I wanted was the solitude of my basement room. I had no desire to speak to anyone. Every time I opened my mouth I was sort of hoping that whoever was facing me would evoke Monsieur. It's as if that man was lodged in my every pore, and always had been. In my mind, I conjured up acts of revenge, sophisticated schemes to make him pay for his silence. Or Monsieur returned to me, saying he didn't know why he had done it. Sometimes, while I was assembling yet another bouquet for yet another customer, floundering among the scattered flowers on the table, I would look up, my eyes scanning the emptiness, my hands mechanically completing the task, and for an infinitesimal moment I thought I could see his tall silhouette or hear his voice. My fingers were badly at risk every time I had to use the pruning shears.

Those were the dark days when Monsieur had stopped answering me, despite the clear signals I sent him. I was going against everything I had ever learned about men. If ever I interrupted my endless stream of communications, even for a couple of days, I was terrified that Monsieur might believe I no longer loved him. So I typed another text, hating myself more with every passing second, thinking I could fool him if I restricted myself to sex, but my words were incoherent with pain. And while I struggled hopelessly with the story the world continued to ignore, I had to face Andrea and my family. I explained to my mother that my bad mood was due to the students' strike, which went on and on. I found excuses not to visit my aunt, to avoid the memories of that birthday dinner and the fact that my uncle knew Monsieur, having worked with him for fifteen years. I couldn't even *look* at my uncle without thinking of Monsieur. I feigned concern when Andrea cancelled one of our dates, and joy when he rearranged it, dreamed up amusing texts to prevent him becoming suspicious. I thought only of my silent mobile phone on the bedside table when we made love. I concealed my broken heart from them all as if it was a contagious illness. Sometimes, in the car with my mother, I would feel a confession rising up my throat, making every single breath a stab of pain. I had to tell somebody how bad he was and that, despite my mistakes, I didn't deserve to suffer like this. I could see myself ditching everything, the beautiful Mandiargues edition in my room, telling my mother about the Wednesday when she'd thought I was playing poker at Timothée's while Monsieur touched me up at the clinic, all the times I'd scampered away from home with a bag of food and lingerie.

But I always summoned the strength to bury the confession because I knew how hurt she would be, and by the time my mother looked at me again, I had fabricated a neutral, or falsely cheerful, face. Those smiles literally splintered me in half. I would return to my small room where the sheets had remained untouched since Monsieur's visit, still displaying the traces of my catastrophe, to my silent mobile, my empty in-box. I lived in a museum dedicated to his glory. And time ticked on.

How I hated the lonely moments when I was overcome by the need to ask myself so many unanswerable questions. As if there was the slightest chance of getting to the truth, I kept blindly assembling clues that might help me understand why Monsieur had gone silent. I was tearing my hair out. I didn't know how to behave with him now, how to know if he had lied to me and, if so, to what purpose. While a part of me began to believe that he had fled to protect me, another part was hanging on to the hypothesis that he was just another arsehole who enjoyed exercising his declining powers on a defenceless girl. It was awful to think I might have fallen into such a clumsy trap – but the truth was childishly simple: Monsieur had had enough of me. And when he felt like that, he just went silent. Over and over I told Babette: 'I *should* have seen it coming. I *should* have known nothing could ever be so simple.'

And Babette, who had been aware of this from the very beginning, would never confirm in words what her sighs meant. What could she have said? The whole world could legitimately mock me. There was a boring logic to laughter.

I remember one morning when I was getting home after a too-long night with Andrea. Still sleepy, I was walking like an automaton along dirty underpasses, when I was sharply assaulted by a trace of Monsieur's fragrance. I had stood motionless for ten minutes, trying to determine where it was coming from, what man, what shadow. I was hurting. I was hurting so much. Smells can be so treacherous. A thousand souls will smell like your beloved. Unknowingly, they walk past you, brush against you, apologize and leave you rooted to the spot, blood draining from your face. Empty to the point of tears, invaded by a battalion of memories, his heartbeat and the softness of his skin.

One Saturday morning, everything went wrong. After weeks of uncertainty, I had concluded that I no longer played any part in his life. I had resigned myself to the fact that he wouldn't answer me again. How had we moved from one extreme to the other in just a few days? How could he ignore a person he had once called 'my love'? Why could he not explain it to me? All I wanted was to understand. And if Monsieur was determined to forget the whole story, why had he sent me, in response to my break-up monologue, this message: 'Please, please, don't stop writing *Monsieur*'?

Of course I had to continue. He was bound to encourage the writing of a book that was all about him. How gratifying to know that a young woman on the edge of despair was exercising her small writing talent in the service of a man she could no longer have.

It was when I received his message that I began to hate myself, to find my lack of dignity contemptible. If I was capable of writing for the love of it or had ambitions to be published, Monsieur had swept them aside, leaving me with only one goal: I had to finish the book so I could see him again. Full stop. The pages I was scribbling were just a pitiful form of bait, an outlet to praise and hate him. So, at the end of the day, there was no longer any difference between the novelist I'd thought I was and those others who found writing cathartic. Writing was a way for me to see Monsieur again; a man who was too much in love with himself to resist the lure of two or three hundred pages devoted to him.

On that particular Saturday morning, while I was humming along and trimming the red roses' stems (the only time I felt alive was when a thorn dug deep into my hand), one of my co-workers approached me, on her way to dropping some cash into the till. She whispered: 'Any news? Has he called you back?'

'Who? Andrea?'

She gave me a quick look and I understood that, alas, she was referring to Monsieur. Of course. It had been ages since a call from Andrea had been a thing of note. At the peak of my relationship with Monsieur, when I'd stood behind the counter at the weekend, frantic with the prospect of seeing him the following Tuesday morning, I had told her about the married forty-six-year-old surgeon, his passion for erotic books and our romance in an obscure Pigalle hotel. Naturally, when the situation had begun to upset me, she had also known. I no longer looked forward to Sunday with excitement. In fact, all I was looking forward to was for work to end so that I could barricade myself into my room, smoking joints with girlfriends or faking happiness in the arms of other men.

'The medic!' she confirmed, her voice hushed, as if the subject of Monsieur was labelled 'Confidential'.

I stared at my dirty hands. 'Nothing's happening,' I said sadly.

'You should drop him. You're better than his sort.'

She was the sort of person who mostly expressed herself in platitudes, but she was often right. 'You're better than his sort' was something she no doubt believed, and because she was not big on compassion or sympathy, I felt myself unwillingly overcome with warmth – unwillingly because if I'd heard those words from someone else, I would have been annoyed. For a brief moment I felt as if only she understood me: she knew my story and was Monsieur's age, thus familiar with men and their ways. Also, she was standing beside me. I just had to speak to someone or I'd explode. So, I opened up: 'Yesterday, he sent me a text and . . .'

I paused to catch my breath and looked into her eyes. She had stopped sorting the buttercup bundles and was listening intently to me.

'. . . I mean, it's been ten days since I'd heard from him, so I was fed up and sent him a message to tell him it was over, even if it was the last thing I really wanted to do. He must have thought I was testing him and that basically all I wanted was for him to change his mind and come back to me.'

In her eyes, I could see she had known from the outset that the whole thing was bound to end like this. That I was too young and vulnerable to hold on to a man like Monsieur.

'He still hasn't responded,' I continued, my voice now shaky. 'And yesterday night, around eleven, I had this text, just the one . . .'

Ellie, shit, you're not going to start crying over this guy! Please don't cry over him. She put a hand on my shoulder – not the sort of thing I appreciate when I'm on the edge of breaking down. I was finding it hard to swallow. I was holding onto the counter, white-knuckled, with all the strength I could muster, thinking that if I concentrated hard enough my chin would stop quivering.

'... just one message in over ten days to say please don't stop writing my book, because I happen to be writing one about him and—' My voice broke, as if something was blocking my throat, and my eyes filled, but I kept trying to speak, my whole body shaking, tears streaming. With all the energy of despair, and ignoring the little old lady who was bringing her cat litter towards my till, I cried, 'The only thing that could force him to answer me is this book I'm writing, singing his praises, right *bastard* he must be. What a fucking bastard!'

She nodded to me, indicating the arrival of our two co-workers to take over the till for the lunch break and I fell silent, sniffing, eyes lowered to my hands, still clutching the dark wood of the counter. They all asked me what the matter was, but I mumbled that I was all right, just tired. That wasn't entirely untrue: my nerves were on edge, even if I seemed to be sleeping all the time.

'Calm down,' she said, pulling her Marlboros from her handbag. 'Let's go outside for five minutes and have a fag.'

I wiped my nose on the moth-eaten sleeve of my pullover, and we went out to lean against a tree, smoking in silence, while in the shop they speculated aloud about what had made me cry.

(So, Babette, when I once told you I'd never allow a bastard like him to make me cry, I was wrong. That day I did cry, and sitting beneath my tree, smoke rising from my cigarette, I swore on everything I held dearest that I would never allow it to happen again. To this day, I have kept that promise.)

Shortly after, I had arranged to spend an evening with Valentine in her top-floor apartment in the fourth *arrondissement*. I'd just left the shop and was writing part of *Monsieur*, sitting in front of her building, waiting for her to get home. It had been so long now since the main character had shown any sign of life that the whole story was like a waking dream. At times, it felt like a painful wound, as memories flowed back. Valentine hooted to attract my attention.

'Get in, kiddo. I have to find somewhere to park.'

'Around here on a Gay Pride Saturday night, when the weather's good?'

'I know some places,' she said, and I sat down next to her, grumbling.

For Valentine, unpunctuality was a way of life, but she would never apologize. We lit our cigarettes and swapped stories while she manoeuvred her little Fiat through the narrow streets around the Île Saint-Louis, glimpsing parking spaces as faster drivers stole them. In rue François-Miron, the café terraces were full, the pavements flowing with slow-moving tourists. Valentine could accept the crowds with a very Parisian serenity, punctuating her speech with muted swear words whenever someone blocked her path.

'What about Monsieur?' she finally asked, as we sat waiting at a red light. 'Any news?'

'No change.' I sighed. 'As I told you, the last time I

heard from him was when he told me not to stop writing the book. As if I ever would.'

'What a bastard,' she said promptly.

'Total radio silence since then. Of course I think of him all the time. But he's so unpredictable. He might still make an appearance some day when he feels like getting down and dirty again.'

'Ah, Monsieur . . .'

From her detachment, I sensed that Valentine wasn't interested and was crushed – she was such a close friend. Before I'd met Monsieur and paid the price, it wouldn't have bothered me. But right now I wanted to talk about it – to a wall, if I had to.

'You're still writing?' she asked me.

'As you see,' I answered, jerking my chin at the black notepad I'd put down above the glove compartment.

'Cool.'

Is it because she was so radiant with happiness that she didn't want to listen to my anguish? Instead she brought the conversation back to her own life and loves, and I kept silent for a while, nodding at intervals, torn between the sadness I felt at finding we were almost strangers now and contemplation of this part of Paris, which she happened to share with Monsieur. I'd just realized that, and was frantically watching the façades of the buildings we passed, as if he might suddenly appear at a window.

'Fuck, this is hopeless,' she decided, sprinting away from the traffic lights. 'I'll just have to go to the car park and move it later tonight.'

'Good idea.' Anyone else would have settled for that ages ago.

The narrow ramp of a Vinci car park opened in front of us and I caught sight of its hoarding and felt what was left of my heart break into a thousand pieces: 'Vinci Pont-Marie Parking', in bold white letters. In my one-track mind I could read the subtitle: 'Darling, I'm about to enter the Pont-Marie car park – the signal might break up. I'll call you back.' Blissfully unaware, Valentine was whistling off-key, a song by Queen.

'This is where he parks,' I whispered, my voice a thin rasp.

'Oh? Shit.'

'Well said.'

It was nine in the evening, the time when Monsieur would likely be on his way home, or had maybe already arrived, and the car park was at risk of turning into 'Where's Wally?'. Nose squashed against the window, I allowed myself to be driven across every level of the underground car park, my heart jumping each time we passed a black four-door saloon similar to his. So many people slamming doors, locking their vehicles, and none of the anonymous silhouettes happened to be his. He must be around here right now. He *couldn't be* anywhere else.

With a rush of perspicacity Valentine, manoeuvring round an awkward corner, said: 'If he lives around here, maybe he has a reserved resident's space.'

At that moment we were gliding past the residents' bays. Fortunately, most were concealed from us by a high wall. For a few seconds, I scanned registration numbers, my heart pounding, then gave up with a deep sigh of resignation. Just the thought of an evening with Valentine made me want to open the car door and run away, like a thief, to go and nurse my pain in one of the gardens around Notre-Dame, where I could imagine Monsieur and his family enjoying a stroll. Alone, I might be able to bear the idea that he climbed those filthy stairs in the car park every day of the working week or took the lift when it wasn't out of order; that, like every inhabitant of the Île Saint-Louis, he paid his outrageous dues to the Vinci guys. While Valentine went on incessantly about her perfect boyfriend, I couldn't mourn in peace. She had a rare mischievous talent for breaking into my daydreams, whether it was with the revelation that her feet hurt or that it would be such a pain in the arse coming down at midnight to move her car from the expensive car park, or how Frédéric, the BF, gave her multiple orgasms. All I could manage was a series of grunts.

We emerged from the subterranean area. Outside, the quai des Célestins was bathed in orange light, which didn't offer me much relief. It was like a stage full of minor characters, waiting for the protagonist. And Valentine kept chatting away, stopping every hundred metres or so to dig in her handbag for fags, keys, mobile phone overflowing with messages. Couldn't she move any faster? Did she really have to show off her happiness and linger so long in this area?

'Oh, Fred's just called me!' she babbled, after a needless halt in the rue du Prévot. 'Do you mind if I call him back for a couple of minutes?'

'Fucking hell, Valentine,' I spat. 'We've been chatting for half an hour and you haven't even noticed how upset I am.'

Holding her mobile, she turned to face me, expectantly.

'I mean, for weeks now my life's been so full of shit. I just want to see Monsieur. I've lost at least four kilos, and you, who've known me for ten years, you haven't noticed anything. What the fuck are we doing now?'

Valentine didn't move. She just looked at me as I stared at her, my cheeks red, wondering what she would say or do now that she was no longer unable to ignore my pain, Monsieur or the way my jeans hung loosely around my waist.

'Shall we go and get drunk?' she suggested.

'I go to bed pickled every night and it's no help.'

'What do you expect from me? A solution?'

'Nothing – from you or anyone else. But I have no wish to spend the next three hours listening to you talk about how supremely happy and blessed you are while I happen to be totally miserable. I'd understand if you stayed away from me, but I've always believed – strongly believed – that friends should at least pretend to be interested when someone close is unhappy. I'm not expecting anything from you except maybe some compassion and the willingness to listen. I've always been there for you in the past when our roles were reversed.'

'Ellie, I do care.'

We were facing each other on the street, the crowds angrily parting around us.

'It's just so difficult for me to understand what you have with Monsieur. Tonight is only the second time

I've seen you since Alexandre dumped you and you're already in the midst of a new relationship. I've never seen you so unhappy because of a man. Of course I noticed, but what could I say?'

'I didn't ask you to say anything, Valentine.'

'I'm listening to you, but you're right. Basically I don't want to hear about it because it makes me so angry. What I've learned about the guy makes me want to spit in his face. Of course I saw how you were feeling in the car park, how much you wanted to come across his car, but let me tell you something. Monsieur should thank God we didn't see it. I'd have scratched "motherfucking cunt" into its bodywork with my keys. The only thing I want to know is what the hell got into you to get involved with a forty-six-year-old guy who's cheating on his wife and is exploiting your talent as a writer to make himself look amazing. Is he good-looking? I doubt you're capable of providing me with any answers.'

'So you've never been hurt by a worthless guy? I remember picking the phone up at four in the morning when Emmanuel was horrible to you.'

Valentine quivered with an impatience I'd never seen in her before, even when we'd argued worse. She slapped her thigh and sighed. 'Fuck it, Ellie! Take a close look at yourself! You're the first to say the guy isn't worth it and you still let him hurt you! And, no, I've never consciously fallen for someone worthless. It's the the sort of thing you find out about later. Like you have. You and I have always tolerated each other falling in love with the wrong guy, because on most occasions they had only good intentions. But this man is evil. He's deliberately hurting you because he finds it exciting. You know that and you're a sucker for punishment.'

'I'm sorry I just happen to be weak!' I protested, praying I wouldn't cry.

'But I know you're not weak, and that's the problem. You're young, pretty, clever. Lovely guys want to fuck you as well as, if not better than, that bastard Monsieur, without making you cry. As for writing a book about him – well, I'm speechless. Don't ask me to mollycoddle you when all you deserve is a kick up the backside. I won't listen to you wallow in it, like Babette or Juliette, because I'm quite capable of finding out his wife's phone number and providing her with all the dirty details. So, as I don't know how to extricate you from this whole bloody mess, I'm keeping quiet. Silly, I know, but it's better than acting like Ines and telling you Monsieur will be back. Of course he will – it's what his type does.'

(A contemptible tremor of delight spread through me from the base of my ponytail.)

'And it'll start all over again, and you'll be even more miserable . . . Ellie, what the hell do you expect? You'll have busted a gut for months on end, writing that book. He'll read it, he'll feel like the king of the castle, and what happens then? How have you turned into such a different person since Alexandre?'

'Oh, stop talking about Alexandre! He never loved or respected me for who I am, and never gave a damn about my writing!'

'The week after Alexandre left you, you were much less of a wreck than you are now. You weren't writing to satisfy the whim of a tyrant.'

'If I can only evoke pity in you, maybe it would be best if I went home.'

'I take pity on you because you're my friend and I want to help you.'

'I don't want to be helped, Valentine.'

'I know. It's Monsieur you want.'

I resorted to my usual technique, face raised skyward, to keep the tears from falling. 'I promise you I'm not in love with him. It's just that I'm obsessed with him and I don't understand why. All I can think of is being fucked by him, touching him, smelling him, and I know it's not love. Love isn't about feeling hurt all the time.'

'You're not cut out to be a sex slave. You can't want a man so strongly without your heart becoming involved. That's why I admire and love you – because you're always in love and it makes you so alive. The only funny thing about you and Monsieur is when you left your shit on him. Is there anything else about him that ever made you laugh? And, if my memory serves me right, he never made you come.'

'Never, but that's another problem. I've never found another man so interesting. And there's nothing more dangerous than intelligence. So, what am I to do?'

Valentine sighed theatrically. 'Right now, I haven't a clue. To begin with, I'd suggest that, in the absence of a lift, we climb all six flights of stairs up to my flat. In the opposite building, there's a guy who's ugly as sin. We could show him our tits – he's a perv, always standing at his window.'

As I stood there deep in thought, pierced by every arrow she'd fired at me, Valentine said: 'OK, I know it's not much of an inducement for you to climb six flights of stairs, but he's *pretty* hideous and *very* pervy. We could even take a photo of him and put it on Facebook. Remember how good I am at that.'

Valentine still smiled as she did when she was fourteen, and I remembered how that year she'd convinced some dirty old man to show her his cock on a webcam. She had sent me the entire conversation and the accompanying screen shots and I'd burst out laughing as I sat at my laptop. Alice thought I'd gone crazy.

'And you can tell me about all your other recent lovers. If I'm to believe Babette, there've been enough to fill a whole Métro compartment.'

I chuckled and, as if by magic, began walking towards Valentine, who was laughing her head off. It was almost painful forgetting Monsieur for a while, and intuition told me he would take his revenge for my having neglected him, but I put my hand into Valentine's and we walked down rue Charlemagne, fags hanging from our lips. I was reminded of years earlier when we'd walked home for lunch through the small alleys of Nogent-sur-Marne, confiding in each other about our breathless adventures with the senior boys, who were close to the adult world.

I mentioned this to Valentine as we reached the third floor of her Parisian Golgotha, and she made a remark that was to stay a long time in my mind: 'Basically, even if their hair has turned grey, the men we see are still babies. You and I, all the girls we know, all we've done is grow mature. The only thing about us that's changed is the size of our arseholes.'

'How vulgar!' a neighbour on a lower floor, hearing us, remarked.

My first hysterical laughter, hyena-like, for a thousand years at least. Oh, God!

JUNE

Separated from my girlfriends, who'd joined their parents in the Hamptons, I fell back on the family house in the Midi, with a gang of my sister's friends. The weather was so hot you could have dropped dead and no one would have noticed. The humidity was overwhelming. At half past three in the afternoon, the silence felt so heavy that even the song of the cicadas seemed muffled. A sizzling halo rose from the asphalt: one of those summer days in which life went on in a frying pan. I was in the swimming-pool, thinking of him, a little stoned after the few joints I'd smoked. Next to me, my sister and Lucy were spreading out a set of tarot cards. I went up to my room, a short journey that had erotic allure, and the quality of the light as it filtered through the old shutters, was identical to that of my childhood memories. A beige sort of light, soft and sensual. Very sensual in the way it floated all the way from the curtains and illuminated the whole room with a deceptive glow. It had been two months since Monsieur had shown any sign of life, and now he was all around me, because of the heat and the light . . . Monsieur and his hazy eyes.

* * *

Alice rushed through my dreams like a cannonball, giving me the crafty look that seldom requires the addition of words.

'Lucy's just laid out the cards.'

I snapped out of it, careful once again not to give the world a hint that I was still under the spell of an older man. My head was full of him but I had to keep up appearances. Outside, the tarot game was in full flow. I fled, like a thief, naked from the waist up. My mind was torn in every direction. What should I do with my phone in which his familiar first name had been replaced by 'Monsieur' in the Contacts list? I was still learning to act with dignity again, reclaiming my pride. Just enough to stop hating myself so much, enough to summon plenty of excuses each time I was on the verge of cracking up, or calling Monsieur and talking to him about the book and my bum. Monsieur adored my bum; surely that would never change. My excuse for today: how to provoke his erection.

Onlookers at their windows that day would have seen a half-naked girl shimmying shoeless across the hot asphalt, with her phone stuck to her ear. Monsieur, of course, wasn't answering. So I left him a long, long message.

I want to hear from you.

I want you to stop being afraid of me.

I want to talk to you about *Monsieur*, which is making progress.

I want to tell you about the swimming-pool. I'm in the South, at our house, with my sister. It's difficult to explain but the heat is so overwhelming that nature is becoming silent. It's the sort of heat you only get in the Midi. A short while ago I was swimming naked, completely stoned.

I was sluggish, numbed by the grass and the heat, so perfectly languorous. And I began to think, God only knows why, that we could have been together in that pool. Just you and me. I imagined you squashing me against the hard edge. And I was saying things like, 'Come on, let's go up to the room. I want to fuck.'

And you answered, 'Fine, but only if you allow me to stare at your cunt for as long as I like.'

I was in total agreement. We left the pool, slowly, to go to my room on the first floor, where the light is dim, just right. I'm sure you'd approve of the light.

You stared for a long time between my legs, but this time it made me happy. I didn't complain, or maybe just a little, the way you like me to. I know we were fucking. I can't really explain how we were doing it. Just imagine. Imagine the way I would hold on to your back.

That's all I wanted to say. It's odd, but I remember that when it was over I said I had no desire for anything else.

Call me back.

Or don't call me back, your choice.

I knew that leaving a voice message for Monsieur was not the best way to get a reaction out of him. I didn't believe it would make any sort of impression on him. I'd never understood how he dealt with his voicemail. It was as if my attempts to contact him were getting lost in a vortex, and as much as I pulled on the wisp of thread that connected us, Monsieur had, without telling me, cut it.

* * *

The following day I got back, drenched with sweat, from the centre of town to find a message waiting for me. I was about to open my mailbox, hoping against hope. It was bound to be a disappointment. Mum? My grandfather, worried about the gas cooker? Zylberstein, thinking of me during his nights on duty?

No. It was Monsieur. Monsieur who said (oh, the beauty of that voice): 'Hello. You wanted to talk to me about the book.' (A short, almost imperceptible hesitation.) 'And also the swimming-pool. Kisses.'

I put my phone down. My heart was thudding. I could no longer hear the cicadas, or the laughter of the people I loved around me. I could no longer understand anything. I think it was the first time I'd felt crushed because of him. I couldn't fathom why this time my silent scream had connected with him. Maybe it was because my message had been so much more to the point than the others. I had tried to appeal to his baser senses, not his mind, and it had worked. He had fallen for it, hook, line and sinker.

Punch-drunk, I climbed up to the terrace, where I could see the others playing volleyball. They were full of irrepressible laughter, but I knew not one of them was buzzing as I was, with the crazy joy of a girl who's been told she's still desirable enough to be fucked. Sitting alone at the table, my sister Flora was rolling herself a cigarette.

'A message from Monsieur,' I explained, my smile ecstatic.

'Really?' she cried, almost swallowing the filter tip she had been holding between her lips. 'What did he say?'

'Yesterday I rang him.'

I fell quiet. How could I explain to an eighteen-year-old virgin why I had called the man who had broken my heart to talk to him about the swimming-pool and my pussy without looking like a fool? Flora was used to my tales of adventure, but you needed to have fucked, to have wallowed in the vocabulary of love, to understand.

'I'll keep it short. I talked dirty to him and Monsieur is fuelled by sex.'

'You should take your time to reply,' she remarked, lighting up, knowing I would answer him sooner rather than later.

This was, after all, Monsieur, the man in the black notebook I was slowly filling with words.

'Of course I'll keep him waiting. It's what he deserves,' I said.

Two and a half hours later my resolve broke.

I rushed outside while the others were cooking and, with the sound of pots and pans in the background, I composed myself, modulating my voice in some semblance of sensuality.

'Hi! I wanted to talk about the book. And the swimming-pool. Call me back.'

A few minutes later I was hating myself again. And as if he had guessed I was far from assured, Monsieur didn't call me back. I spent the following days soothing myself with the fantasies he evoked in me. Under his tutelage, I began to imagine scenes I would never have enjoyed before meeting him. Deviant images assaulted me from every side. But Monsieur failed to appear in them. All he did was trigger my fertile imagination. Slowly his absence felt less cruel and visions of him deserted me. Zylberstein, Édouard, more readily available prey, began advantageously to replace him. My friends filled my days and nights. We clustered together on the terrace playing tarot and smoking countless cigarettes while listening to Michael Jackson. I would write page after page, stimulated by the loving atmosphere, as the house filled with sand, pine needles and long hair. I kept on with *Monsieur* and there was no longer any bitterness in trawling through the memories. I had become something of a doctor: I was studying a human being, dissecting every step of the affair. It was only when I read over what I had written, checking the narrative flow of a scene, that I thought of Monsieur. Strange: on one hand there was Monsieur, the man, and on the other, there was *Monsieur*, the novel.

I read sections of *Monsieur* to Flora, peaceful moments when we lay in the heat across the pink and white mattress. She would close her book and ask: 'Read me a chapter.'

She'd light a cigarette she'd rolled earlier and, awkwardly, I would read aloud my most recent pages, my voice lost among the chirping cicadas, the wind and the music of the Kinks. And Monsieur came alive. Sometimes, attracted by the peace that surrounded us,, Antoine would come and sit beside us, wrapping his arms around his knees; I didn't pause. Have I ever had a better audience? No one made any comment. Once I'd finished, I would close the notebook and the conversation would begin again where we'd left it earlier. Now, others knew about Monsieur, which I liked. He floated above us like a shadow, endowing our holiday with an extra dimension. I wasn't spending my time just sleeping or smoking or kicking my heels in the pool. I was writing. I was assembling a story about a man I had known intimately, but who seemed to the others like some fabulous beast, his existence confirmed by laconic messages. I allowed them to listen to my voicemail; his deep, insolent voice made them all blush.

Oh, how I loved them. In the evening, when our favourite TV programme was on, I made my way to the couch with my notebook and wrote like an automaton, hardly aware of the noise, the laughter, or the joints passing from hand to hand. And it was in the midst of this hubbub that I came up with my best sentences. When I read them again, the next morning, there was nothing I wanted to change. Every comma, every full stop, seemed magically to be in the right place. The pages were covered with chocolate stains and sap from the enormous pine tree that loomed above the terrace, but that only reminded me of something I would otherwise have forgotten and prompted the choice of a particular word. When I wrote alone at siesta time, I was pernickety, too concerned with minute detail, and lost my way.

Although everything that had happened was between me and him, Monsieur will never understand how much he owes to the people who were part of my life down there, the thousand occasions they threw the wet volleyball over my open pages, the thousand times they spilled tomato sauce on the line where I was about to describe a blow-job, a thousand times dripped sun cream on the cover. Without the imprint of their presence on the immaculate white pages spat out by my printer, it's so much less fun. My manuscripts looked like Henry Miller's in his Paris days. They had class.

Because Monsieur had disappeared again from the face of the earth, I fed on what was left at my disposal. Now that he was no longer making me his outlet and I was writing down every one of his caresses, every inch of my flesh stank of sex. I was eating enough for four and smoking like a chimney, hungry only for seduction.

There was Lucy.

The first time I saw her topless, sitting by the edge of the pool, it felt odd, and I knew it shouldn't. Until then, it had never occurred to me that she was as naked as I was beneath her clothes. It set me thinking.

Lucy . . . Lucy likes girls as much as I like boys. I'd seen her grow up, alongside my small sister, running around the garden in her DPAM pyjamas while I was being kissed with a mouthful of braces. I had only recently noticed she had become a woman. I was at her side, a glass of punch in one hand, a joint in the other, watching her move, my mind numbed by the smoke. Her wide black eyes were closed, her skin a delicate brown, her long dark hair flowing across her shoulders. You couldn't have said she was dancing, and she wasn't in a trance. She was lost in the sound of the guitar, locked inside a private world, her legs bending with each new chord. Unbearably sensual. Every young guy there was watching her: an inner fire had ignited in the kid they saw daily at the *lycée* but had never really noticed before. Their mate. How do you pinpoint the precise moment when girls become women and boys become men to the sound of a song by Pink Floyd?

From the moment Lucy had shed her little-girl cocoon, she'd become more than a friend to me, not quite a sister. There was too much confusion surrounding Lucy, contradictory and discordant, for me to categorize her. I spent a lot of time trying to work out why she was the only girl I wanted. I felt a strong need for Lucy, which struck me repeatedly. Every move she made lit the room with the sensuality of the best Pink Floyd songs. She displayed the same quiet charisma as Monsieur, but she was completely unaware of it. It came to her naturally, in all its simplicity. With Lucy, a mundane action, such as unwrapping a cake or setting a pile of plates on the kitchen counter, became a ballet. Even if I was seemingly absorbed in a game of tarot, she was on my mind. And I could feel her when she was near without having to look up.

I didn't desire her as I would a man, but when she was close by all I could think of was her hair, her eyes, her white teeth, and the way she moved with the swiftness of a little animal. Suddenly she would sit next to me, grab my cards and giggle as she showed my hand, shamelessly flirting with me. It infuriated my sister.

'Can't you be discreet, Ellie? You're crazy!' she complained, one night, in the tiny kitchen.

'I can't help it – it's just the way I am.'

'You should try to control yourself!' my sister cried, as

if it were that simple, as if I could ignore the way Lucy stared at me from beneath her heavy lashes, then stole one of my best cards.

That was it: everything for Lucy was a game of tarot. If I attempted a defensive move – she was no prettier than my other girlfriends – she would burst out laughing and produce her winning card. You couldn't have said for certain whether she was beautiful or not until she stood in the right light when all doubt disappeared.

So it came to pass that summer, while I squirmed like a sardine in Monsieur's net, that Lucy came to my rescue and welcomed me into her own. While we stayed in the Midi, I'd somehow kept the situation under control, but things changed when we moved to her country house. I was ashamed to catch myself staring at her for longer than I should.

I deflected the others' attention by pretending to be interested in Antoine, who responded as anyone of his age would. It was yet another thing that got on Alice's nerves: she thought I was trying to seduce all and sundry just to forget Monsieur. I never did seduce Lucy, but thoughts of her continued to assail me, even after I'd seen her cooing in the arms of her girlfriend.

I knew what she really thought behind the furtive glances and seemingly innocent teasing. Over the years, we had built a close friendship so I can't imagine it was only a game. Anyway, I was highly unlikely prey. I'll have to ask her, one day. What do you think, Lucy? I spend so much of my life in the arms of men that maybe I'm a challenge to you. Or is it something else? Something simpler. It's probably unimportant. It's in my nature to ask questions, but I've never asked myself why I liked you so much, despite the smallness of your breasts, your narrow, supple waist, the prominent bump inside your bikini bottoms. You're the only one with whom I could have shared orgasms to the sound of Jacques Brel or Pink Floyd, or established an almost telepathic form of communication, as happened during our stay in the countryside or in the Sologne.

'Maybe we could go for a drive, and later we can play ping-pong.'

Remember? It was two o'clock in the morning and I jumped out of my chair, staring at you as if you were a Fragonard portrait. 'How the hell did you know that was exactly what I was thinking?'

You smiled and we began to dance to '*Do You Love Me?*' by the Contours. Later, I was laughing too much to hit the ping-pong ball, but I could see you clearly. You were beginning to occupy an important place in my life.

One evening, I decided to read you an excerpt from a letter I was writing to Andrea, in which I talked about you at length. This marked the beginning of hostilities.

That evening, you dared me to make a pass at Flora – my sister! – and then at Clara – your girlfriend! – and I realized that, after all, you were far from perfect. Player or manipulator – but was that so bad? I fell asleep that night thinking of making love with you. The following morning, when I came across you, your ponytail askew and pillow lines still marking your cheeks, you smiled at me as if you had read my guilt.

Those days, in an attempt to overcome Monsieur's

absence, I was often on the phone to one of his colleagues, Maxime Zylberstein, thirty-five years old, gynaecologist by trade (and vocation). When I told him about you, he promptly pushed me into your arms. 'Of course,' you'd remark. 'What could be more attractive than two young lesbians together? He couldn't understand why I should hold back because you were my sister's best friend. Had you been a boy, I would long ago have made a move. But, Lucy, think for a moment: how could I have survived had you rejected me? And could I have touched you without appearing naïve or clumsy? I would have loved to invent new caresses for you, kisses that expressed my attraction to you so much better than words. Most men have never understood the fear most women feel in the presence of other women. As if two girls together was no more than a starting point and all their techniques are worthless without a cock involved. And even though I was aware of the techniques and gestures, I had accumulated so many images of the way you might make love that I was terrified of failure with you.

What did I imagine? Your small, precise fingers pretending to discover new erogenous zones – I'm sure you've had enough opportunities to survey every inch of the female body. I don't think of pleasure when I think of you, but of watching you, listening to the sounds you make, learning the taste of your mouth, the savour of your cunt, having the chance to make you as happy as I am when I'm around you.

Thank God, as soon I moved away from the countryside, I could breathe again. Monsieur took his rightful place in my mind and the radio silence continued. This was the life I led, balancing painfully between his absence and your constant chirping.

JULY

My sister, who is evidently unable to choose between her friendship with Lucy and her annoyance over my staring at her, has invited her to Normandy to our father's place. She caught the first available train with her backpack, into which she'd stuffed the essentials: a T-shirt, knickers and grass. Alice and I waited feverishly for her to arrive, as if it had become a matter of life or death. We were bored to death. I was plodding on with *Monsieur*, lacking energy and inspiration away from Lucy and the others. After lunch, we would take narrow paths into isolated parts of the woods where we could smoke with no one to see us. The rest of the day passed so slowly, as if everything was conspiring to make us hate Normandy. We didn't care that we always looked stoned or that our hair smelled of weed. Alice blamed our father for our boredom; she couldn't conceal the redness of her eyes or the reason behind her uncontrollable laughter. At least the garden was large enough for us all to share it without having to cross paths too often.

Lucy arrived on the fourth day. The only day without rain. Coincidence? Or not? That afternoon, we'd splashed and floundered in the miserable stream that ran alongside the walls of the house and cast its dank, muddy smell across the garden. Alice, busy rolling yet another joint, had asked us to go and look for boots in the under-stairs cupboard, and as Lucy was bending over I saw her little bum half revealed by her oversize jeans. It was amazing how masculine she could appear even though she trailed the smell of woman in her wake. Reaching her, I began chatting, and our shoulders touched, generating an electric shock in the small of my back. I was somewhat slow in switching on the light and she remarked: 'The perfect place for rape, no?'

'Perhaps,' I conceded, my heart beating wildly. I was alone with her in the one place in the house where no one, not even Alice, would think of looking for us. Her eyes shone brightly and the white lightning of her teeth pierced the darkness.

'Rape, eh?'

If God had made me just that bit sharper, I would have stopped fumbling for the light switch and the boots, and let her caress me secretly against the shelves and their network of cobwebs. Just imagine the depth of that moment of silence. My hands under her T-shirt, and her lips against mine. Her fingers. I was literally close to a heart-attack, with all sorts of excuses springing to mind: I was wearing an old-fashioned pair of knickers, I'd not showered that morning, I was all hairy. I spoiled the moment: 'So, who's raping whom?'

'I was only joking,' she answered, barely registering my disappointment.

After a few minutes' splashing around in the stream, which was no fun, we had other ideas. We threw the boots back into the under-stairs cupboard where hers landed on top of mine, haloed by a thin ray of sunlight rushing through the open door. A small detail that stayed in my mind: I knew I would write it down later in the notebook.

At nightfall, my father drove us back to Grandma's place. The darkest of nights. Do you remember, Lucy? As soon as we sat together in the back of the car, I felt your mud-spattered brown-skinned thigh graze mine, then come to rest close enough for me to feel your heat radiate in my direction. I moved my right knee, and for the whole journey your golden and my white skin touched, even when my father drove too fast over the humps that were meant to slow us down. I kept watch over Alice, who was arguing with Louise about some Michael Jackson song, and did not dare look you in the eyes. I was thinking of all the men I'd had recently, and how not one had made me shiver like this. It all seemed so clear. The way they triggered me was so much less powerful than this slow-fuse explosion.

Everything, well, almost everything, happened that night, in the small room you shared with Alice. The classic aching-back scenario. I straddled your hard little bum to give you a massage. Alice gave me a filthy look, but I ignored her. I enjoyed kneading your soft flesh and watching you clench your teeth but feign surprise and pleasure. In my mind, I could see myself spoiling it by taking your breasts in my hands. Bypassing them was almost unbearable: there was no hiding the way they swelled under your arms, squashed against the mattress, the fawn light of the bedside lamp playing hide and seek across your skin, *and why should I pretend I was blind?* OK, Ellie, calm down. She's a girl. That's what I was thinking. I don't know if you even noticed how hard I was struggling against the hunger I had for you, against the vision of your hard nipples between my fingers, but you probably did, because a few minutes later you volunteered to massage me. What should we have done?

Maybe what we did: nothing.

'Goodnight, you old bitches,' I mumbled, rising from the bed to go my room.

Alice chuckled, 'You too, old cunt,' but Lucy, her eyes illuminated by the light of the moon, seemed to take the insult too literally. Of course she was smiling. I owed my whole vocabulary to my lovers and everyone knows that you call a lesbian an old bitch as a form of endearment.

'So, how is Monsieur?' Lucy asks, as we sit smoking in a mosquito-infested alleyway.

Alice has just got up unexpectedly and gone to fetch something to rehydrate our parched throats. It's so hot that all the water in our bodies seems to evaporate in an instant, as if a pump were vacuuming it straight out of our mouths.

'Physically? Mentally?' I ask, looking at my knees, uneasy that I've generated so much curiosity among my friends. Since the summer began I've turned Monsieur into one of the main topics of conversation – I hate it .

'How would I know? Just tell me more about him,,' says Lucy, who's never been particularly nosy or asked me for the sordid details I usually enjoy telling Flora or Babette.

'Well, I can definitely say I've never come across another man with whom I've done so many filthy things.'

Lucy wrinkles her nose, visibly unimpressed. Right then, a deafening clap of thunder detonates above us, where a horde of dark grey clouds are gathering, dark and grey like the small house, grey like Normandy. The whole gamut of grey. With a sigh and a shudder, I continue: 'I believe Monsieur is profoundly perverse.'

Lucy half smiles.

'Not just sexually. It's the way he behaves when I'm around that's particularly perverse. As a matter of fact, so is our whole relationship.'

'OK, Ellie, I see, but it's the sort of relationship you were looking for, no?'

'Maybe. Maybe not. I wanted it to be romantic, but maybe not that sort of romance. When I first came across Monsieur I wasn't even in search of a relationship. Stupidly I got caught in a trap. And I can't see my way out.'

Lucy's wide dark eyes look up at me. 'You can't see a way out?'

I meant I just can't see how one day I'll manage to live without forgetting I'd once known him. A few weeks ago, I still believed that everything would be over once and for all when I'd finished writing *Monsieur*, but it won't. What's happened, what I've done with him, is so bizarre that even if I wanted to forget about it, some twisted part of my unconscious would be unable to. Even if he's not worth remembering, which I strongly suspect.

'It's a good thing you're writing about him,' Lucy remarked. '*Monsieur* is a great book. It's *the* book.'

Under my backside, notebook number two, with its purple cover, seems to throb softly, full of pride.

Sometimes Lucy manages to defuse tension before it takes hold. She has temporarily deflected her own status as obsession-in-chief and brought Monsieur back to the surface. Now that it's just the two of us, the silence fills with all the ifs and buts in the history of the world, and I know too well that in an hour or so, I'll be swearing under my breath because I attempted nothing, even something silly like inadvertently touching her hand or pretending to stumble over her, anything she could forgive or use to her own advantage. I do nothing, and I will do nothing because I'm a bloody fool. As I've always known.

The clouds burst one at a time. Lucy and I start to walk home and find ourselves sheltering beneath an oak's heavy branches. She lights a cigarette, unwilling to go on now that the storm we've been expecting since midday has finally broken. I don't know what we're hoping for, waiting in the pouring rain, but it must be something buried deep in our psyche, something powerful, because I've never been able to watch lightning from my window without wishing to be at the very centre of the storm. What lies at the centre of a storm? What's in the air? The idea that anything could happen and there would not necessarily be any lasting consequences? I see the same questions float like mist behind Lucy's dark eyes. Sitting on *Monsieur*, I wonder how I could take advantage of this temporary madness, throw myself at her, pull her down into the grass, stray nettles stinging our arses and lightning racing above my head. I visualize her spread across the ground, huddled against me, her lips blue, her eyes lighting up in fluorescent shades. Fuck. I watch her, watch her cigarette as if was smoking it myself, tasting her saliva. It would be so uncomfortable to roll around in those bushes! Is there any activity, apart from a long siesta, that Normandy is actually cut out for?

Light years away from my lewd thoughts, Lucy has pulled out her phone.

'Alice wants us to join her. She's at home.'

'Tell her to come here. It's so cool to be right in the middle of the storm. It'll make a change from the house.'

But Alice refuses, and the storm isn't making the conversation easy, so Lucy hangs up. 'She says we can watch *The Wall* on the plasma screen.'

'But I want to stay outside!'

'We can go on the terrace.'

Lucy stretches out her hand to clasp mine. The strength of her grip is surprising, maybe because her supple fingers are so long. I don't know how to take her gesture – I may be misinterpreting an innocent touch. Lucy has never given me any indication as to her intentions towards me; but in the midst of my confusion over Monsieur, it bothers me.

I'm playing hopscotch between the puddles as I move along the muddy paths and the rain is beating down. About to turn a sharp corner, I recall a past Sunday in Normandy when I had taken a piss against an immense fir tree overflowing with sap. Over the phone, Monsieur had been delighted to hear about it. Although I didn't want to know how he pictured me in that situation, I had read and reread his message. It had felt so wrong, as I squatted, knickers around my ankles, still dripping.

'I'd love to be there and watch you pee. It would be so good to lick away those final golden drops from your little pussy.'

I had immediately texted back: 'Absolutely not. That's disgusting.' All the time, I was looking around, almost convinced I was being spied on. I felt embarrassed and aroused, unable to stop watching the stream rushing down between my legs, asking myself how I would ever manage to pee in his presence. Or avoid it, and his latest proposal.

The world that surrounds me is full of women who'd shriek at the mere thought of finding themselves in such a situation and men who, God only knows why, could talk for ever about it, were I to bring it up in conversation, their eyes shining as they imagine a woman squatting in a field. In men's imagination, there is seemingly no dividing line between cleanliness and filth: all that matters is whether something makes you hard or not. And where do I fit into that equation? Having spent nineteen years concocting a series of standard female fantasies, I meet Monsieur and, just from reading his texts, find myself besieged by an assortment of daydreams that only the shameless sensuality of a man could conjure. I am twenty, wearing a cotton dress and leggings. My alice band is like a halo across my blonde hair, but beneath my blue eyes, there is a man's brain, a man's precise and perverse mind. I don't know how I can regain my innocence, stop myself staring at Lucy's pretty arms with a man's lustful gaze. These days, my dreams are full of the way Monsieur looks at my cunt when it gapes open and, in the background, his wet cock readies itself for another assault. I no longer spend hours caressing myself thinking of the noise Monsieur makes as he walks into our hotel room, the muted sound of his shoes on the carpet, every step forward like another thrust inside me. Lately it's been fun to make a top ten of my recurring fantasies, starting with Monsieur plunging deep into my throat and coming, while I almost suffocate, unable to distinguish between his cum and my saliva. That, or the idea of two men inside me. My nights are full of indecent close-ups, smells emerging from nowhere; my nights are like Monsieur's hands on my neck, holding me in place, motionless. That's what Normandy is all about, on and on: hundreds of hours spent in silence, with a subterranean network of new imagined perversions. No one could have any idea of the horrors I come up with.

What do I want to be when I grow up? Like Monsieur, I aspire to be perverse.

Sitting on the couch, I'm kicking my heels. I watch Alice and Lucy argue over the computer and twiddle my thumbs. At times like this, I miss Paris so much. I feel impotent in the countryside. The further I am from Paris, the more my power over Monsieur diminishes. Holidaying here is like being in a convent: I can no longer bring to mind the city skyline when I'm confronted by the copper beeches outside. Even the colours are different: there is an overall shade of green that doesn't make sense, and I search in vain for the three hues I'm familiar with: the green of the RATP buses, that of the metal gratings of place Boucicault and, finally, the grey-green that dominates every Parisian statue. The sky is an exceptional blue, and the smell of the rain reminds me of endless days at my grandparents' home, when Monsieur was not yet around to fill my head with nonsense.

The storm has the after-taste of apocalypse: now hailstones as big as my fist are piercing the surface of the pond, and it's the middle of August. Only in Normandy would you find such a climate.

The blues. In Paris, many of the men I see regularly are back from holiday, or are gradually getting ready to leave. For some reason, Zylberstein is the one I'm most often on the phone to. But there is also his friend Octave, who cheered me up by mentioning 'clit' in one of his texts; it made me feel warm inside as I imagined the strident sound of the diminutive word as spoken by a man.

I'm about to suggest we all do something I will no doubt come to regret very quickly, like yet another game of tarot, when my mobile starts vibrating. Almost two weeks since we were last in contact and Monsieur is acknowledging receipt of a mail I can barely remember, but in which I told him about my tribulations with Zylberstein: 'I really enjoyed your letter . . .'

'Hey, it's a message from Monsieur!' I type: 'When was the letter dated? When did you get it? Don't you ever go on holiday?'

I'd crawl across the room on all fours for just a word from Monsieur, and I can't write about sex out of the blue, there and then. When it comes to him, I'm constantly in a state of need and reluctant to let him know it. But talking to him and getting impersonal messages are two very different things. Trying to imagine his voice reading the words to me is as productive as trying to wank with a broken finger. I want to hear his voice so much, and the more I think of it, the more it hurts.

Maybe if I explained things to him, with the right words, black on white, he would come to understand how I live in his absence. Maybe he wouldn't take a whole three days to respond to my texts with all their question marks and 'call me back'. Maybe he would actually call me back.

We're halfway through a game of tarot when, at eight forty-five, Monsieur is calling me. Actually, the words 'unknown caller' flash on the small screen, so it could be anyone, but I instinctively know it's him. I recognize the carnival masks he wears when he's on the phone, but most of all, since I've known him, I've come to experience a spectrum of cramps in the pit of my stomach when he rings. The 'unknown caller' is well known to me. I snatch up my mobile, my arm brushing against the corner of the table, and Lucy immediately understands. I smile at her, suggesting she might follow me outside, the same Lucy who, that afternoon, had defiantly remarked that she had never seen me in a room with a man – me, of all people! Lucy wraps a blanket round her shoulders and leaves the room and the ongoing game, the game with me. I go outside.

'You OK?'

'What about you?' Monsieur answers.

It feels so good, so really good.

'I enjoyed your letter. It reached me this morning,' he adds.

'Only this morning?'

'I read it while I was waiting for a patient. Made me laugh!'

Shoeless in the wet grass, I smile. 'What are you doing right now?'

'Driving home from work, I finished early. So, what did you want to tell me?'

'Not much to say. I'm in Normandy. Bored stiff.'

Monsieur chuckles softly, and I can instantly picture him, his large hands on the steering-wheel, driving by instinct, his mind on our conversation. It's almost two months that Monsieur has been absent from my life, and I'd almost given up hope of speaking to him again. So much so that hearing him now feels as unreal as all those Tuesday mornings I can recall in every detail. Not for a second does he suspect the sort of life I've been living away from him. He sounds blissfully unaware that I have been in pain, or maybe he guessed and enjoyed it in the twisted way peculiar to him. But I'm not about to elucidate. I'd rather die: as far as Monsieur is concerned, Ellie has a life of her own when he's not around. And he's not completely wrong: I write. A book about him.

'*Monsieur* is making steady progress.'

'So you told me in your letter. You said it would be complete by September.'

'I'll let you read it then.'

Monsieur's silences, which follow my peremptory statements, please me. That's how things work with Monsieur: when he doesn't actually say no, I instinctively translate it as yes.

'What about Zylberstein?' Monsieur continues.

'Oh, I stopped seeing him. Enough was enough, don't you think?'

'Did he fuck you up the arse?'

I never quite know how Monsieur will react to any of my answers, Monsieur who's talking to me as if we're still together. I hazard: 'Yes.'

'Did it feel good?'

This is a new form of torture: should I say yes (meaning 'live with it') or lie and not tell him that Zylberstein made me come?

'It was good,' I answer, and as no one, apart from the metal heron in the centre of the pond, can see the expression on my face, I stand proudly, legs apart.

He should understand that I got from Zylberstein all that I could possibly get; he should understand that I came in spite of him, despite the looming shadow floating above me when I fuck that defies me to enjoy anything that it isn't part of. It happened and I can't say that when I came I didn't feel his presence close to me, I can't pretend I didn't feel like screaming his name. No, I can't say anything of the sort as even when I'm alone in my bed he is responsible for every crumb of pleasure I give myself, as I recite the two syllables of his name. Pitifully, I can't stop myself from saying: 'But not as good as with you.'

'Really? Why?'

'Because he didn't do it the same way.'

'How did he do it?'

'You know . . .'

The right mood has been retrieved, in which Monsieur and I act out the roles of eternal lovers, and I relish the thought of revealing to him every detail of my evening with Zylberstein.

'Actually, I was just leaving Édouard's place and—'

'Édouard? Who's Édouard?'

'A friend, who teaches French. I was with him that evening and he'd taken me from behind. Then Zylberstein called me as I was about to go to sleep, and I just felt like seeing him. So I took the Métro and went to his flat.'

'Hold on, hold on. You're telling me you were fucked up the arse by two guys on the same evening?'

Monsieur sounds amazed, as if he'd had a journalistic scoop, that through my contact with him I'd become a true slut. I answer playfully: 'Yeah, well. So then I went to see Zylberstein and—'

'Two guys.' Monsieur sighs.

'And when I told him I'd just been fucked in the arse, do you know what he said?'

'Tell me.'

'"I find that terribly arousing."'

For the first time in weeks, Monsieur and I share a moment of laughter, like partners in crime who find the spectacle of vice awfully amusing. Then there is a delicious instant of silence, followed by his whisper: 'You have such a lovely voice, Ellie.'

There is a hint of sadness in his tone. I take advantage of it, gazing at the strange blue shade of the sky, hating every word: 'Why did you leave?'

'Ellie?'

Forgive me, I think. I hate myself but I have no choice. I must know. I try to sound neutral, hoping that, three hundred kilometres away from me, Monsieur will not notice that my heart is about to shatter. 'I haven't done anything wrong. I just don't understand.'

'What don't you understand, sweetie?'

('Sweetie'. I realize my status has changed: I am now labelled like all the others whose existence I suspect. How does 'my love' turn into 'sweetie'?)

'I can't understand how from one day to the next you stopped calling me, answering me, communicating with me in some way. I can't understand how it can prove easier for you to act like that, instead of just telling me you've had enough.'

'I never did have enough. I—'

'Stop. Please, stop. Let me finish. I know you pretty well and I get the feeling you've had enough. Otherwise you wouldn't have stopped.'

'Ellie—'

'You're like me. As long as things feel fine, you'd carry on.'

'You, of all people, should know it's not easy. All this has nothing to do with my desire for you.'

'So what's the problem, then?'

'I felt we were moving in the wrong direction. Things were becoming dangerous.'

Shit. I freeze. Here we are. The moment when I can choose to believe him or decide that he's lying through his teeth. This is the moment my head splits in two. It'll affect me for days and he, of course, won't have a clue what's going on inside me. Frankly, I have no wish for Lucy to be a witness to this, because right now I no longer have anything in common with the witty and brilliant Ellie I can be when I'm with her. What with my wet ponytail and my father's shapeless sweat-shirt, I look like shit. I try to get my nerves under control, twisting my curls into unwieldy clumps and knots.

'How can I be dangerous? I never asked you for commitment.'

'That's not what I'm talking about. I mean risks I can or cannot take. It's not easy for me, you know.'

'Because of your wife?'

'Because of many things. We were heading in the wrong direction. You know we were.'

I have difficulty in controlling my anger. 'So why the hell are you calling me?'

'I wanted to tell you how much I enjoyed your letter. You put so much of yourself into it.'

'But if you read it all, you will no doubt remember that I ended it by suggesting we meet up again to fuck.'

'That's right,' Monsieur says, and I see his smile light his face. 'It's a part of the letter that charmed me.'

'Just that particular part?'

'And the prospect of fucking you. The thought of your arse.'

For a few more minutes at least, the Ellie Lucy is watching has an opportunity to shine.

'So?'

'So what, sweetie?'

'What do we do, Monsieur? Do we fuck or don't we?'

He explodes with laughter, but for just a second, within the beauty of the sound, the open-throated roar, there is an unmistakable overload of joy that betrays him: Monsieur is uncomfortable. He's probably thinking he had the monopoly on indecent proposals, and the misunderstanding is so typical of our situation. He is totally unaware of the misery he's put me through. I've been playing the game too subtly. Subtlety has to be perceived on both sides of the fence. I have no choice but to be openly wanton: it's the only way I can exploit such brief moments of grace.

'I don't know,' Monsieur answers. 'What should I say, Ellie?'

'Don't you feel like it?' I'm being evasive, in search of a new tone, with all the lascivious inflections of a courtesan putting forward the right arguments.

'I'm dying for it, as you well know. Every time I see you, I get a boner.'

(In many ways, Monsieur is like Pink Floyd's *Eclipse*: on occasion, the words he pulls out burst inside me, taking me light years away from where I stand to unimaginable places where all he says must happen.)

'So, tell me we're going to fuck. It's so simple, you and me in a room, on a Tuesday morning.'

'I'd love to. You know that.'

'So, let's do it! You keep saying "you know that", but I don't seem to know anything. You talk to me as if you're dying to see me, but you seem to spend your life running away from me. It hasn't been easy for me either. From one day to the next you just faded away. If it's over I'd rather you told me so.'

'There is *no way* I could say that to you.'

What is the bastard trying to do to me? Is he dumping me or not?

Through the mist surrounding his voice, I can vaguely hear the soft rhythm of his car's engine and, further afield, the sound of traffic in Parisian streets. I hold back the deep sigh that would let Monsieur know how much I miss the city, how much I would like to be sitting next to him, looking at him, because I know he would want to touch me. Which is all it would take. Night falling across the Marais streets and Monsieur's hands delving under my dress as he explains that our relationship can never work.

'I'm sorry, some of the drivers around here are so awful. Can't you understand that the whole situation is a thousand times simpler for you?'

'How so? Do explain, because from where I stand I'm pretty convinced you're the one who has the advantage.'

'Me?'

'Yes, you. You have your wife, your job, and on the side a chick whose only demand is to be fucked. You have everything.'

'You're looking at it in the wrong way. You're twenty, you have no ties, the whole world belongs to you. I have many obligations. Believe me, you have it easier.'

'That's so WRONG!' I cry out, forgetting that Lucy is listening to me and my father is lighting the barbecue close by. 'It's wrong, and so unfair of you to even think it. You say things like that as if what the two of us have shared hadn't touched me inside, as if I'd already forgotten about it. Has it ever occurred to you I might have an opinion on our relationship? I wasn't asking for much – even "Go to hell" would have been enough.'

'Maybe there was so much violence in our relationship that it called for a violent ending.'

I react to this with a lengthy, indecisive silence, even as the core of me is screaming: 'No way was *that* violent, darling. You merely disappeared off the face of the earth, and I couldn't reach you however hard I tried. It was terribly painful. Speaking bluntly, it was as if you'd run into me with your car and left me for dead on the side of the road. But I wasn't dead. You should have been the one hanging on the telephone, piling up masses of incoherent messages. You should have been in my place and me in yours. That would have been fun, no? Then we'd see if you'd prefer a quick death or an endless one. And I . . .'

But hold on. Hold on hold on hold on. Why is he going on about an ending if . . .?

'If you thought it was over, why did you acknowledge a letter like the one I sent you? All you had to do, yet again, was nothing.'

'I was thinking of you.'

How can you argue with that sort of man? Monsieur always finds a way to turn the situation back to his advantage, so I'm mad with rage and overflowing with joy that he still has me in mind, however briefly, even if his thirst for me can be quenched at will.

'A pretty good reason,' I mournfully concede.

'You seem strange today,' Monsieur remarks, and doesn't know how right he is.

'It's just that I have no clue where all this is leading, and I don't know what to think.'

Monsieur struggles for inspiration. 'I don't know, either. When are you back in Paris?'

'Not sure.'

A single word, a date provided by Monsieur, would be enough for me to go and purchase my return ticket, but I like the way my 'not sure' sounds. I'm not sure and don't give a damn about finding out.

'I'm about to drive into the car park so I have to leave you. I can call back any time you want.'

'As you wish.' I sigh. 'You can call me tomorrow when you go to work.'

'OK.'

Even though I'm desperately biting my lip, I have to squeeze out a PS in a pitiful attempt to counter the indifference I fear I have just conveyed: 'I thought you no longer loved me, that's all.'

'Don't think that, Ellie.'

'No?' My smile has returned.

'No. If I could see you, if it weren't so risky, I would do so as soon as possible.'

'Good.'

'OK, sweetie?'

'OK,' I say, to the voice that is so delightfully nibbling my ear lobe.

'So, all's fine, then. I have to go. I'll call you tomorrow.'

'Tomorrow.'

'Kisses,' Monsieur whispers.

'Me too,' I whisper back, and there is no way for me to describe with any clarity the three or four seconds of silence that follow the end of the conversation, a short eternal instant while I listen to his breathing, wondering if I should say any more, the deep hum of the car's engine and then nothing. It's over. I'm going to have to manage until tomorrow morning, compiling the inventory of

everything else Monsieur and I could have said between
these two parentheses.

I stand, arms hanging at my sides, in the wet grass. So,
Monsieur has returned. From nowhere. I have no idea
how he spent all that time away from me. All I know, and
it makes me perfectly happy, for a couple of minutes, is
that Monsieur is back. Monsieur exists. Monsieur is alive.
I've spoken to him. My whole body is on fire.

'So?' Lucy asks me, approaching me, as she always
does, in total silence.

'I still don't know.'

'He wants to go to bed with you again?'

'Yes. Or I think so. He seems to want to, at least. Unless
he's lying. I never know. This is Monsieur we're talking
about.'

As we walk back to the house, I'm tormented by lack
of understanding. What does he want from me? I know I
shouldn't but I send him a text with a final question: 'Do
you want me to stop squirming in your presence like a
cat in heat?'

Monsieur answers within seconds: 'No.'

Permission to remain happy . . . for the time being.

The following day at a quarter past eight, I'm smoking
my first cigarette of the day in my grandmother's small
garden. As Alice, Lucy and I stayed up late, I have
difficulty in keeping my eyes open. Right now, Monsieur
must be rushing out of the misted-up bathroom, a towel
round his waist. Perfectly shaven, a discreet touch of
cologne behind his ears and across his wrists. I'm sure he
jerks off under the shower, slowly, beneath the streams

of hot water. What he's thinking of when he does so I cannot fathom, but he could possibly be thinking of me. Then he dresses in silence in the muggy heat of the bedroom where his wife is still sleeping. He meets Charles in the corridor, briefly strokes his long hair. In the kitchen Monsieur drinks a cup of coffee and initials Adam's schoolwork. He doesn't sit down, breakfasts in a hurry. It's only at the surgery that Monsieur allows himself to slow down, act with care. It's only at the clinic that he is a genius. In the rest of his life, he runs, is always on the run, no matter what. I've often heard him complain about it, but he would find it difficult to live any differently.

Eight thirty: Monsieur kisses Estelle, who's just emerged from the bedroom in her nightie. The kids have already left.

'See you tonight,' he says, and a few minutes later he is in the car.

His mobile is in the side pocket, connected to a speaker. The world outside appears smoky behind the dark windows. I can see it all without much thought: I imagine his smell in the car, the corners of his lips that would still taste of coffee if I were to lick him there. Monsieur exits the car park, negotiating the sharp corners by instinct, ready to face the new day. Outside, on the quai de la Mégisserie, all pink and pale in the sun, pedestrians nod to him, as if he weren't even there, just a shadow behind the tinted glass of the windscreen. If Monsieur allowed me to cross his car's path, I think I'd stand paralysed in the glare of his headlights.

A quarter to nine: amid the traffic jams, Monsieur is fuming. He speaks to Estelle about the holiday arrangements, but he's not really concentrating on what he's saying as the holidays are still so far in the future. Three operations today, and God only knows how many consultations. His head is full to *bursting*. No space left for thoughts of being alone in the sun with his wife. Or me.

Five to nine: Monsieur parks in front of the clinic's iron gates. As soon as he leaves his car, he's intercepted by a colleague who wants to talk and walks with him to the main building. In the changing room, where he slips on his scrubs, Monsieur leaves his briefcase, his wallet, his mobile and me, and locks them all away. Monsieur is *operating*. Monsieur is a *grown-up*. Monsieur has *responsibilities*.

As I have no genuine responsibilities, I go back to bed. In the bed, my youngest sister turns over, grumbling: 'What's up with you?'

'Nothing. I just couldn't sleep.'

Louise has probably fallen asleep again. The living room is in total darkness. In a few minutes, my grandmother will be up. If I don't doze off by then, I'll be in trouble. What should I do? My hatred for Monsieur is keeping me awake.

Once I've sufficiently annoyed Louise with my fidgeting, I get out of bed. I go to the first floor where Alice and Lucy are sleeping in a blue room full of damp. I squeeze into my sister's bed and, still snoring, she shifts to make room for me. In the depths of my desolation (or should I say my infinite sadness?) the only prospect I can dangle in front of me to reach a blessed state of sleep is the thought of smoking. Since the advent of Monsieur, it's a good thing I have drugs to compensate for his absence.

AUGUST

Tuesday.

I've been in Berlin for a week already, surrounded by a bevy of loving girls, including the now legendary Lucy, whom I greeted with a hearty slap on the back; it was either that or a somewhat more awkward form of contact. I had to make a choice. The heat was leaden on the first day and I initiated the whole gang into the art of smoking, lying on the grass in Monbijoupark, clad only in our underwear, speakers from our iPods at either side of us. I kept staring at the girls, my eyes following one and then another, wondering how long it would be before none of them wanted ever to leave. After barely five minutes spread out like starfish, they had clearly given up all resistance. I had warned them.

Halfway through a game of tarot, Lucy stole *Monsieur* from me, so whatever I had written about her was no longer a secret. She was so wrapped up in her reading that we constantly had to remind her when it was her turn to play. My stomach in knots, I was trying to guess what was going on inside her pretty head, behind her wide dark eyes, whether she believed she was reading fiction or knew she was travelling along the tortured roads of my sexual imagination over which Monsieur and she now sat in judgement. She calmly set the notebook down, not saying a word, as if it wasn't worth debating all the whys and wherefores. When she's around I no longer think of Monsieur but of her, why his cock is no longer as important to me as the idea of her naked body.

Thursday.

If I'm dying to have sex, it's probably because Zylberstein and Landauer are repeatedly calling me, artful doctors' voices enquiring about the fate of a patient. I've been an expatriate for ten days, happy enough for my little fingers to be covered in ink; it appears to be a serious challenge for them and their egos. As soon as I come off the phone to Landauer, Octave calls me up to check he has his facts right: has Ellie Becker actually gone away to spend a whole month without a man? Such a momentous event!

For the sake of accuracy, I could have emphasized 'a month without a *man*'. But to involve Lucy in this circus, imprint her name in the boys' memories and pretend the situation was more significant than it had appeared at first, would have been quite wrong. It would have been tempting Fate to pretend that a period of fast would do me a world of good.

And I'm not convinced that's true.

Anyway, it's meaningless to talk about fasting when, since my arrival in Berlin, I haven't missed a single opportunity to play with myself as I lie in my uncomfortable bed. It's a comfort: despite all the travelling, the world I immerse myself in for ten minutes or so never changes. The protagonists and their attitudes remain immutable: Monsieur, Lucy . . . and me standing in the middle, my will bending under the weight of every possible vice, however unlikely or inexpressible.

I met up with the girls in Viktoriapark, in Mehringdamm. It was so hot we sprawled across the lawn in our swimsuits, surrounded by a pleasant cloud of weed and the honeyed taste of a beer I've never come across elsewhere. By amusing coincidence, every time I opened my eyes I could see Lucy framed between my open thighs.

On the way back, on Kreuzbergstrasse, we found a sort of coffee shop cunningly disguised as a camping-equipment store. The salesman obviously didn't have any grass, but let us have fifteen or so magic seeds. As I write this, we're skipping our way towards Wedding, and I've enough stuff in my backpack to spend a rather pleasant or, alternatively, a most unpleasant evening.

Have I previously mentioned that I find Monsieur stronger than any drug? No artificial paradise can banish him from my thoughts. The girls and I made such a fuss before we swallowed the seeds that I ended up feeling full of love for them. We were ambling between the living room and the wide, shadowy courtyard in a bid to settle our nausea, Lucy leading us. We were almost silent, our conversation interrupted by the unpleasant waves coursing through our stomachs. At first, there were only four of us, by the bicycle sheds; the others had gone for a lie-down. Lucy was puffing at a fag, while I attempted to cheer everyone up with a feeble string of jokes in a bid to hold back my unease. Alice, with sisterly solidarity, sketched a twisted smile then buried her face in my shoulder again. Flora, cross-legged on the lawn, was nibbling her nails and staring into space. There was nothing embarrassing about our silences: it was just our way of placing our respective burdens on some metaphorical pedestal, as we sat hunched, short of breath and about to spew up our guts. It looked as if the salesman had played a bad trick on us, but all of a sudden everything became so warm and beautiful, the air smelling so pleasant, that all thoughts of disaster faded away. I waited.

'Cheer up!' I cried, so sharply I even surprised myself, as acute pain stabbed my stomach.

Alice stood up, lit another cigarette and came to join me, our backs to the wall. 'How long is it since we swallowed the seeds?' she asked.

'Almost an hour,' Flora answered laconically, then also got to her feet, a fag to her lips. 'Can I have a light?'

Lucy's golden arm stretched out: she was holding a lighter.

'Do you think this is going to last much longer?' I heard her ask, lost in a cloud of smoke.

'The nausea? I think it should end soon.'

But the truth was I didn't know. I was pleased that, so far, I'd avoided vomiting. The thought of feeling sick for another eight hours was dreadful.

'Do you all feel funny?' Flora asked.

'I don't know what to say,' Lucy answered. 'I've got awful pains in my thighs. Never felt like this before.'

'I feel . . . odd,' I replied.

'Your pupils are fully dilated,' Alice added, leaning closer to me, her own eyes Lovecraft dark.

'We're mad,' I said, rushing to the glass door to check out my eyes.

'We'd look like a bunch of bloody fools if the cops turned up.' Alice laughed manically.

All I could do was hiccup, then noticed that I couldn't stop smiling. As if some poison carried by the seeds was forcing every muscle in my face to contract.

Five minutes later, we were rolling about, cackling like witches in the block's inner courtyard, our stomachs finally at peace. Mistakenly feeling normal again, Alice and I suggested fetching some music when a tenant on her fifth-floor balcony threatened to call the police. We bolted into the apartment, all trying to get through the door at the same time (I still have a shapely bruise on my arm, which I finger idly as I recall the sheer euphoria of the moment). Clémence then walked out of the room where she had been enjoying a siesta in a bid to control her nausea, followed by Claire and Anne-Lise, and finally Hermance, who appeared when she heard us all shrieking with laughter. It's a moment that will stay with me all my life: ten minutes after she'd arrived on the scene, as we were all frantically trying to describe to each other our overwhelming meaningless happiness, cuddling each other on the couch like a litter of kittens, Hermance stood up, holding her face in her elegant hands. Convinced she had hurt herself, Clémence and Alice jumped up, squeaking, 'Hermi, Hermi, Hermi,' and I was overtaken by hysterical laughter! Hermance began to howl like a banshee, totally out of control, her hands spasmodically moving across her stomach and Flora cried: 'Oh, she's crying! Hermi's crying!'

Yes, she was, but it was for joy. Which we finally realized when she gasped: 'I don't know why I'm crying! I don't even know if I'm crying! Everything is just perfect, everything, everything, everything! This city is perfect, you are all perfect, the music is perfect!' Her chin shaking, and her voice as sharp as a violin, she added: 'It fucking breaks my heart!' And cried even harder as she poured herself another glass of punch.

We enjoyed a whole bunch of further epiphanies throughout the seven hours of that particular evening. The few things I clearly remember: Alice, overcome by unexplained weariness, finding herself unable to hold on to her plate of spaghetti and allowing it to spill over her dress. Laughing. Later, sitting cross-legged in the wicker chair between the two couches, I tried to describe each of the girls present as if she were a fictional household member of the Maison Tellier. The first object of the exercise was to see what type of woman they each corresponded to in the world of the brothel in the Maupassant story where you might come across the Pretty Blonde, the Pretty Jewess, the girl from Normandy. But confronted by all these different faces, observing the diversity of their bodies, the hairstyles, the sheer confusion, I began to flounder. Who cared about the commercial arguments the Madame would put forward to entice the clients? From the outset I could imagine only a single client. I was the only one whose eyes could appreciate how beautiful they all were. How could a man ever understand? Their succulent limbs were relaxing across cushions, their lazy eyelids falling across dark pupils, and every element of the scene gave itself up to the flattery and caresses of the more baroque words in my repertoire. It was an effort to stick to respectable language, not indulge in four-letter words or vulgarity, but I managed it. Even if, where Flora was concerned, I was unable to escape from the mental image of her, head over heels in a wide satin bed, mouth open, hands clenched, in the centre of a huge pillow. Unable to find the right, elegant words to describe the curious loveliness of her face, all I could visualize was her swooning in the arms of some faceless man.

'Flora is like no other,' I said, pulling my legs up under myself.

'And now Lucy!' Clémence shouted.

When it comes to Lucy, her eyes seem to smell of sex and I'll devour her raw as soon as you all have your backs turned, I thought, as I watched her, crouching by one of the low tables, waiting to be judged with a sphinx-like half-smile on her lips. Composing myself, I sighed. 'Lucy . . . Lucy is Lucy. You all know she's impossible to describe.'

Visibly flattered, she lowered her eyes.

Pleased with the effect of my words, I crossed and uncrossed my legs, feeling a rush of heat between my thighs.

Later, she and I went to the swings in the square that bisected the street. Hurling myself high, I felt as if I was about to be consumed by the sky, so full of stars, shining brighter than ever before. My eyes created haloes around each pinprick of light. The world was like a watercolour and, seemingly kilometres below me, Lucy followed my ascent with appreciative shrieks. When the laws of gravity threw me back, I felt euphorically nauseous, drunk with vertigo, and a sensation of freedom, almost as strong as an orgasm, passed through me. My hair was falling back against my forehead, and every breath I took moved straight to my crotch, Monsieur's name flashing like neon behind my closed eyes.

Monsieur.

Can you explain to me how Monsieur appeared unbidden in all this? Why, when I had eyes only for Lucy, did I allow him to take over again? At what point in the evening did it happen?

We were, I think, still in the apartment. Yes, I'm sure that's when it was. God only knows why I was wearing a swimsuit. The conversation was in full swing and I regretfully pulled myself off the couch to pee. A glance in the mirror, the sort of glassy look my parents would instantly have seen through, and I became fascinated by my own reflection. Standing, all of a sudden no longer noticing my bursting bladder, I stroked my cheeks. How amazing! A young woman who looked just like me was facing me, wearing the same black swimsuit, with the same unkempt hair, displaying the same incoherent smile. I kept hearing something chirp in the background.

Reluctantly looking away from the mirror, I sat down heavily. And as I peed, chuckling to myself, the door half opened. Probably just a draught, I realized later, but at that moment I suddenly came to believe that Monsieur was about to make an impromptu appearance. *And why not, after all? Why should I enjoy the most unlikely hallucinations, and not allow him to be part of them?* There I was, my swimsuit around my ankles, stark naked on the throne, my wide dark eyes hypnotized by the gap between the door and the wall, captivated by the vision of Monsieur, standing motionless in the doorway. Monsieur, his gaze digging deep into my flesh. Each flutter of his eyelashes saying, *It's me, me and my cock that always stays hard for you, for you in that particular position, for instance, you pissing with your little deep pink slit all wet because the rest of you is too; if you're having such a hallucination, it's because it makes you wet, no? Tell me the truth, my sweet little whore: at first you were disgusted by the thought of me watching you, but the more you think about it, the more you feel aroused, don't you? Surely an area where Lucy can't compete with me (in truth, could she ever? Ellie?), all these stray thoughts of peeing in front of me emerging from nowhere. She wouldn't understand. She's too young, but I am, dear God, of an age when nothing can shock me. The worst perversions you could think of wouldn't come as a surprise, because I know every single one down to the tip of my fingers and, Ellie, because I always had an inkling all these vices were there inside you, swarming like maggots. So, tell me: did you really think you could forget me for a whole summer? What a joke. Now I'm here, and we're going to have so much fun.*

And I was smiling, like a bitch, watching the doorway. Monsieur leaning towards me, his fingers reaching for me, and right then Alice kicked the door wide open. Monsieur faded and I shook my head, dazed.

'Hurry up, I have to go!' she screamed, sounding like a drunkard.

Later, we went to bed. Flora and Alice had assigned me a bed in their small room. I was about to treat myself to one of those silent pillow-biting orgasms when, from the darkness behind my closed eyelids, Monsieur returned, all cunning looks and a smile full of open-handed spanking, whispering, 'Where were we?'

There, Monsieur. Right there.

Monday.

It was in a small intimate Berlin museum, at an exhibition of black-and-white erotic photography, that Monsieur took his rightful place again, full of his customary spiteful lover's intransigence. I was pacing through the corridors, trying to distance myself from a group of tourists, when I saw them. Saw them, not just noticed. Not right away.

'*Aubrey Beardsley, illustrating Oscar Wilde's Salome,*' I read, before my brain made the right connection at supersonic speed and I remembered all the mails he had sent me in which he had mentioned this particular piece of art, these specific illustrations. I felt for a moment like bursting into tears because I wanted so much to see him, right there in the museum, under the gaze of the attendants, at the heart of the church-like silence.

That night, I came up with the cunning idea. In the morning, the sky still pink, I sent him a text: 'Saw Beardsley's drawings for *Salome* at an exhibition. Wonderful.'

Monsieur responded just a few minutes later: 'Which museum?'

'In Berlin.'

'Have you also seen von Bayros and Kokoschka?'

God only knows why but now that we were discussing art, Monsieur was a fount of conversation. Our dialogue continued throughout the day, barely interrupted by my travels on the U-Bahn and meals taken while still connected to Facebook. Monsieur would learnedly explain everything to me, scandalized by this apparent gap in my education. I had just posted him my lengthy, feverish letter, which ended with an assignation: Monday, 14 September. I was listening to the Rolling Stones on my way to Catherine's and asked him: 'By the way, did you receive my letter?'

Yet another perfect way to reinforce my theory of the Unnecessary Message: Monsieur was suddenly quiet.

Puzzled by his unexpected reaction (or lack of it), I began undergoing a form of mental torture, trying to guess what in particular in my texts could have bothered him to the extent that he had ceased communicating with me in the blink of an eyelid. I didn't believe I'd been too pushy when I was describing my days spent writing. But I came to understand: on occasions, motivated by some random lustful impulse, Monsieur would condescend to answer me. The exchange would last two or three messages despatched at intervals until one of mine became the Unnecessary Message. One too many. Only Monsieur knew when and why we had reached this point. But, with time and experience, I was starting to recognize the triggers: anything banal, pressing demands. Against all expectations, he was capable, with a rudeness that was almost comical, of turning his back on me right in the middle of some torrid exchange, even as I sat drooling over the phone's keyboard. Had he not failed to pick up from his PO box a thick envelope full of pictures of my arse? I could have screamed.

But you get used to anything and, with resignation, I came to accept this type of fragmentary communication, led by his unpredictable impulses.

I arrived at Catherine's with my mobile silent. She was enjoying a siesta and, angry that I was once again journeying down a cul-de-sac, I scribbled a whole ten pages of *Monsieur* while smoking my daily quota of Lucky Strikes.

Two hours later, enter stage left the eponymous character: 'When did you post it?'

Me (frantic): 'A week ago. How odd. One of my friends received his letter yesterday, and I'd posted it later.'

Monsieur (growling): 'What's all this? What letter, what friend? You send the same letter to all your friends?'

Me (roaring with laughter at his cheek): 'Surely I have a right to send letters to whomever I wish – and, anyway, I'm not fucking all my friends! What made you think I'd send the same letter in multiple copies?'

There you are. Another Unnecessary Message, I decided, three hours later, stuffing myself with muffins and watching a German version of *The Young and the Restless* (yearning and disappointment are a universal language).

'Fucking bastard Monsieur,' I was muttering later, in the U-Bahn.

I sent Babette a message: 'I really have to find myself a cooler Monsieur, not a lousy one like the one I happen to have.' Then added: 'But, of course, the problem is that there is only one Monsieur.'

And then, it goes without saying, as I was reaching Mehringdamm, he called me. Halfway through my journey, I leaped out of the carriage, found some space on an empty bench, allowed two trains to roar by, seven minutes apart, even though I'd agreed to be home at precisely eight. You must understand, I had to listen to him with perfect clarity, his beautiful deep voice so full of caresses, creeping beneath my dress, untying my shoelaces. I had spent a month deprived of that particular sound and it would be wrong for me to write, even for the sake of it, 'I just hadn't remembered how lovely it was.' I remembered everything. I recalled with crucifying precision how hatefully arousing Monsieur could be on the phone. He penetrated me. It took me a whole five minutes to realize that I was rubbing myself against the bench, in full view of all. Monsieur's laughter was making me smile, and I was aching to test my wit against his and enjoy more of his laughter, racing like an orgasm through the phone line. Monsieur wanted to come to Berlin. The imperious way in which he said, 'You'll show me everything,' instantly swept away all the months he had eluded me. As ever, Monsieur spoke as if we were getting out of bed. The mere thought of questioning his evasions no longer made sense.

'It's so difficult to reach you on the phone!' I explained, and Monsieur, without my having to prompt him, told me about a fictitious congress in Potsdam, a long weekend hand in hand, me acting as spiritual guide to Berlin nights. Monsieur spoke softly of nights sliding into days and turning again into nights, as we'd lie together naked among the scattered sheets of our Friedrichshain hotel. Finding myself in the very heart of the city, soothed by the warm air of the U-Bahn, I did not dare imagine his shoulder against mine on the bench for fear of screaming aloud. But it was a lovely thought. I was trying to convince myself we could manage it, if only Monsieur could, if only Monsieur *would*. (*Come on, Ellie, it's tough enough to manage a virtual form of communication with him. How do you expect to hold him captive for three or four whole days? Even in a strange town, with barely a word of German, he would still be capable of fading away.*)

'Are you pretty today?' he asked.

'Not particularly.'

He roared with laughter. 'Why?'

'My ponytail's untidy, my jeans are torn . . . I'm not at my best.'

'You're lying,' he replied. 'Look closely at yourself in one of the Métro's glass windows. Now, can you see yourself?'

'Yes.'

Facing me, the reflection of my flushed features, my tiny feet in a dreadful pair of trainers. A woman in love: listening to me babble, that was what any onlooker would have thought. Feeling sick, but only I was aware of that.

'Earlier, I was reading your message again and it made me think of those photos by Bellmer. Have you heard of him? Hans Bellmer.'

'Of course. The dolls.'

'There is one in particular that made me think of you, and the first time I set eyes on you. I didn't even know what you looked like. All I could see was your small pink body between the bed covers, pink like a Bellmer doll.'

'You've never said that to me,' I interjected, not

wanting him to realize how much more I wanted to hear, so many more words of that sort, magic words acting like caresses.

'When are you getting back from Berlin?'

'On the third.'

For a few seconds I bit the inside of my cheeks, but couldn't contain myself: 'Shall we meet up when I'm back?'

'Yes,' Monsieur said, and my whole body suddenly felt lighter, just like that, for no particular reason, as if he was no longer in a position to go back on his word, and I floated, floated, even when the network disconnected us, floating across the sound of *'Honky Tonk Women'* and my feet didn't touch the ground until I reached the Steglitz station.

Once in my bed, as if this called for an unorthodox form of celebration, I brutally inserted the hairbrush handle into myself and lay momentarily on the brink of tears. Not having Monsieur at my disposal, I needed something to fill the emptiness he had just reopened, summoning back all the sensations he triggered at the heart of my being.

Thursday.

All too often, returning from Berlin, I would find myself bored to tears sprawled across my bed. It's mostly the scent of the streets I miss, the air full of pollen, the green waters of the Spree and the smells from all the street stalls scattered along the pavements. I miss the people. I miss the general feeling of euphoria. Skipping along on my own without being a hostage to time-keeping. But now that I have Monsieur to look forward to, Monsieur who is only fifteen kilometres away, boredom tastes different. We've been on the verge of disaster for two nights, and all because of the telephone landline. And because I'm so bloody stupid. Why did I think of calling him from a phone number he didn't know? I was taking refuge in the study and left a message on his answer machine, just telling him he should under no circumstances try to reach me on this number. The reason: it was my uncle's, and it would only take him a couple of seconds to sniff out any monkey business. But I knew that Monsieur never had the time or the patience to pick up his messages from the machine, where thirty or so out-of-date calls were usually waiting for him. Fifteen minutes later, as I was about to call him again, the phone rang. I was writing at my desk. First ring: the sound of people running around, on the floor above my sister rushing towards the phone. Second ring: in an instant, I realized my fate was about to be sealed if the person calling was miraculously the one I was thinking of, and I jumped up, knocking to the floor a whole shelf of pants, screaming, 'It's for me!' The telephone at my ear felt as hot as a piece of flaming coal.

'Hello,' Monsieur said. 'You called, but I don't recognize the number.'

'It's me.' I smiled, my heart beating fast.

'Who?'

'Me, Ellie. Best check your answer machine – I asked you not to call me back here. I'm at Philippe's.'

But Monsieur was no longer listening to me, repeating my name gleefully, as if my call had just shone a ray of light over his whole day. 'How are you, sweetheart? It's so good to speak to you!'

'I'm OK. You?'

'Work, as ever, nothing new. You're in Paris?'

'I came back yesterday. Did you get my letter?'

'Still no. What a palaver. What did you write in it?'

Curled up tight in my bed, in the foetal position, I was squeezing my arms hard between my thighs.

'All sorts of things, about Berlin, the fact I haven't been to bed with a guy for a whole month. Too much to talk about over the phone.'

'I know. When do we see each other?'

'I was thinking of the fourteenth.'

'It's long time till the fourteenth.'

Monsieur is unaware how true his words are, cutting, steel sharp. Another ten nights before I see him.

BOOK III

BOOK III

SEPTEMBER

At the end of the day, what I know of Monsieur can fit into a single sentence, both subtle and concise: 'It would be so great, if only I had enough time.'

If I had enough time, Monsieur and I would enjoy long conversations on the phone. We would sip coffee at bar terraces. Maybe we would dine in the Italian restaurant he considers the best in Paris. He would invent out of nowhere some seminars in the provinces, as he has no doubt done for others. In the world of imagination, Monsieur and I lead an exciting life, the sort of life any married man would enjoy with his mistress; and if I don't get this, it's not down to lack of time, as he so often tells me, but that I'm not worth it. While he fucks me and I feel nothing, I consider this hypothesis: I'm not worth it, but I don't know which of the two of us is the most wretched. He who deigns to mount me, or me below him moaning with lust. I can effortlessly count every kiss and word I have been granted prior to penetration, and I'm already counting the minutes until he comes, so we can discuss the subject.

It's on this particular Tuesday morning in September that I feel the initial seeds of rebellion rise inside me. If I'd had the slightest trace of will-power, I could have spent my holidays learning to despise him by remembering the collateral damage, the disappointment, the slow degradation, the terrible disorientation, by weighing up the total mess versus the few seconds of euphoria. But I'd adopted the wrong attitude, assembling all my memories in a row, like relics, making a hero of the man and finding paradise in his arms. Monsieur is just another guy and I've turned him into something else altogether.

He hasn't changed. Above me, he pours out a cascade of filthy words and obscene instructions, but I'm no longer caught between the fires of arousal and awkwardness. 'Touch yourself,' he whispers, and I feel like telling him to go to hell. That, whatever happens, I won't come. And if he needs to watch a porno movie, he should invent one in which my thighs are thinner, my virtue less evident, my pussy wetter.

But Monsieur systematically goes on fucking. The quest for an orgasm, not customarily his main goal, preoccupies him. And if he grips me with such strength, it's mostly to avoid my eyes. But wasn't I the one who suggested we meet up again? I asked him to fuck me. So we fuck.

I picture myself two days earlier on the phone with Monsieur, telling him about a conversation I'd had with my girlfriends during which they had actually taken his side, thoroughly approving of his obsession with seeing me touch myself. The main argument Ines had come up with: 'Having reached the age of forty-six, he realizes he'll never manage to make you come on his own.'

His hackles raised, Monsieur had snapped: 'Tell her from me that I'm quite capable of making her come for a whole bloody night, should she ever be game!'

My initial thought, confused by my need to see him and the disillusion growing inside me, was *Just start by making me come, just me! Any time!*

But all I could tell Monsieur, with a faint smile on my lips: 'You'll never be able to make anyone come, ever!'

And he dutifully followed my instructions.

After love, Monsieur looks at me distractedly, the way you look at a still warm cadaver. My legs are spread open across the bed and I feel like a doll that's been torn apart, caught in the web of his fascination with what he's done to me, made of me. I have toothmarks on the inside of my thighs. As I make a feeble attempt to turn onto my back, Monsieur grasps me in a vice-like grip, somehow trying to communicate the necessary, clumsy tenderness that men who have become indifferent to us feel obliged to express after the act of love. But, with one of his arms braced around my neck and the other across my stomach, it makes me think of a snake suffocating its victim, following a hail of deadly bites.

A few minutes later, I'm lying on my back and I can see us in the mirror on the right-hand wall of the room, me deep in my obsession: how could I ever have believed that I could one day control this man? Monsieur's muscles are delicate, seemingly designed to capture prey and escape from predators in a flash. And you have merely to look briefly at me to know that I'm the sort of creature who is fleet of foot and tricky only in the bedroom. Otherwise

I'm like a slug, round and heavy and moving in eternally slow motion.

'Did you fuck in Berlin?' Monsieur suddenly asks me.

'I told you, it was a sexual desert,' I answered, sliding against his back, grazing his flanks.

'With all those guys at your beck and call, you did nothing?'

'None of them came to Berlin.'

Monsieur drapes his arm across my chest, turns and looks at me. There is a hint of a dimple in his cheek, the pattern of a smile in its early stages. 'Of course, I remember now, the hairbrush.'

'I made it very clear I wanted you never to refer to that episode again.'

'But it's a funny story, isn't it?'

In an attempt to turn Monsieur's mind away from the ridiculous image of me with a hairbrush sticking out of my cunt, I continue: 'Zylberstein, Atlan, Landauer, they're all guys I'm willing to fuck, but not to the extent of having them around for two whole days.'

'Tell me . . . Zylberstein, Atlan, Landauer . . .'

'I know. All my lovers happen to be Jewish. God knows why, no particular reason.' And God only knows why I added: 'Jewish and doctors.'

Monsieur's face develops the sort of vexed pout my father always adopts when hearing of my fibs. 'That's bad.'

'What is?'

'To fuck just doctors.'

'It's not . . . my choice. It just happens that way. I met

one, then another, and yet another . . . and as they all know each other, there's no end to it.'

Monsieur remains silent, as if satisfied by my explanation. But the way his mouth curls tells me he is already coming up with some new fantastical theory: maybe this would-be romantic writer and careerist tramp is excited by collecting doctors – perhaps it makes her story more exciting, if predictable. A theory I decry, but sadly I haven't the energy to defend myself.

My three *Monsieur* notebooks are under my pillow. I pull them out and leaf through them as I look at him, full of arousal and consumed by anguish. His eyes, with their customary hunger, swiftly move across the lines. My heart beats out of control. With every successive paragraph, I want to snatch the notebook away from him. Towards the final chapter (the one, of course, which looks at his wife and the couple they form from every possible angle), his grey eyes land softly on a word, maybe a sentence, and I find the situation remarkable. My life suspended. Just as slowly, Monsieur looks up at me, a harsh question racing across his thick lips, the tone of his voice much too calm for me not to worry: 'How would you know if my wife was cheating on me?'

'I wouldn't,' I said (I'm scared to death, dear God, *terrified*). 'It was just a supposition. But it's not impossible.' I add, defensive like a coward. 'It's not me who says it. It's just a character.' I take a breath, continue: 'Anyway, I've naturally changed all the names, including yours.' Monsieur slowly turns the pages, unmoved. I cunningly add: 'I even changed your wife's name.'

'You should still explain to me what my wife has to do with all this.'

'But . . . so much! You can't imagine all that the story implies. It's evident that mentioning your wife is significant. Even though I know nothing about her. *Particularly* as I know nothing about her. That's what I keep saying throughout *Monsieur*.'

He's now deciphering the inside covers of the notebooks where, from the very beginning, I've been in the habit of jotting down my witticisms, my still unformed ideas, my rambling thoughts. A whole jumble of incomprehensible sentences to anyone but myself, apart from words once said by Monsieur, hastily remembered and jotted down between cautious inverted commas, black on white, all the wonderful obscenities he would whisper to me on Tuesday mornings and that I was afraid I'd forget (I'm certain that in fifty years' time they will still resonate as strongly in the memory of the old woman I will be): 'Touch your sweet pussy for me.' That, and so many others murmured in the darkness, that I wanted to incorporate into my story: 'Monsieur's cock nestling inside his trousers. Monsieur when he is jerking off. Monsieur's balls?' (Having written page after page about what he did to me, I had realized I had no precise visual memory of his impressive set of balls . . . Bizarre.)

I can easily imagine the coldness of his incomprehension, the anguish that fills him as he confronts all the topsy-turvy sentences that refer to him, 'Monsieur' written down a thousand times in a thousand different ways. My notebooks are like the walls psychopaths deface, every available inch covered with photos of victims, cuttings from newspapers, locks of hair. He enters the lair, noting how I've retained so many details of us that he now no longer remembers. Maybe he thinks I'm pathological, but as far as I'm concerned, this was the only way to be objective about our affair and also to keep him alive, as the fire he lit inside me just won't go out, despite his absence. I watch him woefully as he feeds on my secrets, enters the pink and black little-girl world I have unwittingly brought to life. I am already indignant at the prospect of how he will judge it.

Closing the final notebook, he knits his brows and exhales a long, long sigh, with all the finality of a guy presented with a *fait accompli*.

'How do you refer to me in your book?'

'As Monsieur. You already know that.'

'What sort of job have you given me?'

'Surgeon. I've already told you I couldn't change that. It's you.'

Once again Monsieur sighs with dismay, whispering as if to himself: 'Everyone will know.'

I feel like screaming, but say softly, 'You're not the *only* surgeon in Paris.'

'I'm the only one who is known for his appreciation of erotic literature.'

'So what? Should I make Monsieur a doughnut vendor who reads pulp thrillers?'

The outline of a smile appears on Monsieur's lips, defusing the tension.

I come to realize that, having read these two pages, it's not just that Monsieur is scared: he understands that the clever idea of getting me to write a book about our relationship has now turned against him. Of course, it makes him nervous. I can no longer read on his face what he is thinking. Staring at him through my eyelashes, I ask: 'You hate me now?'

'Me, hate you?' he remarks, with a look of genuine shock. 'Why should I hate you, sweetie?'

'You don't approve of anything I do or show you.'

'On the contrary, I approve of everything you do.'

'You think I'm trying to land you in the shit?'

'You're not landing me in the shit,' he answers (translate as *I will not allow you to land me in the shit*). 'I just don't want to hurt anyone. Understand?'

'I have as much to lose as you do.'

'I have nothing to lose! There's no point in hurting people. That's why you must change all the names.'

'I will.'

Discreetly, I pull the notebooks back to my side of the bed. Now, it's just Monsieur, me and our now unfamiliar bodies. Chin tucked into the fold of his armpit, I am no longer listening to his darling voice commenting on my book. I silently study his features. Monsieur is beside me, but kilometres away, his tirade against the supposed rashness of my book now just a detail. He is on this bed, and so am I, but *we* (the abstract but instantly recognizable concept of 'we') have missed the boat.

'I have to leave,' he proclaims, at ten to eleven, a mere half-hour after his triumphant arrival.

'You're kidding.' I jump off the bed, staring at him with incredulity. 'Now? You've only just arrived!'

'I know, but what can I do? It's all I could manage. Actually, I almost didn't come at all.'

Half an hour. That's what I get for my efforts. I pout, which seems to affect Monsieur as, still naked on his knees in the tangle of sheets, he groans. 'Don't look at me like that. You know that if I could do otherwise I would.'

'That's just it. I don't know. All I can do is *think* I know.'

'So accept it. I have no choice.'

I respond bitterly: 'You sure haven't courted me much of late.'

'When?'

'Last weekend, for instance.'

As he doesn't appear to understand, now busy looking for his trousers, I continue: 'I remember the first times we saw each other. You had as much work as you do now on your plate, but you made time. You spent your life on the phone to me, sending me texts. And now, fuck all. Until the very last moment, I was even unsure whether you'd turn up today.'

'I do what I can. It's lack of time, for everything. You can't imagine how it is. I'm working fourteen hours a day, think of that.'

'I've always known you were busy. That's not what I'm talking about.'

'These days it's worse.'

Holding his trousers in one hand, Monsieur is deep in thought. Then he asks: 'When did we start seeing each other?'

'It began in May,' I answer mournfully, unable to look him in the eyes and control the horrible thought flashing through my mind: *Monsieur passed through my life like a ghost*.

'May . . . Must have been the recession. I had less work.'

Monsieur, his beautiful eyes so accustomed to lying, insolently holding my gaze. I recognize this shaky form of poise. Like him, I am capable of lying, but Monsieur doesn't know this, believing he owns the copyright to every subterfuge in the book.

I light my joint again in an attempt to fill the awkward silence. Clumsily exhale the smoke.

'Do you distrust me now?'

Isn't it preposterous that you can brush away your whole life with one swipe of the hand, like emptying a table of hot dishes? But it isn't funny. It would take only a word or two for Monsieur to antagonize his wife, alienate his children, become the object of ridicule at work and be laughed at by his friends. I am twenty, just a clumsy sketch of a woman, and I have the power to do all this. It's like holding a gun. Sometimes I'm dying to pull the trigger, but my conscience keeps my fingers away from the firing mechanism.

Monsieur kneels in search of his second sock, his face turned towards mine. 'No. No, I don't distrust you.'

'You'd never say so, but I see it in your eyes. *Monsieur* worries the hell out of you.'

'If you changed all those things people close to us might recognize, why should I be distrustful? Hell, on the contrary! It's your first novel! I always encouraged you to write, no?'

'True.'

'All I'm saying is, we still have some time before they start printing thirty thousand copies. Time enough to make the characters opaque.'

'Thirty thousand copies seems a lot,' I remark, eyes glazed.

I probably look the picture of disappointment, and Monsieur moves over to stroke my knee.

'Believe me, you're a born writer. I knew it from the moment I read your piece in *Stupre*.'

'Oh, by the way . . .' I grabbed my bulging handbag, from which the pink cover of my last copy, duly inscribed, had been peeping out.

With a broad smile, Monsieur took the magazine, folding and unfolding the yellowing cover, exploring every page with expert attention. 'It's beautiful!' he exclaimed, and for those two words, repeated over and over again, I would have given him my life.

Why did I attach so much importance to Monsieur's approval? Every compliment he bestows on me has always been measured, distilled, analysed, formatted, and I'm not even talking about the dreadful flattery with which he bombards me while I squirm below him as we make love, an immediate consequence of all the cum accumulating in his brain. When Monsieur says something is 'beautiful', the word is filled with brightness.

'I wrote you a great dedication.'

While others would only see the words 'cock' and 'cunt', you truly saw Lucie, and understood her. So I place this copy in your expert hands. 'For Monsieur C.S., Ellie Becker.'

His charming lips parted, uncovering a row of superbly white teeth.

'It's for me?' Monsieur asks shyly, surprisingly coy.

'I promised I'd give you a copy.'

'This magazine is great. Thank you.'

I already imagine my slot in the library on the Île Saint-Louis, among the ribald books in which Monsieur conceals my letters. No one can even guess at the assortment of fictional orgies permanently taking place in that study, which in my mind is alternately a boudoir and a castle. All the great books are there, their dust communing with the fat smell of old pages, a thousand concepts battling away, overlapping. And, from tonight, I will be there too, with my vagina-pink cover still carrying the smell of printer's ink and my quiet teenage fantasies.

But it's already eleven and Monsieur has to leave. The few minutes we have left are spent looking for his clothing scattered across the room (not that I remember such a tornado occurring on his arrival).

'Don't look so sad, please.'

'I'm not sad. It's just been too short.'

'I know. For me too.'

I crawl away and sit near the desk, pretending to look for something on my laptop. Monsieur carefully laces his ankle-boots, his face serious. Then, upright and solemn, he rises, takes hold of his sunglasses and casts his eyes across the room, the deserted bed, the crumpled sheets. I already know what he is going to say once he's completed his visual search for things that might have inadvertently fallen from his pockets: 'You'll check everything after I've gone?'

His final words at the end of every single encounter, as I've only just realized.

'I'll check.'

'Thanks.'

He moves, disturbing the blanket of air that surrounds us, and it already feels cold, like outside. Dragging poetic currents in his wake – the smell of me on his precious clothes – as I close my eyes against the growing pain. It's taken me months to get Monsieur here for just an hour and it's going to take me twice as long at least to manage it again. I'm exhausted at the mere thought.

'Did you have company yesterday?' he asks, as he stumbles over a Japanese restaurant's carrier-bag.

'My girlfriends.'

'Which ones? Babette and Ines?' Monsieur ventures.

'My sister and our girlfriends. Lucy, Flora, Clémence.'

'They knew why you were here?'

Monsieur's worried eyebrows, almost a caricature.

'They knew I was waiting for you, yes.'

'Do they know who I am?'

I'm silent for a moment, horror-stricken that Monsieur might be hoping I did not confide in my best friends. Me. A *girl*. I manage to stammer: 'But . . . of course they know who you are!'

'They know my name?'

I lie: 'No. They only know you as Monsieur.'

Just half a lie: that's how they refer to him, if only because, traumatized by the two crushing syllables of his first name, I do.

'You have to be careful. Rumours can spread so fast.'

315

'I know my girlfriends well. They have no contact with people who know you.'

Monsieur sighs again, with undue exaggeration. 'How can you be sure? This is Paris.'

'Trust me.'

Why should I? Monsieur might have asked himself. We wouldn't be discussing the matter of trust if I'd kept my mouth shut. But he leans towards me and gently kisses my forehead. 'I have to go.'

I give him what I hope is a dirty look. 'So go.'

Monsieur steps away.

'You want to see me again?'

'Of course.' And, still motionless and holding my gaze, he adds: 'When we met each other, I had less work on my plate. Now the recession is over, or it seems that way, business is picking up. Which is welcome . . .' His eyes travel from my neck to my hips. 'Or unfortunate, whichever the case may be.' The lust warming Monsieur's features fades to make way for a cold, dispassionate medical mask. 'It's just the way it is.'

I nod, displaying neither sorrow nor joy.

'Let me kiss you, anyway,' Monsieur pleads, as if I intended not to.

His lips have already lost their indolent warmth. Everything about him now belongs to his wife and his clinic. My tummy brushes against him and I whisper: 'So call me, then.'

'I will.'

He is visibly ill at ease in making me this promise, after so many false ones. He looks like my sister does when our grandmother gets her to promise to send a postcard during the holidays: a two-minute phone call is too much of a challenge so a three-word postcard is like a mountain to climb. Grandmother already knows she is unlikely to get any written news of our holidays and, to make it worse, is already smiling and forgiving us. Through her eyes, I stare at my ungrateful godson who's come along in the line of duty and picked up his present. Quite right, too, that the miserable sod should feel guilty as he walks down the stairs. Compared to what I might have said or done, he's getting off lightly.

Unable to watch him leave, I get back into bed, facing the mirror, and tuck myself between the sheets. I try to sleep, but keep thinking of Monsieur in ways that make it impossible. More to the point, I can't find the way! I can no longer imagine the torrid scenes that usually accompany me on my journey to sleep. The gap between fantasy and reality, that cruel abyss, is acting as a censor to all my daydreams.

I stare at myself, holding the remains of the joint in one hand. Ash falls across the sheets where the smell of Monsieur lingers, elusive, between the folds. The bites on my thighs are no longer a gift, the spreading heat in my stomach just a memory, an expression of his lust and the way he takes advantage of me. Barely two minutes following his departure, I already feel the emptiness of need. All the prayers and supplications in the world would fail to move Monsieur, who will be incapable of clearing some five minutes for me in his busy timetable, should the sudden wish to fuck assail him.

I already know what I will tell Babette on the phone. The guy is a monster. He doesn't love me, has never loved me. He's the worst kind of bastard, always unwilling to let me know until the last minute whether he's coming to see me or not. He gets here late, leaves early, and in between accumulates recriminations, almost blaming me for the fifty-six minutes we spend together, as if I've stolen an hour from him, with a knife to his throat. The guy lands on my doorstep overflowing with all the compliments I've paid him throughout the summer, full of the hope I've invested in him, the case of fantasies in which I've assigned him the leading role, and dares to stand in front of me full of his own importance. He mounts me before I'm even wet, making fun of my desire to communicate. I'm writing a book about him, but all he sees in me is the danger I pose, ready to consume his marriage, his life, danger advancing towards him on gifted literary legs and in search of revenge, and he pisses off with the audacity to make me further promises, *letting me pay for the room even*, but I forgive him, Babette. I forgive him everything. I am in love.

OCTOBER

'Hello?'

'Yes, it's me.'

'Who's me?'

'But . . . *me!*' I frown, like a customer of the Martinez Hotel in Cannes, who feels she has no need to give her name.

'Who? I can barely hear you, sorry.'

'Ellie!' I spit out indignantly.

'*Ellie?*'

'Yes!'

Shuffling at the other end of the line. I can hear Monsieur's shoes elegantly clattering along the hospital tiles.

'I'm sorry. Who's that on the line?' There is a sharpness in his voice. Which I don't recognize.

Hurt, I repeat: 'Ellie. Can't you hear me?'

'Look, listen, I'm at the clinic, it's a bad line and I haven't time to struggle over the phone for long, so *who are you?*'

'*Ellie!*'

'Ellie who?'

'Becker. Ellie Becker!' I'm red with shame, my mood turning black, spoiling the rest of my day.

It's humiliating enough to have your dress accidentally tucked into your tights or to tumble down the steps in the Métro, but it's something else altogether not to be recognized by a man you're writing a book about.

'Ellie Becker,' Monsieur repeats, his voice warming. 'Hello. How are you?'

'How many Ellies do you know?' I ask him, annoyed.

Monsieur bursts out laughing, and it's like a slap in the face in the middle of lovemaking.

NOVEMBER

Friday. I recall it with utter precision. I was rather proud to have engineered a meeting with Monsieur but I hated myself. There was no real need to see him, no urgent reason. This was something I was inflicting on myself, the texts putting off the rendezvous ten, twenty, thirty minutes, standing waiting in the cold on rue François-Miron. I was like those smokers who've undergone six dreadful months without a cigarette, then allow themselves one puff and instantly regret it. You should never stop smoking. Guilt is already enough of a burden to have to add to it. Babette, whom I'd called to take my mind off my freezing toes, had responded with a lengthy sigh.

'So, where are you right now?'

'I'm . . . outside. Waiting for Monsieur.'

'Outside? It's bloody freezing!'

'If I go into a café, I won't be able to smoke.'

'Since when have you been unable to function without a fag?'

'Since the advent of Monsieur. I've been waiting for half an hour. Seeing how anxious I am, that's a fag for every five minutes. You do the sums.'

'Is he late or is he standing you up?'

'He had a call from the hospital just as he was leaving. I'm the one who agreed to wait, Babette.' I sniffed discreetly. 'But I'm catching a cold here.'

'That's *so* unlucky, the call from the hospital,' Babette remarked.

'You said it. Absolutely.'

'But why are you waiting for him? He'll chat to you for barely ten minutes on the street corner, then fuck off.'

That was how understanding Babette now was. Back in June, Valentine had been unsupportive and now my best friend was moving in the same direction. My props were crumbling one by one. 'I *have* to see him. You know that.'

'And when he gets there, he'll just spit in your face and you'll thank him.'

'Why do you have to say things like that?' I protested, left short of breath by her unexpected sharpness.

'I'm sorry, Ellie . . . but why are you such a sucker for punishment? This has been going on for too long, come on!'

'Going on?'

'Listen, there are times when it's right and proper to grieve and be all over the place, but you've gone too far. Seriously, the guy is not worth seven whole months of your life. It's crazy.'

'I know. That's why I have to speak to him. I need answers.'

'Answers to what?'

'For my book. I can't write things that turn out to be unfair.'

'An unfair book. Are you taking the piss? With all

the pain that book's causing you, you won't owe him anything whatsoever for the rest of your life.'

'I know, but—'

'And do you really believe that once you're face to face with him you'll want to ask all those questions? When you know all too well that they'll get on his nerves?'

'So, you just assume I'll keep doing the wrong things?'

'Let me guess: you've dressed to kill?'

A quick appraisal. Dress, suspenders, and split crotch Bensimon knickers. The epitome of modern chic. For Monsieur's eyes only. 'Not at all.'

'You don't sound like a girl who's wearing Snoopy pants. Or a student who's been to lectures this morning.'

Exasperated, I barked: 'Oh, fuck you!' And, in a foul mood, hung up. Fortunately, while we'd been talking, Monsieur had sent me a text asking me to meet him five minutes later in the Vinci Pont-Marie car park. *The* car park. The antechamber to hell.

I sat down on the dirty steps. My heart was beating wildly, loud enough to silence the soothing background music played in all such places, although no one is ever likely to stay around long enough to listen to it. Apart from me. And Monsieur. Then, head down, tying my laces, I caught a faint movement to my right, the sound of the door's electric lock falling into place, a rush of displaced air. I looked up and Monsieur was there, his appreciative eyes running over my body. He was holding the door open, as if I was one of his patients, and when I brushed against him to pass through the door, I felt the space between us sizzle, heated in an instant by the guilty, wary lust this man inspired in me.

'You said you had questions?'

'For *Monsieur*. There are matters I need to shed light on, things I haven't quite understood.'

'What, for instance? Look at me.'

For a thousandth of a second, I looked into his eyes and regretted my audacity. I began again, gabbling: 'I haven't understood why we don't see each other any more – if you tried to explain it, I couldn't come to terms with it – why you don't communicate with me any longer when it's obvious we have so much to give to each other, why—'

'Slow down, slow down,' Monsieur interrupted. 'You're talking too fast.'

I bit my lower lip, trying to catch my breath.

'Are you stressed because I'm here?'

'You're *very* full of yourself.'

'I'm stressed too. Let me take your pulse.'

Before I could protest, Monsieur had clasped my wrist between his fingers. Raising my eyes to the heavens, irritated but smiling, I muttered: 'There is *nothing* wrong with my pulse.'

'It's fast,' Monsieur replied, almost in a whisper. 'Just like mine.'

'It's not going fast at all,' I concluded, snatching away my still madly throbbing wrist.

But, however curt I was trying to appear, I was already falling headlong into Monsieur's fly-trap, unable to conceal anything from him. Not even what was hidden beneath my clothing: I was getting wet. I liked the way Monsieur was so elegantly invasive, able to see through me on every occasion. Because of the rising heat, I took off my coat, and his eyes opened wide when he noticed my cleavage. And the distinct lack of lingerie obscuring the view.

'You're crazy going out in public like that! It's dangerous!'

'I keep my coat buttoned up when I'm in the street. Like everyone does.'

'I can see all of your breasts in that dress,' Monsieur observed, swaying between concern and appreciation, while his fingers cautiously pinched one of my hard nipples.

'What are you doing?'

Not even looking me straight in the eyes he smiled, unperturbed by the unusually aggressive reluctance I was displaying.

'Would you mind terribly if I touched you a little while we speak?'

'What's the point of you doing that if we can't fuck any more? Do you have any idea how I feel by the time I have to go home?'

'What about me? Look!'

Peering down, I caught sight of the erection inside the smart trousers of his suit. Oh, God, how good it would be to open his flies. Just that. Once his cock was out, Monsieur would become another man altogether. He would soon forget to glance at the clock every couple of minutes, and the guillotine blade looming above us would fade away. Cold air streaming across warm skin would remind him of the harbour of my body. But, over the past months, I had changed, and no longer reacted in the same way to his boldness and bad manners and even though, today, Monsieur was rock hard under his trousers, a whole world separated us. Disturbed, I looked away. 'What do you want me to say? Just look at you. What's all this provocation leading to?'

'What provocation? It's just a normal fact of life that I should desire you. Look at me.'

Monsieur took hold of my chin between his fingers, and his smile widened, unveiling his fascinating, carnivorous teeth. 'You are so beautiful,' he said. 'I think you're even prettier than you used to be.'

I answered him bitterly: 'I don't think that's of much use to me.'

'Ellie, it's not that I don't want to see you. I'd love to. I just *can't*.'

We looked each other in the eye, as Monsieur sang his customary litany: 'We'll both end up miserable, you know. If I had enough time, I'd be with you constantly. I feel like seeing you all day long, talking to you, taking you in my arms. Nothing would please me more than to discuss literature over a glass of something. I can't think of anyone I'd like to chat to more about books than you.'

Eyes fixed on the steering-wheel, he shook his head, perplexed. 'Maybe our relationship could be platonic.'

Astounded, I roared with laughter, sounding like a dog barking. 'Look at you! Look at your trousers! How do you think we'd manage that?'

'The more I see you, the more I realize it wouldn't be possible,' Monsieur admitted sorrowfully.

'No. Neither of us could. This is going nowhere.'

Moving between anger and dismay, I crossed and uncrossed my legs. All these hours of waiting, just to hear Monsieur wonder if we could ever be in the same room together and not end up in bed.

'I can't see you,' he continued, 'because ninety per cent of my life would be badly affected. I have my family, my work, and I'd need a whole new life to make enough space for you, the space you deserve.'

'And . . . how do the others manage, all the other men who cheat on their wives?'

'How do they do it?' Monsieur choked back a sardonic laugh. 'It's easy! They meet up once a week in a hotel room, undress while listening to the story of each other's week, fuck and go their own way. Maybe she'll ask, "How's your wife?" He'll say, "Very well, thank you," and there you are. You see how simple it is. But that's not what I want.'

'So what the hell have we been doing? It sounds just like what you've described.'

'That's not how we were,' Monsieur replied, shaking his head, visibly shocked by my vision of things.

'Oh yes we were. Last time, in the fifteenth *arrondissement*, that's exactly how it went.' I looked at him sadly. 'You arrived, we fucked, spoke for half an hour, and then you left.'

'You think that's all it was, really?'

'I'm writing a novel about you. If that's all it had been, a simple sordid story, a comic strip would have sufficed.'

At times, I could feel Monsieur's jubilation at being in a book. I now know one thing: the relationship became so complicated, from its beginning to what is in all likelihood the end, partly because he can't distinguish between reality and fiction. The life lovers lead in literature seems too beautiful to him, too exciting to fit into everyday routine. But what appears heroic or romantic in a book by Stendhal is just endless pain for someone like me, who only has real life to fall back on.

Monsieur couldn't help peering at my suspenders, and probably wanted me to notice the insistence of his gaze. 'It's cool what you're wearing.'

With all the bruised modesty I had gained from my contact with unsuitable lovers, surgeons, married men, forty-year-olds, passionate or full of vice, but never all at the same time, I hitched my dress up a little. I had no intention of provoking him: my body took the decision to do so, and it felt awful. I saw Monsieur smile, spurred on by this new challenge.

'Let me see,' he continued, his hand diving under my coat.

As it made its way towards my stomach, I leaned forward, determined to make it as difficult for him as I could, twisting my knees to repel his attack. Monsieur moved closer and whispered: 'Don't move. Don't be afraid.'

I flinched a little.

'All I want to do is touch that pretty little breast of yours. Don't be afraid.'

His large hand was the perfect shape and size, surrounding me with such softness and heat that I became wet inside my open-crotch knickers. I could feel my breast shudder and convulse in his hand, my nipple held between his fingers screaming, 'Yes yes yes,' to his furtive touch. Then Monsieur journeyed all the way down my stomach and inserted his hand between my thighs. I bucked and stepped back; he withdrew, a smile dawning.

'You shouldn't be afraid of me,' he kept repeating, caressing my cheek with his elegant fingers.

'Am I afraid of you?' I said haltingly, and in the cold crypt of his car my breath hung like heavy mist in the air, full of the fear I had for him.

'Kiss me on the mouth.' Monsieur imperceptibly moved his heavy lips towards me, as if daring me not to find them the very incarnation of seduction.

'Why on earth should I do such a thing?'

'Because we're just friends,' Monsieur said. I burst out laughing and he joined in.

'Friends? Are you taking the piss?'

'Aren't we friends?' Before I could say anything, Monsieur answered his own question: 'We *are* friends. Kiss me.'

I allowed my small chapped mouth to meet Monsieur's immense, welcoming lips. Not for long, half a second maybe. A half-second that reminded me of the days when Monsieur's kisses were legal tender, and didn't trigger my present mix of analysis and reluctance. But I never kiss my friends on the mouth. Now I know why: you can be a friend or you can be a lover, and when you happen to be lovers and enemies, like Monsieur and me, you end up with a broken heart.

'It would be so much easier for me if you were married or had a full-time boyfriend.'

I dared not tell Monsieur the truth about Édouard. Or all the others who would have willingly taken his place if he'd allowed them to do so.

'If you had any feelings for me, you'd lie to me! You'd have the guts to tell me you don't want to see me again!'

'I can't do that,' Monsieur replied. 'I can't lie when it comes to things like this.'

His wide grey eyes would never provide me with an answer, however long I might seek one. It was as though an immovable wall separated me from everything Monsieur might be thinking about. I could have left it at that, but I could already picture myself walking towards the Métro platform with all those thoughts swirling inside my head, like a washing-machine in full flight. I raised my chin. 'Swear.'

'What do you want me to swear?'

'Swear you're not saying that just to keep me on the hook.'

Monsieur's face was unreadable, his unreadable eyes looking straight into mine. 'But I *don't* want to keep you on the hook!'

'No?'

'Of course not. The situation is already painful enough.'

He glanced at his watch. I could feel him itching to leave. Monsieur had to leave, Monsieur was about to leave, and until the next occasion, I would hate myself for not having done or said anything in an attempt to hold him back. Already his eyes were drawn to the passing crowds. Mentally he was in their anonymous midst, his long silhouette and expensive clothes cleverly fading into the mediocrity of all those other people. Maybe he was imagining himself in the arms of his wife. I stepped back, moving towards the Métro platforms. As he also moved away, he placed his hand on my face, took my nose between two fingers, and said: 'You're beautiful, Ellie.'

'Farewell, then,' I said, my face showing all the sadness in the world.

'Why "farewell"?' Monsieur asked.

Instead of answering, I gave a thin smile and kept walking away, until all I could see of him was a flap of ultramarine silk scarf, tucked inside the high collar of his Lanvin coat. Where others would have seen an assembly of expensive materials, I recognized the essence of Monsieur, his perfume, and beneath it the fragrance of his skin. I hadn't been close to it for months but I knew it by heart.

As I jogged towards the Métro, Monsieur called after me and briefly walked alongside me. 'Have you found an ending for the book?'

'Not really.'

'Maybe a violent one,' Monsieur remarked.

'I'm thinking about it.'

I had already thought of an ending, neither violent nor spectacular, that would have seen us bringing the relationship to a conclusion in which we were both equals. But I wasn't about to exhaust myself by explaining all this to him, why I wished we could end things not owing each other anything. *Owing?* Owing what? Monsieur would ask. Love is not a set of accounts. And how would I have responded to that? How could I have explained over the telephone in two and a half minutes that love is never unilateral? Or that at the age of twenty I still keep a record of all the points scored during our skirmishes, alongside the count of my lovers. It would annoy

Monsieur out of all proportion and confuse matters now that I had seen his true colours this evening.

'One of us could die,' he suggested, and I held back a mocking laugh.

'I'm writing a true story, you know. Not a novel.'

'I know, but how can you bring things to a proper conclusion if no one dies? You need something powerful and strong. Maybe one day she could learn of Monsieur's death.'

I'd slowed my pace, if only to savour the sound of his voice and his interest in discussing my masterwork. It was only weeks later that I realized he had understood what was reality and what was fiction in the three hundred pages I was so proud of. We weren't much different from the characters in the book. We needed a violent ending, something irreversible. Without a clean break, we could go on like this for years and years. Or I could. There was no place for tiredness in this weary game where I collided with Monsieur on every corner. Sometimes he wouldn't notice, and at others he would look back and generously take five minutes to stroke my head, but every time I was with him, I couldn't predict how he would react. And I dearly *wanted* to know if my shameful ability to give him a hard-on was still effective. All a bit breathless. Of course, Monsieur found it fun, as much, if not more so, as I did. Getting rid of him in the book would not get rid of him in reality. In fact, I could already imagine myself, depressed by my crime, rushing to the clinic, waiting for him to cross the courtyard and, wordless, throwing myself against him, if only to feel his warmth, the beat of his heart against my cheek, the overflow of his life.

Killing Monsieur off was the most effective way to get back to the start; so banal. Surely there must be a way, dear God, to find the right ending.

I thought back to something he had said on the phone a few days earlier (not that Monsieur ever says anything in total innocence): 'One day I will die. And when that time comes, I will regret that I didn't spend more time with you.'

I had never thought in that way before: one day Monsieur would die. It was bound to happen. And when it did, I would be much older myself, maybe the age Monsieur was now, or more. With a husband, kids, a life. Of which Monsieur was no longer a part, I hoped. I prayed that I would only hear of it from a newspaper. Or never hear of it at all.

JANUARY

OK, so I said I was leaving. Bra, stockings, dress, cape. Shoes. My knickers are too far across the room. If I move any closer to the bed, he'll wake up and, bloody hell, he'll know why I'm leaving. And there's no way I can let him know that without appearing rude.

Tuesday, half past noon, and I'm going home, or I think I am.

The door weighs a few tonnes. It says 'Olivier Destelles' on the card. If it works out this time, if I'm confident enough, it will have been the last time I read his name, the last time I touched the door handle, the last time I saw his face, the last time I confronted my own in his lift's glass mirror.

I have a thousand transport connections to make before I get home, and right now my face is squashed against the window of a bus moving between Balard and the twelfth *arrondissement*, an area from which it will prove easier to reach my home. It's not looking easy, but I've been in cruise control since I rushed out of the Destelles apartment. I'm not even sure if I managed to sleep. He'd snored. I'd cunningly switched my iPod on while still in the bed and listened to *Atom Heart Mother*. It didn't move me as much as usual, and my idle brain had conjured up an elaborate theory about the parallels between Pink Floyd and Wagner. The first original thought I'd had in ages and I'd promised myself to write it down, although not quite now because of the awkward circumstances. I'd been having great difficulty writing down word after word, but this morning, on the bus, in the state I was in, it was virtually impossible. How I mourned all the frantic business of the past summer when I could sit at a table for hours, writing. Now inspiration goes walkabout every time I look at a sheet of paper. And I'm going out too much. I'm smoking too much. Too many vodkas. Too many guys. Too many days that begin at four in the afternoon. Too much sleep. I've become an expert at throwing myself into situations that never allow me any form of productivity.

I think about it a lot, on my way back from those evenings. Head against the glass window of the bus, cold to the bone: I'm drowning. This never-ending search for Monsieur, which once made sense and felt far from unreasonable, has become a total nightmare. My mother often suggests this is so – even my friends drop heavy hints, but it's only at moments like this that I understand it. For the past few weeks, I've convinced myself I've reached my limit, but a part of me insists on ignoring this as I travel down the same path again and again, to avoid having to face all those early mornings on the Métro home, tired from lack of sleep and self-disgust. I suppose it could have been worse. Surely the RER line won't take a whole *twenty-one* minutes to get me home. I'm falling asleep, my limbs are rigid, I'm too cold and too hot, sitting on the hard, narrow seat is torture, but I'd scream if I were to lie down, and there's just nowhere I'd feel comfortable, but please please please let all these people around me just disappear so I can find the right position for hours on end, and settle down. I'm itching with the impossible desire to be *elsewhere*, wherever that might happen to be. Music and reading are my only escape, but I have nothing to read and Pulp, in my earphones, is of no more use than a sublime Beethoven symphony. Six songs speed by, which I'm unable to follow or enjoy; all I know is that '*Bar Italia*' will always remind me of Olivier Destelles, his parties and all the hours when the brutal explosion of my life looms closer on the horizon.

The song has everything. The hysterical overlapping waves of the synthesizer and, at its core, Jarvis Cocker's voice emerging just slightly behind the beat; the high-pitched whining and then the unfurling, madly joyful chorus. Listening to it now makes me feel just a little better. But later the music will only recall my general unease, as if I was experiencing it all over again. Not sure if I'll ever be capable of listening to the whole three minutes and forty-four seconds again, even though it's the sort of song whose lyrics I adore. It's incredible that something has the power to make you want to be sick and dance. Fuck. The shattering influence of the song, the inspired insight of the lyrics, it's almost making me cry. And who is galloping back towards me on his black mount as I come to this shattering realization? Who emerges again from the fog of forgetfulness where months of absence have exiled him? The only person in the world I could bear to see, who'd help me forget that today, right now, I feel so bad. Monsieur would take me in his arms and, for once, his know-it-all attitude, the certainty of everything he'd achieved before I came along, would no longer be a source of irritation but would reassure me. I could say to him time and again, 'I'm hurting, I'm hurting,' until I felt better or collapsed out of sheer weariness, and I know that he would understand, would not make unkind comments at seeing me so sad. Monsieur knows the cost of curiosity. I would tell him about *'Bar Italia'* at breakneck speed, not allowing him to interrupt me, and he would stroke my hair to calm me, and we would experience again the thrill of pleasure we'd shared with *Irene's Cunt*.

I'm sick to the bone of writing about all these hypothetical situations.

I thought of him a number of times yesterday. It was snowing heavily as I left the Baron on the arm of Olivier Destelles, literally so, as he just dragged me along. It was four o'clock and Paris was empty and dirty, but looking up at the sky you would have thought you were in the Chanel advert featuring Estelle Warren. I had never felt like that before, swinging in turn between euphoria and depression. I was gasping for breath, feeling like death, slurring every word. I had a sudden urge to pee and stopped in the street behind a parked car covered with snow; but once I was squatting with my knickers down, I stared at Olivier with despair in my heart, asking him why I couldn't piss – why, *why*? His eyes, which I wished, in view of the situation, could have been Monsieur's, looked down at me and he explained that there was nothing unusual about it. I'd manage to pee later. He said it so lewdly that I found him utterly disgusting, my blood boiling, and realized how little I was attracted to him, the prospect of fucking him. Instead I yearned for something more transcendental, more solemn, like a scene from Bataille's *Madame Edwarda*. I was almost sitting with my bare arse in the snow, the rest of me concealed by my black cape, my face peering out from under the hood, like something out of the book, actually.

Olivier was leading us back to his car, but every three steps, I stopped to ask him some ridiculous question, soliciting promises I didn't want him to keep – *did he even understand me*? The dilemma was all mine. I told him about my life, in the most intimate detail, stumbling and holding onto his shoulder, convincing myself that in spite of everything that separated us, everything I disliked about him, he might have a better measure of me than all the other guys. Occasionally, the repugnance he inspired in me froze me to the spot. Turning a corner, I leaned back against a building, legs apart, my skirt pulled up to unveil my thatch, encouraging him to lick me, there, now. I can't describe the look in his eyes as he said no; he just laughed. I liked that. But I would have liked it even more if he could have been overflowing with vice.

Walking past a bus shelter, everything changed. Halfway through a particularly personal monologue, talking to him as if he were my alter ego, I suddenly lost all desire to be with him. I could see passers-by watching us, me with my fifteen-year-old face and my clenched jaw, my absurd high heels, Olivier in his formal suit, his long coat, his father-figure features, his devil-like face. What had made me think I could tell him all those things? Standing on the pavement, I was overcome with boredom. But a powerful surge of adrenaline set off more babbling, and I betrayed all my worthless secrets to him, like a breathless whore on the make. I'd briefly come to my senses by the time we reached and climbed into his car and Olivier whispered: 'We're made for each other. You know it, Ellie.' (We spoke to each other rather formally, straight out of a Mills & Boon novel.)

I smiled bitterly and thought, Monsieur Monsieur Monsieur, so fervently that perhaps he inexplicably woke up at that moment, wherever he was, right then in the middle of the night. I believe in intuition. I believe in it because, straight after that, it was as if Monsieur could see me on all fours on Olivier's sofa, navigating between yawns and ridiculous 'Yes, yes, yes' cries, too high to get wet, a run in one of my stockings, the other twisted around my ankle. *Ellie, what the hell are you doing here? Isn't it enough that this guy is a pervert and a millstone around your neck to drag you down even further to the lower depths? It's all so tasteless, and not a pretty sight. You could be advertised on some twisted Internet site, something catchy like 'young high-as-a-kite slut willing to be fucked by all and sundry' and there would be comments like 'poor soul' or 'pathetic'. You really worry me, Ellie. Did I not say to you, in my car, on your birthday, 'Be careful'? And, nodding, you replied, 'I don't see why you should worry, you never call me and we never see each other.' You were pig-headed, pretending not to understand, although you knew exactly what I meant; that's why I'm worried for you. I could see all this coming and how much you'd come to regret it, and regrets are the worst thing. The stink of men who don't know how to touch you or that you are unwilling to instruct in all the right ways is all over you. I saw it when you gave a start as I first called you 'my tiny love', as if it were inconceivable that I could love you for ever. Did I not tell you about the way your eyes look when I fuck you up the arse, blurred, and how you cease all movement? Now you're giving him that look, which rightly belongs to me, you allow the fool to squirm all over you, whispering filth in your ears, even calling you 'darling', although it makes you simper and turn your cheek the other way, and he doesn't even realize, eh, Ellie? How can he not feel how stiff your body is, the tightness in your neck and the reluctance with which you accept his kisses? You hate him so much he should surely be aware of it. You would, wouldn't you, if you were in his skin? Does he think it's because you're high? How can you be such a fool? I have another theory: maybe he does understand the ferocious loathing you have for him but doesn't give a fuck. As long as you don't scream for him to stop, he'll go on playing your game. And you're not the kind to scream, are you? You just wait for it all to pass and then you can write it down, the mediocrity, the humiliation, the banality. You'll try out all sorts of guys before you come to understand, but one thing is obvious, Ellie, you don't belong to this world where a man just fucks a girl to listen to how she sounds in the throes of lovemaking. You should get out of there, even if you have nowhere to go. I'd rather know that you're walking the streets at five in the morning in this polar cold than lying warm beneath this fat pig. Wouldn't it be preferable?*

A final insult, something I had not previously been aware of and should have told me I was doing the wrong thing: Olivier Destelle's fragrance is Habit Rouge. That was when I knew I had to put a stop to it or it would kill me. An ultimatum to myself that lasted barely a second, but that I will never forget.

I own a superb and ageless edition of Baudelaire's *Les Fleurs du mal*, which he gave me for my twenty-first birthday. It's so large I can't close my handbag when I carry it around, which is all the time. Not that everyone understands why I used to go out with an older guy, or at least nobody asks. Inside the book, a small piece of paper I clumsily unfold: 'Offered by C.S., 14/12/2009'. I usually hide Monsieur's presents under a pile of screwed-up old clothing, but my mother recently tried to tidy things up, and I was lucky she didn't come across the note, in which his treacherous name was written in big, bold letters. He and I, however, know that this pretty piece of paper is now the only thing that connects us, which is why it goes everywhere with me. Which is also why now, taking refuge on the bed in a foetal position, in a house that is waking to the day, I keep the note next to me at face height. So, navigating between alcohol fumes and an aching jaw, I am able to recall that December Wednesday in his car. It's easy to screen those ten minutes all over again, the only moment of late that my heart has truly been beating, out of love, naturally.

I have taken the decision not to write any more about the telephone calls and banal assignations that Monsieur reluctantly grants me. In a few months, I will in all likelihood barely remember more than two or three things about these final contacts, and before I fall asleep I make a note of them.

I now have two particularly beautiful books in my library.

Even if I am no longer full of the rage of belonging to him, I still need to speak to him. And speaking to him makes me want to fall in love again.

It might be, after due reflection, that Monsieur also loves me, and our relationship is like a play by Racine in which everything appears to keep the lovers apart. But in this particular instance, it doesn't make the central drama at the heart of the story any more attractive: his black car has come to replace the Tuesday-morning hotels, we see each other for a quarter of an hour in the car park or double-parked, and Monsieur doesn't even bother to take off his sunglasses. I continue to wear suspenders for him. I've introduced a note of sarcasm into our dialogue and he fails to understand my mood; the smallest things annoy him and he turns against me when my answers prove too evasive. Against all logic, he refuses to admit that lovers can bear to be very far from each other for more than a day, and we are therefore of another kind. And whatever we happen to be is no fun but, hey, it's all I've got.

Here, I think I've come up with the right allegory, so forget all the stupid things I've previously conjured up: it's like a cartoon that's lasted too long, with a worn-out grey mouse lazily wiggling its bum in the presence of the fat, overfed cat. Doomed to keep fighting because life would be too bizarre without the endless run and chase.

MARCH

Monsieur slowly slipped his finger inside my arse and I contracted around him, with a spontaneity that makes me ashamed of myself.

'Yes, darling,' Monsieur soothed me, with a note of tenderness in his voice, as I, with a total lack of discretion, rubbed myself against the roughness of the sheets (the combination was, oh, God, enough to make you scream). 'Yes, darling.'

The thought of him knowing to what extent I felt heavy, swollen, unable to control the treacherous overflow generating between my arse cheeks, the folds of the sheets spreading me apart, forcing me to convulsively grind my teeth.

'Your little pussy,' Monsieur articulated, his low voice vibrating with quiet assurance. 'How pretty it is, darling, your pussy. Just wet the way I like it.'

'Oh, slide your fingers inside me,' I mewed, sounding like a porno actress about to swoon, shivering with pride (now I sound like a chat-line heroine!).

But the hand making its way down to fulfil my demand couldn't help itself and smacked me hard instead, the sort of smack that resonated all the way across my arse like a bolt of electricity.

'I'll put in so much more than my fingers. Just be patient.'

I can't recall clearly what happened next. I probably buried my face in the pillow, angered by the perfect configuration of the sheets and his finger inside my arse, where it had been joined by his tongue, which I now found rather elegant.

One thing led to another, and he began to eat me, holding my arse cheeks apart, carefully and teasingly avoiding my cunt, even when I flung myself back in protest towards his face, the edge of his chin the only part of him in contact with my overflowing wetness. All of me just a quantity of expectant, throbbing flesh, immoderately swollen. Months before (it felt like millennia) it would have been inconceivable for me to respond to Monsieur while he was licking out my arse but the need was now so strong that, my arse cheeks quivering like jelly against his nose, I managed to gurgle: 'Do something, for God's sake!'

'What do you want me to do?'

I withdrew into the pillow, unable to express ways in which he could pleasure me better, his fingers or his mouth, maybe even his cock. How could I choose? The multiple answers to Monsieur's question were making me feel dizzy, and his long, artful tongue, hard and invasive, was not making things any easier. I frowned and mumbled: 'Do something with my cunt!'

Somehow I regained control over myself. I continued: 'It's bloody irritating, you being so careful not to touch it.'

In a flash, he looked away from me, and behind the

half-moons of my arse, I stared at him, my eyes still only half open. That luscious mouth of his was swollen by its travails to prepare me for his entry, and Monsieur in his excitement looked like an animal. My small unsteady voice was about to issue some further demand when he turned me over, and rested on his knees facing my wide-open legs, his cock unfolding, bruising the skin of my tummy with its hardness. He looked anything but a surgeon. In truth, thus unclothed, Monsieur was just a long, thin body, with his cock at its centre, the sole master of his movements, of my fate. Long gone was all the sophistication I had evoked a thousand times, outrageously praised to my girlfriends, written and dreamed about, and sought in vain in others. What now seemed to be unfolding in Monsieur's mind was as old as the world, making his lips curl up as he said loudly, his eyes fixed on my oozing slit: 'Don't move. Let me watch you.'

Without looking away, he took hold of his cock and, out of embarrassment, I burrowed deeper into the pillow. Roughly he took hold of my neck with his free hand, and in my panic, I'm sure my eyes squawked, *Surely you're not going to strangle me?* Because it would have required just a touch of extra pressure for his fingers to force their way deeper into the soft flesh and break the pink cartilage. I must have been looking at him with intense terror in my eyes when Monsieur stroked my cheek with his thumb, whispering: 'Don't be scared, baby mine.'

The embrace slowly relaxed and I caught my breath. Monsieur's cock quivered in his right hand and I was gaping open, unnerved by his presence. *I must look a right mess,* I thought, forcing myself to hold his gaze as he loomed above me.

You look like a whore, Monsieur's eyes replied. *I can see your arse, your cunt, I can even see inside you and you look like a whore. Enough for me to be hard as rock just looking at you on the sheets, with your now silent mouth. As if your mouth had anything to say. As if your second mouth had more things to say. You can hide wherever you wish, even tighten your legs, if you wish, but I know what lurks between them, how voracious and willing your little cunt is as it cries with the energy of despair to be filled. Listen to yourself. Your stomach is wide open, your gullet is dilated and you want to keep your eyes closed. What does it all mean, Ellie? Why can't I own both, your soul and your arse? What right have you to place an embargo on all those twisted ideas rushing though your little blonde head, when I clearly see in front of me an interlocutor capable of so much more sincerity than you, an interlocutor willing to kill for the gift of my fingers, my cock, even my mouth. And you think you can give this to someone else? Ellie? Every time, I pass through your life with the speed of the breeze. In a few days, you will frenetically touch yourself as you recall this occasion because you're not brave enough to live it now, right now, when you have all the tools at your disposal to come properly and lacerate my back with your nails. You'll hate yourself and will compromise yourself with a series of messy, badly organized texts, and all they will say to me is that you miss me. So, look at me. Let your small slim fingers swim across the sliminess of your slit while your eyes defy me to find another slut as beautiful as you on this planet. Allow your fingers to move lower. Touch yourself.*

But I would not. My lips wet, I ordered Monsieur: 'Lick my cunt.'

Lick my cunt!

He laid both his hands at the apex of my thighs, spreading me. The wetness of the sound made me jump. This was what it meant to be open, truly open, monstrously so. His thumbs grazing across my opening made a slow bee-line towards my lips, meeting at the perfect spot, with the assurance of someone who can calculate to the nearest millimetre (surgical exactitude). I felt like a butterfly pinned to a board. Monsieur, studying my face as I became overwhelmed, quickly took hold of me between his forefinger and his second finger, as you pinch a child's nose. Even with my eyes closed, I sensed the hardness of his gaze, its penetrating intensity.

Driving in two fingers, he opened me like a wound, with his customary grave delicacy, unveiling the velvet flesh that is seldom bared, while I twisted on the bed, mumbling words I couldn't finish, the primitive language of love.

Babette and I had often wondered what silent question passed across the lips of men for us to keep saying, 'Yes, yes, yes,' when we made love. Just as there are rhetorical questions, there are also ornamental answers that do not involve or commit you: the yes born of that specific moment, precisely forming in your throat, is a form of unchallenged approval, the very essence of approval. It does not mean that you are saying yes to fingers or a cock, however interchangeable they might be, even if at that precise instant they form the central axis of the momentary parallel world you are wading through. It's a total surrender to the moment, pleasure, feeling completely happy, way beyond anything that's ever happened before or might take place later. The only thing you can say is 'Yes.'

And I thought again of the way Henry Miller described the sound of a finger delving inside a cunt, a sort of *squish-squish* micro-sound, while below my stomach Monsieur was distilling wet gurgles my words could barely disguise, suction noises miles away from the more elegant *squish-squish* that would rightly belong to a nineteenth-century boudoir. I heard myself say: 'Kiss me.'

Displaying not an ounce of resistance (he probably thought I was totally under his thumb), Monsieur promptly aligned his lips against mine. In a trance, I stared at the man's head between my thighs, the hands and fingers digging small pits in the flesh of my arse cheeks. I could feel but not hear his warm breath.

'You smell so good . . . Your cunt smells so good!'

As I caught my breath again, in anticipation of my next series of frenzied yelps, Monsieur began to lap at me, at first slowly enough for me to feel every square inch opening as his tongue travelled across my private surface, *almost as if he was licking the back of a stamp!* That was the thought that sprang to mind before he deepened his assault as if to fuck me with his tongue, and the sensation of being only partly filled set my nerves on edge. My thighs were shuddering to a maddening rhythm beside his ears. Neutralizing my frantic movements with a sharp parting of my knees, he continued to peck at me. I could almost see myself swell and harden under his lips, jut like a small, wet nipple between his teeth, between his fingers as his whole mouth encompassed my opening, drinking from me, drinking, drinking, drinking again, again and again. It had taken him only a few minutes to turn the torture, the endless wait, the months of mortification, into a necessary road travelled to reach this sublime moment of supernatural communion. The language of love is a construct of thighs rubbing against each other, the muted sound of sheets crinkling, sudden hardness and, of course, 'Yes, yes, yes'.

It was when I least expected it (I was drowning in a whirlpool of pleasure) that Monsieur, with no word of warning, slipped two fingers into my arsehole, and I almost screamed, dear God. Actually, I think I did. I joined the ranks of the women who *know*: the small proportion of readers who will truly understand the exquisite and disgusting violence I experienced. My guts felt twisted from the speed with which I had been opened and closed again, and there I was babbling away, my legs in the throes of paralysis.

'I'm going to fuck you in the arse now,' Monsieur whispered. 'I'm going to fuck you in the arse, Ellie.'

'Do it facing me, please,' I muttered, my breath sticking in the back of my throat.

'Yes, it'll be wonderful, my cock inside your small arsehole while just above I watch your dripping cunt.'

Monsieur rose slowly above me. His cock shone in the pink darkness of the room (I had forgotten how wet some men's cocks appear after you've briefly blown them).

'Use your fingers, spread yourself open further.'

I obeyed, holding my hole wide, subterranean sounds rising from my tight throat. Monsieur created a passage for himself, forcing open the breach he had already wetted with his spit. A brief flash of pain coursed through me as he thrust himself forward and half buried inside me, whispering: 'That's it, darling . . . I'm in.'

I felt his hairs brush against my bum cheeks, and hot flesh filling me to the brim, *filled like a whore.*

'It's there, Ellie. Deep inside your arse.'

'Yes, yes, yes . . .'

'Talk to me, tell me how you feel, how good it feels when I fuck you in the arse.'

'It's good,' I confirmed, my voice unsteady. 'Your cock is so . . .' (total contrition as my vocabulary betrayed me while, above me, he waited for me to find the right adjective) '. . . so good!'

'Just look at you.' Monsieur smiled.

I stared at his chin, disgusted by the obscene swelling of my cunt as it gaped wildly, lazily, wet and carmine. I instinctively felt I should conceal it from his gaze and began to touch myself. Monsieur immediately spread-eagled me with his outstretched hands and there I was, wallowing on the hotel bed, my thighs held apart at what seemed an impossible angle, my belly full (and that feeling of being filled was as much ecstasy as it was sheer torture), half of a painfully hard cock sticking out from my arsehole and then thrusting back inside me to its full length, and right above it, my slit gaping open. And while I felt like the lowest of the low, Monsieur kept fixing me with intense concentration, light years away from repugnance, visibly delighted by the dichotomy of my shuddering body and the remnants of civilized propriety still visible on my face. A face he often described as *doll-like.* But as the waves of pleasure rose inside me, civilization was losing ground, rapidly losing its foothold, and the whole world beneath my half-open eyelids was turning hazy, my heart was beating faster, my nerve endings were growing harder by the second. The air around us thickened. All of a sudden, everything was more beautiful, warmer, as if, without renouncing Monsieur, I was once again alone in the room, totally unconcerned that anyone could be watching me. Until Monsieur decided on something even more obscene: brutally withdrawing from my arse, he stood still, facing me like a statue, his hands still holding me down, and gazed at me, his cock high against his stomach.

'Don't do that!' I breathed out, terrified by the sheer crudeness of the situation and by the thought – somewhat pragmatic in view of the circumstances, but after all I'm only a girl – that my cunt was so wide open it could have right there and then have hoovered up all the air in the room.

But Monsieur, on the other hand, was only a man, and the collateral damage this sort of situation could cause didn't appear to bother him in the slightest and he just kept on standing there, his fingers holding my knees back so he could watch my arsehole and my cunt in all impunity while I squirmed with embarrassment. Or maybe he was quite aware that I did not dare move even an ear, fearful the mood might change. And so I found myself pinned down motionless, just my hands frantically wriggling out of my control, half hoping not to have to picture what I looked like, all my openings open to the wind. I mumbled:

'Fuck me!'

'Let me look at you a little longer,' Monsieur kept saying, as he swept the burning tip of his cock along the ridge separating my arsehole from my cunt.

'Please,' I begged, hoping my submission might weaken his resolve.

'Keep touching yourself,' he said.

OK, OK, I thought, my pride dented. *But there's a distinct lack of cock in all this.*

And while Monsieur, fascinated, could not find it in himself to cut the spectacle short, I impaled myself on him in one single thrust, arse first, locking my legs around his back so he couldn't slip away. One of those long hands I loved and feared made its way to my neck, *Very good*, Monsieur said, and filled my cunt with God only knew how many fingers, still fucking me to a steady rhythm – is there a word to describe the perfect rhythm men sometimes miraculously come across following an eternity of trial and error? It almost brought tears to my eyes.

'You're quite a slut, Ellie,' he smiled as I kept on warning him that I was about to come any moment now.

My name, in his mouth and this particular context, felt like the bite of a carefully handled whip. I could not hold on any longer (but the mere thought of having to *hold back* was like a victory over life and the whole wide world) to hear his sublime final remark with any semblance of precision, but I remember it with clarity in the midst of my screams, as the wave rolled over me, and he just thundered in the distance, his voice like a choral accompaniment to my orgasm:

'You're so damn wet, my darling . . .'

Then came a few seconds when all I could think of was to begin breathing again, floating in cotton, the sole sensation of my wet thighs and Monsieur's still hard cock reaching me through a thick curtain of fog. Bathing in a sentiment of full plenitude, wallowing like a sow in the undone bed, I caught hold of my breath as best I could, now indifferent to his remaining movements all over me, the sudden stiffness of his cock deep inside my weary moist innards. It's when he dug his nails into the flesh of my thighs, kneading me hard enough to raise bruises, that I opened a grim eye. Monsieur's orgasm began like a soft breeze skimming across the surface of water; under my gaze, his torso and then his neck were caressed by a shimmering wave, and in response, his eyelashes began to flutter. Beneath his half-open eyelids two deep grey pupils searched for mine. *Fuck, he's so beautiful*, I remember thinking. The thin-winged nose and quivering nostrils, so familiar from their endless journey between my arse and my knees. The mouth that is always partly open when he makes love, the thick lower lip. His long eyelashes. The scandalous smoothness of his skin, a girl's skin on a male body. The harshness of his features, the violent beauty of his face when it vibrated, as it did now, above mine, hovering between struggle and surrender. Monsieur was no longer struggling. Monsieur watched me as we held on to each other, as my arsehole sucked at his cock, and I was overtaken by passion, observing how his lips quivered and his eyes could barely stay open.

'I'm coming,' he whispered, his fingers wrapping themselves around my hair.

I love you, I thought, stroking his cheek with the back of my hand. 'Come.'

He threw himself back, holding his cock in his hand, veins throbbing, bones, ligaments, even, a whole unthinkable architecture exposed. I let him endlessly ejaculate across my pussy. A last drop lingered and I caught it on the tip of a finger before bringing it to my mouth, begging him hoarsely: 'Take me in your arms.'

In the yellow room, the silence sheltered a world of tenderness that reminded me of siestas with my parents when I was five. My voice a thin whisper, I said: 'I don't want to talk banalities with you. We see so little of each other that I hate the fact I've already wasted so much time chatting about uni, my friends, all those meaningless things.'

'Those meaningless things interest me,' Monsieur replied, his hands still firmly pressed against my chest. 'Everything about you interests me.'

'I want to talk about literature. It's what binds us. And I have so many things I want to tell you, ask you, it's almost like suffocating.'

I turned to face him fully. 'Stay with me a little longer so that we can at least talk about Bataille.'

'Ellie, do you really believe we can say all there is to say about Bataille in two or three hours? It's not the way, debating literature at a moment's notice. It's normal that we talk about our lives.'

'I agree, but you never stay long enough to get past the preliminaries, and that's all I'm left with.'

Despondent, I lowered my chin and Monsieur suddenly rose, his hands still grasping my neck. 'All my obligations weigh on me, you know.'

'Yes.'

'So what can we do, Ellie? Do you think we should stop seeing each other?'

'I'm not sure. It's been some time since I've had any idea.'

'You don't want to see me?'

'*I don't know!*'

For a few seconds, I buried my face in the pillow, trying to conceal my irritation. 'You see, I treasure the rarity of our encounters, that I can sometimes count them on the fingers of one hand in an entire season. It makes it seem a much less banal story.'

'Is that good or bad?'

'It works both ways, you know that.'

'I didn't want us to live like ordinary people. We're both worth so much more than that, you and I.'

Monsieur always spoke with such assurance that I didn't have the heart to argue. Hiding my face in his shoulder, I continued: 'Fine, but maybe I would have preferred it if our relationship had been less extraordinary and I'd seen more of you. Maybe I would have liked to join you every week in a hotel and ask you how your wife was while you undressed. It would have been better than five minutes every three months or so and never having the opportunity to talk. It might sound terribly banal, but there wouldn't have been any harm in it. If other people act that way, it means it works.'

I felt his lips purse, buried in my hair, and knew that he was pouting. That was how his scorn manifested itself.

'Do you think a story that just anyone could have lived through would have inspired you to write a book?'

'I would still have been happier if I'd seen you more often. Sorry! Do you even know how many of the three hundred pages of my book were written because I couldn't see you and had to find a way to speak to you?'

Monsieur sighed, massaging my small breasts.

'You don't give a damn.'

'Of course I do! Why are you saying such things? If I could spend more time with you . . .'

'But you never have time. Time is the one thing you don't have. I know that. And I'm sick and tired of sentences beginning with "if".'

'It's true I seldom have time. I work fourteen hours a day and have a family.'

'So why won't you tell me it's over?'

'Because I don't want it to be!'

What struck me right there and then? What came to my mind first? Was it *What a selfish bastard* or *He doesn't want to leave me*? Was I relieved or dismayed? My eyes dry, I looked ahead but could see nothing with any clarity.

'So would you rather I went on following you, always crying or dripping with wet from my cunt?'

'What can I say, Ellie? That I no longer wish to see you? I can't lie to you.'

'I can't stand this going on indefinitely.'

'If I said, "It's over," it wouldn't change your need for me or mine for you.'

'I can pretend. I'll move on to something else. I'm only twenty-one.'

Taken aback, Monsieur removed his warm hands from my hips. I let go of his arm, which flopped against mine, and said: 'I don't want still to be in love with you when I'm forty-five. This is the other side of the coin: our story is so far from banal that I'll remember you all my life.'

'So it's not a bad thing, is it?'

'And you, when you're seventy, you'll think of me. Haven't we found a wonderful way to be ever miserable?'

And, for the first time, Monsieur pulled me against him, asking: 'So what do we do?'

'I don't know,' I answered.

I had to give him enough time to feel scared. I wanted him to stop asking me what we should do, take a firm decision, beg me to break the awful silence. For once, if only for a few seconds, he would know how it felt. But my resolve broke.

'I don't want to follow in your wake. It leads nowhere. It makes me sad.'

'What makes you sad?' Monsieur leaned towards me, his long hand working its way across my stomach, automatically mapping every curve to my intersection. If I'd closed my eyes, I would have felt closeted with a somewhat unconventional psychiatrist.

'I've—' My throat tightened, and I dived into the refuge of the pillow again. Monsieur took my chin between his fingers, but I was already full of tears and knew that within a few seconds I'd have two streams of thick snot escaping my nose and my eyes would be all puffy, not what was needed right now.

'Leave me alone!' I protested, but he flattened himself

against me, his long warm body surrounding me, taking my face between his hands.

'What is it, sweetie?'

'And stop calling me "sweetie". You call everyone "sweetie".'

'What's making you sad?'

'You're so clever, you're so damn *clever*, and you still have no clue?'

'I still don't know you well enough, Ellie.'

Motionless in his embrace, I tried to avoid his gaze, hoping I could conceal my tears and raw nostrils from him. But Monsieur pursued me. 'I have no idea what goes on inside your head. What you expect of others, what you'd like to become, what you expect from me.'

'It's all your fault. I—'

'I know, darling, I know,' Monsieur interrupted, kissing my forehead, then the tip of my nose.

'If you'd given me time, I would have told you everything about me. You could have known me so much better than all the others.' I sobbed uncontrollably, and the kiss he gave me to calm me tasted of salt. 'It makes me sad never to be able to reach you on the phone, that you never answer my messages, that you never call me back, that you invariably offer me false hope, then let me down at the last moment. There's no way you can learn about me. Over ten months of frantic comings and goings you've never managed to free yourself for one lousy evening to spend it with me, and you have the cheek to tell me you don't want it to end!'

'Ellie . . .'

'And neither do I know you. I've written a book about

you, but maybe I've got it all wrong. All I know of you is what you've been willing to let me see in just a few hours.'

I raised my eyebrows in the way that Babette says gives an inkling of what I might look like in twenty years. I hate it when I do that.

'So, in a nutshell, that's what makes me sad. Not to know you, and being a semi-stranger to you makes me sad. And to know none of this affects you makes me sad.'

'Who says it doesn't make me sad too?'

'No one, actually. Everything you think I have to read between the lines. You never say anything to me.'

'It does make me sad,' Monsieur says, his nose rubbing against mine, 'that I don't know enough about you, that I don't see you, speak to you. It's all so horrible.'

I realised there was no point in saying anything more, I could just remain there coiled up against him, my face all sticky, and the situation would continue for some months still, conditions unchanged, with the faint hope of catching his attention, attracting his favours looming over an improbable horizon. We'd been stuck here for almost a year now. It wasn't after a whole year I was likely to find a place for myself between Monsieur and his wife, isolated from his likely other girlfriends, in the margins, considered when he felt distracted, remembered when convenient. Forcing strangled sounds from my throat, I suggested:

'So tell me it's over, then.'

'I can't do such a thing.'

'How bloody selfish you are!'

EMMA BECKER

I rose on the bed, shamelessly wiping my nose, now on my knees facing Monsieur who was still lying down, his mouth opening to come up with further objections.

'You just don't want to exclude the possibility of being able to fuck me whenever you feel like it. It's all too human, but do understand how unhappy it makes me feel.'

'You knew when we first began seeing each other how little time I had. Every time I see you, they happen to be minutes stolen from my time-table, my work, my . . .'

'Don't start mentioning her.'

Her. Since when do I talk like a common mistress?

'Don't talk to me about your wife. I've always had the good taste to never include her in all the obstacles preventing us from seeing each other. I've never wanted to be in competition with her.'

'I never saw you competing with her, but it's also because she exists that I can't look after you better. It's the life I chose, long ago.'

'Or maybe you just don't give a damn about it all.'

Monsieur suddenly grew stiff, and his fingers gripped the sheets, with all the white-knuckle intensity he usually displayed before he came. A bad sign. His voice full of fatherly aggravation, as if a single extra expression of rebellion would see him explode.

'When will you ever cease thinking that I don't give a damn?'

'When you do something to prove the contrary,' I answered, convinced he could never raise his hand to me, whatever the provocation. 'When you have the guts to tell me it's over, because you accept you will never have the time to properly spend w

'Should I call you more often? Is
is all about?'

'Who said there was a problem

A knot in my throat, I slipped

'For over eight months now, I'.

at your feet, hoping you'd notice me, start talking to
as if I were an adult. Maybe I'm the one who was wrong,
or you were wrong to let me act in this way, but these are
the facts: I can't go on like this.'

'I never wanted to make you unhappy.'

'I know. No one ever wanted to make someone else
unhappy. No one ever wants to make someone else
unhappy, but it happens.'

'As far as I'm concerned, I still want to keep on seeing
you.'

He sounded like a child who's been sent to the corner,
and it made me want to throw myself into his arms. It
might have been a gentle deception, clever manipulation,
I had no proof that Monsieur was genuinely in pain. Or
experiencing as much pain as I did. That the thought
of no longer having regular contact with me was truly
affecting him. That just saying my first name had become
painful, or even thinking it. I had a choice between
throwing myself into his arms or hating myself for not
doing so, or staying there like a pillock on my knees and
come to regret months later a final occasion to breathe in
his perfume, feel his whole body surround me. Clenching
my fists, I nervously laughed, like a door closing, unable
to look into his eyes.

'Neither do I want us to stop seeing each other. It's the

g I want to do. Do you think I have anyone else in
te who can talk to me about Aragon or Mandiargues
e way you do?'

'We can always talk, no need to make love,' Monsieur earnestly suggested.

'You know all too well it's impossible. I'll still be consumed by the need to touch you. And you'll always feel compelled to mess about with me under café tables. I will see so little of you. Even less than now. But it will still be enough to remind me of how things used to be, having you as mine. It won't change anything.'

'So what, Ellie? We stop calling each other, talking, finding out how we are?'

'I stop calling you, talking to you, asking after you. And you continue as you've always done.'

'So we're saying it's over?'

I clenched my teeth, exasperated by Monsieur's repetitive propensity for pushing me all the way, ignoring how much I had shed my naivety away from him. So, a final form of provocation, my heart beating wildly, I cried out:

'Yeah, it is, it's over.'

Then, reassuring myself:

'A decision had to be reached.'

I could have fainted a hundred times over as I got dressed. Leggings. Knickers. High-collared Claudine dress. Bensimon trainers. Monsieur kept on watching me, as if he was holding an invisible piece of string keeping my nose pointed straight in his direction so that I might gauge his reaction but mostly I was gradually becoming aware of the fact I would never be seeing him again. It was difficult to get my mind around it. His eyes followed my movements with such calm equanimity confirming my deepest conviction: he had known, all evening, that I would be leaving him. That, in some way, I'd partly left him some time ago. And that my final flight had, consciously or not, long been planned. So why, oh why was he staring at me like this? Why did it feel as if he felt offended at the spectacle of my escape?

I fixed my ponytail, twisting it around three times, using two separate elastic bands.

I sat on the edge of the bed so I could lace up my shoes properly.

I pretended to send four text messages.

I was biding my time. Doing everything on automatic pilot, feeling dead inside. Finally, hands crossed over my knees, I realized there was nothing else for me to do but leave. Monsieur watched as I shivered and whispered my name. Head held low, below the shield of my hair, I saw his hand slowly moving towards me, open, unthreatening. And then, in a flash, it disappeared and I felt it in my hair, journeying backwards across my head, reaching halfway down my back. I briefly glanced at Monsieur, silently saying *but what in hell do you want me to do?*

'Go,' he said laconically, and it felt so much worse than 'Stay'.

The whole extent of the tragedy taking place in the room swept across me. What a huge, bloody mess. Hundreds of people had just died in an earthquake in Chile, Earth had possibly changed its course in the heavens, there'd been the thing in Haiti and the only drama I had been involved in, the only thing that could make me cry was leaving this man, eight months of my life, and it felt like my whole life. Like in the cartoons, my eyes had probably gone all red, and I threw myself at him, burying my nose into the softness of his neck, sobbing, my tears flowing, draining through the prickliness of his unshaven morning face. Monsieur dug his nails into my back with such fierceness that it left a mark for some time, a few days at least: three initially pink moon-shaped crescents, which would later turn to red and brown. As I silently sobbed, my cheek against his, he took my tear-stained face between his hands.

'Look after yourself, please. And don't forget me.'

'OK,' I promised, sniffing away.

'OK?'

'You too, take care of yourself . . .'

'Swear you will,' Monsieur said, his nose touching mine, as I looked straight into his long lashes and grey eyes, finding no indication of emotion, just his customary neutrality.

'I swear,' I hiccuped, pulling my face away from his hands.

Right then, did he even have a clue of everything I'd just lived through? I was standing up with difficulty (and how did I even manage that?) while Monsieur was still seated, the wet and sticky shadow of my cheeks on his. I just had to say something, for fear of losing what was left of my sanity, so I added, almost talking to myself:

'Don't talk to me of memories or farewells. I don't believe in farewells.'

'Neither do I.'

'You know,' I said, as I stood yet again on the brink of collapsing, 'I was fifteen years old when I experienced my first sentimental break-up. I missed an afternoon class because I was so sad. I remember, my father and I walked to the bakery to buy girdle cakes, I was shedding tears like a fountain. I knew he didn't know what to or say to make me feel better – you never could discuss those sort of things with my father – and he said to me *you always come across the people who mean something to you or once meant something again.*

Turning my head away to wipe my snot on my collar, I continued:

'That's all I can think of right now. Such a stupid thing to say.'

'No, it's a lovely, thoughtful thing to say.'

'Maybe a bit of both,' I conceded, slipping my jacket on.

Mid-season: it was still March, but May was fast approaching. The air smelled like last year. The chestnut trees were flowering. The sweetness of mangoes. A blend of Habit Rouge, dust and floor polish. The sky the same shade of blue. Was it a clue, the logical conclusion, the closing of circle I had always been unable to decrypt? I would have enough time to think about this on the Métro, as I knew no single track on my iPod would be able to interrupt the frantic flow of my thoughts. Nearby conversation would sweep over me, people would embrace, laugh, listen to the Beatles, read their copies of *Cosmopolitan*. Fucking hell, the world would go on! How was it possible? How could individual universes collapse on themselves and leave the rest of the world unaffected?

As I leaned over to pick up my handbag, I willed myself to faint. But it wasn't that easy.

'So I'll never see those panties of yours again?' Monsieur said, sounding neither provocative nor funny I must say. Neutral. An open book.

Never again. Sometimes there are words, standing next to each other, that make you want to feel sick.

I don't believe that a single man is worth those favourite panties that witnessed my first orgies, watched me straddle my first conquests, and tentatively step into my first alien bedrooms. It wasn't a question of price, even if at the time it felt outrageously expensive: the noblest hands, the most precious hands had pulled on its elastic like the strings of a harp. The worthiest of eyes had devoured the plump spectacle of my flesh below the polish of its lace. I had leaked into its material so many times, in the most extravagant of places. At the Baron, chaperoned by Olivier Destelles. A few weeks later, high as a kite, I would drift through Thomas Pariente's apartment starkers but for them and an Hermès scarf. Some years earlier, seeing them for the first time, straight from the precious small Agent Provocateur carrier-bag, Alexandre had remarked that they were my 'heart-attack panties'. My whole sexual life was inscribed inside the black satin folds. I'd lost weight, put on weight again, and lost it again, but they'd never offended me by becoming too loose or tight. As by miracle, the material adhered to my flesh like a second skin. Those panties were *mine*.

'Here you are,' I said to Monsieur, with an uneasy smile.

As soon as he held them in his hands, still looking

attentively at me, he brought them to his nose, smelling the imprint of my cunt, his languid pupils like those of a perfumer facing the most exquisite of fragrances. This was why I had loved this man, the very reason I had fallen head over heels: the way his face lit up when I opened my legs. The greediness of his lust.

'These panties are much too beautiful for you to give them to me,' Monsieur noted, as his fingers wrapped themselves around the lace.

'Wasn't our relationship beautiful too?' I said, with a fatalistic sigh that I instantly felt ridiculous, reciting platitudes like a sitcom actress.

He smiled at me.

As I took my first step towards the door, my body felt surprisingly light, considering I would never see Monsieur again. I was weightless. The wooden floor under my feet indelicately squeaked: I wanted to escape in total silence, unnoticed. I could feel Monsieur's eyes behind me, scanning one last time my pantie-less silhouette (that promise of nudity had always had such a cataclysmic effect on him) and, for a man so at ease with words, he was struggling to somehow break the silence. Maybe he knew deep down inside he no longer had anything left to say. That there was a form of pain, like pulling out a splinter, which was impervious to words.

I opened the door, struggling madly against the thought of turning back. The absence of sounds was the same, in the room and in the corridor. Inside me the silence was screaming. Surrounding me was a silence of mourning. Biting my lips, I turned the handle, a final whiff of Habit Rouge reached me, floating across my cheeks, and that was it.

That was it.

That feeling of getting away with it cheaply can prove terribly fragile. When I began to walk again, the carpet felt soft and deep, sickeningly soft. The smell of lilies washing over the landing was unbearable, the walls aggressively orange-coloured. I feared hearing Monsieur move behind me, just a few metres away, inside the room. The sound of the door handle turning.

I ran down the steps four at a time, rushed past the reception desk like the breeze, refusing to look around the hotel I would never return to, ever, mumbling 'thank you, have a good day', my voice a ghost-like trickle (*I've never wanted to reveal the name of this seventeeth arrondissement landmark of sorts, mentioning it just brings back the nausea. All I have to do is silently spell out the word and for ten seconds or so the people facing me, the world all around, the music I'm listening to, the silence even, they all freeze, lose colour, turning into those sort of silvery old photographs that cause my heart to tighten*).

It was midday on Rue des Dames. Standing on the small flight of steps I stared ahead at the continuous flow of grey passers-by, gasping for air. All the buildings seemed to rise to terrible heights, their windows like dead eyes. With no great conviction, I put a foot forward and walked down one step and a determined young executive almost bumped into me, instinctively mumbling *'pardon!'* out of mere habit, and I leapt back like a cat to my original position, on the door's threshold.

It felt like being drunk, the way you become terribly clumsy after the third glass. Alone, mostly. Lost. Stranded halfway between two equal catastrophes, on one hand ready to melt back into all the waves of insignificance, on the other the desire to rush back towards the soft, cotton-like heat of the hotel, where Monsieur sat waiting for me, with his wolf-like smile. I'd often wondered if others also experienced the same sort of total loss of motivation, of frames of reference. If italicized sentences came to life in their mind, out of nowhere like they did to me.

If you go back inside it will fuck everything up. But if you run away, it's all the same. So, what are you left with, at the end of the day? Nothing. No desire to read, write, fuck or see people, no inclination to sleep or be alone, so what have I got left, damn? Have I ever really thought through what it would be like to never see Monsieur again? Don't do it. If you do it, you'll scream. You won't see him again, not at the clinic, not at Philippe's, not at the hotel, nor in his car, nowhere. There is no place left on this planet that will bring you together. I loved Monsieur more than anything else in the whole wide world. I will not see him again. Our two lives will now follow parallel tracks, I . . . I will grow older without him being aware of it. I will know nothing of his life. He will forget you, he's bound to. Or worse, he will never forget you.

'Ouch.'

You will never forget him. All I have left are these memories but oh God I now remember so little, oh God I've even forgotten his face, that face that never appeared to be the same in photographs. I just have fleeting images, and soon they will disappear like all the rest. Even if you write. Writing won't stop time racing by, erasing everything in its passage. What's

worse? Forgetting? Or the contrary? But I don't want to, me!
I don't want to forget! I don't want him to forget me, dear
God, to forget my arse, my smell or all the messages I used
to send him, my name and my pitiful devotion, my dog-like
devotion to him, I . . . oh fuck, who cares if he forgets me, as
I'll NEVER see him again. Breathe. I can't breathe. I'm scared,
the fear is killing me. So is the cold. I . . . sit down. You can't
allow yourself to collapse to the ground in front of all these
strangers. Sit down, light yourself a fag. Hold it between your
small trembling fingers. Oh, I just don't want to be myself. I
just want to wake up on the day when Monsieur's name will
have disappeared, has been expunged from my memory, when
the thought of him barely raises a smile on my lips. Will it ever
happen? Can I manage it? Will you ever be able to look at a
photograph of him without it feeling like a slow-motion slap
against your cheeks? I don't want to be me ever again. I don't
think I can bear all this pain much longer. Or rather I know I
will: I know I will take the Métro like any normal person, that
I will find my way back home like a normal person, even if I'm
crying or choking or snot is pouring from my nose throughout
the journey, because who cares after all? I feel like being sick.
I'm going to be sick. Swallow all that saliva down. Breathe,
breathe. Don't make the mistake and stop breathing.

If my recollection of that moment is correct, fleeting
as it is, it's because Monsieur found me, slumped against
the wall, at the top of the steps leading to the hotel door,
sheltered away from the passing crowds, my eyes wide
open, my cheeks wet with a river of tears, stinging me
like lemon juice, choking my anguished sounds inside the
cup of my hands. I felt an imperceptible shadow close by
me and couldn't care less. I was scared and my stomach

was so twisted up inside that I could feel nothing, felt no need to regain any form of dignity. Wildly sobbing under my breath. Everything around me was just too large. I could no longer understand how I was allowed to walk the streets of such a large city on my own. How anyone could trust me in any way.

I glanced to my left, brushing away a wet, salty strand of hair, saw Monsieur and his suit jacket, the careful alignment of his side pocket warped by my scrunched-up panties. I didn't stop crying. He must have known as soon as I had walked out onto the landing that my legs wouldn't take me far. It was of no consequence, I was only twenty-one. An age where you rush ahead in overdrive without ever feeling pain or weariness. It just happens, like that, out of the blue, on hotel steps right in the middle of your mad run to nowhere.

'I beg you, don't cry,' he said, his voice so dreadfully overflowing with tenderness it hurt. I lowered my hands from my face to try and mumble something and thought, for a moment, that Monsieur was about to touch me, but before I had a chance to say anything, he'd pulled a large bone-coloured silk handkerchief from his inside pocket, his initials C.S. sewn into the bottom right hand corner.

'Take it,' I heard, and half a second later I was holding between my fingers the most exquisite velvety piece of material Man has ever created, fabric evoking an endless, armless, bodyless embrace, but an embrace nonetheless.

With an effort I summoned up from deep inside my soul, I sketched a thin smile, looked at Monsieur who was also smiling at me, the shadow of grief spreading across his small wrinkles, a sight I had never witnessed before. We looked at each other for ages, impervious to the outside world. Then my heart that I'd already thought shattered broke into a thousand pieces again and I buried my face into the handkerchief that smelled of Guerlain, opened my mouth, but already Monsieur had taken flight, his eyes lowered, hopping down the twelve small steps leading to the street four at a time. Stretching my neck until it hurt, my eyes followed him for a few metres, the blue of his scarf a point of reference, but he soon turned a corner, disappeared as he knew how to do so well, and all that was left was Ellie, rue des Dames, Ellie and her handkerchief smelling of Habit Rouge.

Sometimes you pull a splinter out. Sometimes you are the splinter. Everything else is unimportant. All the rest is just a long process of falling out of love by which all little girls return to shores where they unlearn the pain, the compromise, the sacrifice, the torment. A place where grief is less poignant and pleasure is weaker.